VINTAGE CRIME

A Crime Writers' Association
Anthology

Edited by Martin Edwards

This is a **FLAME TREE PRESS** book

Collection copyright © 2020 Crime Writers' Association
Introduction copyright © 2020 Martin Edwards
For a full list of copyright information please see the back of this anthology

FLAME TREE PRESS
6 Melbray Mews, London, SW6 3NS, UK
flametreepress.com

US sales, distribution and warehouse:
Simon & Schuster
100 Front Street, Riverside, NJ 08075
www.simonandschuster.com

UK distribution and warehouse:
Marston Book Services Ltd
160 Eastern Avenue, Abingdon, OX14 4SB
www.marston.co.uk

Publisher's Note: This is a work of fiction. Names, characters, places, and
incidents are a product of the authors' imaginations. Locales and public names
are sometimes used for atmospheric purposes. Any resemblance to actual
people, living or dead, or to businesses, companies, events, institutions or
locales is completely coincidental.

Thanks to the Flame Tree Press team, including:
Taylor Bentley, Frances Bodiam, Federica Ciaravella, Don D'Auria,
Chris Herbert, Josie Karani, Molly Rosevear, Mike Spender,
Cat Taylor, Maria Tissot, Nick Wells, Gillian Whitaker.

The cover is created by Flame Tree Studio with
thanks to Nik Keevil and Shutterstock.com.
The font families used are Avenir and Bembo.

Flame Tree Press is an imprint of Flame Tree Publishing Ltd
flametreepublishing.com

A copy of the CIP data for this book is available from the British Library
and the Library of Congress.

HB ISBN: 978-1-78758-548-5
HB (Deluxe) ISBN: 978-1-78758-549-2
US PB ISBN: 978-1-78758-546-1
UK PB ISBN: 978-1-78758-547-8
ebook ISBN: 978-1-78758-550-8

Printed and bound in Great Britain by Clays Ltd, Elcograf S.p.A.

VINTAGE CRIME

A Crime Writers' Association
Anthology

Edited by Martin Edwards

FLAME TREE PRESS
London & New York

CONTENTS

Introduction 1
Martin Edwards

Money is Honey 3
Michael Gilbert

Strolling in the Square One Day. 25
Julian Symons

The Service Flat 36
Bill Knox

Footprint in the Sky 44
John Dickson Carr

The Woman Who Had Everything 60
Celia Fremlin

The Nuggy Bar. 71
Simon Brett

Inspector Ghote and the Noted
British Author. 96
H.R.F. Keating

The Perfect Alibi. .119
Paula Gosling

Cuckoo in the Wood 130
Lesley Grant-Adamson

In Those Days. 136
Liza Cody

Turning Point 143
Anthea Fraser

The Hand That Feeds Me. 157
Michael Z. Lewin

Cold and Deep. 161
Frances Fyfield

Moving On 175
Susan Moody

The Woman Who Loved Elizabeth David 191
Andrew Taylor

Nowhere to be Found 205
Mat Coward

Interior, With Corpse 221
Peter Lovesey

The Egyptian Garden. 234
Marjorie Eccles

Melusine. 250
Martin Edwards

Top Deck 267
Kate Ellis

Sins of Scarlet. 281
Robert Barnard

All She Wrote 291
Mick Herron

Biographies 301

Sources. 307

Crime Writers' Association

The CWA was founded in 1953 by John Creasey – that's over sixty-five years of support, promotion and celebration of this most durable, adaptable and successful of genres. The CWA runs the prestigious Dagger Awards, which celebrate the best in crime writing, and is proud to be a thriving, growing community with a membership encompassing authors at all stages of their careers. It is UK-based, yet attracts many members from overseas.

INTRODUCTION

It's a pleasure to welcome readers to the latest anthology of stories by members of the Crime Writers' Association. This is a collection with a difference, celebrating the work of CWA members since the Association was founded in 1953. The aim is to present a wide range of stories which are entertaining in their own right and also demonstrate the evolution of the crime short story during the CWA's existence, from the Fifties up until the early twenty-first century.

There are countless gems of crime writing in the CWA archives, as this book demonstrates. Leading names of the past are well-represented, along with several great names of the present. The book also includes a number of hidden treasures by less familiar writers. The first CWA anthology, *Butcher's Dozen*, appeared in 1956, and was co-edited by Julian Symons, Michael Gilbert and Josephine Bell; I've been the series editor since 1996. Prior to the 1990s, stories in the anthologies were quite often reprinted from other sources; one example here is John Dickson Carr's contribution, the earliest story in the book, which appeared in the memorably titled *The Department of Queer Complaints*, published in 1940.

More recently, the anthologies have focused almost exclusively on newly written fiction. Over the past quarter of a century, the series has yielded many award-winning and nominated stories in the UK and overseas by such luminaries as Ian Rankin, Lawrence Block and Reginald Hill. This book itself includes one story, by Kate Ellis, which was shortlisted for the CWA Short Story Dagger and another, by Robert Barnard, which won the same honour. The CWA has also produced a couple of collections of essays about real life crimes as well as a special anthology, *Mysterious Pleasures*, to celebrate the CWA's golden jubilee.

For this project, the CWA has teamed up with a highly enterprising publisher, Flame Tree Press, and my thanks go to Nick Wells, Josie Karani and their colleagues for their enthusiasm for this project and their work in putting the book together. I'm also grateful to each and every one of the contemporary writers who have graciously agreed to allow the reprinting of their stories, as well as to the estates and agents of the deceased members for their willing co-operation with my attempt to translate an intriguing concept into an enjoyable reality.

Martin Edwards

MONEY IS HONEY

Michael Gilbert

"For the Dear Lord's sake, go down and deal with Mallet direct," said Mr. Craine, senior partner of Horniman, Birley and Craine, solicitors, of Lincoln's Inn, to his young partner Mr. Bohun. "He was on the telephone to me yesterday afternoon for two hours. My left ear still feels the size of a watermelon. You know as much about his blasted companies as I do. Ask yourself down to lunch. It's only ninety minutes out of Liverpool Street. You'll like Humble Bee House. It sounds a sort of stockbroker Gothic joke; actually it's early Victorian and rather nice—"

Further telephoning followed, and at half past twelve Henry Bohun stood at the wrought iron gates of Humble Bee House. He saw at once what Craine had meant. The place had been built as a gentleman's residence at a very bad period of English domestic architecture, but time and nature had dealt kindly with it. Myrtle, privet and laurustinus had lost planned formality and had run together to turn the driveway into a funnel of light and shade. Halfway along, on the left of the drive, a formal sunken garden had slipped back to the simple grassy glade from which it had been hewed; its ledges supported a colony of blue-and-white hives, eight or ten small ones clustered round a large one. In the September sunlight the bees were pottering about, making their last preparations for winter.

Next moment he was startled to see a fox look out at him. He stopped. The fox grinned, crossed the drive, and disappeared silently. Bohun wondered if he ought to do something about it. Would it be correct to shout *View halloo*? He was too much of a Londoner to feel any certainty about the matter.

The door was opened by a middle-aged maid. He announced his business, and was shown into a large, dark room intersected with bookcases, and branching out into unexpected window seats and embrasures, so that it had the appearance of three or four separate rooms in one.

"By the way," said Bohun, as the maid was about to withdraw, "I don't know if you knew – but you've got a fox in your front garden."

"There's a badger, too,' said the maid. "They belong to Master Norman. I'll ask if Mr. Mallet can see you."

Reflecting that he had come all the way from London at Mr. Mallet's express invitation, it seemed to Bohun conceivable that he might. However, he merely nodded and sat down. The maid withdrew and Bohun opened his briefcase and sorted out the papers dealing with the Mallet-Sobieski Trustee and Debenture Corporation.

Click-click-click-click. Clickety-click.

Bohun looked up from his papers.

Click-click. Clickety-click-click-click.

Too regular for a cricket. Too loud for a death-watch beetle.

After standing it for a few minutes he put down his papers and moved softly across the carpet. The noise seemed to come from behind a parapet of bookshelves in the far corner of the room.

When he rounded the corner he was surprised to find that he had not been alone in the room after all. A tall man with a thick moustache and one eye was sitting on the edge of the window-seat. He was rattling three dice in his large, brown right hand, and turning them out on to the table in front of him.

"Morning," he said. "You the lawyer?"

"That's right," said Bohun.

"Bloody house, isn't it? Poker dice. Fancy a game? My name's Rix – Major Rix."

"Mine's Bohun," said Bohun. "No, thank you. I'm just waiting to see Mr. Mallet."

"Doubt if you'll be able to," said Rix. "He's pretty ill, you know."

Bohun looked surprised.

"It must have been very sudden," he said. "He spent most of yesterday afternoon talking to my partner on the telephone. I gather he was in rather strong form."

It was Rix's turn to look surprised. "I wouldn't know about that," he said. "He's been in bed for a week. Had a stroke or something. Oh, there's that bloody man Morgan. Morgan, I say—"

"Sir?"

Although he had heard nothing the voice came from directly behind Bohun's right shoulder. A middle-aged man, in dark clothes, had come quietly into the room and added himself to the party.

"Oh, Morgan. Someone has locked the corner cupboard."

"Yes, sir. I locked it, on Mr. Mallet's orders."

"Then kindly unlock it."

"There was something you wanted?"

"You're damned right there's something I wanted," said Major Rix. "That's where the whisky lives."

Morgan moved across to the cupboard, selected a key from a ring of keys and opened the cupboard. He then went over to the sideboard, opened that, and took out a tumbler. Into the tumbler he poured a very reasonable quantity of whisky, replaced the bottle in the cupboard, relocked the cupboard, and handed the glass to Major Rix.

He did all this in the most serious manner possible.

"There is a syphon of soda in the sideboard – if you require it, sir," he said. "That is not locked."

Major Rix said nothing at all. He simply picked up the tumbler and swirled the whisky round in it.

"Perhaps you would care to come with me," said Morgan.

"Oh – certainly." Bohun recovered himself with an effort. As he looked back he saw that the major was still sitting in his chair. His single eye had a frosty, faraway look in it.

Bohun followed Morgan up the stairs. As they reached the top a door opened and a woman came out. Pre-war Oxford, thought Bohun at once. About thirty-five. Bluestocking, but overlaid now with a certain amount of country moss.

"Good morning?" she said, managing to turn it into a question.

"This is Mr. Bohun, Miss Rachel. He's here to see your father on business."

"Business." Miss Mallet sounded upset. "But – is Daddy well enough to see this gentleman?"

"I expect it will be important business," said Morgan. "Some matter which *has to* be attended to. You understand."

"Oh – yes, I expect that's it." Miss Mallet turned to Bohun, drawing him aside with her glance in a way which seemed to exclude Morgan from the whole conversation.

"You must be as quick as you can, Mr. Bohun. If you've brought something – something for him to sign, get it done as quickly as possible. He's a dying man."

"He's—"

"If you'd come this way," said Morgan loudly. Miss Mallet laid a hand on his arm. "I want you to promise me," she said.

"I'm afraid," said Bohun carefully, "that there may be some mistake. The business I have to discuss with your father – it isn't family business at all. It's to do with his work in London. We've got quite a few important decisions to make. However – I'll certainly be as quick as I can, I promise you that."

All the time that he had been speaking she had kept hold of his arm. Morgan had taken a step forward and seemed almost ready to grasp him by the other arm. Penelope and the Suitors, thought Bohun. He was inclined to let the scene develop but it was broken up by a noise from below.

Major Rix had come out into the hall.

The drink which Morgan had poured for him must have been stronger than it looked, for even from above it could be seen that he was swaying very slightly on his feet, and he fumbled with the door handle for a few moments as he closed the door.

Miss Mallet had dropped Bohun's arm and was looking down into the hall. The expression on her face reminded him of a visitor at the zoo, some adult, intellectual spinster, peering down into the trough of the Reptile House. Detached, intrigued, very faintly nauseated.

"If you'd come along now," said Morgan.

When they had turned the corner of the corridor he halted. It was too dark for Bohun to see his face.

"I expect you haven't met Miss Rachel before," he said.

"I haven't had the pleasure—"

"Nor Master Norman?"

"No, I've never met him."

"You don't want to pay too much attention to what either of them say. They're both a little bit – you know."

Before Bohun could say anything more he had turned, knocked at a big, double door and opened it without waiting for an answer.

The room was in half-darkness, and what light there was came from a reading lamp placed slightly behind the bed in such a way that it deepened the shadows on the face of the man who lay there.

Bohun was considerably startled at the picture. But he was even more startled when Mr. Mallet sat up vigorously from his supporting pillows. His voice, when he spoke, showed no trace of weakness.

"Where are the children, Morgan?"

"Miss Rachel has gone downstairs. Mr. Norman is out with his birds."

"Then draw the curtains back a bit. We must have some light. Fetch Mr. Bohun a chair. That's right, we can use this table. Now, Bohun – this holding company. I tried to explain it to Craine, but he seemed to find it very difficult to understand. Perhaps I oughtn't to say so, but he seems to be losing his grip a bit—"

Fortunately Bohun had met Mr. Mallet before; most people in a certain line of business in the City ran across him sooner or later. Rumour had it that he had been a sergeant major in one of the administrative branches during the First World War and had made a pile out of the barter of vehicle spare parts. Whatever truth there may have been in this was now buried in the drift of time. The early Twenties had been spent in company flotation, as audacious as it was profitable. After this he had transferred his energies to the field of the Trust Corporation. At sixty he was rich and practically respectable.

"He's quite a character," Mr. Craine had warned him. "He shouts and bangs and swears and insults you and roars with laughter and sends you a dozen bottles of Scotch for Christmas. One year he sent me a box of exploding cigars. In some ways he's got a lot in common with the late Joe Stalin—"

At the end of two hours, although he had been sustained with a plate of sandwiches and a glass of milk, brought up by Morgan, Bohun felt limpish. The table was littered with papers, and Bohun was beginning to wonder whether it was he who was advising Mr. Mallet on the effect of the latest Finance Act, or vice versa. However, they had reached some sort of conclusion when steps sounded in the passage. Mr. Mallet swept the papers together, stuffed them under his pillow, turned off the second light, and sank back with a loud groan.

The door opened, and Morgan came in.

Mr. Mallet came to life at once.

"Thought it was Rachel," he said. "That's all right then. If anything further's needed, I'll telephone Craine tomorrow. I think you've got a good grasp of it, quite a good grasp."

"Thank you," said Bohun faintly.

"One other thing. If you happen to talk to either of my children before you go, would you mind remembering that I'm a dying man? I had a stroke at the beginning of the week which paralysed my left side. It hasn't affected my brain in any way, but if I should have another – which seems very possible – it may well finish me. You understand?"

"Oh, certainly," said Bohun. "I'm sorry to hear—"

"Not at all," said Mr. Mallet. "Stay to tea if you like. Morgan will drive you to the station in time for the five o'clock train."

It was two mornings later before Bohun got round to discussing the Mallet family with Mr. Craine.

"You've never seen such a crazy setup in your life. Either the father's mad, or the children are mad, or they're all mad—"

"I've never noticed anything actually mad about Mallet," said Craine. "You're certain he wasn't really ill?"

'I'm not a doctor," said Bohun. "Strokes are funny things. But in my view he was no more ill than—"

"Blast that telephone," said Mr. Craine. "Excuse me a moment. Who? Mr. Mallet? Oh, young Mr. Mallet. Put him through, please—"

The telephone squeaked and bumbled. Whoever was speaking at the other end had a lot to get off his mind, and was determined to unload it fast.

At last Mr. Craine succeeded in breaking in.

"I've got Mr. Bohun here with me," he said. "Yes – that's my partner. He came down to see you two days ago. He knows all about it. When? Oh, right away. If he gets the next train he should be with you before lunch."

He rang off.

"Look here," said Bohun, "I've got Lady Maidsmoreton coming—"

"Mallet's dead," said Craine. "He died this morning. The house is in an uproar. You'll have to go and cope. Take the will with you. I've got it here. I'm sole executor so you've got my full authority to spend any money and take any steps you like. I expect you may have to be down there a couple of days, so I'll get John Cove to look after your work. Miss Thwaites, would you mind getting hold of a taxi?"

"Oh dear," said Norman Mallet. "Oh dear. I'm so g-glad you've g-got here, Mr. – Mr. Bohun. I'm sure it will make a great difference having you here. I'm sorry you had to walk up from the station. I couldn't find Morgan and I couldn't – I mean, he always k-keeps the keys of the car on him, so it was very awkward." He had a slight, rather pleasant stammer.

"How did it happen?" said Bohun.

"Last night. Just as he always s-said it would. Quite suddenly. Like that—" Norman snapped his fingers, then seemed to find the gesture slightly indecorous and restored his hand to his trouser pocket.

"It was between n-nine and eleven. Rachel saw him at nine. She usually went in to see him last thing at night, to tuck him up and give him his – well, to make him comfortable. When Morgan went up at eleven o'clock to settle him for the night, he found him d-dead. We sent for the doctor, of course. That's Dr. Runcorn. He's up there now. You'll be able to see him."

"Did Dr. Runcorn know that your father was ill?"

"Of course. He's been father's d-doctor for years."

"But he knew about the stroke?" persisted Bohun.

"Oh, yes, he knew about that."

"Was he attending him?"

"Well, there was nothing much he could do."

The parlourmaid appeared. She had been crying.

"Will Mr. Bohun be staying?" she inquired.

"Why, yes – certainly. That is, I hope you'll be staying—"

"I'd like to stop to lunch, if it wouldn't be troubling you," said Bohun. "I've booked a room at the Black Goats."

"I expect you'll be more c-comfortable there," said Norman, without making a great deal of effort to conceal his relief. "Placket, would you show Mr. Bohun up – he'd like a word with the doctor."

"It's quite all right," said Bohun. "I know the way."

He was halfway up the stairs when the study door opened and Major Rix appeared. He snapped his fingers at Bohun and said, "Come on down here a moment, there's something I want to tell you."

"I must—"

"It's important," said Rix. "You'd better hear it."

"Oh, all right," said Bohun.

"They'll tell you Mallet died of a stroke," said Rix, as soon as the library door was shut. "Nothing further from the truth. The doctor's an old fool. He wouldn't know a stroke from German measles."

"I—" said Bohun.

"Just let me tell you this," said Rix urgently. "Mallet was murdered. Morgan did it. I don't know how. Poison or something, I should think. There's enough poison in this house to finish off the French Navy. Herbal muck. Rachel brews it. Another thing. What did Morgan slip up to London for last Thursday? Mallet never sent him. But I saw him. I was up there on business. He was coming out of some place off the Gray's Inn Road. Lot of shady chemists' shops in that district. Don't tell me he was up to nothing."

Bohun hardly liked to point out that if there was plenty of poison in the house it seemed a waste of time to go all the way up to London to buy more. But Rix was beyond such considerations. He was also more than a little drunk.

"Have you any idea," he said, "why Morgan should want to do that?"

"Of course," said Rix. "You know it as well as I do. Mallet had left him five thousand in his will. He was going to change it when Rachel married me. Morgan was afraid he'd get left out of the new one. I needn't tell you."

"Er – no," said Bohun. He had Mr. Mallet's will in his pocket and was reasonably familiar with its contents. "Well, I think perhaps you ought to be rather careful about saying things like that to anyone—"

"I wouldn't say them to anyone," agreed Rix handsomely. "After all, you're just a bloody lawyer. You're paid to have things said to you."

"Quite so," said Bohun. It was a view of his professional duties which had been expressed to him before, though never quite so bluntly. He went upstairs to find the doctor.

Dr. Runcorn was just finishing. He was a dignified little sheep with a respectable crown of smooth, white hair, and muddy grey eyes. He shook Bohun's hand and said, "I'm glad you've come. The lawyer takes on where the doctor leaves off. Very sad, a busy man like him. But businessmen often go that way."

"It was the stroke, then."

"A recurrence of the stroke, yes."

That seemed to be that.

Bohun said, "I know nothing about strokes, of course, but I saw him two days ago and he seemed so alert and vigorous."

"Vigorous enough in mind," said the doctor. "That's often the way. It attacks the body first."

"He seemed comparatively vigorous in body, too."

"I'm afraid I don't follow you," said Dr. Runcorn." I saw him myself on – let me see – Monday morning, and he was completely paralysed. He could only move his head and neck."

"Then he'd made a remarkable recovery," said Bohun. "When we were discussing business on Tuesday afternoon he sat up without apparent effort, handled the various papers extremely vigorously and generally behaved like a man who was perfectly well, but happened to be taking a day's rest in bed."

"Did you see him out of bed?"

"Well – no."

"You're quite sure you're not exaggerating his other movements?"

"I'm not in the habit of exaggerating," said Bohun.

"Well, it's very remarkable. But, then, nature is remarkable. It is of academic interest now, poor fellow."

"There was more to it than that," said Bohun steadily. "Once or twice in the course of our conversation he suggested that the whole of his illness was a sham. Something intended to deceive his children."

Dr. Runcorn went very red and his mouth tightened disagreeably.

"Am I to understand that you are suggesting that he deceived his medical adviser, too?"

"Well, it would be possible, wouldn't it? Who's to know? A man says to you, 'I've had a stroke. My mind is quite clear but my body won't move.' There's nothing to show, is there? Or is there?"

"There can be certain secondary symptoms—"

"Were these present in Mallet's case?"

"To a limited degree. But I'm afraid I cannot see where this is taking us. Are you suggesting that he is not dead now?"

"No," said Bohun softly, looking at the sheeted figure on the bed. "No. That is a fact that I think we will have to accept."

"Then what do you suggest, pray?"

"Perhaps a further examination into the cause of death."

"I have made my examination."

"Then I suggest a second opinion."

"And your authority for making the suggestion?"

"The lawyer," said Bohun unkindly, "takes on where the doctor leaves off. I act for the sole executor – who happens to be my partner. I will obtain his written directions if you insist."

Dr. Runcorn went white. "Really," he said, "I think you are making a mountain out of a molehill. You realise, I hope, what you are doing. Perhaps you would like the police in the house as well—"

The door crashed open. The noise and urgency of it made both men jump. It was Major Rix. He looked almost sober.

"Morgan's been shot," he said. "I just found him in the spinney at the back of the house."

"Well, now," said Inspector Franks patiently, "and where do you come into this?"

Bohun told him where he came in.

Inspector Franks spelled his name out carefully, and said, "It's a long shot, but you wouldn't by any chance happen to know a Superintendent Hazlerigg?"

"Yes. He was a Chief Inspector when I knew him."

"Then you're the chap who doesn't go to sleep?"

"The eye that never closes," agreed Bohun.

"Ah," said Inspector Franks. He thought for a minute, and then said, "I expect it'll be a help to me, having an independent inside view, as you might say. If you've no objection."

"None at all," said Bohun. "But don't expect too much. I've known Mallet for some time, but I only met Rachel when I came down on Tuesday – and I actually saw Norman for the first time this morning."

"Norman and Rachel," said Franks. "Those would be the only children?" He turned back the pages of his book. "I've seen both of them, but I couldn't make much out of them. Both a bit young for their age, I thought."

"Retarded adolescence," agreed Bohun. "Stern parent. Not much contact with the outside world. Norman keeps foxes and badgers. Rachel brews herbs."

"Well now," said Franks. "Herbs?"

"Just before we go on with this," said Bohun, "there's a point I'd like to be quite clear on. Which death are you investigating?"

"Both, at the moment," said Franks. "Morgan could be suicide – but I don't think it is. Mallet could be natural causes. I'm keeping an open mind about that."

"Have you got someone doing the necessary?"

"Police surgeon. Yes. He won't miss much."

"Good," said Bohun. "As long as that's settled."

"I've got one or two other people to see. Perhaps you'd like to listen in. Representing the next of kin."

"That's very good of you," said Bohun, trying to conceal his surprise. It occurred to him that Hazlerigg must have given him an exceptionally good ticket.

The middle-aged maid came. Her name was Placket.

"Such a good master," she said, "and such a kind father."

"Really, now," said Franks. "No trouble at all?"

"A happy, united family," said Placket. "The children stopping at home, and not rushing off the very moment they were out of the schoolroom."

"Let me see. Mr. Norman is just forty and Miss Rachel is thirty-five?"

"She was thirty-five last month. I still make them each a cake on their birthday. Thirty-five candles. It has to be a big cake."

"So I should think," said the Inspector, impassively. "You say they were a happy, cheerful family? I suppose Mr. Mallet spent a lot of time up in town. What did the children do all day?"

"Employed themselves as country people should," said Placket, rather tartly. "Master Norman had his studies. He's a great naturalist. What he doesn't know about birds and beasts – but there! You'll have seen for yourself. And Miss Rachel, she collects herbs. She's published a book—"

She went over to the shelf and pulled out a volume. It was a solid-looking book and published, Bohun saw, by a well-known firm. *The Herbs and Plants of East Anglia: Their Uses in Medicine and Cookery* by Rachel Mallet.

The Inspector looked happier. "I'd like to keep that for a bit."

"I expect Miss Rachel would sign it for you if you asked her," said Placket.

"Happy family?" said Major Rix. "Don't you believe it. I've never seen such a little hell-kitchen in my life. Wogs, Wops and Wuzzies – I've seen them all. Believe me, for real hating you want to come to the English Shires."

"Well, now; that's very interesting—"

"Old Mallet was a pirate, you see. He'd got the pirate mentality. When he'd made his haul, he liked to put it in a chest and sit on it. He liked his bits and pieces all round him, where he could see 'em. Rachel and Norman were bits and pieces. If he'd had his own way, he'd just like to have had them sitting round, quietly, as if they'd been carefully preserved and put under glass. Only human nature doesn't work out like that. All it did was to make 'em branch out in other ways. Norman and his birds and bees, and Rachel and her herbs. That sort of thing. The more they tried to lead lives of their own, the more he tried to stop them. First he tried to argue them out of it – no good. Then he tried to laugh them out of it. Do you know, he got a chap to write a sort of skit of Rachel's herb book – not very funny really. I read some of it. I reckon he had to pay through the nose to get *that* published—"

"Rather an elaborate joke," said Franks.

"Oh, he was like that. Go to any lengths for a laugh. As long as it made someone else uncomfortable. Very like a man I once knew in Jamaica – trained a tortoise to drink rum. However, that's another story. Lately it's been leg-pulling. Country superstitions and that sort of thing. Norman knows 'em all. Swallows go up at night, good weather coming. Rooks fly round the trees, it's going to rain. Norman believes in 'em all."

"There are certain scientific explanations—" began Bohun, but he caught a look from Inspector Franks and subsided.

"Well, I don't know about that," said Rix. "Prefer a barometer myself. However, Mallet used to pull his leg about it properly. When they had visitors. Particularly when they had visitors. I've heard Mallet say, 'Oh, Morgan, when I was out in the garden this morning, I saw the bees flying backwards round the hive. What do you suppose that means?' And Morgan would say, solemn as a judge, 'I am given to understand, sir, that it signifies that Consols will rise two points before the next account.' And so on. The more he bullied 'em the quieter they hated him."

"Not a very happy family," said Franks.

"You're telling me."

"But you were proposing to marry into it?"

"Yes. But I wasn't going to live with them afterwards."

"You didn't anticipate any trouble, then."

"Marriage always leads to trouble," said Major Rix frankly. "It's just one of those things you've got to put up with. My last wife used to shoot at me with an air gun."

"Hmph," said Inspector Franks. "Now, about the evening of Mr. Mallet's death."

"I know just what you're going to say," said Major Rix, "and I know it didn't sound good, all that stuff I was telling you about Rachel and Norman hating their father. But it doesn't mean they killed him. It wasn't them at all. That sort of hating doesn't lead to killing. You can take my word for that. It was Morgan. I never trusted him an inch myself. Then, after he'd done it he got cold feet and went out and shot himself. I've seen that happen before."

"Yes," said Franks. "No doubt it's one of the solutions we shall have to investigate. Thank you very much for what you have told us. Meanwhile—"

"There was one thing," said Bohun. "When you found Morgan this morning – were you certain he was dead?"

"Of course I knew he was dead. I've seen lots of dead men before."

"Did you disturb the body in any way?"

"Did I – certainly not."

"To be quite specific," said Bohun. "Did you take a key from the ring of keys in his hip pocket?"

Involuntarily the Major turned to look over his shoulder at the corner cupboard. It was ajar.

"All right," he said. "Very smart of you. I borrowed the key of the drink cupboard."

"Why did you do that?" said Franks sharply.

"Well, really," said Rix. "Just because the bloody man had shot himself, I saw no reason to put all the whisky into pawn."

"Well, now," said Franks. "You'll be doing me a service if you tell me what you make of all that?"

It was evening, the oil lamp had been trimmed and lit, and they were alone in the coffee-room of the Black Goats, an ancient apartment approached by so many twisted stairs and winding corridors that it seemed improbable that anyone else should ever find his way to it.

"I don't mean the routine bits," he went on. "I shall have to wait for the reports to come in tomorrow. There's the doctor's report on Mallet and on Morgan and I've had an expert look at the gun which killed Morgan – it's an ordinary twelve-bore sporting gun from the case in the gun room, but it might tell us something. And there's the fingerprints and photographs and so on. They might be useful." He spoke as a man who has not got a great deal of faith in fingerprints and photographs, but Bohun was not deceived.

He did not know much about police routine, but he did know that most cases were solved by simple hard work on matters of detail by a great number of policemen.

"It's the shape of the thing that rattles me. Usually you can see which way a thing goes, right at the start. Man or woman gets killed – in nine cases out of ten it's the husband or wife who did it. That's one of the things about marriage. You do know where you are. Or else perhaps it's a professional – breaking and entering and so on. You just look up the list. But this—" He spread his hands despairingly.

"It is a bit confusing," agreed Bohun. He got up, trimmed the lamp, and sat down again sympathetically.

"First of all you've got Mallet, if that *was* murder. Even allowing for it being an inside job, you've got plenty of candidates. Norman and Rachel who hated him – according to Rix. Morgan who wanted his money—"

"Oh, there's nothing in that one," said Bohun. "I've got the will here. So far as I know it's the only will Mallet made, and he never had the slightest intention of changing it. Morgan got five hundred pounds in either case – not five thousand."

"It's not always what's in a will that causes the trouble," said Franks.

"It's what people think may be in it. Can you tell me what happened to the rest?"

"Oh yes, I think I can do that. There are a few other little gifts – five hundred pounds to Placket – the others are people in his London office. Then the rest goes into two parts. One half to Norman and one half to Rachel. Only she can't touch her capital. It's tied up in the usual way to prevent a husband getting hold of any of it."

"Do you suppose Rix knew that?"

"Even if he did, he was on to quite a good thing when Mallet died. They couldn't touch the capital, but Rachel's income would have been about six thousand a year. That would have done very nicely to pay the bills – he'd have had free board and lodging, food and drink for the rest of his life. Particularly drink."

"So far as money goes, then, Rix and Morgan both had motives. Only Morgan's may have been smaller than he imagined."

"That's about it," said Bohun.

"When you look at the means," said Franks, "there's nothing to choose between them. We make it as difficult as we can for people to buy poison, but the law hasn't yet got round to stopping them making it for themselves. Mallet used to have a hot whisky at nine o'clock. Almost anyone got it ready and took it up. There was no rule about it. Norman and Rachel say Morgan took it up that night. Placket says she thinks Norman did. Rachel certainly went up to see him at nine o'clock."

"And what about Morgan's death?"

"There's even less there. The gun was in a cupboard with the cartridges – not locked. Anyone could pick it up, follow Morgan into the spinney – and shoot him. No one would take any notice. The fields are full of those automatic bird-scarers. They go off about once an hour."

"Then perhaps Morgan did shoot himself."

"If he did," said Franks. "All right. He's the obvious candidate for Mallet. Then the thing's reasonably straight. But if he didn't – it doesn't seem to have any shape at all. There's a piece missing somewhere."

"I'm only here to make suggestions," said Bohun. "You do the work. I'm under no delusions about that. I quite agree with what you said – the middle piece is missing, and the other pieces won't match up till you find it. All I've got at the moment is three questions in my head. The first's a tiny matter of fact. What was Morgan doing up in London last Thursday?"

"I've got an inquiry going," said Franks. "I circulated a photograph. Unfortunately it's not a very good one – and there are quite a lot of shops in and around the Gray's Inn Road."

"All right," said Bohun. "It may be nothing."

The lamp was smoking again, and he got up to adjust it, first turning the flame right down, then carefully up again, talking as he worked. "The second question is, were the two deaths connected? I don't necessarily mean, did the same person do both. But were they logically connected? And, if so, how? The third point seems to me to be the oddest of the lot. Suppose that the postmortem on Mallet shows that his stroke was a fake. Then what was the point of it? Mallet was a notorious joker, but his jokes always seemed to end with a big belly laugh for Mallet and someone else feeling all kinds of a fool. This one doesn't seem to have worked out quite like that. *What went wrong?*

"First report," said Franks next morning, "from the doctor, on Mallet. No sign of any cerebral congestion or haemorrhage. In plain English, no stroke."

"So much for old Uncle Runcorn."

"Yes. Not very good. But there's more to it than that. Equivalent of three grains of hyoscine or hyoscyamine in the stomach and digestive organs. Not *materia medicastuit.* Vegetable origin. Derived from distillation of the seeds of henbane, alias hogsbean, alias stinking nightshade. Probable that the dose was taken after Mallet had his evening meal but before midnight. To be continued."

"Quite enough to go on with," said Bohun.

"I thought you'd like it. Second report. Doctor on Morgan. Suicide barely possible, but most unlikely. Position of wounds – direction of wounds – powder burns, etc., etc. You can read it for yourself."

Bohun did so." It certainly sounds acrobatic," he agreed. "Muzzle at least twenty-four inches away from the head, but pointing practically straight at it. I really think you can rule out suicide."

"I had already done so," agreed Franks. "Listen to this. Report number three. Absolutely *no fingerprints* on the gun of any sort. Morgan wasn't wearing gloves. Tell me how he could shoot himself without leaving any prints on the gun."

"All right," said Bohun. "That's that. Anything else on Morgan?"

"General state of health. State of clothing. Contents of pockets—"

"Let's have that one."

"Wallet, money, old letters, bills. Nothing recent. Handkerchief, packet of fags. Lighter. Large pocketknife. Key ring—"

"Key ring?"

"That checks up with Rix's story. The key of the drink cupboard was missing – and we picked up half a possible Rix fingerprint on one of the other keys. He probably touched it when he was removing the first key."

"A cool customer," said Bohun. "What other keys?"

"Two house doors, cellar and two safe keys."

"Hmph," said Bohun. "House. Cellar. Safe. Hmph?"

"One other small point. He'd got three recent bee stings. Two on his right arm, one on his left wrist."

"Had he though?" said Bohun.

He went off to telephone Craine.

"You'd better stay down there," said Craine. "I suppose there's bound to be an inquest. When they've finished cutting him up perhaps you can get him buried. The instructions are in the envelope with the will."

After lunch Franks reappeared. He had a look in his eye which meant more news.

"I've got a good identification of Morgan on his shopping expedition," he said. "The shop assistant picked the photograph straight out of a dozen without even stopping to think, bless him. I'll give you three guesses what he went up to London to buy."

"I'm not that good," said Bohun. "You tell me."

"A dictaphone. The sort of thing a businessman keeps on his desk to breathe his secret thoughts into. Not very big" – Franks demonstrated with his hands – "a small dispatch-case would hold it. But powerful, and up to date. Records on a roll and the typist plays it back later into earphones."

Bohun digested this.

"Have you found it yet?"

"I've got every man I can lay hands on, busy now taking the house apart. If it's there I'll find it before dusk." Dusk came. And dark. But no dictaphone.

At one o'clock in the morning Bohun was sitting by himself in the wheel-back rocking chair in the coffee-room. He had got the wick of the lamp adjusted to a nicety now and the oil flame spread its low, warm, kind light over the dingy old room.

He was not asleep, nor even sleepy, because he suffered from para-insomnia and rarely slept more than an hour in any night. None of the doctors who had examined him had agreed about any point in his rare complaint except that one day he would drop down dead.

He knew, by experience, when he was due to sleep and until that moment it was a waste of time even to go near his bedroom. He found the night hours useful. Sometimes he wrote, sometimes he read, sometimes he thought – a luxury which few normal people can fit into their crowded waking lives.

He was thinking at that moment and he was making quite reasonable progress. For example, he was certain, now, that the double murderer was Norman Mallet. He was the only man with a real motive. As Major Rix had pointed out, people often got angry over their family's idiosyncrasies, but they very rarely killed each other on account of them. With Norman it was different. If he believed that his father was using his money to coerce Rachel into a loveless marriage with Rix, then he might well think it his duty to stop it. More particularly if he was convinced that his father was dying already. And most particularly if he saw a lawyer coming to the house. Lawyers meant settlements and new wills or codicils. From that point of view his own visit had probably timed the murder. It had set it off. And this despite the fact that both Norman's assumptions were false. His father had *not* been dying, and Bohun's visit had been *nothing* to do with his will.

Where motives were concerned, as the Inspector had so truly remarked, it wasn't what actually happened, but what people thought was going to happen that produced results.

As for the killing of Morgan, Norman had given himself away at his very first meeting. Bohun had not observed the fact at the time, but had remembered it afterwards. Apologising for not coming to the station to fetch him, he had said, "Morgan always keeps the keys of the car on him." Now that was not true. A search of Morgan's body had shown a number of keys, but they were house keys, not the garage key, and not the car key. It seemed logical to suppose that the reason Norman had been unable to meet him was that he had been too busy murdering Morgan.

Why he had done so, and what sort of connection it could have with the death of Mr. Mallet, was the final step in this tangled business.

Franks had been right about that. There was a piece missing. It was the middle piece of the jigsaw puzzle, and when he saw it, all the other little edges and twists would fall into position, and a recognisable whole would appear.

What had been the point of Mallet's last great pointless practical joke?

What connection had it, if any, with his previous jokes? His ridiculing of his children's love of birds and animals and country life and country superstitions?

What use had he for a dictaphone? Why had it to be obtained secretly? And where was it now if it wasn't in Humble Bee House?

How had Morgan managed to get his wrists and arms stung three times?

There is enormous virtue in sequence. It is conceivable that if Bohun had asked himself these questions in any other order he might not have spotted the truth which, by now, was staring him in the face.

Feeling a little shaken in spite of himself he got to his feet and made his way to his bedroom. From his suitcase he took a torch and from the pocket of his coat a pair of gloves. It would be dark but there would be light enough for his purpose. And in any event, night was the best time, as Morgan had no doubt discovered. As he was leaving the inn he saw, in the corner of the hall, a heavy stick, and after a moment's hesitation he added this to his equipment.

Half an hour later he was standing once more at the gate of Humble Bee House. The driveway was a tunnel of darkness. It was the hour of false dawn, and, standing quite still, he could hear life moving in the thickets which bordered the drive. He opened the gate as quietly as he could, and the ghost of a wind set the leaves whispering, so that the news of his arrival seemed to run ahead of him up the drive.

He went silently, on the turf edge, and presently he found himself by the glade of beehives. The large one in the middle was clearly the place. He could have wished that he knew more about bees.

Putting down his torch and stick he grasped the roof very gently with both hands. It came up, in one piece, together with the top section of the hive. Underneath was nothing more alarming than a folded blanket.

He listened very carefully, and in the stillness he sensed rather than saw the legion of sleeping bees. Very gently he raised the blanket and, sure enough, there was the dictaphone, a box-like affair above the first comb-section, with its receiver immediately behind the ventilation grille in front of the hive. Carefully he lifted it, carefully replaced the blanket and hive-top. Then he tiptoed away with his spoil into the thickest part of the shrubbery.

A quarter of an hour later he was back in the bee glade. He lifted the top and replaced the dictaphone exactly where he had found it. He stood for a moment as if undecided. Then, with a quick, almost abrupt gesture, he pulled a pencil and notebook from his pocket and, using his torch guardedly, scribbled a note. When he had finished it, he tore out the page, folded it in four, and wrote a name on the outside. Then, with the paper in his hand, he made his way up the drive, towards the sleeping front of Humble Bee House.

It was eleven o'clock on the following morning when Bohun reached Humble Bee House once again, and rang the front door bell. The door was opened by Placket, who had no word to say to him. The Inspector was behind her in the hall.

"It's all over," he said. "Perhaps you'd better come up."

Norman and Rachel Mallet were sitting, upright, in chairs on either side of the empty hearth in their father's room. It was difficult, in the shadows, to realise that they were dead, so quietly and calmly they sat. Almost as if they had been carefully preserved, thought Bohun, and put under glass. The words formed an echo in his head.

"They took the same stuff as they gave the old man," said Franks. "Norman left a note – just to say that he was responsible for both his father and Morgan. Not much explanation. He says it was him, not his sister, but she knew about it – afterwards. I don't suppose we shall ever understand the whole of it now."

"On the contrary," said Bohun. "If you'll come out in the garden I'll do my level best to explain it to you."

"I wouldn't try to open it now, not unless you happen to be a skilled apiarist," said Bohun. "But inside that large central hive you'll find the dictaphone Mallet and Morgan bought for the consummation of their final stupendous joke."

"Joke?"

"So elaborate. So funny. So much in character. What's the best-known and oldest superstition about bees? That if there's a death in the house, they must be the first to be told about it. Can't you imagine it? After a week or ten days of preparation and preliminary fun, getting everyone in the mood for it, Morgan suddenly comes down last thing at night with the news that the master has had a second stroke and passed away. Chaos and confusion and the doctor to be sent for, and the lawyers to be telephoned. And in the middle of it all, Norman creeps down to the hive and whispers the news to the bees."

"I see," said Franks. "And the message is picked up on the dictaphone."

"That's right. To be preserved, forever and ever as the joke of a lifetime. I think it must have been due to take place that very evening. You can imagine Morgan's feelings when he went along to arrange for the culmination of the jest – *and found his master really dead.*"

Franks thought this out. He brushed off a bee which had settled on his coat.

"Later," said Bohun, "I don't suppose he thought of it at once, but later. Perhaps in the early hours of next morning, when things had settled down, it did just occur to him to wonder. So he went off to the hive. The dictaphone had run down by that time, but he wound it back and listened in – and heard what I venture to think was one of the plainest and most singular confessions of murder which has ever been made – a *confession unmistakably identified by a slight stutter.*"

"You mean to say," said Franks, "that after he'd done the job Norman went off and told the bees all about it."

"Certainly," said Bohun. "You must never keep anything from the bees."

Another bee came past, and settled on Franks' sleeve. The Inspector looked at it in silence. The bee looked back, for a moment, impassively, then flew off.

"After that," went on Bohun, "Morgan re-hid the dictaphone in the safest place – back in the hive. The bees must have been a bit more active by then. I think that's when he got stung."

"He got stung a lot harder when he tried to blackmail Norman next morning," said Franks thoughtfully.

"Yes. Bad tactics to blackmail a desperate man."

"That's not entirely guesswork, I take it." Franks nodded towards the hive.

"I'm afraid not. I thought it all out last night. I've listened to the confession. You won't find *my* fingerprints on the dictaphone, because I wore gloves. But I'm prepared to bet you'll find Morgan's."

"I see." The Inspector sat, swinging his legs. He seemed to be in difficulties over something. At last he said, without looking up, "I take it you told him. Sent him a note or something."

"Without prejudice to my having to deny it later," said Bohun, "and since you haven't found it, I gather he must have destroyed it – yes, I did."

"I see," said Franks. "Best way out, really. I don't see much of this coming to light now. What exactly did you say to him?"

Bohun got to his feet, and started down the drive with Inspector Franks beside him. They had reached the gate before he spoke.

"It is a couple of lines of verse. I've known them all my life – though I couldn't tell you, even now, who wrote them. They go like this:

> *'Money is honey, my little sonny*
> *And a rich man's joke is always funny.'"*

Behind them, Humble Bee House dozed in the morning sun.

STROLLING IN THE SQUARE ONE DAY

Julian Symons

Francis Quarles walked across Trafalgar Square on a clear blustery November day. Wind blew the fountains' spray towards him, slightly wetting his suede shoes. Round his feet pigeons cooed and strutted. A small girl stood with arms outstretched holding food, unable to contain her laughter as the birds scrambled over her hands, shoulders and head.

As Quarles watched, smiling benevolently, a pigeon jumped on to his own head. He stood in the Square, a big man wrapped in a teddy-bear overcoat, leaning on his walking stick, a pigeon perched on his head. A photographer clicked his camera.

"Very nice, sir. Three for five shillings, post-card size. I'll just take another to make sure."

Quarles waved his hand dismissively, shook off the pigeon, and walked away. Two minutes later he was in the lift going up to his office in Soames Buildings, overlooking the Square. He went in from the corridor entrance and pressed down the switch for Molly Player. She came in.

"We have a visitor," Molly announced. "Wants to see you, urgent, won't give her name."

"What sort of woman?"

"Late thirties, I should say. Elegant. You'll like her." Molly made a face. "Class. Money. Doesn't know I exist. Looks familiar, somehow, but it may be just that air of breeding."

It was possible to tell a good deal about a woman's education and background, Francis Quarles believed, by such small things as the way she sat in a chair. The woman who now sat opposite his desk seemed perfectly at ease. The light from the big window that faced her showed smoothly classical features, a little inexpressive perhaps, but that might have been the result of her deliberate self-contained calm.

She wore a plain blue suit, severe and simple. Yet the impression she produced was, curiously, one of controlled passion.

An intelligent woman, Quarles concluded, and potentially a dangerous one.

He offered her a cigarette. She took it and inhaled deeply.

"Mr. Quarles? I have heard that you are the sort of man who doesn't betray a confidence." He merely nodded. "My name is Lesley Riverside."

"Of course. Silly of me."

Lord Riverside was Under Secretary to the Ministry of Home Security. He had married, about ten years ago, a woman much younger than himself, the beautiful Lesley Stoneham, who had had a reputation for gaiety and wildness. Her name had been linked with those of half a dozen young men; but all that, as far as Quarles knew, was in the past.

"Mr. Quarles," she said with faultless composure, "I have been very stupid. I want you to get back a photograph for me – a photograph showing me with a man. It is a perfectly innocent photograph. It was taken out there in the Square."

"In Trafalgar Square?"

"Yes. We were standing under one of the Landseer lions. This little photographer came up to us, clicked his camera, and said that he had taken a snap. We told him that we didn't want it." She added in her even voice, "We should have smashed his camera."

"Nothing else happened? He took no second photograph?"

"No. I want the negative of that photograph back, Mr. Quarles."

He met her gaze with one as steady as her own. "Why?"

"It is embarrassing," she said, but she showed no embarrassment. "Quite a long while ago I had an affair with a man named Tony Hartman. George – my husband – knew about it. I had to promise never to see Tony Hartman again. George is a jealous man – I might even say, pathologically jealous. He said that if I ever met Tony again he'd—"

"Yes?"

"George said he would kill him."

"And the man with you in the Square—"

"Yes. The man with me was Tony Hartman."

"When was this photograph taken?"

"A week ago."

"It may have been destroyed by now. What makes you think you're in any trouble?"

"This came today."

Quarles read the letter she pushed across the desk. It said: 'You and your friend make a lovely pair. A certain person would be interested. Send £20 in ones to James Johnson, c/o Charing Cross Road Post Office.'

"Are you going to pay it?" Quarles asked.

"Certainly not. That's why I've come to you."

"All right," Quarles said, although he thought it was far from all right. "But this will cost you money."

She wrinkled her nose distastefully. "As long as it is understood that I am *buying* it. You can go up to fifty pounds."

"That's not very high."

"I have no intention of being blackmailed for a large sum of money, Mr. Quarles. I might go to seventy-five."

"Tell me what you can remember about the man who took the photograph."

"He was a small man, rather grubby, fair hair, brown suit, very fancy suede shoes, a bad squint in his left eye."

Quarles was glad that his own suede shoes were under the desk.

"You're very observant, Lady Riverside. Did you notice whether he was wearing a badge?"

"A badge? No, I'm sure I should have noticed it. Is there anything else you want to know?"

"I don't think so. I'll report to you when I have some news."

"By telephone, please, between ten and eleven o'clock each morning. I shall answer the telephone then."

She did not extend her hand as she got up to go. Quarles watched her from his window as she crossed the Square, unhurried and unruffled, and waited for a taxi. Molly came in and stood beside him.

"What was she like?"

"An intelligent icicle. She says she's being blackmailed."

"And is she?"

"That's what I'm going to find out."

*   *   *

Trafalgar Square is one of the three or four places in Central London (Westminster Abbey and the Tower of London are two of the others) where street photographers cluster, cameras ready, to snap gaping Americans, innocent Europeans and those up from the provinces to see the sights of London. Some of the photographers are licensed by the L.C.C. and wear badges to say so, but others operate independently and without permission.

Quarles's guess that the man he was after would prove to be an independent operator was proved correct. Two of the official photographers recognised Lady Riverside's description as that of a man named Joe James, and one of them, who knew Quarles, was able to give him James's address.

"You want to be careful with Joe James, Mr. Quarles. What do you want him for?"

"It might be blackmail. Would he be up to that?"

"He'd be up to anything. He only uses this camera pitch as a come-on for mugs. I wouldn't trust him further than I could throw him."

The address Quarles had been given was in Fendy Street, near Paddington Station. Fendy Street proved to be a cul-de-sac of condemned, or at least eminently condemnable, Victorian houses. Children played in the gutters while their older brothers and sisters, drainpiped and lipsticked, lounged against the walls. The eyes that followed Quarles's bulky figure as he walked down the street wearing his teddy-bear overcoat, carrying his loaded stick, were definitely hostile.

The number that Quarles had been given was 22. There were five bells outside the house. Quarles pressed one. Nothing happened.

A small greasy-haired girl in a soiled red frock, her face angelic beneath layers of dirt and dust, said, "They don't work, mister. Who d'yer want?"

"Joe James."

"He'll be at the Black Horse round the corner. Least, he usually is, this time of day."

"Thank you." She stared at him as though he were speaking an unknown language, and looked unbelievingly at the shilling he gave her.

Saloon or Public, Quarles wondered, and pushed open the Saloon bar door. A couple of minutes later an unobtrusive man wearing a grey trilby hat and a threadbare grey suit, who had tailed Quarles from his office, followed him in.

Quarles recognised Joe James immediately. The photographer leaned against the bar with a glass of beer in front of him. Quarles tapped him on the shoulder.

"Mr. James?"

The squint was very marked. "Who wants him?"

"Or Mr. James Johnson, if you like that better." Quarles added mildly, "It's a mistake to use your own initials, or part of your real name, when you're sending letters like that. Let's talk, shall we?"

Joe James was less shaken than Quarles had expected him to be. James led the way to a table in the corner. "Have you brought the money?"

"No."

"Then you can get out. Who are you, anyway? How'd you find me?"

"My name is Quarles. I'm a private detective, and I've got friends who know you. Blackmail is a serious offence."

"Don't give me that. She'd never dare."

"Why not?"

One eye looked at Quarles. The other stared fixedly at the door. "You don't know much, do you? She's sent a boy to do a man's job."

"My client wants the negative of that photograph."

"She's got a hope. When I spotted her photo in a picture paper the other day – at my dentist's it was – I said to myself, Joe, boy, you're fixed for life. Don't kill the goose that's going to lay the golden eggs, I said. A nice steady twenty pounds a month I reckon it's worth. She can afford it, and that's what she's going to pay."

"It's not worth it."

The squinting eye roved wildly. "Let her go to the police, then."

"Let me see a print of it."

"Look." Joe James's forefinger jabbed at Quarles's chest. "*You're* not seeing anything. *She* knows what picture I took, and she knows I've only got to send it to a certain party and she'd be—"

"Yes?" Quarles said, as Joe James stopped suddenly. "What would happen?"

The little man smacked down his glass on the table. His voice was low but intense. "I don't believe you know what it's all about. You just go back and tell her to pack up that money and send it like I said. And if you know what's good for you, get out of here."

"I'm here to buy the negative. Thirty pounds for it."

"Don't make me laugh."

"Fifty."

"Not for sale."

"A hundred."

It was a cold day, but the little man's brow was thick with sweat. He did not answer.

"Five hundred pounds," Quarles said softly. "Suppose I offered you five hundred pounds for the negative. Should I get it then, Joe?"

"Get out." Joe James's hand moved downward. The empty glass he was holding broke on the table edge, and he raised the jagged fragment menacingly. Quarles brought up his walking stick and sent the fragment of glass flying. In the hubbub that ensued he left quietly. He did not notice the man in the grey trilby hat and the threadbare grey suit, who stayed on, nursing his half pint of bitter.

*   *   *

On the following morning, just after ten o'clock, Quarles picked up the telephone. The voice at the other end said, "Yes?"

"Lady Riverside? This is Francis Quarles."

"Oh, yes." The voice became one degree colder. "I won't require your services any further, Mr. Quarles. If you send in your bill I will see that you receive a cheque."

Whatever Quarles had expected, it was not this. "But my report—"

"Is of no interest to me. The matter has been settled." The line was disconnected. Quarles stared at the telephone.

"I was listening," Molly Player said when he went to the outer office. Not without malice she added, "Her ladyship doesn't soil her hands with the lower orders more than is necessary. Where are you going?"

Quarles's face was dark with anger. "Back to Fendy Street." He went out into a London which today was yellow with fog – a fog so palpable that a knife could slice it. The photographers were gone from the Square, buses crawled, even the pigeons were muted.

When Quarles reached Fendy Street it was empty and silent. Even the teenagers and the children had disappeared. He went to the door of Number 22, ignored the bells, and plied the knocker heavily.

The door was opened by the little girl to whom he had given the shilling. Her frock looked a little dirtier, her hair a little greasier, than they had done the day before.

"Oh, it's you. Joe James ain't in."

Quarles looked at his watch. "It's too early for the pub."

"That's right. 'E ain't out either. What I mean is, there's his milk. 'E always takes it upstairs for his tea. What I mean is," she said triumphantly, "'e ain't 'ere."

"I'll just take up the milk and make sure. He's first floor, isn't he?"

"Second." This time she accepted the shilling as a matter of course.

Quarles took up the half pint of milk to the second floor and knocked. There was no reply. He turned the door handle, and the door opened.

The room was full of fog. Joe James lay on the floor in his pyjamas, his tongue hanging out of a discoloured face. The cord pulled round his neck was so tight that it had cut into his skin.

Quarles did not touch the body, but he examined the room. It was full of fog because the window had been left wide open. He crossed over to it, looked out and saw, to one side and below, the flat roof of an extension. It would have been easy enough for any moderately active man to climb up on to that roof and thence to this window.

The room was in utter disorder, with the contents of drawers strewn on the floor and the bedding cut to ribbons. Empty gin and whisky bottles lined the walls. In one corner stood a metal filing cabinet, its drawers gaping.

Quarles carefully went through the notes and photographs inside, and saw without surprise that at least half a dozen people would have had good reason for wanting Joe James dead. The little man had not confined his photography to the streets.

But Quarles found no photograph or negative relating to Lady Riverside.

The papers from the dead man's wallet were scattered on the floor. Among them was a clipping from a newspaper five days old, headed *EXPULSION OF IRON CURTAIN DIPLOMAT. CHARGE OF SPYING.* The story went on to say that a particular Iron Curtain country had been notified that the British Government had information to the effect that Max Nafescu, a Third Secretary in the Embassy, had been engaged in espionage activities, and that his presence in this country was no longer acceptable. The Embassy had protested strongly, but Nafescu had been sent home. There was a photograph of him, smiling and looking engagingly boyish, and another photograph which showed him, coat collar up, boarding an aeroplane.

Quarles read and reread this clipping, and then put it in his pocket.

★　　★　　★

It took him more than an hour to get back to Trafalgar Square in the fog. He telephoned Lady Riverside, and spoke to a manservant who asked his name, went away, and returned.

"Lady Riverside is not at home."

"I think you're mistaken. Tell her that it is in connection with a friend in—" and Quarles named the Iron Curtain country.

"But, sir—"

"Just tell her that. I'll hold on."

It was just a minute later when he heard her icy voice. "Mr. Quarles? I haven't the least idea what you're talking about."

"Joe James is dead."

"I have never heard the name."

"And I am talking about Max Nafescu."

There was a silence. Then she said, "What do you want?"

"To see you. Today."

"It is inconvenient. I have a dinner party this evening."

"It won't take more than a few minutes."

"Very well. Come here at seven o'clock."

The house was in Kensington Square, tall, narrow and elegant. He was shown into a first-floor drawing-room, which had French windows leading out to a balcony. Quarles walked over to these windows, parted the curtains, and stared out at the fog.

When he turned she was standing in the doorway, and she had spoken his name. She wore a dark blue dress that reached the ground, and there was a blaze of diamonds at her throat. Her cheeks were flushed. She was one of the most beautiful women he had ever seen.

"Mr. Quarles, I owe you an apology. I should have explained to you this morning why I wanted no further investigation made. I was unnecessarily brusque. Forgive me."

He said nothing.

"Last night I spoke to my husband. I told him about Tony Hartman, about the photograph. I told him that whatever had been between us was over. I had misjudged my husband. He forgave me, he understood. We could afford to laugh at this petty blackmailer. You see?"

"It won't do," Quarles said. "You're very good, but it won't do. You're not worried about Tony Hartman, and you haven't told your husband anything. You're worried about a charge of treason, Lady Riverside."

She walked across to the mantel and put her bare arm on it. "That is ridiculous."

"Let me tell you a story – the story of a beautiful woman who liked excitement, and was bored with her life. Somehow – at a party, a reception – she met a handsome young man, Third Secretary in an Embassy. Was there a love affair between them? Possibly, but it wasn't important. The important thing was that her husband was in the Government, and she was in a position to pass on secrets. Perhaps at first she did it as a kind of lark, a kind of adventure. Later it became more than that.

"They met in, of all places, Trafalgar Square. But after all, why not? It is crowded – the people are preoccupied with the birds, the fountains, each other. It was bad luck that a photographer took a snap of them together. But still, this wasn't important – it became important only when the Third Secretary was accused of espionage, had to leave the country, and the photographer saw the story in the paper. And from then on the bad luck piled up.

"The photographer saw a picture of her in a glossy magazine, and he remembered the two who had been so insistent that they didn't want to be photographed. He realised that this photograph was worth a lot of money. By a further piece of bad luck, he was a petty blackmailer. So he wrote a blackmail note.

"And what was our society hostess to do now? I can tell you what she did." Quarles's dark eyes were angry. She did not meet his gaze. "She went to a private detective and told him a cock-and-bull story which he partly believed. She wanted him to find the photographer, that was all. She told somebody at the Embassy, and they had the private detective followed. He found the photographer for them. Then they killed him, and searched for the negative."

"I didn't want—" she began, and stopped. Then she said defiantly, "You have no proof."

"They didn't find the negative, did they?"

She stared. "You mean that you've found it?"

"It is in a safe place."

"What do you want for it?" Her composure had broken at last. She came over and clutched at his coat. "How much?"

"It is not for sale."

"I don't understand."

He disengaged her hands from his coat. "You can't understand, can you, that some things are not for sale?"

"But-but what *do* you want?"

"I shall deliver the negative to the proper place tomorrow morning. Unless circumstances make it unnecessary."

Her whole body seemed to sag for a moment, then she was all ice and iron again. "I think I understand now."

"Scandal is always undesirable. And I should say this: if anything happens to me, it will not help you."

In a low voice she said, "Nothing will happen. I've done with all that."

He left her staring into the looking glass over the mantel. He let himself out of the house and walked into the fog. His footsteps on the pavement were muffled, as though he were walking in cotton-wool.

★　　★　　★

On the next day the fog had lifted. A watery sun shone from a pale-blue sky. Molly had the paper ready for him when he entered the office.

"Isn't it terrible about Lady Riverside?" Quarles raised his eyebrows. "She went out for a walk last night – had a bad headache after a dinner party – and stepped right in front of a passing car. She was killed at once."

"It was the end she chose," Quarles said. He told the story to Molly, who listened spellbound.

"She was really selling secrets?"

"Giving them away, I guess – just for the thrill of it. She was that sort of woman," Quarles said.

Molly bit one of her fingernails. "There's one thing I don't see. How did you get hold of the negative?"

"I didn't," Quarles said. "There wasn't any negative. I knew that when she first came here and told me that the photographer had clicked his camera just once. These street photographers never take a film on speculation that way – they simply click the camera once to stop you, then go into their sales talk, and if you want a photograph, then they really take one. James didn't have a picture to sell – he was bluffing, as I found out when I offered him five hundred pounds for the negative. I was bluffing too – but I had more luck.

"She was a beautiful woman," he added, and sighed. "And intelligent too. But not quite intelligent enough."

THE SERVICE FLAT

Bill Knox

Marion Lister was thirty, brunette, attractive rather than good-looking, and lived alone in her small, top-floor service flat, one of three situated within the house in Garroway Court, a quiet, still reasonably fashionable part of Glasgow. She worked nine till five, five days a week, as private secretary to an advertising consultant.

That meant that from nine till five the flat should have been locked and empty... Marion Lister did her own housework.

Yet it was three weeks now since the small things had suddenly begun to show. The trace of cigarette ash, the telephone receiver replaced the wrong way round, a cushion rumpled, all the other minute, personal details which shrieked only one message.

Someone was using her flat while she was out. Nothing taken, nothing damaged...but Marion Lister had begun to know the pulsating terror of coming home and putting the key in her own doorlock, the concentrated fear that one evening the flat wouldn't be empty when she went in.

"All right, so you say you can't call the police." Her friend Vi Taylor shrugged as they turned off the rain-puddled road and walked up the short driveway to the house. "Ever thought of staying off work for a day and just waiting to see if anyone comes in? Now, don't look at me like that – I'm just joking. Trying to, anyway!"

"I tried that." Marion Lister's voice was quiet, resigned. "I waited, all day. Nothing happened. That's why I invited you home tonight – to talk about it to somebody who'd listen. Vi, I went to work as usual the next day. When I came home at night, it had happened again."

They went into the big gloomy hall with its old-fashioned wallpaper and dark-stained woodwork. An elderly woman gave a curt, barely friendly nod of recognition as they went past, then turned back to talk to the stockily built young man by her side.

"Neighbours?" Vi Taylor glanced back as they climbed the stairs. The young man had gone out, the woman was returning to her task of polishing the heavy brass palm-pots which decorated the entrance area.

"Mrs. Johns, the caretaker. And her son Danny – he's an engineer, on night shift. They live in the basement." Marion Lister searched her bag for her key as they reached the last flight of steps and neared her door.

"He's too young for me." Her friend gave a chuckle, then followed her in as the door was opened. "Well, what do we do? Try under the bed?" She sighed, touched her companion lightly on the arm, and shook her head. "Sorry. That wasn't funny."

"Just stay here." Swiftly, systematically, Marion Lister checked through the flat...the tiny kitchenette and bathroom, the bedroom, the combined living-room and lounge. When she finished, she trembled a little as she showed her friend a small blue china ashtray.

"This morning, last thing before I went out, I stubbed a cigarette in this. Now it's clean."

"You're sure?" Vi Taylor frowned. "Maybe somebody had a reason for being in. Or maybe you made a mistake."

"Nobody had a reason. And the stub was there."

"Who's got a passkey? Mrs. Johns?"

"Just Mrs. Johns."

"Then let's talk to her," decided her friend.

*   *   *

Mrs. Johns was still polishing when they reached the foot of the stairs. She listened, her face growing stonier by the moment.

"You told me this once before, Miss Lister." She gave a sniff of sheer disbelief. "I told you then – nobody's been in your place. Unless you're suggestin' that Danny or me—"

"I'm just trying to find out—"

"And I'm just tellin' you!" Hands on hips, Mrs. Johns glared back at her. "Nobody calls me a thief – not me or my son."

She broke off as the main door opened. The woman who came in first was in her late sixties, grey-haired, walking slowly with the aid of a stick. She gave them a vacant smile, and headed towards the door at the end of the corridor. The blonde, plain-faced girl who followed swept them with young, sullen eyes as she passed.

"I'm sorry, Mrs. Johns. Perhaps there's a mistake," Marion Lister broke off the incipient battle.

"Huh." Mrs. Johns gave another sniff.

"What about these two?" As they turned away, Vi nudged her companion and nodded towards the women going into the ground floor flat. "Asked them?"

Marion Lister nodded. "Miss Congreave couldn't climb the stairs on her own. The girl is her niece, Anna – Anna Lewis. She's stupid or lazy, I don't know which. They said they knew nothing."

"That just leaves the flat on the middle floor."

"I haven't spoken to them yet." Marion Lister pursed her lips. "But I will. Now. They're a man called Rowan and his wife. He's a violinist – plays in a theatre orchestra. She says she's an invalid – floats around most of the time in a kimono."

Mrs. Rowan answered the doorbell. Thin, middle-aged, blonde hair dark at the roots, she wrapped her bright yellow silk kimono around her while Marion Lister repeated her story.

"Well, I haven't heard anything." She gave a faint smirk of disbelief. "Charlie!"

Charlie Rowan was in his forties. He came to the door dressed in dinner jacket and black tie, ready to leave for work.

"The show starts in half an hour," he explained. "No, I'm like Jean. Can't help you. Haven't heard or seen anything."

They thanked him and headed back up the stairs. From below, Jean Rowan's stage whisper to her husband reached their ears.

"Time she got married and had something more to occupy her mind."

★   ★   ★

"I'm not saying she's right," said Vi Taylor later, as they washed up after a gloomy meal. "But, Marion, you could be imagining it. If you had a holiday, got away from work for a spell…"

"Vi, I'm not going mad. It's really happening." Marion Lister drained the last of the washing-up water from the sink, and lit a cigarette with shaking hands.

Her friend shrugged. "Well, then, it must be somebody who is able to watch every morning and make sure you've left for work. Look, what about the old trick of gumming a piece of thread across the bottom of your door when you go out? If the thread's broken when you come back, you'll know you've had a visitor."

For Marion Lister, any idea was better than none. Next morning, as she left for work, she gummed a small piece of dark thread across her door, low down.

She came home that evening, the thread paramount in her mind. But Mrs. Johns blocked her way in the ill-lit hallway, a bewildered Miss Congreave by her side.

"It's a disgrace, that's what it is," declared the caretaker, the previous evening's clash forgotten in her excitement. "You'll never guess! That girl Anna just upped and left poor old Miss Congreave. Packed her case and nipped off while the poor old soul was out for a walk. Nipped off without a soul seein' her!"

"You've no idea where she's gone, Miss Congreave?" Marion Lister tried to muster suitable sympathy.

"No note, no warnin', just nipped off..." Mrs. Johns broke off as, feet loud on the stairway, Charlie Rowan clattered down from the first floor. Halfway towards them he turned and waved up towards the stairs. "Bye, Jean."

They caught a brief glimpse of the yellow kimono flicking back into the flat above, then heard the door close.

"Heard about Anna Lewis, Mr. Rowan?" demanded Mrs. Johns.

"You told me yourself," reminded Rowan. "Terribly sorry – I'm late. Conductor doesn't like it."

He dashed out of the building.

When Marion Lister finally reached her top floor flat, the thread across the door was broken. Her visitor had been back – but she felt a sudden, savage joy at the sight. This was her proof – proof beyond denial.

Or was it? Couldn't others say she'd faked it all? Psychiatrists had a name for that kind of behaviour...

The next morning Marion Lister rose at her usual hour. She dressed, made breakfast, washed up, and then, as usual, went downstairs and out of the building, heading in the direction of the local bus stop.

But, just short of the stop, she turned off the main road. Five minutes later she walked along the lane which ran behind Garroway Court, sneaked in through the back entrance to the house, crept on stockinged feet through the empty hall and up the stairs and, moments later, was inside her flat.

After an hour, the telephone rang.

She ignored it.

Ten minutes later, she heard the sound of a key in the lock and darted behind the shelter of the floor-length window drapes.

Cautiously, Danny Johns entered the room, closed the door behind him, and began to look round.

"Danny?" She stepped into view when he was only a few feet away.

"Heck!" The caretaker's son gulped. "You're home, then?"

"Something you didn't expect." Marion Lister eyed him warily. He stood between her and the telephone, and somehow she was beginning to doubt the wisdom of what she'd accomplished. "Has it been you, Danny – all along, I mean?"

Danny Johns flushed. "Me? You mean, me pokin' my nose in while you're—" He gave a growl. "Look, I'm here because my Ma sent me up. She thought she heard a noise, and what with the fuss you've been makin' she told me to check. Wait a minute."

He opened the door and gave a shout. In a moment, Mrs. Johns had joined him.

"You!" The caretaker's eyebrows formed twin question marks.

"Hidin' behind the curtains, Ma," grunted her son. "Popped out like a ruddy jack-in-the-box and started off at me."

"I didn't know—" Marion Lister wasn't allowed to finish.

"Hidin' and spyin' and makin' trouble! I've heard of women like you!" Mrs. Johns was furious in her rage. But, disgust on his face, her son pulled her away. They went out, the door banged shut, and Marion Lister collapsed into a chair, close to tears.

Moments later, she rose again as the doorbell chimed.

"Mr. Rowan!"

Charlie Rowan, in off-duty sports shirt and corduroy slacks, shifted awkwardly. "I...that is, I heard the noise from down below. Came up to see if you were all right." He frowned. "You need a drink. Any brandy in the flat?"

She shook her head.

"No? Well, I'll bring a bottle up. Sorry I can't invite you to my place, but Jean's resting. You know how it is – she needs her rest."

He went out, leaving the door open. Marion Lister crossed to the couch and lifted her cigarettes and lighter. She fumbled, the lighter dropped, and then slid down between the back of the couch and the loose seat-cushions. Shaking her head, she reached into the space, retrieved the lighter, then, puzzled, reached back in again and pulled out the other object her fingers had brushed against.

It was a button. A large, gaudy button with an ornamental metal centre. A button she'd never seen before.

"Miss Lister..."

She looked up. Mrs. Johns stood in the doorway, eyeing her awkwardly. "Eh...c'n I come in?"

She nodded.

"Maybe I was a wee bit hasty." Mrs. Johns bit her lip. "About what I said, I mean—"

"Let's forget it, Mrs. Johns." Marion Lister was quietly earnest. "This button...ever seen it before?"

"Anna Lewis has a costume wi' buttons like that." Mrs. Johns' interest flared. "Where'd you find it?"

"In the couch." Marion Lister stopped, uncertain, as Rowan re-entered the flat, carrying the promised brandy bottle.

"Spot of this'll buck you up," he said. "Now, glasses."

She watched as he crossed the room, opened the small cupboard beneath the upright desk in the far corner, and produced three of the wine glasses she kept there.

"Mr. Rowan – how did you know where the glasses were?"

"Glasses? Well..." Rowan flustered.

"You've never seen them produced before, Mr. Rowan. Not when I've been here." In the doorway she saw Danny Johns. He stopped and waited, listening. "Is the reason this button? Anna Lewis's button? That's how you know, isn't it? Because you've been here – with her?"

"Nonsense." Rowan snapped the word. "I came here to help and... and...I'm going!" He turned.

Mrs. Johns gave an aggressive sniff. "Danny."

Her son leaned across the doorway. "Stay a moment, mate," he said. "Till we hear what Ma has to say, anyway."

"It's about the passkey." Mrs. Johns stroked the tip of her nose. "I just remembered. Anna Lewis did borrow it once. Said she'd forgotten her own, and that her aunt was out."

"She could have had it copied." Marion Lister looked at the button in her hand. "I took the cushions off the couch three days ago, when I was cleaning. The button wasn't there then."

"I'm not staying." Rowan shoved against the younger man in the doorway, was pushed back, swung angrily with the bottle, and next second was sent flying wildly back across the room, crashing to the floor and bringing down the telephone with him.

"Where's Anna, Mr. Rowan?" insisted Marion Lister. "Nobody saw her go. Do you know where she is – or what happened to her?"

He picked himself up from the floor, blood flowing from a cut on his forehead. "All right—" he shook his head in a dazed fashion, took out his handkerchief and held it to the wound. "We were using your flat. It was – well, it made things easier."

"And yesterday?"

"We were here. Then we had a quarrel, and she walked out." He glanced from one face to another, in growing agitation. "I know where she is. If you want, I'll arrange for her to...to telephone you this afternoon."

They were still unconvinced.

"I mean it." Rowan's voice changed to a pleading note. "Look, my wife doesn't know. I – the shock would be bad for her. You know she's got a weak heart. Anyway, we're leaving in a week or so. I've got a new job, another orchestra, out of town. That's what caused the quarrel. I told Anna we were leaving, and that was the finish as far as we were concerned."

Marion Lister lifted the telephone from the floor, replaced it on its stand, and shook her head. "I'll believe you – if you call the girl right now and I speak to her."

Rowan hesitated, lifted the receiver, then slowly lowered it.

"He's right." Danny Johns tried the instrument for himself.

"No dialling tone."

"You've got a 'phone, Mr. Rowan." Marion Lister inspected him with the cold anger engendered by weeks of fear and uncertainty. "Use it. We'll come with you."

"But my wife..." Rowan's protests died as Danny Johns gripped him by the arm. They went downstairs together.

"I'll use the passkey." Mrs. Johns opened the Rowans' door.

The telephone was on a small table just inside the little hallway.

But they stopped short as the inner door of the flat opened.

"Charlie..." Anna Lewis's voice turned to a strangled gasp of fear. And she was wearing Mrs. Rowan's yellow silk kimono.

"It's another question now, Mr. Rowan," said Danny Johns softly. "What happened to your wife?"

Rowan looked at Anna Lewis. Neither of them spoke.

Slowly, carefully, Marion Lister lifted the telephone.

FOOTPRINT IN THE SKY

John Dickson Carr

She awoke out of confused dreams; awoke with a start and lay staring at
the white ceiling of her bedroom for a minute or two before she could
convince herself it was anything but a dream.

But it was a dream.

The cold, brittle sunlight poured in at the open window. The cold,
brittle air, blowing the curtains, stirred a light coating of snow on the
windowsill. It stirred briskly in that little, bare room; it should have set
the blood racing, and Dorothy Brant breathed it deeply.

Everything was all right. She was at the country cottage, where she
and Dad and Harry had come down for the skating on the frozen lake;
possibly even a little mild skiing, if the snow came on according to the
weather forecast. And the snow had fallen. She should have been glad
of that, though for some reason the sight of it on the windowsill struck
her with a kind of terror.

Shivering in the warm bed, the clothes pulled up about her chin,
she looked at the little clock at her bedside. Twenty minutes past nine.
She had overslept; Dad and Harry would be wanting their breakfast.
Again she told herself that everything was all right: though now, fully
awake, she knew it was not. The unpleasantness of yesterday returned.
Mrs. Topham next door – that old shrew, and thief as well...

It was the only thing which could have marred this weekend. They
had looked forward to the skating: the crisp blades thudding and ringing
on the ice, the flight, the long scratching drag as you turned, the elm
trees black against a clear cold sky. But there was Mrs. Topham with
her stolen watch and her malicious good manners, huddled up in the
cottage next door and spoiling everything.

Put it out of your mind! No good brooding over it: put it out of
your mind!

Dorothy Brant braced herself and got out of bed, reaching for her dressing gown and slippers. But it was not her dressing gown she found draped across the chair; it was her heavy fur coat. And there were a pair of soft-leather slippers. They were a pair of soft-leather moccasins, ornamented with beadwork, which Harry had brought back from the States; but now the undersides were cold, damp and stiff, almost frozen. That was when a subconscious fear struck at her, took possession, and would not leave.

Closing the window, she padded out to the bathroom. The small cottage, with its crisp white curtains and smell of old wood, was so quiet that she could hear voices talking downstairs. It was a mumble in which no words were distinguishable: Harry's quick tenor, her father's slower and heavier voice, and another she could not identify, but which was slowest and heaviest of all.

What was wrong? She hurried through her bath and through her dressing. Not only were they up but they must be getting their own breakfast, for she could smell coffee boiling. And she was very slow; in spite of nine hours' sleep she felt as edgy and washed-out as though she had been up all night.

Giving a last jerk of the comb through her brown bobbed hair, putting on no powder or lipstick, she ran downstairs. At the door of the living room she stopped. Inside were her father, her cousin Harry and the local Superintendent of Police.

"Good morning, *miss*," said the Superintendent.

She never forgot the look of that little room or the look on the faces of those in it. Sunlight poured into it, touching the bright-coloured rough-woven rugs, the rough stone fireplace. Through side windows she could see out across the snow-covered lawn to where – twenty yards away and separated from them only by a tall laurel hedge with a gate – was Mrs. Topham's white weather-boarded cottage.

But what struck her with a shock of alarm as she came into the room was the sense of a conversation suddenly cut off; the look she surprised on their faces when they glanced round, quick and sallow, as a camera might have surprised it.

"Good morning, miss," repeated Superintendent Mason, saluting.

Harry Ventnor intervened, in a kind of agony. His naturally high colour was higher still; even his large feet and bulky shoulders, his small sinewy hands, looked agitated.

"Don't say anything, Dolly!" he urged. "Don't say anything! They can't make you say anything. Wait until—"

"I certainly think—" began her father slowly. He looked down his nose, and then along the side of his pipe, everywhere except at Dorothy. "I certainly think," he went on, clearing his throat, "that it would be as well not to speak hastily until—"

"*IF* you please, sir," said Superintendent Mason, clearing his own throat. "Now, miss, I'm afraid I must ask you some questions. But it is my duty to tell you that you need not answer my questions until you have seen your solicitor."

"Solicitor? But I don't want a solicitor. What on earth should I want with a solicitor?"

Superintendent Mason looked meaningly at her father and Harry Ventnor, as though bidding them to mark that.

"It's about Mrs. Topham, miss."

"Oh!"

"Why do you say 'Oh'?"

"Go on, please. What is it?"

"I understand, miss, that you and Mrs. Topham had 'words' yesterday? A bit of a dust-up, like?"

"Yes, you could certainly call it that."

"May I ask what about?"

"I'm sorry," said Dorothy, "I can't tell you that. It would only give the old cat an opportunity to say that I had been slandering her. So that's it! What has she been telling you?"

"Why, miss," said Superintendent Mason, taking out a pencil and scratching the side of his jaw with it, "I'm afraid she's not exactly in a condition to tell anything. She's in a nursing-home at Guildford, rather badly smashed up round the head. Just between ourselves, it's touch and go whether she'll recover."

First Dorothy could not feel her heart beating at all, and then it seemed to pound with enormous rhythm. The Superintendent was looking at her steadily. She forced herself to say:

"You mean she's had an accident?"

"Not exactly, miss. The doctor says she was hit three or four times with that big glass paperweight you may have seen on the table at her cottage. Eh?"

"You don't mean – you don't mean somebody *did* it? Deliberately? But who did it?"

"Well, miss," said Superintendent Mason, looking at her still harder until he became a huge Puritan face with a small mole beside his nose. "I'm bound to tell you that by everything we can see so far, it looks as though you did it."

This wasn't happening. It couldn't be. Afterwards she remembered, in a detached kind of way, studying all of them: the little lines round Harry's eyes in the sunlight, the hastily brushed light hair, the loose leather wind-jacket whose zip fastener was half undone. She remembered thinking that despite his athletic prowess he looked ineffectual and a little foolish. But then her own father was not of much use now.

She heard her own voice. "But that's absurd!"

"I hope so, miss. I honestly hope so. Now tell me: were you out of this house last night?"

"When?"

"At any time."

"Yes. No. I don't know. Yes, I think I was."

"For God's sake, Dolly," said her father, "don't say anything more until we've got a lawyer here. I've telephoned to town; I didn't want to alarm you; I didn't even wake you – there's some explanation for this. There must be!"

It was not her own emotion; it was the wretchedness of his face which held her. Bulky, semi-bald, worried about business, worried about everything else in this world – that was John Brant. His crippled left arm and black glove were pressed against his side. He stood in the bright pool of sunlight, a face of misery.

"I've seen her," he explained. "It wasn't pretty. Not that I haven't seen worse. In the war." He touched his arm. "But you're a little girl, Dolly; you're only a little girl. You couldn't have done that."

His plaintive tone asked for confirmation.

"Just a moment, sir," interposed Superintendent Mason. "Now, miss! You tell me you *were* outside the house last night?"

"Yes."

"In the snow?"

"Yes, yes!"

"Do you remember the time?"

"No, I don't think so."

"Tell me, miss: what size shoes do you wear?"

"Four."

"That's a rather small size, isn't it?" When she nodded dumbly, Superintendent Mason shut up his notebook. "Now, if you'll just come with me?"

The cottage had a side door. Without putting his fingers on the knob, Mason twisted the spindle round and opened it. The overhang of the eaves had kept clear the two steps leading down; but beyond a thin coating of snow lay like a plaster over the world between here and the shuttered cottage across the way.

There were two strings of footprints in that snow. Dorothy knew whose they were. Hardened and sharp-printed, one set of prints moved out snakily from the steps, passed under the arch of the powdered laurel hedge, and stopped at the steps to the side door of Mrs. Topham's house. Another set of the same tracks – a little blurred, spaced at longer intervals where the person had evidently been running desperately – came back from the cottage to these steps.

That mute sign of panic stirred Dorothy's memory. It wasn't a dream. She had done it. Subconsciously she had known it all the time. She could remember other things: the fur coat clasped round her pyjamas, the sting of the snow to wet slippers, the blind rush in the dark.

"Yours, miss?" inquired Superintendent Mason.

"Yes. Oh, yes, they're mine."

"Easy, miss," muttered the Superintendent. "You're looking a bit white round the gills. Come in here and sit down; I won't hurt you." Then his own tone grew petulant. Or perhaps something in the heavy simplicity of the girl's manner penetrated his official bearing. "But why did you do it, miss? Lord, why did you do it? That's to say breaking open that desk of hers to get a handful of trinkets not worth ten quid for the lot? And then not even taking the trouble to mess up your footprints afterward!" He coughed, checking himself abruptly.

John Brant's voice was acid. "Good, my friend. Very good. The first sign of intelligence so far. I presume you don't suggest my daughter is insane?"

"No, sir. But they were her mother's trinkets, I hear."

"Where did you hear that? You I suppose, Harry?"

Harry Ventnor pulled up the zip fastener of his wind-jacket as though girding himself. He seemed to suggest that he was the good fellow whom everybody was persecuting; that he wanted to be friends with the world, if they would only let him. Yet such sincerity blazed in his small features that it was difficult to doubt his good intentions.

"Now look here, old boy. I *had* to tell them, didn't I? It's no good trying to hide things like that. I know that, just from reading those stories—"

"Stories!"

"All right: say what you like. They always find out, and then they make it worse than it really was." He let this sink in. "I tell you, you're going about it in the wrong way. Suppose Dolly did have a row with the Topham about that jewellery? Suppose she *did* go over there last night? Suppose those are her footprints? Does that prove she bashed the Topham? Not that a public service wasn't done; but why couldn't it have been a burglar just as well?"

Superintendent Mason shook his head. "Because it couldn't, sir."

"But why? I'm asking you, why?"

"There's no harm in telling you that, sir, if you'll just listen. You probably remember that it began to snow last night at a little past eleven o'clock."

"No, I don't. We were all in bed by then."

"Well, you can take my word for it," Mason told him patiently. "I was up half the night at the police station; and it did. It stopped snowing about midnight. You'll have to take my word for that too, but we can easily prove it. You see, sir, Mrs. Topham was alive and in very good health at well after midnight. I know that too, because she rang up the police station and said she was awake and nervous and thought there were burglars in the neighbourhood. Since the lady does that same thing," he explained with a certain grimness, "on the average of about three times a month, I don't stress *that*. What I am telling you is that her call came in at twelve-ten, at least ten minutes after the snow had stopped."

Harry hesitated, and the Superintendent went on with the same patient air: "Don't you see it, sir? Mrs. Topham wasn't attacked until after the snow stopped. Round her cottage now there's twenty yards of clean, clear, unmarked snow in every direction. The only marks in that snow, the only marks of any kind at all, are the footprints Miss Brant admits she made herself."

Then he rose at them in exasperation.

"'Tisn't as though anybody else could have made the tracks. Even if Miss Brant didn't admit it herself, I'm absolutely certain nobody else did. You, Mr. Ventnor, wear size ten shoes. Mr. Brant wears size nine. Walk in size four tracks? Ayagh! And yet somebody did get into that cottage with a key, bashed the old lady pretty murderously, robbed her desk, and got away again. If there are no other tracks or marks of any kind in the snow, who did it? Who must have done it?"

Dorothy could consider it, now, in almost a detached way. She remembered the paperweight with which Mrs. Topham had been struck. It lay on the table in Mrs. Topham's stuffy parlour, a heavy glass globe with a tiny landscape inside. When you shook the glass globe, a miniature snowstorm rose within – which seemed to make the attack all the more horrible.

She wondered if she had left any fingerprints on it. But over everything rose Renée Topham's face, Renée Topham, her mother's bosom friend.

"I hated her," said Dorothy; surprisingly, she began to cry.

★   ★   ★

Dennis Jameson, of the law firm of Morris, Farnsworth and Jameson, Lincoln's Inn Fields, shut up his brief case with a snap. He was putting on his hat and coat when Billy Farnsworth looked into the office.

"Hullo!" said Farnsworth. "You off to Surrey over that Brant business?"

"Yes."

"H'm. Believe in miracles, do you?"

"No."

"That girl's guilty, my lad. You ought to know that."

"It's our business," said Jameson, "to do what we can for our clients."

Farnsworth looked at him shrewdly. "I see it in your ruddy cheeks. Quixotry is alive again. Young idealist storms to relief of good-looker in distress, swearing to—"

"I've met her twice," said Jameson. "I like her, yes. But merely using a small amount of intelligence on this, I can't see that they've got such a thundering good case against her."

"Oh, my lad!"

"Well, look at it. What do they say the girl did? This Mrs. Topham was struck several times with a glass paperweight. There are no fingerprints on the paperweight, which shows signs of having been wiped. But, after having the forethought to wipe her fingerprints carefully off the paperweight, Dorothy Brant then walks back to her cottage and leaves behind two sets of footprints which could be seen by aerial observation a mile up. Is that reasonable?"

Farnsworth looked thoughtful.

"Maybe they would say she isn't reasonable," he pointed out. "Never mind the psychology. What you've got to get round are the physical facts. Here is the mysterious widow Topham entirely alone in the house; the only servant comes in by day. Here are one person's footprints. Only that girl could have made the tracks; and, in fact, admits she did. It's a physical impossibility for anybody else to have entered or left the house. How do you propose to get round that?"

"I don't know," said Jameson rather hopelessly. "But I want to hear her side of it first. The only thing nobody seems to have heard, or even to be curious about, is what she thinks herself."

Yet, when he met her at the cottage late that afternoon, she cut the ground from under his feet.

Twilight was coming down when he turned in at the gate, a bluish twilight in which the snow looked grey. Jameson stopped a moment at the gate, and stared across at the thin laurel hedge dividing this property from Mrs. Topham's. There was nothing remarkable about this hedge, which was some six feet high and cut through by a gateway like a Gothic arch. But in front of the arch, peering up at the snow-coated side of the hedge just above it, stood a large figure in cap and waterproof. Somehow he looked familiar. At his elbow another man, evidently the local Superintendent of Police, was holding up a camera; and a flash-bulb glared against the sky. Though he was too far away to hear anything, Jameson had a queer impression that the large man was laughing uproariously.

Harry Ventnor, whom he knew slightly, met Jameson at the door.

"She's in there," Harry explained, nodding towards the front room. "Er – don't upset her, will you? Here, what the devil are they doing with that hedge?"

He stared across the lawn.

"Upset her?" said Jameson with some asperity. "I'm here, if possible, to help her. Won't you or Mr. Brant give some assistance? Do you honestly think that Miss Brant in her rational senses could have done what they say she did?"

"In her rational senses?" repeated Harry. After looking at Jameson in a curious way, he said no more; he turned abruptly and hurried off across the lawn.

Yet Dorothy, when Jameson met her, gave no impression of being out of her rational senses. It was her straightforwardness he had always liked, the straightforwardness which warmed him now. They sat in the homely, firelit room, by the fireplace over which were the silver cups to denote Harry's athletic and gymnastic prowess, and the trophies of John Brant's earlier days at St. Moritz. Dorothy herself was an outdoor girl.

"To advise me?" she said. "You mean, to advise me what to say when they arrest me?"

"Well, they haven't arrested you yet, Miss Brant."

She smiled at him. "And yet I'll have bet that surprises you, doesn't it? Oh, I know how deeply I'm in! I suppose they're only poking about to get more evidence. And then there's a new man here, a man named March, from Scotland Yard. I feel almost flattered."

Jameson sat up. He knew now why that immense figure by the hedge had seemed familiar. "Not Colonel March?"

"Yes. Rather a nice person, really," answered Dorothy, shading her eyes with her hand. Under her light tone he felt that her nerves were raw. "Then again, they've been all through my room. And they can't find the watch and the brooch and the rings I'm supposed to have stolen from Aunt Renée Topham, Aunt Renée!"

"So I've heard. But that's the point – what are they getting at? A watch and a brooch and a couple of rings! Why should you steal that from anybody, let alone from her?"

"Because they weren't hers," said Dorothy, suddenly looking up with a white face, and speaking very fast. "They belonged to my mother."

"Steady."

"My mother is dead," said Dorothy. "I suppose it wasn't just the watch and the rings, really, that was the excuse, the breaking point, the thing that brought it on. My mother was a great friend of Mrs. Topham. It was 'Aunt Renée' this and 'Aunt Renée' that, while my mother was alive to pamper her. But my mother wanted me to have those trinkets, such as they were. Aunt Renée Topham coolly appropriated them, as she appropriates everything else she can. I never knew what had happened to them until yesterday.

"Do you know that kind of woman? Mrs. Topham is really charming, aristocratic and charming, with the cool charm that takes all it can get and expects to go on getting it. I know for a fact that she's really got a lot of money, though what she does with it I can't imagine: and the real reason why she buries herself in the country is that she's too mean to risk spending it in town. I never could endure her. Then, when my mother died and I didn't go on pampering Aunt Renée as she thought I should, it was a very different thing. How that woman loves to talk about us! Harry's debts and my father's shaky business. And *me*."

She checked herself again, smiling at him. "I'm sorry to inflict all this on you."

"You're not inflicting it on me."

"But it's rather ridiculous, isn't it?"

"Ridiculous," said Jameson grimly, "is not the word I should apply to it. So you had a row with her?"

"Oh, a glorious row. A beautiful row. The grandmother of all rows."

"When?"

"Yesterday. When I saw her wearing my mother's watch."

She looked at the fire, over which the silver cups glimmered.

"Maybe I said more than I should have," she went on. "But I got no support from my father or Harry. I don't blame Dad: he's so worried about business, and that bad arm of his troubles him so much sometimes that all he wants is peace and quiet. As for Harry, *he* doesn't really like her; but she took rather a fancy to him, and that flatters him. He's a kind of male counterpart of Aunt Renée. Out of a job? – well, depend on somebody else. And I'm in the middle of all this. It's 'Dolly, do this,' and 'Dolly, do that,' and 'Good old Dolly; she won't mind.' But I do mind. When I saw that woman standing there wearing my mother's watch, and saying commiserating things about the fact that we couldn't afford a servant, I felt that something ought to be done about it. So I suppose I must have done something about it."

Jameson reached out and took her hands. "All right," he said. "What will you do?"

"I don't know! That's just the trouble."

"But surely—"

"No. That was one of the things Mrs. Topham always had such sport with. You don't know much about anything when you walk in your sleep."

"Ridiculous, isn't it?" she went on, after another pause. "Utterly ludicrous. But not to me! Not a bit. Ever since I was a child, when I've been overtired or nervously exhausted, it's happened. Once I came downstairs and built and lit a fire in the dining room, and set the table for a meal. I admit it doesn't happen often, and never before with results like this." She tried to laugh. "But why do you think my father and Harry looked at me like that? That's the worst of it. I really don't know whether I'm a near – murderer or not."

This was bad.

Jameson admitted that to himself, even as his reason argued against it. He got up to prowl round the room, and her brown eyes never left him. He could not look away; he saw the tensity of her face in every corner.

"Look here," he said quietly, "this is nonsense."

"Oh, please. Don't you say that. It's not very original."

"But do you seriously think you went for that woman and still don't know anything about it now?"

"Would it be more difficult than building a fire?"

"I didn't ask you that. *Do* you think you did it?"

"No," said Dorothy.

That question did it. She trusted him now. There was understanding and sympathy between them, a mental force and communication that could be felt as palpably as the body gives out heat.

"Deep down inside me, no. I don't believe it. I think I should have woken up. And there was no – well, no blood on me, you know. But how are you going to get round the evidence?"

The evidence. Always the evidence.

"I did go across there. I can't deny that. I remember half waking up as I was coming back. I was standing in the middle of the lawn in the snow. I had on my fur coat over my pyjamas; I remember feeling snow on my face and my wet slippers under me. I was shivering. And I remember running back. That's all. If I didn't do it, how could anybody else have done it?"

"I beg your pardon," interposed a new voice. "Do you mind if, both figuratively and literally, I turn on the light?"

Dennis Jameson knew the owner of that voice. There was the noise of someone fumbling after an electric switch; then, in homely light, Colonel March beamed and basked. Colonel March's seventeen stone was swathed round in a waterproof as big as a tent. He wore a large tweed cap. Under this his speckled face glowed in the cold; and he was smoking, with gurgling relish, the large-bowled pipe which threatened to singe his sandy moustache.

"Ah, Jameson!" he said. He took the pipe out of his mouth and made a gesture with it. "So it *was* you. I thought I saw you come in. I don't want to intrude; but I think there are at least two things that Miss Brant ought to know."

Dorothy turned round quickly.

"First," pursued Colonel March, "that Mrs. Topham is out of danger. She is at least able, like an after-dinner speaker, to say a few words; though with about as much coherence. Second, that out on your lawn there is one of the queerest objects I ever saw in my life."

Jameson whistled. "You've met this fellow?" he said to Dorothy. "He is the head of the Department of Queer Complaints. When they come across something outlandish, which may be a hoax or a joke but, on the other hand, may be a serious crime, they shout for him. His mind is so obvious that he hits it every time. To my certain knowledge he has investigated a disappearing room, chased a walking corpse, and found an invisible piece of furniture. If he goes so far as to admit that a thing is a bit unusual, you can look out for squalls."

Colonel March nodded quite seriously. "Yes," he said. "That is why I am here, you see. They thought we might be interested in that footprint."

"That footprint?" cried Dorothy. "You mean—?"

"No, no; not your footprint, Miss Brant. Another one. Let me explain. I want you, both of you, to look out of the window; I want you to take a look at the laurel hedge between this cottage and the other. The light is almost gone, but study it."

Jameson went to the window and peered out.

"Well?" he demanded. "What about it? It's a hedge."

"As you so shrewdly note, it is a hedge. Now let me ask you a question. Do you think a person could walk along the top of that hedge?"

"Good lord, no!"

"No? Why not?"

"I don't see the joke," said Jameson, "but I'll make the proper replies. Because the hedge is only an inch or two thick. It wouldn't support a cat. If you tried to stand on it, you'd come through like a ton of bricks."

"Quite true. Then what would you say if I told you that someone weighing at least twelve stone must have climbed up the inside of it?"

Nobody answered him; the thing was so obviously unreasonable that nobody could answer.

Dorothy Brant and Dennis Jameson looked at each other.

"For," said Colonel March, "it would seem that somebody at least climbed up there. Look at the hedge again. You see the arch cut in for a gate? Just above that, in the snow along the side of the hedge, there are traces of a footprint. It is a large footprint. I think it can be identified by the heel, though most of it is blurred and sketchy."

Walking quickly and heavily, Dorothy's father came into the room. He started to speak, but seemed to change his mind at the sight of Colonel March. He went over to Dorothy, who took his arm.

"Then," insisted Jameson, "somebody did climb up on the hedge?"

"I doubt it," said Colonel March. "How could he?"

Jameson pulled himself together. "Look here, sir," he said quietly. "'How could he?' is correct. I never knew you to go on like this without good reason. I know it must have some bearing on the case. But I don't care if somebody climbed up on the hedge. I don't care if he danced the tango on it. The hedge leads nowhere. It doesn't lead to Mrs. Topham's; it only divides the two properties. The point is, how did somebody manage to get from here to that other cottage – across sixty feet of unbroken snow – without leaving a trace on it? I ask you that because I'm certain you don't think Miss Brant is guilty."

Colonel March looked apologetic. "I know she isn't," he answered.

In Dorothy Brant's mind was again that vision of the heavy paperweight inside which, as you shook it, a miniature snowstorm arose. She felt that her own wits were being shaken and clouded in the same way.

"I knew Dolly didn't do it," said John Brant, suddenly putting his arm around his daughter's shoulders. "I knew that. I told them so. But—"

Colonel March silenced him. "The real thief, Miss Brant, did not want your mother's watch and brooch and chain and rings. It may interest you to know what he did want. He wanted about fifteen hundred pounds in notes and gold sovereigns, tucked away in that same shabby desk. You seem to have wondered what Mrs. Topham did with her money. That is what she did with it. Mrs. Topham, by the first words she could get out in semi-consciousness, was merely a common or garden variety of miser. That dull-looking desk in her parlour was the last place any burglar would look for a hoard. Any burglar, that is, except one."

"Except one?" repeated John Brant, and his eyes seemed to turn inward.

A sudden ugly suspicion came to Jameson.

"Except one who knew, yes. You, Miss Brant, had the blame deliberately put on you. There was no malice in it. It was simply the easiest way to avoid pain and trouble to the gentleman who did it."

"Now hear what you really did, Miss Brant," said Colonel March, his face darkening. "You did go out into the snow last night. But you did not go over to Mrs. Topham's; and you did not make those two artistic sets of footprints in the snow. When you tell us in your own story that you felt snow sting on your face as well as underfoot, it requires no vast concentration, surely, to realise that the snow was still falling. You went out into it, like many sleepwalkers; you were shocked into semi-consciousness by the snow and the cold air; and you returned long before the end of the snowfall, which covered any real prints you may have made.

"The real thief – who was very much awake – heard you come back and tumble into bed. He saw a heaven-sent opportunity to blame you for a crime you might even think you had committed. He slipped in and took the slippers out of your room. And, when the snow had stopped, he went across to Mrs. Topham's. He did not mean to attack her. But she was awake and surprised him; and so, of course, Harry Ventnor struck her down."

"Harry—" The word, which Dorothy had said almost at a scream, was checked. She looked round quickly at her father; then she stared straight ahead; then she began to laugh.

"Of course," said Colonel March. "As usual, he was letting his — what is it? — his 'good old Dolly' take the blame."

A great cloud seemed to have left John Brant; but the fussed and worried look had not left him. He blinked at Colonel March.

"Sir," he said, "I would give my good arm to prove what you say. That boy has caused me half the trouble I ever had. But are you raving mad?"

"No."

"I tell you he couldn't have done it! He's Emily's son, my sister's son. He may be a bad lot; but he's not a magician."

"You are forgetting," said Colonel March, "a certain size ten footprint. You are forgetting that interesting sight, a smeared and blurred size ten footprint on the side of a hedge which would not have held up a cat. A remarkable footprint. A disembodied footprint."

"But that's the whole trouble," roared the other. "The two lines of tracks in the snow were made by a size four shoe! Harry couldn't have made them, any more than I could. It's a physical impossibility. Harry wears size ten. You don't say he could get his feet into flat leather moccasins which would fit my daughter?"

"No," said Colonel March. "But he could get his hands into them."

There was a silence. The Colonel wore a dreamy look, almost a pleased look.

"And in his unusual but highly practical pair of gloves," the Colonel went on, "Harry Ventnor simply walked across to the other cottage on his hands. No more than that. For a trained gymnast — as those silver cups will indicate — it was nothing. For a rattle-brained gentleman who needed money it was ideal. He crossed in a thin coating of snow, which would show no difference in weight. Doorsteps, cleared of snow by the overhanging roof, protected him at either end when he stood upright. He had endless opportunities to get a key to the side door. Unfortunately, there was that rather low archway in the hedge. Carrying himself on his hands, his feet were curved up and back over the arch of his body to balance him; he blundered, and smeared that disembodied footprint on the side of the hedge. To be quite frank, I am delighted with the device. It is crime upside down; it is leaving a footprint in the sky; it is—"

"A fair cop, sir," concluded Superintendent Mason, sticking his head in at the door. "They got him on the other side of Guildford. He must have smelled something wrong when he saw us taking photographs. But he had the stuff on him."

Dorothy Brant stood looking for a long time at the large, untidy blimp of a man who was still chuckling with pleasure.

Then she joined in.

"I trust," observed Dennis Jameson politely, "that everybody is having a good time. For myself, I've had a couple of unpleasant shocks today; and just for a moment I was afraid I should have another one. For a moment I honestly thought you were going to pitch on Mr. Brant."

"So did I," agreed Dorothy, and beamed at her father. "That's why it's so funny now."

John Brant looked startled – but not half so startled as Colonel March.

"Now there," the Colonel said, "I honestly do not understand you. I am the Department of Queer Complaints. If you have a ghost in your attic or a footprint on top of your hedge, ring me up. But a certain success has blessed us because, as Mr. Jameson says, I look for the obvious. And Lord love us! – if you have decided that a crime was committed by a gentleman who could walk on his hands, I will hold under torture that you are not likely to succeed by suspecting the one person in the house who has a crippled arm."

THE WOMAN WHO HAD EVERYTHING

Celia Fremlin

The effort of opening her eyes was enormous, and no sooner had Maggie achieved it than the light pounced like knives, and she closed them again.

She thought at first that it was the sun, that she was sunbathing, sunbathing for too long, on a scorching Mediterranean beach, on holiday somewhere or other. This must be heat-stroke she'd got, she felt so weak and numbed, almost paralysed. Even her jaw would not move, her teeth were clenched in some sort of tension whose cause she could not at the moment recall; so that when she tried to speak, the words would not come.

"I think I'm getting heat-stroke, darling," she wanted to say, reproachfully, in a feeble effort to arouse Rodney's sympathy and concern. "I've been lying here too long, why didn't you wake me...?"

But it was no good, something seemed to be blocking the sounds, choking them back into her throat; and anyway, Rodney wasn't listening.

Well, of course he wasn't. He never listened to her, these days. Maybe he wasn't even there; maybe he'd wandered off by now, bored and restless, eyeing desultorily the other female figures spread-eagled on the sand, and thinking about his work.

He never thought about anything else any more, at home or away; a far cry indeed from those golden holidays in the first years of their marriage, when he'd sit or lie beside her hour after hour, rubbing oil on her brown body, murmuring into her ear nonsense to make her laugh or endearments to make her glow – face down on the hot sand – with secret joy.

Maybe he *was* still sitting there after all, right beside her? Reading, of course, and making notes. Going over those eternal papers and documents which he lugged with him everywhere, even on holiday; the dry, convoluted paragraphs curling under the Mediterranean heat, the sand seeping into the interstices of his bulging, important briefcase.

To hell with Rodney's importance, his rocketing success! Success had come suddenly, attacking her marriage like a fast-growing cancer, with metastases spreading into every corner of their relationship.

"Rodney...?" She tried to put appeal, reproach and pathos into the syllables; but once again, no sound came from her throat.

And now a memory...a suspicion...an unease lurched inside her, and she forced herself once more to open her eyes, to peer through the dazzle with narrowed, burning lids.

*　*　*

No beach. No blazing Mediterranean sun. Only a reading-lamp – and a shaded one at that – casting its mild sixty watts across the littered desk; and straight in front of her, propped carefully at eye-level, just where she had left it, was her suicide note.

So she was still alive. The thought was a neutral one to Maggie at first – neither surprising nor unsurprising. Nor did she feel either relieved or dismayed at this miscarriage of her plans.

Her plans? What, actually, *were* her plans? What had the whole thing been about? Letting her lids fall closed again against the baffling light of Reality (Reality? Oh, not *again*...!), Maggie set herself to fumbling through the cotton wool that right now was her brain, seeking the relevant connections, trying to recall, through the confusion of her thoughts and the singing in her ears, the sequence of events that had landed her here, in her husband's own special wing-chair, in his own well-ordered study, with an empty bottle of sleeping-pills at her elbow.

No, not empty. Half the pills were still there – no, more than half – the blur of blueness reached way up the glass sides, two-thirds up at least.

So what had gone wrong? She'd intended to take the lot, of that she was certain. What had prevented her? Had she been overcome by unconsciousness before she'd had time to swallow more than a dozen or so of the things? Or had she, on the very verge of oblivion, somehow lost her nerve...?

This, of course, would explain why she was still alive, she reflected, with slow, laborious logic; and still she could feel neither pleased nor sorry at the outcome. She could, though, feel a weak stir of anger about it all. It was so unfair! Why was everything, for her, always so difficult? *Other* people commit suicide in their hundreds of thousands, all over the world, why should *she* be the one who never managed to bring it off?

Because this wasn't the first time she had tried – oh, by no means. In these past two or three years – the years since Rodney's spectacular promotion at the Foreign Office had changed him from a shy, pleasant young man into a dynamo of ruthless energy – during these years, Maggie had made two other suicide attempts – three, if you counted that first one of all, which (as she now admitted to herself) hadn't really been an attempt at all, but merely a ruse for getting attention – *forcing* attention, indeed, at pistol-point – from her increasingly remote and preoccupied husband.

She'd worked it out so carefully, too. He was to have come home (late, as usual) to find his wife dead in a gas-filled bathroom. He was to have kicked and battered on the bathroom door: "Let me *in*, darling, let me *in*!" he was to have yelled, white-lipped at the keyhole, rattling and bashing, shaking the handle loose from its moorings, pushing until the hinges groaned and the door finally caved in before him. She saw him dragging her limp figure out of the bath, across the landing, long mousy hair dripping like Ophelia's, and finally laying it on the bed, covering it with kisses.

"Wake up, my darling... Oh, wake up!" he was to have sobbed, distraught with grief and with remorse. "Oh, Maggie, Maggie, come back to me! I love you...I need you...!"

Too late the kisses. Too late the wild words of love. His tears of remorse would fall upon her dead face in vain.

Or would they? It would be a shame, when you came to think about it, to be missing it all. How about if she stirred and murmured his name at some point in the proceedings, when he had suffered enough, had repented enough of his shortcomings? "Rodney...Rodney...!" she would whisper with her first faint breath of returning life: and from there to his promising to give up his demanding job and stay home in the evenings would be but a few delicious, night-long steps...

With a surge of steaming water, Maggie had lurched upwards into a sitting position and turned off the unlit jets of the water heater, leaving only the pilot to do its feeble worst. Then she lay back once more into the water, warmed through and through, and blissfully expectant.

And after all that, he hadn't come into the bathroom at all! Hadn't smelt the gas seeping out under the door – nothing! She'd lain there in the cooling water from midnight until a quarter past one, only to hear him slam the front door and go straight upstairs to the bedroom, closing the door behind him.

For several minutes, Maggie had lain there, incredulous. Surely, when he saw the empty bed, he would come in search of her? She waited; the minutes passed; and presently, chilled and desperate, she dragged herself out of the now nearly cold water, wrapped a towel round her shivering body, and went to investigate – only to find him snoring peacefully on his own side of the big double bed.

"I thought you must have stayed the night at your sister's or somewhere," he'd explained offhandedly the next morning: and on Maggie's insisting that she "might have died!" he'd merely said "Ridiculous!" – then added: "You'd better phone the gas people and get them to send someone. It's a waste of gas to have a pilot that keeps blowing out" – and with that he'd gone off to the office as if nothing had happened.

"Ridiculous," indeed! *I'll show him,* she thought; and a couple of months later she did – or nearly. The occasion had been the "official entertaining of a Scandinavian diplomat – blond, and not a day over thirty-five – from which duty Rodney had come home at one in the morning to find a policeman at his door and an urgent summons to the local hospital.

She'd intended, of course, that he should find the policeman at his door; also that he should have to rush to the hospital. But she *hadn't* intended – well, of course she hadn't – that as soon as he reached the hospital he should be told there was nothing to worry about. "She'll be all right; she's coming round nicely!"

"Nothing to worry about" – when the whole aim and object of the harrowing, nerve-racking episode had been to *make* him worry! These damned interfering medicos – she hadn't meant to "come round" at all, let alone as quickly as this, before Rodney had had so much as fifteen minutes of real anxiety! How could *she* have known that forty tranquillisers wouldn't be enough to finish her off! Or that consuming them on a park bench on a freezing February night would actually detract from, rather than add to, their efficacy?

"The cold gives a shock to the system, it delays the onset of coma," Sister explained, with a touch of malicious triumph, pulling down Maggie's lower eyelids, one after the other, while she spoke, and examining their inner surfaces for God knows what sign or symptom (dying was no simple thing, Maggie had discovered; it seemed to involve the most unexpected areas of the body, and to expose you to the most complicated and irrelevant procedures at all hours of the day and night). "And anyway," Sister continued, still smugly, "you can't kill yourself with tranquillisers no matter how many you take; they're not strong enough."

How could Maggie have known? How *did* people find out these things?

And likewise, how could she have known, the very next summer, on holiday, that if you can swim at all, however poorly, then it is impossible deliberately to drown?

They'd gone to Ibiza this time for their holiday – if you could call it a holiday with Rodney working all day and all night on his wretched report – scribbling, crossing out, jotting down figures, frowning, staring blind as a stone into the glory of the summer sea: seeing nothing, saying nothing, as unaware of Maggie as if she were dead. It was on the sixth day of this holiday, a day of blue water and white, shimmering heat, that he'd told her, quite casually, at lunchtime, that he had to fly back to London that very afternoon. Yes, it was an awful shame; and yes, he'd try to get back within two or three days; but just *supposing* he couldn't make it before the end of their three weeks, then...

Then Maggie must stay on and enjoy herself. Just like last summer, and the summer before that, not to mention the Easter holiday they'd had in Madeira. It was always the same...Maggie staying on and enjoying herself in some awful foreign hotel where she didn't know a soul…a surplus woman, eyed by her fellow-guests, served pityingly by the waiters, dragging out the remaining days of her "holiday" as if it was a prison sentence.

And as if this weren't enough, there'd been the quarrel as well – and this, too, followed the familiar pattern: But it's my *job*, darling, don't you see? Your job, your job, always your damn job, you never think of anything else, can't you ever think of *me* for a change? Think of *you* – hell, who do you think I'm slaving away earning the money *for*? I notice you're not behindhand in *spending* it – new kitchen unit – new curtains – wall-to-wall carpets! Hell, you've got *everything*! And expensive holidays thrown in! Do you realise what this hotel costs? – just bed and breakfast alone comes to—?

Shut up, shut up, shut up, all you ever think of is money! Money, money, money! I hate your money, I don't want your money, I just want you to love me, like you used to do…

Oh Lord, oh God, don't start *that* again! Look, dear, do *please* try to pull yourself together. I have to be at the airport by five, and I was hoping we could have one last swim…

One last swim. Rodney must have been surprised at Maggie's sudden silence, and at the way all the temper seemed to drain out of her. All of a sudden, she became quiet and co-operative, agreeing to join him for his swim…even walking into the sea ahead of him…

How *do* people drown? How *do* they decide to swim *this* stroke, but not the next one…?

At first, swimming away from the shimmering beach, away from Rodney fixing his snorkel in the middle distance, it had all seemed so easy. All she had to do was to go on swimming, on and on, through the warm silky water, until the end came.

HOLIDAY BATHING TRAGEDY – she saw the headline in her mind's eye; thought about Rodney seeing it too – covering up his eyes, perhaps, to shut out the terrible words…the terrible remorse… the despairing realisation of how much he had loved her…a realisation that had come too late…

A small wave, whose coming she had not noticed, slapped against her face, a little peremptorily, and she spluttered for a second or two, coughed, and went on swimming – noticing, for the first time, that the water seemed colder than it had a little while ago. Her arms were beginning to ache, and her back too.

YOUNG WIFE SWIMS TO HER DEATH.

Well, fairly young. Thirty-three isn't *old*, and the reporters would naturally want to make a meal of it if they could. *MYSTERY OF DROWNED BLONDE* – well, not blonde exactly, but they could hardly say *DROWNED MOUSE*, could they – and then the coroner's questions. Did the dead woman have any worries? Was she depressed? In financial difficulties? No, poor Rodney would have to answer: No, and No, and No. No, she had everything. *Everything.*

THE WOMAN WHO HAD EVERYTHING – that would be the next headline. On the second day, that would be – the day after tomorrow.

The day after tomorrow. As soon as that, she, Maggie, just wouldn't be there any more. Sooner, actually. Much sooner. By this evening, probably. By the time the lights along the shore were switched on tonight, she just wouldn't be there to see them.

Another wave spluttered in her face…and another. Out here, the water was getting choppy, and very cold. She thought of turning back, then remembered why she was here.

She was tired, though; so very, very tired. Little cramps were running down her legs, and there was a sort of heavy numbness in her limbs which made it hard to keep going.

How *do* people drown? How *do* they? How do they prevent their exhausted, obstinate muscles from swimming just one more stroke…and then another? Exhausted, frozen, tied in triple knots with cramp, still the damn things keep on functioning…one stroke…another…another…

Another wave slopped into her face; and almost before she had got her breath, came a second one. They were coming at her faster now, more spitefully. She was aware of a threat in them now, veiled as yet, but unmistakable…each time it was harder to get her breath, to cough away one little dollop of water before the next sloshed against her nostrils.

It would get harder still. This, of course, would be the way the end would come. The moments of recovering her breath would become fewer and fewer, the coughing more desperate until, at last, that wave would slosh into her lungs which couldn't be coughed away at all. Not ever.

With what seemed like her last strength, she swivelled over on to her back so that her face need not take the brunt of every oncoming wave; raising her weary head for a second she glimpsed, terribly far off, the line of the beach, and the tiny, sunlit holiday-makers, like dolls in the distance. This is it, she thought; now I *can't* get back; and with the thought, there came into her body a huge and terrible force, surging from somewhere behind her ribs and spreading everywhere, into every limb. It gripped her as a terrier grips a rat, carrying her triumphantly where it intended she should go.

"Had a good swim, darling?" asked Rodney, not raising his eyes from the journal he was reading; and Maggie, slumped down on the sand beside him, could not believe that he would not, in a few moments, notice her shuddering limbs, her face; hear the thundering of her heart.

But he didn't; and within minutes the shuddering had begun to subside, the heartbeats to slow down. Colour was returning to her face, and she lay there in the hot sand hating her body for its flawless functioning, for the perfection of its survival mechanisms, and for the speed with which it knew how to recover from almost anything. Of what use was her decision to die, in the face of her body's tigerish determination to stay alive? All those billions of cells in there, what did *they* care about the misery, the humiliation and the futility of her existence? *They* were all right, Jack, multiplying and dividing and regenerating, carrying on with their petty little life cycles, with never a thought of what it all added up to for *her*! *She* was the one who had to take the consequences of their blind, idiot determination to keep going, damn them!

Damn them! Damn them!

* * *

It must be past midnight by now – well past. Slumped deep in the wing-chair, Maggie stirred a little; tried, feebly, to sit up straight; but the whole thing was too difficult. The muted lamplight still seemed too bright for such sensitive retinas as hers, newly returned from the dead, and so she closed her eyes once more. Against the swirling blackness behind her lids she tried to picture Rodney's home-coming – which surely could not be delayed much longer, so late as it was?

There was no possibility, this time, that he'd be able to ignore the thing, she'd set the scene much too carefully. To start with, she'd left the milk on the front step ever since this morning; to come home after midnight and find two full milk bottles still outside the front door would surely arrest any man's attention? On top of this, she had left the back door swinging open into the black, blowy garden, so that the first thing Rodney would feel as he stepped into the hall would be the icy November draught sweeping through the house. What the *hell* is going on, he would inevitably wonder, striding across the hall and into the kitchen to slam the back door. And then – angrily at first, but presently with growing anxiety – he would go in search of his wife.

Not in bed? Not watching television? Not in the bathroom? And she couldn't be out, not possibly, for neither of them ever went out without locking the back door and all the windows. And as he moved, with growing unease, from room to room, he would notice – if he hadn't noticed it already – that the whole house was in darkness. What could she be doing, sitting in total darkness, making never a sound...? And now, at last, his heart would begin to thump with fear...

But there was something wrong somewhere. This delectable vision of Rodney's anxiety and concern contained some discrepancy... there was something that didn't fit properly... Her brain, with slowly returning clarity, groped uneasily for what it was that could be amiss; but it was not until, by some chance, she blinked her eyes open again for a moment that the thing hit her with a sledgehammer.

The lamp! The reading-lamp, casting its dim beams across her field of vision – it shouldn't have been on at all! *She* hadn't switched it on – she knew with absolute certainty that she hadn't. It had been bright afternoon, the room bathed in slanting autumn sunlight, when she'd sat down here to take the pills – there was no possibility at all that she'd have had the lamp on...and now, with an awful growing suspicion, she noticed something else.

The desk. Rodney's big desk, wide open, and all that litter of papers – it hadn't been like that this afternoon! It had been shut and locked – as Rodney was always accustomed to leave it – and her suicide note had been standing in solitary state on the bare polished surface – not flanked, as it was now, by papers, files, documents...

The terrible suspicion grew, it became a certainty, monstrous and almost beyond belief. Rodney must have already come in! Come in here, switched on the lamp and seen her! Seen the note: seen her unconscious, the pills beside her! Seen her – and gone away! He had done nothing – attempted nothing – to save her! He must even – so monstrous was his unconcern – have pushed right past her dying body to get at his desk!

And what then? What does a man do next, after he has looked down at his wife's unconscious face, and decided to let her die? Where does he go from there?

Away, of course. He gets the hell out of it all. And now a new vision, hallucinatory in its intensity, took over behind Maggie's eyelids. She saw Rodney, guilty and secretive, padding about this room in the dim lamplight, hastily shuffling together his most important documents, cramming them into his briefcase, all the time keeping his eyes averted from the awful figure in the chair, who might or might not be dead, and who might yet, like some avenging spirit, rise up and accuse him...

And what next? Off upstairs to pack an overnight bag? By a tragic chance, Your Honour, I happened to be away from home that night... By the time I got back, it was too late...

Something like that...and swift upon this thought, followed another in Maggie's brain: *perhaps he is still here*! Perhaps, if I got out of this chair, and tiptoed up the stairs very quietly?

And it was only now that Maggie discovered that she actually *couldn't* move. It wasn't, as she had supposed, mere weakness and lethargy, the aftermath of her overdose; it was actual paralysis of every limb, against which her muscles seemed to brace themselves in vain. Only her head was still mobile, and raising it a little she looked down, and saw, with numbed incredulity, the ropes which bound her legs and arms; felt the bruises and the weals; and identified the strange stiffness of her jaws as a gag, professionally secured.

And so Maggie got her headlines after all.

DIPLOMAT'S WIFE, BOUND AND GAGGED, DEFIES FOREIGN SPY RING

*COURAGE OF YOUNG WIFE SAVES SECRET
GOVERNMENT PAPERS*

BLONDE FOILS INTRUDERS SINGLE-HANDED

Reading, in column after column, of her courage, her re-source, her
cool-headedness, Maggie did not know what to think, or which way to
turn: she did not even know how to counter the undeserved admiration,
the hugs and kisses, which Rodney was lavishing upon her. He didn't
seem to *want* to listen to the true story.

If it was the true one? What Maggie presumed had happened was
that the intruders had seized on this extraordinary chance of getting
into the house without breaking in, had made their way to Rodney's
study, switched on the light – and seen Maggie. They would not have
stopped to ask questions, they were professionals, binding and gagging
her would have been a matter of seconds.

Was it the strange, unresisting limpness of her body that had scared
them? Or the suicide note, which they would have seen as soon as they
began to rifle the desk? Whichever it was, they plainly had not wanted
to get mixed up in it, and had fled.

That was how it probably was. Almost certainly. And yet...and
yet...? There *were* these bruises, over and above the marks of the rope.
Wasn't there just the possibility that Maggie *hadn't* been quite dead to
the world when her assailants had arrived? That she *had* fought back,
protecting her husband's interests, powered by some blind, enormous
instinct below the threshold of consciousness, and far beyond the reach,
now, of her drugged memory? An instinct as enormous and as invincible
as the one which last summer had wrenched her out of the depths of the
sea? Had she indeed mysterious powers inside her – an untested courage
of which, in ordinary life, she knew nothing?

The courage, maybe, *actually* to commit suicide? Or even, just
possibly, the courage to face the consequences of loving an ambitious,
highly strung man stretched almost beyond his limits by responsibilities
and pressures such as he had never known?

THE NUGGY BAR

Simon Brett

Murder, like all great enterprises, repays careful planning; and, if there was one thing on which Hector Griffiths prided himself, it was his planning ability.

It was his planning ability which had raised him through the jungle of the domestic cleaning fluids industry to be Product Manager of the GLISS range of indispensable housewives' aids. His marriage to Melissa Wintle, an attractive and rich widow with a teenage daughter, was also a triumph of planning. Even his wife's unfortunate death three years later, caused by asphyxiation from the fumes of a faulty gas heater while he was abroad on business, could be seen as the product of, if not necessarily planning, then at least serendipity.

But no amount of planning could have foreseen that Melissa's will would have left the bulk of her not inconsiderable wealth to Janet, daughter of her first marriage, rather than to Hector, her second husband.

So when, at the age of fifty-two, Hector Griffiths found himself reduced to his GLISS salary (generous, but by no means sufficient to maintain those little extras – the flat in Sloane Street, the cottage in Cornwall, the Mercedes, the motor-boat – which had become habitual while his wife was alive) and saddled with the responsibility of an unforthcoming, but definitely rich, step-daughter, he decided it was time to start planning again.

Hector Griffiths shared with Moses, Matthew, Mark, Luke, John and other lesser prophets and evangelists the advantage of having written his own Bible. It was a series of notes which he had assembled during the planning build-up to the launch of NEW GREEN GLISS – WITH AMMONIA, and he was not alone in appreciating its worth. No less a person than the company's European Marketing Director

(Cleaning Fluids) had congratulated him on the notes' cogency and good sense after hearing Hector use them as the basis of a Staff Training Course lecture.

Hector kept the notes, which he had had neatly typed up by his secretary, in a blue plastic display folder, of which favoured Management Trainees were occasionally vouchsafed a glimpse. On its title page were two precepts, two precepts which provided a dramatic opening to Hector's lectures and which, he had to admit, were rather well put.

A. EVEN AT THE COST OF DELAYING THE LAUNCH OF YOUR PRODUCT, ALWAYS ALLOW SUFFICIENT TIME FOR PLANNING. IMPATIENCE BREEDS ERROR, AND ERROR IS EXPENSIVE.

B. ONCE YOU HAVE MADE YOUR MAJOR DECISIONS ABOUT THE PRODUCT AND THE TIMING OF ITS LAUNCH, DO NOT INDULGE SECOND THOUGHTS. A DELAYED SCHEDULE IS ALSO EXPENSIVE.

A third precept, equally important but unwritten, dictated that before any action was taken on a new product, there should be a period of Desk Work, of sitting and thinking, looking at the project from every angle, checking as many details as could be checked, generally familiarising oneself with every aspect of the job in hand. Thinking at this earlier, relaxed stage made it easier to deal with problems that arose later, when time for thought was a luxury and one had to act on impulse.

It was nearly three months after Melissa's death before Hector had time to settle down to the Desk Work for his new project. He had been busy with the European launch of GLISS SCOURING PADS and had also found that clearing a deceased's belongings and sorting out a will, even such a simple and unsatisfactory one as Melissa's, took a surprising amount of time. Janet had also needed attention. Her mother's death had taken place at Easter, which meant that the girl had been home from her Yorkshire boarding school. Janet, now a withdrawn fifteen-year-old, had unfortunately been asleep at the time of Melissa's accident, had heard nothing and so been unable to save her. Equally unfortunately, from her step-father's point of view, she had not been in the bathroom with her mother when the gas fumes started to escape, which would have solved his current difficulties before they arose.

But, as Hector always told the eager young men in beige suits and patterned ties on the Staff Training Courses, success rarely comes easily, and the wise manager will distrust the solution that arrives too readily.

No, Janet was still with him, and he did not regret the time he had devoted to her. His plans for her future had not yet crystallised but, whatever it was to be, prudence dictated that he should take on the role of the solicitous step-father. Now she was such a wealthy young woman, it made sense that he should earn at least her goodwill.

He smiled wryly at the thought. Something told him he would require more of her than goodwill for the occasional handout. The flat in London, the cottage in Cornwall, the motor-boat and the Mercedes demanded a less erratic income. He needed permanent control of Janet's money.

But he was jumping to conclusions. He always warned Management Trainees against prejudging issues before they had done their Desk Work.

Hector Griffiths opened the blue folder on his desk. He turned over the page of precepts and looked at the next section.

1. NEED FOR PRODUCT (FILLING MARKET VOID, INCREASING BRAND SHARE)

It took no elaborate research to tell him that the product was needed. Now Melissa was dead, there was a market void, and the product required to fill it was money.

Unwilling to reject too soon any possibility, he gave thought to various methods of money-making. His prospects at GLISS were healthy, but not healthy enough. Even if, when the Marketing Director (UK) retired and was replaced by the European Marketing Director (Cleaning Fluids), Hector got the latter's job (which was thought likely), his salary would only rise by some 25 per cent, far off parity with the wealth he had commanded as Melissa's husband. Even a massive coincidence of coronaries among the senior management of GLISS which catapulted Hector to the Managing Director's office would still leave him worse off.

Career prospects outside GLISS, for a man of fifty-two, however good a planner, offered even less. Anyway, Hector didn't want to struggle and graft. What he had had in mind had been a few more years of patronising his underlings in his present job and then an early, dignified and leisured retirement, surrounded by all the comforts of Melissa (except for Melissa herself).

So how else did people get money? There was crime, of course – theft, embezzlement and so on – but Hector thought such practices undignified, risky and positively immoral.

No, it was obvious that the money to ease his burdens should be Melissa's. Already he felt it was his by right.

But Janet had it.

On the other hand, if Janet died, the trust that administered the money for her would have to be broken, inevitably to the benefit of her only surviving relation, her poor step-father, desolated by yet another bereavement.

The real product for which there was a market void, and which would undeniably increase Hector Griffiths' brand share, was Janet's death.

2. SPECIFIC DESCRIPTION OF PRODUCT

Fifteen-year-old girls rarely die spontaneously, however convenient and public-spirited such an action might be, so it was inevitable that Janet would have to be helped on her way.

It didn't take a lot of Desk Work to reach the conclusion that she would have to be murdered. And, following unhappy experiences with the delegation of responsibility over the European launch of GREEN GLISS SCOURING PADS, Hector realised he would have to do the job himself.

3. TIMING OF LAUNCH

This was the crucial factor. How many products, Hector would rhetorically demand of the ardent young men who dreamt of company Cortinas and patio doors, how many products have been condemned to obscurity by too hasty a schedule? Before deciding on the date of your launch, assess the following three points:

A. HOW SOON CAN THE PRODUCTION, PUBLICITY AND SALES DEPARTMENTS MAKE THE PRODUCT A VIABLE COMMERCIAL PROPOSITION?

B. HOW LONG WILL IT BE BEFORE THE MARKET FORCES WHICH REVEALED A NEED FOR THE PRODUCT ALTER? (N.B. OR BEFORE A RIVAL CONCERN ALSO NOTES THE NEED AND SUPPLIES IT WITH THEIR OWN PRODUCT?)

C. WHAT SPECIAL FACTORS DOES YOUR PRODUCT HAVE WHICH CREATE SPECIAL NEEDS IN TIMING? (e.g. YOU DO NOT LAUNCH A TENNIS SHOE CLEANER IN THE WINTER.)

Hector gave quite a lot of Desk Work to this section. The first question he could not answer until he had done some serious Research and Development into a murder method. That might take time.

But, even if the perfect solution came within days, there were many arguments for delaying the launch. The most potent was Melissa's recent death. Though at no point during the police investigations or inquest had the slightest suspicion attached to him, the coincidence of two accidents too close together might prompt unnecessarily scrupulous inquiry. It also made sense that Hector should continue to foster his image of solicitude for his step-daughter, thus killing the seeds of any subsequent suspicion.

The answer to Question A, therefore, was that the launch should be delayed as long as possible.

But the length of this delay was limited by the answer to Question B. Though with a sedately private matter like the murder of Janet, Hector did not fear, as he would have done in the cut-throat world of cleaning fluids, a rival getting in before him, there was still the strong pressure of market forces. The pittance Melissa had accorded him in her will would maintain his current lifestyle (with a conservative allowance for inflation) for about eighteen months. That set the furthest limit on the launch (though prudence suggested it would look less suspicious if he didn't run right up against bankruptcy).

In answer to Question C (what he humorously referred to to his Management Trainees as the "tennis shoe question"), there was a significant special factor. Since Janet was at boarding school in Yorkshire, where his presence would be bound to cause comment, the launch had to be during the school holidays.

Detailed consideration of these and other factors led him to a date of launch during the summer of the following year, some fifteen months away. It seemed a long time to wait, but, as Hector knew, IMPATIENCE BREEDS ERROR.

4. RESEARCH AND DEVELOPMENT OF PRODUCT (A. THEORETICAL)

He was able, at his desk, to eliminate a number of possible murder methods. Most of them were disqualified because they failed to meet one important specification: that he should not be implicated in any way.

Simplified, this meant either a) that Janet's death should look like an accident, b) that her step-father should have a cast-iron alibi for the time of her death, or, preferably, c) both.

He liked the idea of an accident. Even though he would arrange things so that he had nothing to fear from a murder inquiry, it was better to avoid the whole process. Ideally, he needed an accident which occurred while he was out of the country.

A wry instinct dissuaded him from any plan involving faulty gas heaters. A new product should always be genuinely original.

Hector went through a variety of remotely controlled accidents that could happen to teenage girls, but all seemed to involve faulty machinery and invited uncomfortably close comparisons with gas heaters. He decided he might have to take a more personal role in the project.

But if he had to be there, he was at an immediate disadvantage. Anyone present at a suspicious death becomes a suspicious person. What he needed was to be both present and absent at the same time.

But that was impossible. Either he was there or he wasn't. His own physical presence was immovable. The time of the murder was immovable. And the two had to coincide.

Or did they?

It was at this moment that Hector Griffiths had a brainwave.

They did sometimes come to him, with varying force, but this one was huge, bigger even, he believed, than his idea for the green tear-off tag on the GLISS TABLE-TOP CLEANER sachets.

He would murder Janet and then change the time of her murder.

It would need a lot of research, a lot of reading books of forensic medicine, but, just as Hector had known with the green tag, he knew again that he had the right solution.

4. RESEARCH AND DEVELOPMENT OF PRODUCT (B. PRACTICAL)

One of Hector's favourite sentences from his Staff Training lecture was: "The true Genesis of a product is forged by the R and D boys in the white heat of the laboratory." Previously, he had always spoken it with a degree of wistfulness, aware of the planner's distance from true creativity, but with his new product he experienced the thrill of being the real creator.

He gave himself a month, the month that remained before Janet would return for her summer holidays, and at the end of that time he wanted to know his murder method. There would be time for refinement of details, but it was important to get the main outline firm.

He made many experiments which gave him the pleasure of research, but not the satisfaction of a solution, before he found the right method.

He found it in Cornwall. Janet had agreed to continue her normal summer practice of spending the month of August at the cottage, and early in July Hector went down for a weekend to see that the place was habitable and to take the motorboat for its first outing of the season. While Melissa had been alive, the cottage had been used most weekends from Easter onwards and, as he cast off his boat from the mooring in front of his cottage and breathed the tangy air, Hector decided to continue the regular visits.

He liked it down there. He liked having the boat to play with, he liked the respect that ownership of the cottage brought him. Commander Donleavy, with whom he drank in the Yacht Club, would often look out across the bay to where it perched, a rectangle of white on the cliff, secluded but cunningly modernised, and say, "Damned fine property, that."

The boat was a damned fine property, too, and Hector wasn't going to relinquish either of them. Inevitably, as he powered through the waves, he thought of Melissa. But without emotion, almost without emotion now. Typical of her to make a mistake over the will.

She came to his mind more forcibly as he passed a place where they had made love. During the days of their courtship, when he had realised that her whimsical nature would require a few romantic gestures before she consented to marry him, he had started taking her to unlikely settings for love-making.

The one the boat now chugged past was the unlikeliest of all. It was a hidden cave, only accessible at very low tide. He had found it by accident the first time he had gone out with Melissa in the boat. His inexperience of navigation had brought their vessel dangerously close to some rocks and, as he leant out to fend off, he had fallen into the sea. To his surprise, he had found sand beneath his feet and caught a glimpse of a dark space under an arch of rock.

Melissa had taken over the wheel and he had scrambled back on board, aware that the romantic lover image he had been fostering was now seriously dented by his incompetence. But the cave he had seen offered a chance for him to redeem himself.

Brusquely ordering Melissa to anchor the boat, he had stripped off and jumped back into the icy water. (It was May.) He then swam to the opening he had seen and disappeared under the low arch. He soon found himself on a sandy beach in a small cave, eerily lit by the reflection of the sun on the water outside.

He had reappeared in the daylight and summoned Melissa imperiously to join him. Enjoying taking orders, she had stripped off and swum to the haven, where, on the sand, he had taken her with apparent, but feigned, brutality. When doing the Desk Work on his project for getting married to Melissa, he had analysed in her taste for Gothic romances an ideal of a dominant, savage lover, and built up the Heathcliff in himself accordingly.

It had worked, too. It was in the cave that she had agreed to marry him. Once the ceremony was achieved, he was able to put aside his Gothic image with relief. Apart from anything else, gestures like the cave episode were very cold.

When, by then safely married, they next went past the cave opening, Melissa had looked at him wistfully, but Hector had pretended not to see. Anyway, there had been no sign of the opening; it was only revealed at the lowest spring tide. Also by then it was high summer and the place stank. The council spoke stoutly of rotting seaweed, while local opinion muttered darkly about a sewage outlet, but, whatever the cause, a pervasively offensive stench earned the place the nickname of "Stinky Cove" and kept trippers away when the weather got hot.

As he steered his boat past the hidden opening and wrinkled his nose involuntarily, all the elements combined in Hector's head, and his murder plan began to form.

4. RESEARCH AND DEVELOPMENT OF PRODUCT (C. EXPERIMENTAL)

Commander Donleavy was an inexhaustible source of information about things nautical, and he loved being asked, particularly by someone as ignorantly appreciative as Hector Griffiths. He had no problem explaining to the greenhorn all about the 28-day cycle of the tides, and referring him to the tide tables, and telling him that yes, of course it would be possible to predict the date of a spring tide a year in advance. Not for the first time he marvelled that the government didn't insist on two years in the regular Navy as the minimum qualification for anyone wishing to own a boat.

Still, Griffiths wasn't a bad sort. Generous with the pink gins, anyway. And got that nice cottage over the bay. "Damned fine property, that," said Commander Donleavy, as he was handed another double.

The cycle of the tides did not allow Hector Griffiths to become an "R and D boy" and get back into "the white heat of the laboratory" again until his step-daughter was established in the cottage for her summer holiday. Janet was, he thought, quieter than ever; she seemed to take her mother's death hard. Though not fractious or unco-operative, she seemed listless. Except for a little sketching, she appeared to have no interests, and showed no desire to go anywhere. Better still, she did not seem to have any friends. She wrote duty postcards to two elderly aunts of Melissa in Stockport, but received no mail and made no attempt to make new contacts. All of which was highly satisfactory.

So, on the day of the spring tide, she made no comment on her step-father's decision to take the boat out, and Hector felt confident that, when he returned, he would still find her stretched lethargically in her mother's armchair.

He anchored the motorboat in shallow water outside the cave entrance, took off his trousers (beneath which he wore swimming trunks), put on rubber shoes, and slipped over the side. The water came just above his knee, and more of the entrance arch was revealed. On his previous visit the tide cannot have been at its very lowest. But the entrance remained well hidden; no one who didn't know exactly where it was would be likely to find it by chance.

He had a flashlight with him, but switched it off once he was inside the cave. The shifting ripples of reflection gave enough light. It was better than he remembered. The cave was about the size, and somehow had the atmosphere, of a small church. There was a high pile of fallen rocks and stones up the altar end, which, together with the stained-glass window feel of the filtered light, reinforced the image.

But it was an empty church. There was no detritus of beer-cans, biscuit packets or condoms to suggest that anyone else shared Hector's discovery.

Down the middle of the cave a seeping stream of water traversed the sand. Hector trod up this with heavy footsteps, and watched with pleasure as the marks filled in and became invisible.

The pile of rubble was higher than it had at first appeared. Climbing it was hard, as large stones rocked and smaller ones scuttered out under the weight of his feet. When he stood precariously on the top and looked down fifteen feet to the unmarked sand below, he experienced the sort of triumph that the "R and D boys" must have felt when they arrived at the formula for the original GLISS CLEANING FLUID.

In his pocket he found a paper bag and blew it up. Inflated, it was about the size of a human head. He let it bounce gently down to the foot of the rubble pile, and picked up a large stone.

It took three throws before he got his range, but the third stone hit the paper bag right in the middle. The target exploded with a moist thud. Shreds of it lay plastered flat against the damp sand.

Hector Griffiths left the cave and went back to get his step-daughter's lunch.

5. PACKAGING (WHAT DO YOU WANT THE PRODUCT TO LOOK LIKE? WHAT DOES THE PUBLIC WANT THE PRODUCT TO LOOK LIKE?)

"The appearance of your product is everything," the diligent young men who worried about their first mortgages and second babies would hear. "Packaging can kill a good product and sell a bad one. It can make an original product look dated, and an old one look brand new."

It could also, Hector Griffiths believed, make the police believe a murder to be an accident and an old corpse to be a slightly newer one.

As with everything, he planned well ahead. The first component in his murder machine was generously donated by its proposed victim. Listless and unwilling to go out, Janet asked if he would mind posting her cards to Melissa's aunts in Stockport. She didn't really know why she was writing to them, she added mournfully; they were unlikely ever to meet again now Mummy was dead.

Hector took the cards, but didn't post them. He did not even put stamps on them. You never knew how much postal rates might go up in a year. He put them away in a blue folder.

There wasn't a lot more that could be done at that stage, so he spent the rest of his time in Cornwall being nice to Janet and drinking with Commander Donleavy at the Yacht Club.

He listened to a lot of naval reminiscences and sympathised with the pervading gloom about the way the world was going. He talked about the younger generation. He said he had nothing to complain of with his step-daughter, except that she was so quiet. He said how he tried to jolly her along, but all she seemed to want to do was mope around the cottage or go off on long walks on her own. Oh yes, she did sketch a bit. Wasn't that her in a blue smock out by the back door of the cottage? Commander Donleavy looked through his binoculars and said he reckoned it must be – too far to see her clearly, though.

If he was in the Yacht Club in the evening, Hector might draw the Commander's attention to the cottage lights going off as Janet went to bed. Always turned in by ten-thirty – at least he couldn't complain about late hours. She was a strange child.

Commander Donleavy laughed and said there was no accounting for the ways of women. Good Lord, within a year that little mouse could have turned into a regular flapper, with boyfriends arriving every hour of the day and night.

Hector said he hoped not (without as much vigour as he felt) and laughed (without as much humour as he manifested). So the holidays passed.

When he got back behind his desk at GLISS, he found a letter telling him that an international domestic cleaning exhibition, INTERSAN, would be held in Hamburg from the 9th to the 17th of September the following year.

This was better than he had dared hope. He called in his assistant, a former Management Trainee, who was in charge of the undemanding and unexciting GLISS SPOT-REMOVER range and who constantly complained about his lack of responsibility, and asked him to represent the company at the exhibition. Hector knew it was a long way off, but he thought it would give the young man something to look forward to. He was beginning to feel his age, he added tantalisingly, and thought there might be other responsibilities he would soon wish to delegate.

On 14 September, Hector Griffiths set aside that day's copy of the *Daily Telegraph*. He put it with the postcards in the blue folder.

There was little more he could do for the time being, except to go over his planning in detail and check for flaws. He found none, but he still thought there was something missing. He needed one more element, one clinching piece of evidence. Still, no need to panic; it'd come. Just a matter of patient Desk Work. So, while he devoted most of his energies to the forthcoming launch of GLISS HANDY MOPPITS (IDEAL FOR THE KITCHEN, NURSERY OR HANDBAG), he kept a compartment of his mind open to receive another inspiration.

So the months passed. He and Janet Christmassed quietly in London. To his relief, she did not appear to be fulfilling Commander Donleavy's prognostications; if anything, she was quieter still. The only change was that she said she hated school, was getting nowhere there, and wanted to leave. Her indulgent step-father suppressed his glee, thought about the matter seriously, and finally agreed that she should leave at the end of the summer term, then join him for August at the cottage, so that they could decide on her future.

6. PUBLICITY (MAKE SURE EVERYONE KNOWS ABOUT YOUR PRODUCT EXACTLY WHEN *YOU* WANT THEM TO.)

This was the only one of Hector Griffiths' headings which might, while vital for any GLISS product, seem to be less applicable in the case of a murder.

But publicity is not only making things public; it is also keeping things secret until the time is right, and Hector's experience at GLISS had taught him a great deal about this art. Though lacking the glamour of military secrets, cleaning fluid secrets were still valuable and had been the subjects of espionage. So Hector was trained to keep his plans to himself.

And, anyway, there was going to come a time when publicity of the conventional sort was necessary, indeed essential. If the police never found Janet's body, then the plan was incomplete. Not only might there be difficulties in releasing her money to her step-father, he might also have to suffer the stigma of suspicion. As with the launch of a product, what was important was the moment of public revelation. And the timing of that, with this product as with any other, Hector would dictate personally.

It was, incidentally, while he was thinking of publicity that he came upon the missing element in his campaign. Some months before the launch of GLISS HANDY MOPPITS (IDEAL FOR THE KITCHEN, NURSERY OR HANDBAG) Hector had to go to his advertising agency to agree the publicity campaign for the new product. He enjoyed these occasions, because he knew that he, as Product Manager, was completely in command, and loved to see his account executive fawn while he deliberated.

One particular ploy, which gave him a great deal of satisfaction, was simply delaying his verdict. He would look at the artwork, view the television commercial or listen to the campaign outline, then, after remaining silent for a few minutes, start talking about something completely different. The executive presenting to him, fearful above all else of losing the very lucrative GLISS account, would sweat his way up any conversational alley the Product Manager wished to lead him, until finally Hector relented and said what he thought.

After seeing the television commercial for GLISS HANDY MOPPITS (IDEAL FOR THE KITCHEN, NURSERY OR HANDBAG), Hector started playing his game and asked what else the executive was working on.

The young man, a fine sweat lending his brow a satisfying sheen, answered sycophantically. His next big job was for one of the country's biggest confectionery firms, the launch of a brand new nut and nougat sweet – the NUGGY BAR. It was going to be a huge nationwide campaign – newspapers, cinema, television, radio, the lot. The product was already being tested in the Tyne-Tees area. Look, would Mr. Griffiths like to try one? Nice blue and gold wrapper, wasn't it? Yes, go on, try – we've got plenty – the office is full of them.

Well, what did Mr. Griffiths think of it? Pretty revolting? Hmm. Well, never mind. Yes, take one by all means. Well, anyway, whatever Mr. Griffiths thought of them, he was going to be hard put to avoid them. After the launch on 10 September, he would see them in every shop in the country.

Hector Griffiths glowed inwardly. Yes, of course there was skill and there was planning, but there was also luck. Luck, like the fact that the old GLISS FLOOR POLISH tin had adapted so easily to metric standards. Luck, like suddenly coming across the NUGGY BAR. It was a magnetism for luck that distinguished a great Product Manager from a good Product Manager.

The NUGGY BAR was secure in his pocket. His mind raced on, as he calmly told the account executive that he found the GLISS HANDY MOPPITS (IDEAL FOR THE KITCHEN, NURSERY OR HANDBAG) commercial too flippant, and that it would have to be remade, showing more respect for the product.

7. RUN-UP TO LAUNCH (ATTEND TO DETAILS. CHECK, CHECK AND RECHECK.)

Hector Griffiths checked, checked and rechecked.

In June he went to an unfamiliar boat dealer in North London and bought, for cash, an inflatable dinghy and outboard motor.

The next weekend he went down to Cornwall and, after much consultation with Commander Donleavy, bought an identical dinghy and outboard from the boatyard that serviced his motorboat.

Three days later he bought some electrical time-switches in an anonymous Woolworths.

Then, furtively, in a Soho sex shop, he bought an inflatable woman.

In another anonymous Woolworths, he bought a pair of rubber gloves.

At work, the GLISS HANDY MOPPITS (IDEAL FOR THE KITCHEN, NURSERY OR HANDBAG) were successfully launched. Hector's assistant, in anticipation of his exciting trip to Hamburg for INTERSAN, took his holiday in July. One of his last actions before going away was to prepare the authorisation for the continued production of GLISS SPOT-REMOVER. This was the formal notice to the production department which would ensure sufficient supplies of the product for November orders. It was one of those boring bits of paperwork that had to be prepared by the individual Product Manager and sent to the overall GLISS Product Manager for signature.

Hector's assistant did it last thing on the day he left, deposited it in his out-tray, and set off for two weeks in Hunstanton, cheered by the fact that Griffiths had said he was going to take a longer holiday that summer, all of August plus two weeks of September. Another indication, like INTERSAN, that the old man was going to sit back a bit and give others a chance.

So Hector's assistant didn't see the old man in question remove the GLISS SPOT-REMOVER authorisation from his out-tray. Nor did he see it burnt to nothing in an ash-tray in the Sloane Street flat.

Janet left her Yorkshire boarding school as quietly as she had done everything else in her life, and joined her step-father in London. At the beginning of August they went down to Cornwall.

She remained as withdrawn as ever. Her step-father encouraged her to keep up her sketching, and to join him in occasional trips in the motor-boat or his new rubber dinghy. He spoke with some concern to Commander Donleavy in the Yacht Club about her listlessness. He pointed her out sketching outside the cottage, and the Commander almost saw her figure through his binoculars. Once or twice in the evening, Hector commented to the Commander about the early hour at which she switched the lights out.

On 16 August, Hector Griffiths went out fishing on his own and unfortunately cut both his hands when a nylon line he was reeling in pulled taut.

That evening he tried to talk to his step-daughter about a career, but found it hard going. Hadn't she discussed it with friends? With teachers at the school? Wasn't there someone he could ring and talk to about it?

After a lot of probing, she did give him the name of her French mistress, who was the only person she seemed to have been even slightly close to at the school. Had she got her phone number? asked Hector. Yes. Would she write it down for him? Here, on this scrap of paper.

Reluctantly she did. She didn't notice that the scrap of paper was a piece torn from a copy of the *Daily Telegraph*. Or that the only printing on it was most of the date – "14 September, 19…"

Her step-father continued his uphill struggle to cheer her up. Look, here was something he'd been given. A new sort of chocolate bar, nut and nougat, called the NUGGY BAR. Not even on the market yet. Go on, try a bit, have a bite. She demurred, but eventually, just to please him, did take a bite.

She thought it was "pretty revolting".

8. THE LAUNCH

The spring tide was to be at its lowest at 19:41 on 17 August, but Hector Griffiths didn't mention this when he persuaded his step-daughter to come out for a trip in the motorboat at half-past six that evening. Janet wasn't keen, but nor was she obstructive, so soon the boat, with its rubber dinghy towed behind, was chugging along towards "Stinky Cove". Her step-father's hands on the wheel wore rubber gloves, to prevent dirt from getting into the wounds made by his fishing line the previous day.

Janet seemed psychologically incapable of enthusiasm for anything, but Hector got very excited when he thought he saw an opening in the rocks. He steered the boat in close and there, sure enough, was an archway. The stench near the rocks was strong enough to deter any but the most ardent speleologist – in fact, there were no other vessels in sight – but Hector still seemed keen to investigate the opening. He anchored the motorboat and urged Janet into the dinghy. They cast off and puttered towards the rocks.

Instructing his step-daughter to duck, Hector lined the boat up, cut the motor, and waves washed the dinghy through on to the sand of a hidden cave.

With expressions of wonder, Hector stepped out into a shallow stream, gesturing Janet to follow him. She did so with her usual lethargy. Her step-father pulled the dinghy some way up on to the sand. Crowing with childlike excitement about the discovery they'd made, he suggested exploring. Maybe this little cave led to a bigger one. Wasn't that an opening there at the top of the pile of rubble? He set off towards it. Without interest, but co-operative to the last, Janet followed.

It was on the precarious top of the pile that Hector Griffiths appeared to lose his balance and fall heavily against his step-daughter. She fell sideways down the loose surface to the sand of the cave floor. Fortunately she fell face down, so she didn't see the practised aim of the rock that went flying towards her head.

The damp thud of its impact was very similar to that an earlier missile had made against a paper bag, but louder. The commotion was sufficient to dislodge a shower of small stones from the roof of the cave, which gave very satisfactory credibility to the idea that Janet had been killed by a rockfall.

Hector also found it a source of satisfaction that she had landed away from the stream. When her body was finally discovered, he didn't want her clothes to be soaked through; it must be clear that she had entered the cave in the dinghy, in other words, at the lowest ebb of a spring tide.

Hector stepped carefully down the rubble. Keeping his feet in the stream, he inspected Janet. A little blood and brain from her crushed skull marked the sand. She was undoubtedly dead.

With his gloved hands, he slipped the scrap of *Daily Telegraph* with her French mistress's phone number and the opened NUGGY BAR with its blue and gold wrapper into Janet's pocket.

He then walked down the stream to the opening, already slightly smaller with the rising tide, waded into the sea and swam out to the motorboat.

On board he removed a tarpaulin from his second rubber dinghy, attached its painter to the back of the larger boat and cast it behind. Then he chugged back to his mooring near the cottage, as the tide continued to rise.

9. THE VITAL FIRST MONTH (YOUR PRODUCT IS YOUR BABY – NURSE IT GENTLY.)

Hector Griffiths still had nearly a month of his six-week holiday in Cornwall to go, and he passed it very quietly and peacefully. Much of the time he was in the Yacht Club drinking with Commander Donleavy.

There he would complain to the Commander, and anyone else who happened to be listening, about his step-daughter's reticence and ask advice on what career he should guide her towards. Now and then at lunchtime he would point out the blue smock-clad figure sitting sketching outside the back door of the cottage. At night he might comment on her early hours as he saw the cottage lights go off.

In the mornings, before he went out, he would check the time-switches and decide whether or not to use the inflatable woman. He didn't want the sketching to become too predictable, so he varied the position of the dummy in its smock and frequently just left it indoors. Once or twice, at dusk, he took it out in the dinghy past the harbour and waved to the fishermen on the quay.

At the end of August he posted Janet's cards to Melissa's aunts in Stockport. Their messages had the timeless banality of all postcard communications.

In the first week of September he continued his nautical rounds and awaited the explosion from GLISS.

Because the cottage wasn't on the telephone, the explosion, when it came, on 5 September, was in the form of a telegram. (Hector had kept the sketching dummy out of the way for a few days in anticipation of its arrival.) It was from his assistant, saying a crisis had arisen, could he ring as soon as possible.

He made the call from the Yacht Club. His assistant was defiantly guilty. Something had gone wrong with the production authorisation for GLISS SPOT-REMOVER. The factory hadn't received it and now there would be no stock to meet the November orders.

Hector Griffiths swore – a rare occurrence – and gave his assistant a lavish dressing-down. The young man protested he was sure he had done the paperwork, but received an unsympathetic hearing. Good God, couldn't he be trusted with the simplest responsibility? Well, there was nothing else for it, he'd have to go and see all the main buyers and apologise. No, letters wouldn't do, nor would the telephone. GLISS's image for efficiency was at stake and the cock-up had to be explained personally.

But, the young man whimpered, what about his forthcoming trip to INTERSAN in Hamburg?

Oh no! Hector had forgotten all about that. Well, it was out of the question that his assistant should go now, far too much mopping-up to be done. Damn, he'd have to go himself. GLISS must be represented. It was bloody inconvenient, but there it was.

After a few more demoralising expletives, Hector put the phone down and, fuming, joined Commander Donleavy at the bar. Wasn't it bloody typical? he demanded rhetorically, can't trust anyone these days – now he was going to have to cut his holiday short just because of the incompetence of his bloody assistant. Young people had no sense of responsibility.

Commander Donleavy agreed. They should bring back National Service.

Hector made a few more calls to GLISS management people, saying how he was suddenly going to have to rush off to Hamburg. He sounded aggrieved at the change of plan.

On his last day in Cornwall, the 6th of September, he deflated the dinghy and the woman. He went a long way out to sea in the motorboat, weighted them with the outboard motor and a few stones, and cast them overboard. The electrical time-switches and the rubber gloves followed.

That evening he said goodbye to Commander Donleavy in the Yacht Club. He confessed to being a little worried about Janet. Whereas previously she had just seemed listless, she now seemed deeply depressed. He didn't like to leave her in the cottage alone, though she spoke of going up to London, but he wasn't sure that he'd feel happier with her there. Still, he had to go on this bloody trip and he couldn't get her to make up her mind about anything...

Commander Donleavy opined that women were strange fish.

As he drove the Mercedes up to London on 7 September, Hector Griffiths reviewed the necessary actions on his return from Hamburg. Because of the GLISS SPOT-REMOVER crisis, he could legitimately delay going back to Cornwall for a week or two. And, since the cottage wasn't on the phone and she hadn't contacted him, he'd have to write to Janet. Nice, fatherly, solicitous letters.

Only after he had received no reply to two of these would he start to worry and go down to Cornwall. That would get him past the next low tide when the cave was accessible.

On arriving and finding his letters unopened on the mat (he would first search the cottage for a copy of the *Daily Telegraph* for 14 September and, if he found one, destroy it), he would drive straight back to London, assuming that he must somehow have missed his step-daughter there. He would ring her French mistress and Melissa's aunts in Stockport and only after drawing blanks there would he call the police.

When they spoke to him, he'd mention Janet's talk of going up to London. He'd also mention her depressed state. He would delay as long as possible mentioning that his rubber dinghy appeared to be missing.

Then, preferably as much as four months after her murder on 17 August, by which time, his reading of forensic medicine told him, it would be difficult to date the death with more than approximate accuracy, he would remember her once mentioning to him a hidden cave she'd found at low tide round "Stinky Cove".

The body would then be discovered.

Because of the lack of accurate timing from its state of decomposition, the police would have to date her death from other clues. The presence of the dinghy and the dryness of her clothes would indicate that she had entered the cave at a spring tide, which at once limited the dates.

Local people would have seen the dinghy, if not the girl, around until shortly before Hector's departure on 7 September. But other clues would be found in the girl's pocket. First, a NUGGY BAR, a new nut and nougat confection which was not available in the shops until 10 September. And, second, a phone number written on a scrap of newspaper dated 14 September. Since that was the date of a spring tide, the police would have no hesitation in fixing the death of Janet Wintle on 14 September.

On which date her step-father was unexpectedly, through a combination of circumstances he could not have foreseen, in Hamburg at INTERSAN, an international domestic cleaning exhibition.

So Hector Griffiths would have to come to terms with a second accidental death in his immediate family within two years.

And the fact that he would inherit his step-daughter's not inconsiderable wealth could only be a small compensation to him in his bereavement.

10. IS YOUR PRODUCT A SUCCESS? (ARE YOU SURE THERE'S NOTHING YOU'VE FORGOTTEN?)

On the day before he left for Hamburg, Hector Griffiths had a sudden panic. Suppose one of Melissa's aunts in Stockport had died?

They were both pretty elderly and, if it had happened, it was the sort of thing Janet would have known about. She'd hardly have sent a postcard to someone who was dead.

He checked by ringing the aunts with some specious inquiry about full names for a form he had to fill in. Both were safely alive. And both had been so glad to get Janet's postcards. When they hadn't heard from her the previous year, they were afraid she had forgotten them. So it was lovely to get the two postcards.

Two postcards? What, they'd got two each?

No, no, that would have been odd. One each, two in all.

Hector breathed again. He thought it fairly unlikely, knowing Janet's unwillingness to go out, that she'd sent any other postcards, but it was nice to be sure.

So everything was happily settled. He could go abroad with a clear conscience.

He couldn't resist calling GLISS to put another rocket under his assistant and check if there was anything else urgent before he went away.

There was a message asking him to call the advertising agency about the second wave of television commercials for GLISS HANDY MOPPITS (IDEAL FOR THE KITCHEN, NURSERY OR HANDBAG). He rang through and derived his customary pleasure from patronising the account executive. Just as he was about to ring off, he asked, "All set for the big launch?"

"Big launch?"

"On the tenth. The NUGGY BAR."

"Oh God. Don't talk to me about NUGGY BARS. I'm up to here with NUGGY BARS. The bloody Product Manager's got cold feet."

"Cold feet?"

"Yes. He's new to the job, worried the product's not going to sell."

"What?"

"They've got the report back from the Tyne-Tees area where they tested it. Apparently forty-seven per cent of the sample thought it was 'pretty revolting'."

"So what's going to happen?"

"Bloody Product Manager wants to delay the launch."

"Delay the launch?"

"Yes, delay it or cancel the whole thing. He doesn't know what he wants to do."

"But he can't pull out at this stage. The television time's been contracted and the newspapers and—"

"He can get out of most of it, if he doesn't mind paying off the contracts. He's stuck with the magazine stuff, because they go to press so far ahead, but he can stop the rest of it. And, insofar as he's capable of making a decision, he seems to have decided to stop it. Call came through just before lunch – Hold everything – The NUGGY BAR will not be launched on the tenth of September!"

The Mercedes had never gone faster than it did on the road down to Cornwall. In spite of the air-conditioning, its driver was drenched in sweat.

The motorboat, too, was urged on at full throttle until it reached "Stinky Cove". Feverishly Hector Griffiths let out the anchor cable and, stripping off his jacket and shoes, plunged into the sea.

The water was low, but not low enough to reveal the opening. Over a week to go to the spring tide. He had to dive repeatedly to locate the arch, and it was only on the third attempt that he managed to force his way under it. Impelled by the waves, he felt his back scraped raw by the rocks. He scrambled up on to the damp sand.

Inside all seemed dark. He cursed his stupidity in not bringing a flashlight. But, as he lay panting on the sand, he began to distinguish the outlines of the church-like interior. There was just enough glow from the underwater arch to light his mission. Painfully, he picked himself up.

As he did so, he became aware of something else. A new stench challenged the old one that gave the cove its name. Gagging, he moved towards its source.

Not daring to look, he felt in her clothes. It seemed an age before he found her pocket, but at last he had the NUGGY BAR in his hand.

Relief flooded his body and he tottered with weakness. It'd be all right. Back through the arch, into the boat, back to London, Hamburg tomorrow. Even if he'd been seen by the locals, it wouldn't matter. The scrap of *Daily Telegraph* and the dry state of Janet's clothes would still fix the date of her death a week ahead. It'd all be all right.

He waded back into the cold waves. They were now splashing

higher up the sand, the tide was rising. He moved out as far as he could and leant against the rock above the arch. A deep breath, and he plunged down into the water.

First, all he saw was a confusion of spray, then a gleam of diluted daylight ahead, then he felt a searing pain against his back and, as his breath ran out, the glow of daylight dwindled.

The waves had forced him back into the cave.

He tried again and again, but each time was more difficult. Each time the waves were stronger and he was weaker. He wasn't going to make it. He lay exhausted on the sand.

He tried to think dispassionately, to recapture the coolness of his planning mind, to imagine he was sitting down to the Desk Work on a cleaning fluid problem.

But the crash of the waves distracted him. The diminishing light distracted him. And, above all, the vile smell of decomposing flesh distracted him.

He controlled his mind sufficiently to work out when the next low tide would be. His best plan was to conserve his strength till then. If he could get back then, there was still a good chance of making the flight to Hamburg and appearing at INTERSAN as if nothing had happened.

In fact, that was his only possible course.

Unless… He remembered his lie to Janet. Let's climb up the pile of rubble and see if there's an opening at the top. It might lead to another cave. There might be another way out.

It was worth a try.

He put the NUGGY BAR in his trouser pocket and climbed carefully up the loose pile of rocks. There was now very little light. He felt his way.

At the top he experienced a surge of hope. There was not a solid wall of rock ahead, just more loose stones. Perhaps they blocked another entrance…a passage? Even an old smugglers' tunnel?

He scrabbled away at the rocks, tearing his hands. The little ones scattered, but the bigger ones were more difficult. He tugged and worried at them.

Suddenly a huge obstruction shifted. Hector jumped back as he heard the ominous roar it started. Stones scurried, pattered and thudded all around him. He scrambled back down the incline.

The rockfall roared on for a long time and he had to back nearer and nearer the sea. But for the darkness he would have seen Janet's body buried under a ton of rubble.

At last there was silence. Gingerly he moved forward.

A single lump of rock was suddenly loosed from above. It landed squarely in the middle of his skull, making a damp thud like an exploded paper bag, but louder.

Hector Griffiths fell down on the sand. He died on 8 September.

Outside his motorboat, carelessly moored in his haste, dragged its anchor and started to drift out to sea.

★　　★　　★

It was four months before the police found Hector Griffiths' body. They were led to it eventually by a reference they found in one of his late wife's diaries, which described a secret cave where they had made love. It was assumed that Griffiths had gone there in his dinghy because of the place's morbidly sentimental associations, been cut off by the rising tide and killed in a rockfall. His clothes were soaked with saltwater because he lay so near the high tide mark.

It was difficult to date the death exactly after so long, but a check on the tide tables (in which, according to a Commander Donleavy, Griffiths had shown a great interest) made it seem most likely that he had died on 14 September. This was confirmed by the presence in his pocket of a NUGGY BAR, a nut and nougat confection which was not available in the shops until 10 September.

Because the Product Manager of NUGGY BAR, after cancelling the product's launch, had suddenly remembered a precept that he'd heard in a lecture when he'd been a Management Trainee at GLISS...

ONCE YOU HAVE MADE YOUR MAJOR DECISIONS ABOUT THE PRODUCT AND THE TIMING OF ITS LAUNCH, DO NOT INDULGE SECOND THOUGHTS.

So he'd rescinded his second thoughts and the campaign had gone ahead as planned. (It may be worth recording that the NUGGY BAR was not a success. The majority of the buying public found it "pretty revolting".)

The body of Hector Griffiths' step-daughter, Janet Wintle, was never found. Which was a pity for two old ladies in Stockport who, under the terms of a trust set up in her mother's will, stood to inherit her not inconsiderable wealth.

INSPECTOR GHOTE AND THE NOTED BRITISH AUTHOR

H.R.F. Keating

Perched up on a creaking wobbly chair in the office of the Deputy Commissioner (Crime), the peon put one broken-nailed finger against Inspector Ghote's name on the painted board behind the DCC's desk. He swayed topplingly to one side, scraped hold of the fat white pin which indicated "Bandobast Duties", brought it back across in one swooping rush and pressed it firmly into place.

Watching him, Ghote gave an inward sigh. Bandobast duties. Someone, of course, had to deal with the thousand and one matters necessary for the smooth running of Crime Branch, but nevertheless bandobast duty was not tracking down breakers of the law and it did seem to fall to him more often than to other officers. Yet, after all, it would be absurd to waste a man of the calibre of, say, Inspector Dandekar on mere administration.

"Yes, Dandekar, yes?"

The DCC had been interrupted by his internal telephone and there on the other end, as if conjured up by merely having been thought of, was Dandekar himself.

"Yes, yes, of course," the DCC said in answer to the forcefully plaintive sound that had been just audible from the other end. "Certainly you must. I'll see what I can do, *ek dum.*"

He replaced the receiver and turned back to Ghote, the eyes in his sharply commanding face still considering whatever it was that he had promised Dandekar.

And then, as if a God-given solution to his problem had appeared in front of him, his expression changed in an instant to happy alertness. He swung round to the peon, who was carefully carrying away his aged chair.

"No," he said. "Put the bandobast pin against – er – Inspector Sawant. I have a task I need Inspector Ghote for."

The peon turned back with his chair to the big painted hierarchy of crime-fighters ranging from the Deputy Commissioner himself down to the branch's three dogs, Akbar, Moti and Caesar. Ghote, in front of the DCC's wide baize-covered desk, glowed now with pure joy.

"It's this Shivaji Park case," the DCC said.

"Oh yes, DCC. Multiple-stabbing double murder, isn't it? Discovered this morning by that fellow who was in the papers when he came to Bombay, that noted British author."

Ghote, hoping his grasp both of departmental problems and the flux of current affairs would earn him some hint of appreciativeness, was surprised instead to receive a look of almost suspicious surmise. But he got no time to wonder why.

"Yes, quite right," the DCC said briskly. "Dandekar is handling the case, of course. With an influential fellow like this Englishman involved we must have a really quick result. But there is something he needs help with. Get down to his office straightaway, will you?"

"Yes, sir. Yes, DCC."

Clicking his heels together by way of salute, Ghote hurried out.

What would Dandekar have asked for assistance over? There would be a good many different lines to pursue in an affair of this sort. The murdered couple, an ice-cream manufacturer and his wife, had been, so office gup went, attacked in the middle of the night. The assailants had tied up their teenage son and only when he had at last roused the nearest neighbour, this visiting British author – of crime books, the paper had said, well-known crime books – had it been discovered that the two older people had been hacked to death. Goondas of that sort did not, of course, choose just any location. They sniffed around first. And left a trail. Which meant dozens of inquiries in the neighbourhood, usually by sub-inspectors from the local station. But with this influential fellow involved…

Emerging into the sunlight, Ghote made his way along to Dandekar's office which gave directly on to the tree-shaded compound. He pushed open one half of its batwing doors. And there, looking just like his photograph, large as life, or even larger, was the Noted British Author. He was crouching on a small chair in front of Dandekar's green leather-covered desk, covering it much like a big fluffed-up hen on one small precious egg. His hips, clad in trousers already the worse for the dust and stains of Bombay life, drooped on either side while a considerable belly projected equally far forward. Above was a beard, big and sprawling as the body beneath, and above the beard was hair, plentiful and inclined to shoot in all directions. Somewhere between beard and hair a pale British face wore a look of acute curiosity.

"Ah, Ghote, thank God," Dandekar, stocky, muscular, hook-nosed, greeted him immediately in sharp, T-spitting Marathi. "Listen, take this curd-face out of my sight. Fast."

Ghote felt a terrible abrupt inward sinking. So this was how he was to assist Dandekar, by keeping from under his feet a, no doubt, notable British nuisance. Even bandobast duties would be better.

But Dandekar could hardly produce that expected rapid result with such a burden. He squared his bony shoulders.

Dandekar had jumped up.

"Mr. Peduncle," he said, in English now, "I would like you to—"

"It's not Peduncle actually," the Noted British Author broke in. "Important to get the little details right, you know. That's what the old shell-collector in my books – he's Mr. Peduncle – is always telling his friend, Inspector Sugden. No, my name's Reymond, Henry Reymond, author of the Peduncle books."

The multitudinous beard split with a wide, clamorously ingratiating grin.

"Yes, yes," said Dandekar briskly. "But this is Inspector Ghote. He will be assisting me. Ghote, the domestic servant of the place has disappeared – a Goan known as John Louzado. They had no address at his native-place, but we might get it from a former employer. Will you see to that? And Mr. Ped – Mr. Reymond, who is expressing most keen interest in our methods, can attach himself to you while I talk with the young man who was tied up, the son, or rather adopted son. I think somehow he could tell a good deal more."

Ghote put out his hand for Mr. Reymond to shake. He did not look forward to dealing with the numerous questions likely to arise from that keen interest in Bombay CID methods.

As Ghote drove the Noted British Author in one of the branch's big battered cars down Dr. D.N. Road towards Colaba where the fleeing servant's former employer lived, he found his worst forebodings justified. His companion wanted to know everything – what was that building, what this, was that man happy lying on the pavement, where else could he go?

Jockeying for place in the traffic, swerving for cyclists, nipping past great lumbering red articulated buses, Ghote did his best to provide pleasing answers. But the fellow was never content. Nothing seemed to delight him more than hitting on some small discrepancy and relentlessly pursuing it, comparing himself all the while to his Mr. Peduncle and his "The significant variation: in that lies all secrets". If Ghote heard the phrase once in the course of their twenty-minute drive, he seemed to hear it a dozen times.

At last, when they were waiting at the lights to get into Colaba Road, he was reduced to putting a question of his own. How did it come about, he interrupted, that Mr. Reymond was living in a flat up at Shivaji Park? Would not the Taj Hotel just down there be more suitable for a distinguished visitor?

"Ah yes, I know what you mean," the author answered with an enthusiasm that gave Ghote considerable inward pleasure. "But, you see, I am here by courtesy of Air India, on their new Swap-a-Country Plan. They match various people with their Indian equivalents and exchange homes. Most far-sighted. So I am at Shivaji Park and the writer who lives there – well, he has written some short stories, though I gather he's actually a Deputy Inspector of Smoke Nuisances and a relation of your State Minister for Police Affairs and the Arts, as it happens – well, he at the present moment is installed in my cottage in Wiltshire, and no doubt getting as much out of going down to the pub as I get from being in a flat lucky enough to have a telephone so that people are always popping in and, while they're looking up a number in the little red book, talking away like one o'clock."

The Noted British Author's eyes shone.

"Yes," Ghote said.

Certain queries had occurred to him. Could there, for instance, be an exchange between a police inspector in Bombay and one in, say, New York? But somehow he could not see himself getting several months' Casual Leave, and he doubted whether many other similar Bombayites would find it easy.

But he felt that to voice such doubts aloud would be impolite. And his hesitation was fatal.

"Tell me," Mr. Reymond said, "that sign saying 'De Luxe Ding Dong Nylon Suiting'..." And, in a moment, they had struck full on another "significant variation".

Desperately Ghote pulled one more question out of the small stock he had put together.

"Please, what is your opinion of the books of Mr. Erle Stanley Gardner? To me Perry Mason is seeming an extremely clever individual altogether."

"Yes," said the Noted British Author, and he was silent right until they reached their destination in Second Pasta Lane.

Mrs. Patel, wife of a civil servant and former employer of John Louzado, was a lady of forty or so dressed in a cotton sari of a reddish pattern at once assertive and entirely without grace.

"You are lucky to find me, Inspector," she said when Ghote had explained their business. "At the Family Planning office where I undertake voluntary work, Clinic begins at ten sharp."

Ghote could not stop himself glancing at his watch, though he well knew it was at least half-past ten already.

"Well, well," Mrs. Patel said sharply, "already I am behind schedule. But there is so much to be done. So much to be done."

She darted across the sitting-room, a place almost as littered with piles of papers as any office at Crime Branch, and plumped up a cushion.

"Just if you have the address of John's native-place," Ghote said.

"Of course, of course. I am bound to have it. I always inquire most particularly after a servant's personal affairs. You are getting an altogether better loyalty factor then. Don't you find·that, Mr. – I'm afraid I am not hearing your name?"

She had turned her by no means negligible gaze full on the Noted British Author. Ghote, who had hoped not to explain his companion, introduced him with a brief "Mr. Reymond, from UK."

"Yes," said Mrs. Patel. "Well, don't you find – Ah, but you are *the* Mr. Reymond, the noted British author, isn't it? Most pleased to meet you, my dear sir. Most pleased. What I always find with criminological works is the basic fact emerging, common to many sociological studies, a pattern of fundamental human carelessness, isn't it? You see—"

But, river-spate rapid though she was, she had met her match.

"One moment – I am sorry to interrupt – but there is a slight discrepancy here. You see, there are two different sorts of crime books involved. You are talking about sociological works, but what I write are more crime novels. Indeed, it's just the sort of mistake my detective, Mr. Peduncle, the old collector of sea shells, is always pointing out. 'The significant variation: in that lies all secrets.'"

"Ah, most interesting," Mrs. Patel came back, recovering fast. "Of course I have read a good deal of Erle Stanley Gardner and so forth, and I must say..."

She gave them her views at such length that Ghote at last, politeness or not, felt forced to break in.

"Madam, madam. If you will excuse. There is the matter of John's native-place address."

"Yes, yes. I am getting it."

Mrs. Patel plunged towards a bureau and opened its flap-down front. A considerable confusion of documents was revealed, together with what looked like the wrappings for a present bought but never handed to its intended recipient.

Prolonged searching located, first, an address-book, then "a list of things like this which I jot down" and finally the back of a notebook devoted to household hints clipped from magazines. But no address.

"Madam," Ghote ventured at last, "is it possible you did not in fact take it down?"

"Well, well, one cannot make a note of everything. That is one of my principles: keep the paperwork down to the minimum."

She gave the British author some examples of Indian bureaucracy. Once or twice Ghote tried to edge him away, but even a tug at the distinguished shirtsleeve was unsuccessful. Only when he himself began explaining how British bureaucracy was a crutch that fatally hampered people like Inspector Sugden in his own books, did Ghote act.

"Madam, I regret. Mr. Reymond, sir. We are conducting investigation. It is a matter of urgency."

And with that he did get the author out on to the landing outside. But as Mrs. Patel was shutting the door with many "Goodbye then" and "So interesting, and I must try to find one of your books," Mr. Reymond broke in in his turn:

"Inspector, there is a small lacuna."

Ghote stared.

"Please, what is lacuna?"

"Something missing, a loose end. You haven't asked where Louzado worked before he came here. Mr. Peduncle would have a word to say to you. If there's one thing he always seizes on it is the little lacuna."

The bursting-out beard parted to reveal a roguish smile.

"Yes," said Ghote. "You are perfectly correct. Madam, do you have the address of John's former employer?"

"Why, yes, of course," Mrs. Patel replied, with a note of sharpness. "I can tell you that out of my head. John was recommended to me by my friends, the Dutt-Dastars."

And, mercifully, she came straight out with the address – it was somewhat south of the Racecourse – and Ghote was even able to prevent her giving them a detailed account of the posh-sounding Dutt-Dastars.

*　　*　　*

Since their route took them past Crime Branch HQ, Ghote decided to risk the Noted British Author re-attaching himself to Inspector Dandekar and to report progress. Besides, if he could install Mr. Reymond in his own office for ten minutes only it would give him a marvellous respite from relentlessly pursued questions.

So, a peon summoned and Coca-Cola thrust on the distinguished visitor, Ghote went down to Dandekar.

"Well, Inspector," he asked, "did the son have more to tell?"

"More to tell he has," Dandekar answered, sipping tea and dabbing his face with a towel. "But speak he will not."

"He is not one hundred per cent above-board then?"

"He is not. I was up there at Shivaji Park within half an hour of the time he freed himself from those ropes, and I could see at a glance the marks were not right at all."

"Too high up the wrists, was it?"

"Exactly, Inspector. That young man tied himself up. And that must mean he was in collusion with the fellows who killed the old couple. How else did they get in, if he did not open the door to them? No, three of them were in it together and the Goan and a notorious bad hat from the vicinity called Budhoo have gone off with the jewellery. You can bet your boots on that."

"But the young man will not talk?" Ghote asked.

"He will not talk. College-educated, you know, and thinks he has all the answers."

Ghote nodded agreement. It was a common type and the bane of a police officer's life. His determination to push forward the case by getting hold of John Louzado's address redoubled.

"Well," he said, "I must be getting back to Mr. Reymond, or he will come looking for us."

In answer Dandekar grinned at him like an exulting film villain.

But, when he got back to his office, he found the Noted British Author doing something more ominous than looking for Dandekar. He was furiously making notes on a little pad.

"Ah," he said the moment Ghote came in, "just one or two points that occurred to me in connection with the case."

Ghote felt this last straw thump down.

"Oh yes," he answered, as waggishly as he could. "We would be very delighted to have the assistance of the great Mr. Peduncle and his magical shell collection."

"No, no," the noted author said quickly. "Mr. Peduncle's shells are by no means magical. There's a slight discrepancy there. You see, Mr. Peduncle examines shells to detect their little variations and equally he examines the facts of a case and hits on significant variations there."

"The significant variation in which are lying all secrets," Ghote quoted.

Mr. Reymond laughed with great heartiness. But in the car, heading north up Sir J.J. Road, he nevertheless explained in detail every single discrepancy he had noted in his little pad.

It seemed that, in the comparatively short time between the apparently distraught son coming to say he had been set upon and Inspector Dandekar bringing him to Crime Branch HQ, he had accumulated a great many facts and bits of hearsay. All of them must have been boiling away in his fertile mind. Now to spume out.

Most were trivialities arising from the domestic routine of the dead couple, or of his own flat or the flats nearby. To them Ghote succeeded in finding answers. But what he could not always sort out were the queries these answers produced. "Significant variations" seemed to spring up like buzzing whining insects in the first flush of the monsoon.

Only one point, to Ghote's mind, could be said to have any real connection with the killing, and that was so slight that in any other circumstances he would have thrust it off.

But it was a fact, apparently, that Mr. Reymond's servant, an old Muslim called Fariqua, or more precisely the servant of the absent Indian author of some short stories, had been discovered on the morning of the murder asleep inside the flat when he ought to have been in the distant suburb of Andheri, where since the author's arrival he had been boarded out – "Well, I mean, the chap actually seemed to sleep on the couch in the sitting-room, and I thought that was a bit much really" – and he had provided no explanation.

"Now," Mr. Reymond said, turning in his seat and wagging his finger very close to Ghote's face, "he must have hidden himself away in the kitchen till I'd gone to bed. And isn't that just exactly the sort of variation from the normal which my Mr. Peduncle would seize upon, and which my Inspector Sugden would try to shrug off. Eh, Inspector?"

Ghote felt the honour of the Bombay force at stake.

"Certainly I do not shrug off this at all, Mr. Reymond," he said. "After we have seen the Dutt-Dastars I will have a word with Fariqua. But then, since you would be at home, perhaps you would care to rest yourself for the afternoon. I know this humid weather makes visitors most extremely fatigued."

He held his breath in anxiety. To his delight Mr. Reymond, after consideration, acquiesced.

And if at the Dutt-Dastars' he got Louzado's address…

The Dutt-Dastars, it appeared, were a couple entirely devoted to art. Their house was crammed with Mrs. Dutt-Dastar's oil-paintings, sprawling shapes in bus-red and sky-blue, and Mr. Dutt-Dastar's metal sculptures, jagged iron masses, inclined to rust and a considerable menace, Ghote found, to trouser bottom and shirtsleeve. And in the Bengali way their devotion was expressed as much in words as in acts.

Mr. Reymond they seized on as a fellow artist, blithely ignoring any occasion when he tried to point out a discrepancy, lacuna or significant variation. And equally ignored, time and again, were Ghote's attempts to get an answer to the one question he still saw, despite the somewhat odd behaviour of Mr. Reymond's Fariqua, as the plain and simple way to get their evidence: "Do you have the address in Goa of your former servant John Louzado?"

At last, when he had established to his complete satisfaction that a couple as utterly vague could not possibly have recorded, much less retained, a servant's address, he planted himself abruptly full in front of Mrs. Dutt-Dastar just as she was explaining the full similarity between her painting *Eagle Figure with Two Blue Shapes* and Mr. Reymond's book *Mr. Peduncle Caught in Meshes*, which she had yet actually to read.

"Madam, kindly to tell: who was the previous employer of John Louzado?"

"John Louzado?" Mrs. Dutt-Dastar asked, seemingly totally mystified.

"The servant you recommended to Mrs. Patel, of Second Pasta Lane."

"Ah, John. Yes, what to do about John? He did not suit, not at all – it was sheer madness to have taken him on from someone like Shirin Kothawala, a dear person but with no understanding of the artist – but I could not sack the fellow just like that. And then I remembered that funny Mrs. Patel. Well, she would never notice what a servant was like, would she?"

"Madam, the address of Mrs. Shirin Kothawala?"

"Well, but of course. In one of those divine but madly expensive flats in Nepean Sea Road. A block called Gulmarg. Anybody will tell you."

"Mr. Reymond, I am departing to proceed with inquiries."

"Oh, yes. Yes. My dear fellow. Coming, coming."

On the way back, thanks to Ghote's unequivocal assurance that he would immediately interrogate Fariqua, for all that he privately knew nothing would come of it, the author's questions were at least confined to the sociological. But before they arrived Ghote decided to issue a warning.

"Mr. Reymond, in India – I do not know how it is in UK – servants often have matters they are wishing to conceal from their masters, like for instance the true cost of vegetables in the bazaar. So, you see, it would perhaps be better if you yourself were not present when I question Fariqua."

He regarded the author with apprehension. But it seemed he need not have worried.

"Excellent idea, Inspector," Mr. Reymond replied. But then he added: "Though there is one small discrepancy."

Ghote knew it had been too good to be true.

"Please?" he asked resignedly.

"Oh, just that we don't have servants in England now. It's why I find it difficult to know how to behave with them."

"Well, you behave with them as if they were servants," Ghote said. "But if you do not wish to be present at the interview, perhaps that would be best."

So he had the pleasure of tackling the Muslim unimpeded by any bulky British shadow. It was a good thing too, because Fariqua proved every bit as evasive as he had told Mr. Reymond servants could be. He needed, when it came down to it, to use a little tough treatment. And he had a notion that cuffs and threatened kicks would not be the way Mr. Peduncle conducted an interrogation.

But, after ten minutes in which Fariqua noisily maintained he had not been in the author's flat at all the previous night, he caved in quite satisfactorily and produced a story that might well be true. He had been playing cards with "some friends" and it had got too late to catch a train to Andheri. So he had bided his time, sneaked back into the author's flat before the door was locked and had hidden down between the stove and the wall till he had been able to take what, he implied, was his rightful place on the sitting-room couch.

Ghote gave him another couple of slaps for impudence.

"Now, what are the names of your card-playing friends?"

"Inspector, I do not know."

But this time Ghote had hardly so much as to growl to get a better answer.

"Oh, Inspector, Inspector. One only am I knowing. It is Kuldip Singh, sir, the driver of Rajinder Sahib at Flat No. 6, Building No. 2."

"Achchha."

Ghote let him go. He ought to walk round to Building No. 2 of the flats and check with the Punjabi gentleman's driver, but that must wait. The Noted British Author might change his mind and want to come with him. And he would get that address, the simple key to having a solid case against the three of them, much more quickly unencumbered.

It turned out, however, that the Parsi lady's "divine but madly expensive" flat was not, as Mrs. Dutt-Dastar had said, in a block called Gulmarg in Nepean Sea Road but in a block of that name in Warden Road on the twin prominence of Cumballa Hill. But at least Mrs. Kothawala, sixty, exquisitely dressed, precise as a crane-bird, was helpful. She knew to a week just how long she had employed Louzado. She knew to an anna just how much he had cheated her by. She remembered having warned Mrs. Dutt-Dastar about him, and that Mrs. Dutt-Dastar had clearly forgotten before the telephone conversation was halfway through. And she knew for a fact that she had never had John's address in Goa. But, of course, she was able to tell Ghote where he had worked before he had come to her.

But sorting out Mrs. Dutt-Dastar's error had taken a long time and Ghote found that having dutifully telephoned Inspector Dandekar and made sure there was no sign of the Noted British Author – their suspect was still unshaken too, he heard – he had time that evening to make only this one inquiry. And that proved as exasperating as the others, worse even, since instead of getting at least the name of Louzado's next earlier employer he had to be content with the name only of a lady who would be "sure to remember".

Before trying her next morning he gritted his teeth and put in a call to Mr. Reymond, who, of course, was only too keen to come with him – "I had been thinking of looking in on Inspector Dandekar actually" – and only by wantonly altering the geography of Bombay did he persuade him that it would be more economical for him to stay at Shivaji Park until after he had made this one inquiry, which he promised would be rapid. But in fact the task proved immensely troublesome since the possibly helpful lady had moved house and no one nearby seemed to know where to. Application to the postal-wallahs met with a certain amount of bureaucratic delay and it was not until the very end of the morning that he had an address to go to. So he telephoned Mr. Reymond once more and dolefully arranged to collect him after lunch.

"No sleep for me this afternoon, Inspector," the cheerful voice had assured him. "I've a lot I want to ask you."

"Yes," said Ghote.

The first thing the Noted British Author wanted to know was why Fariqua had not been arrested. Ghote produced the fellow's explanation for the "significant variation" in his behaviour.

"Ah, so that accounts for it," Mr. Reymond said, for once apparently happy. "I'm glad to hear it. I wouldn't like to think I was getting my breakfast scrambled eggs from the hands of a murderer."

Ghote gave a jolly laugh. It came to him all the more easily because he had felt sure there would be some lacuna or loose-end to pursue. But the journey passed with no more than questions about the peculiarities of passers-by until they were almost at their destination, a house just inland from Back Bay in Marine Lines.

Then the author, after a silence that had prolonged itself wonderfully, suddenly spoke.

"Inspector Ghote, I can no longer conceal it from myself. There is a lacuna."

"Yes?" Ghote asked, misery swiftly descending.

"Inspector, you did not, did you, check Fariqua's alibi with Mr. Rajinder's chauffeur? And I think – I am almost sure – Mr. Rajinder is the man who left on holiday by car three days ago."

"Then I will have to make further inquiries," Ghote said glumly.

But he forced himself to brighten up.

"In any case," he said, "perhaps we shall learn here just where John Louzado is to be found in Goa, and then, who knows, a single telephone call to the police there and they would have the fellow behind bars and we would have evidence in plenty, even some of the stolen jewellery, if we are lucky."

"Yes," Mr. Reymond said, "but Fariqua's invented story still leaves a loose-end."

Yet the interview at the Marine Lines flat looked from the start as if it was going to be all that Ghote and Inspector Dandekar had been counting on.

"Oh, John, yes," said the deliciously beautiful occupier, Mrs. Akhtar Hazari. "Yes, we should have an address in Goa. Not for John himself but for a priest – John was a Christian – who was to provide a reference. In fact, it was when we heard that John had a criminal record that we decided he must go. My husband imports watches and we often have valuable stock in the flat."

Ghote was possessed of a sudden feeling that everything in the world was simple. Confidence bubbled in his veins. It would not be as direct a way of wrapping up the case as he had spoken of to Mr. Reymond but the whole business might still be dealt with inside a few days.

"Of course it was two or three years ago now," Mrs. Hazari said. "But I always seem to keep letters. I will look. Will you take tea?"

So they sat in her big cool sitting-room, Ghote on a fat pile of cushions, the Noted British Author swinging rather apprehensively in a basket chair suspended by a chain from the ceiling.

Time passed.

The servant came back and inquired whether they would like more tea. Mr. Reymond hurriedly refused for both of them. Ghote would in fact have liked more tea, but even better he would have liked to see that letter. He asked Mr. Reymond, who seemed to feel it necessary to speak in swift hushed tones, a few questions about his books. But the answers were not very satisfactory.

And then at last Mrs. Hazari returned.

"Inspector," she said, "I must tell you that after all I have not got that letter. I had thought it was in an almirah where I put old papers like that. I even knew exactly the box it should be in. But my memory played me false. I threw out a lot of junk about a year ago, and it must have been in that."

Ghote felt like a child robbed of a sweetmeat. And now, he realised, with gritty dismay, he would solemnly have to pursue Mr. Reymond's theory about Fariqua.

"And John came straight to you from Goa?" he asked Mrs. Hazari desolately.

"No," she said. "He did have one short job first. He went to a family where at once the wife died and the man no longer needed so many servants. That was why we took him without a reference. It was a business acquaintance of my husband, I think. And unfortunately he's in Delhi. But if you would give me a ring tonight, I could perhaps tell you then."

With that Ghote had to be content. That, and the dubious gain to be had from dealing with Fariqua's final lie.

Happily by the time they got back to Shivaji Park Fariqua had left for Andheri, earlier than he should have done but not so much so that there was any reason to suppose he had run off like John Louzado. To placate Mr. Reymond Ghote sadly confirmed that the Kuldip Singh with whom Fariqua had claimed to be playing cards on the night of the murders had indeed already left Bombay by then.

Perhaps, Ghote thought as he turned from saying a last goodnight, down at HQ the boy would have broken his obstinate silence and admitted the truth and then there would be no need to pursue next morning this surely – surely? – unsatisfactory loose-end. Or was it a lacuna?

But Inspector Dandekar had no good news. Indeed he seemed considerably worried.

"I had the damned boy in the interrogation room today for eight solid hours," he said. "I have kept him standing up. I have been drinking tea and smoking cigarettes in front of him. I have had a trestle set up and Head Constable Kadam standing there swinging a Iathi. But nothing has moved him one inch."

"Inspector," Ghote said with some hesitation, "is it possible that those ropes on his wrists had been altogether badly tied by the real miscreants and not faked only?"

Dandekar sat in silence glaring down hook-nosed at his desk. "Well, yes, anything is possible," he said at last. "But damn it, I cannot believe it. I just cannot believe it."

*   *   *

So Ghote was up at Shivaji Park before eight next morning, waiting for the tricky Fariqua and telling himself that there was no reason why the fellow would not come to work as usual.

But the surge of relief he felt when the Muslim did appear made him realise how much he was now expecting everything about the affair to go wrong. He pounced like a kite dropping down on a tree-rat.

It did not take long to reduce the fellow to a state of abject fear. And then he talked.

"Aiee, Inspector. No. No, Inspector Sahib. I swear to God I had nothing to do with it. Inspector, I just got to know those fellows. We used to sit and talk when I was sleeping here. Inspector, I did not know they were bad-mash fellows. Inspector, I am swearing to you. And then that night, that one Budhoo – Inspector, he is a really bad one that one, a devil, Inspector – Inspector, he said more than he was meaning. He said something was going to happen that night. We were in the kitchen of their flat, Inspector. All of them were out, Sahib, Memsahib and the boy. I did not know it was going to be murder, Inspector. I thought they had a plan only to take the jewellery, Inspector. They were saying she had jewellery worth one lakh, Inspector. They would hide under a bed. But no more were they telling me. And then they threatened that I should stay with them. But after they said I could go, Inspector. Then it was too late to go to Andheri. But Reymond Sahib had his door open still and I was able to creep in. I swear to you, honest to God, Inspector, I am never knowing anything about killing. But they said also that they would kill me if I spoke. Inspector, will you be saving me, is it? Is it, Inspector? Is it?"

Ghote stood looking down at the shrunken cringing figure. Was he letting the fellow trick him again? It did not really seem likely. What he had said this time had been more than simply logical, like the story of card-playing with the Punjabi's driver. This account of inconclusive talk with two of the murderers in the kitchen of the dead couple's flat had rung true through and through. No wonder the fellow had tried to set up an alibi if that had happened. Of course, there had been no mention of any involvement by the son. But then the other two would have kept quiet about that. Yes, what he had learnt would scarcely help Dandekar.

"You will be safe enough from your friends," he growled at Fariqua. "In the lock-up."

Without the rest of them there would not be a case worth bringing as an accessory before the fact. But no harm to have the fellow to hand.

He marched him off.

He gave the Noted British Author the news by telephone. A witness who had heard and not properly heard the criminals' plans: hardly the sort of thing for the pages of *Mr. Peduncle Plays a Joker*. A man induced by threats to join a robbery and then let go before it had begun: not exactly the sort of event for *Mr. Peduncle Hunts the Peacock*.

And indeed questions and doubts poured out so fast that he was reduced at last to pointing out sharply that Mr. Reymond was now without a servant. At that the Noted British Author betrayed signs of disquiet. So Ghote explained he could get a replacement by talking to his neighbours and was rewarded by the author quite hastily ringing off.

Encouraged by this, he hurriedly set out for the address he had got from Mrs. Hazari late the night before. It was, her husband had said, a Mr. Dass whose wife, now dead, had first briefly employed John when he had come to Bombay. He lived in a block of flats in B Road behind Churchgate.

Climbing up the tiled stairway of the building, Ghote found he was retaining, despite the rather shabby air of the place, all his optimism. Louzado's trail had been long, but now it must be near its end. This was, after all, where the fellow had had his first Bombay job. They could go no further back. But it was equally the most likely place for an employer to have noted that Goa address.

On the door of the flat a small tree-slice nameboard had painted on it in much-faded script "Mr. and Mrs. Gopal Dass." It must, Ghote reflected, have been a long while since there had been a Mrs. Dass if it was her demise that had brought Louzado's first Bombay job to its abrupt end. And certainly the little irregularly shaped board had a strong look of dusty neglect.

He rang the door bell.

There was such a long silence that he almost became convinced he was to experience yet another defeat. He was even turning towards the next-door flat to make inquiries when the door opened by just a crack.

He swung round.

"Is it Mr. Gopal Dass?"

The door opened a little more. Ghote saw in the bright light from the room beyond a man who had once been fat.

Afterwards he was able to account in detail for the instantly stamped impression. It had come in part from the old European-style suit, its jacket drooping from the shoulders in deep encrusted folds, the trousers hanging in baggy rucks from the hips. But even the face had shown the same signs: flesh seemed to sag from it.

"What is it you are wanting?"

The voice, too, appeared to be coming from someone no longer there, hollow and without force.

Rapidly Ghote introduced himself and stated his problem. He felt that the slightest chance might cause the tall empty man to close the door so barely opened.

Mr. Dass heard him out, however. Then he sighed, driftingly like a puff of night breeze with hardly the strength to ruffle lonely waters.

"Oh, no, no," he said. "No addresses. Everything like that went when my wife left me for another life. Everything."

He turned slowly and looked into the room behind him. Ghote saw over his shoulder that it was almost completely bare. No curtains, no carpet, no pictures of the gods. Just a small table with a brass bowl, a brass tumbler and a packet of Mohun's cornflakes on it, and in a corner a bed-roll.

"Yes," Mr. Dass said. "I got rid of everything. My life is at an end, you know. At an end."

And very slowly, and without any sense of discourtesy, he turned and closed the door.

And I too, Ghote thought in the thick sadness he felt billowing from the shut door with its once gay tree-slice nameboard, I too have reached an end. The end of my hunt for John Louzado.

But one part of the affair certainly was not over. The Noted British Author would undoubtedly be out pursuing his loose-ends before much longer. He might be doing so already. One conversation could well have found a new servant.

He ran clatteringly down the empty echoing stairway, drove full-out back to HQ, glancing wildly at Dandekar's office as he came to a gravel-squirming halt, and ran for his telephone.

"Ah, Inspector Ghote."

The British author's enveloping smile seemed to come all the way down the line. "Ah, good. I was just setting out to see you. You're speaking from your office?"

"Yes," Ghote answered. "That is – no. That is…"

"There seems to be a bit of a discrepancy," the plummy voice said.

"Not at all," Ghote answered with sharpness. "I am at office, and I shall be here all morning."

But when the Noted British Author arrived he was magnificently insulated from him. Within two minutes of his call Inspector Dandekar had asked him to take over his interrogation. It had been something of an admission of defeat for Dandekar. He had told Ghote he felt he dared no longer leave unexplored the possible trails in the Bombay underworld. If the boy was innocent despite everything, then inquiries through the usual network of touts and informers must be pursued now with extra vigour.

"Mind you," he had concluded, "I still swear young Raju is guilty as hell. I hope you can break him."

So, with Dandekar gossiping to thief acquaintances in such places as the stolen goods mart of the Chor Bazaar and thus safe from any British botheration, Ghote felt perfectly justified in leaving the author to cool his heels.

And in the meanwhile he faced young Raju, cocksure graduate of Bombay University, adopted son of the murdered ice-cream manufacturer, and, as Dandekar had discovered at Shivaji Park, openly mutinous at having been given the fairly humble job in his new father's firm of going round to shops and restaurants instead of having a fat sum given him to start up on his own.

It was with this point that Ghote began.

"Sit down, sit down," he said. "I have been going over your answers to Inspector Dandekar, and there is one small thing I cannot understand. You wanted a sum to start up a business. But it is not at all clear what is the business."

The boy sat down on the hard chair in front of Ghote's table and with deliberate casualness put one leg over the other.

"You are not catching me that way, bhai," he said, "All along I am denying and denying I asked for money."

Ghote sighed.

"But we have a statement from a neighbour to whom you yourself complained," he said. "Two others also heard loud quarrelling."

"Lies," Raju answered contemptuously.

Ghote did not let himself be discomposed. But for all the calmness with which he went back to the point and for all the reasonableness of every other question he asked in the next two hours, he got, it seemed, nowhere. Some of the hard and shiny contempt left the boy's voice and the two of them eventually might have been friendly acquaintances, but the answers, though different in tone, were never one whit helpful. So when a constable came in with a chit saying Inspector Dandekar had returned Ghote felt decidedly relieved. He had not really hoped for success where Dandekar had failed, but a small gleam in him had licked at the possibility. And now he knew it would not be.

Dandekar he found equally gloomy.

"Nothing," he said in answer to a query about his luck with the informers. "Not a whisper. Of course there may be something still, you know. When the newspapers get on to a case people hold out. But I did not get one word."

And if you did not, Ghote thought, no one else could.

"The boy is also the same as ever," he said. "I talked and cajoled and urged but he did not give one thing, except to stop back-answering."

"That little rat. I am going to have him, Ghote. I am going to get him talking if it is the last thing I do. I am going now."

And, all solidly compact determination, he marched out.

Ghote sat where he was on the small chair beside Dandekar's desk. He felt he could not face the waiting British author. He had used every atom of his patience with young Raju. He leant forward, banged the brass bell on the desk and when the peon came ordered tea.

He took his time sipping at the hot milky liquid and had not quite finished when suddenly the batwing doors clapped back with a noise like a pair of quick-following pistol shots and Dandekar came striding in again.

But now his face was alight with a dark joy.

"Got him," he said. "Got him. I knew I would, and by God I did."

Ghote's first feeling – he tried to overcome it – was chagrin. He had had Raju all morning and had ended up where he began: Dandekar had had him for scarcely twenty minutes and had broken him. But, never mind who had done it, the boy had talked.

"He confessed everything?" he asked Dandekar. "Faking the ropes, planning it all with Louzado and that Budhoo?"

"Everything. Thanks to you, Ghote."

"To me?"

"Oh yes. When I heard you had taken that soft line I thought that perhaps now one good hard push would do it. And it did. They did not set out to murder, of course. But when that Budhoo found not one lakh of jewellery but four or five rings only he went mad. That accounts for all those wounds."

"Shabash, Inspector, shabash," Ghote said, a rush of warmth swirling through him.

But Dandekar, slumping down into his chair, opening a drawer and pulling out a towel to dab his sweaty face, had begun to look less triumphant.

"It is all right, Ghote," he said. "But you know as well as I do that when it comes to court, as likely as not, young Raju will shamelessly deny every word."

"Yes," Ghote said. "We need Budhoo, though we would be lucky ever to find that one. Or we need John Louzado."

He began recounting how that trail had ended. But in a minute a look of wide-eyed staring came on Dandekar's hook-nosed face. Slowly Ghote turned, though he knew almost for a certainty what he would see.

And there it was, looming over the top of the doors like a bristling hairy moon, the face of the Noted British Author.

Resignedly Ghote pushed himself to his feet.

"Mr. Reymond," he said, his voice ringing with brightness. "I was just coming to tell you. We have broken the case."

But congratulations did not come as freely as he felt they should. Indeed, as out in the sunshine his story progressed, the bushy beard gaped wide more than once with hardly restrained interjections.

Loose-ends, Ghote thought. Lacunas. Significant variations. Surely there could not be more.

And at last he ran out of words and had to face the author's objections.

"Inspector, I feel bound to point out a few things. You and Inspector Dandekar have been most kind to me. I can see that as soon as I get home I shall write a story called *Mr. Peduncle and the Indian Inspector.* And it would be nothing short of a betrayal if I kept silent."

"Most kind. But I assure—"

"No, Inspector, it is the least I can do. First then, let me say that I know young Raju well. He and I often had long, long talks when he came to phone friends in Delhi and other places. And I promise you, Inspector, he is not the chap to set criminals on to rob his own benefactors. There's a simple discrepancy between what the boy is and what you say he did. But that's not all."

"No?" Ghote said.

"No. You see, there's one piece of the puzzle which still doesn't fit. And time and again my Mr. Peduncle has said to Inspector Sugden

'You've got to fit in every bit, my dear fellow, every bit of the puzzle'."

"But—"

"No, Inspector, hear me out. I know this can't be easy to take, but you can't get away from pure logic. What you heard from Fariqua this morning simply didn't add up. You've only to think about it. And if he's lying there can be only one reason. Young Raju wasn't the third man: Fariqua was."

Ghote stood there fuming. Who was this detective-story writer to come telling them what was and was not so? Him and his logic and his lacunas.

But, even as he encouraged the rage to squirt and bubble inside him, he also felt a streak of cold doubt.

Logic. Well, logic was logic. And suspects had been known to confess under pressure to crimes they had not committed, even to murder. And Dandekar, first-class though he was, certainly could put pressure on.

Was it possible that, despite what seemed plain facts, that story of Fariqua's, seemingly unlikely but perfectly in accord with the way things happened, was just a story?

One thing was certain. The shame, the ridiculousness, of having an author of detective books get to the right answer first must not make them ignore that answer. If only they were not relying wholly on that confession but had Louzado and Budhoo in a cell too. If only the trail of addresses had not—

And then, like a last monsoon storm coming winding rapidly in across the sea long after the monsoon ought to have ended, bringing a last welcome sudden coolness, an idea came winding and leaping into his mind.

"Sir, sir," he said. "Come with me straightaway, sir, if you please."

And without giving the author a chance to reply he bundled him into the car and set off into the darting traffic.

They made it to the Shivaji Park flat in record time. There, still begging for patience, Ghote took one fast look round the sitting-room – couches spread with cotton counterpanes, bookshelves, two tables, and, yes, the telephone.

And next to it "the little book" in which, so the Noted British Author had told him soon after they met, people from nearby looked things up. His mention just now of Raju telephoning distant friends had at last brought it to the front of his mind. He flicked at the indexed pages with sweat-slippery fingers. L for Louzado. And yes. Yes, yes, yes. There it was. The address.

He seized the phone, dialled furiously, shouted instructions for a Lightning Call and miraculously was speaking to the Goa police in Panjim in minutes. And got splendid co-operation. They knew the place, they would find the man, no doubt they would find his share of the missing rings. The fellow would be behind bars in half an hour.

It was almost as if he was putting a hand on his shoulder himself.

He turned from the telephone and looked the bursting-bearded British author full in the face.

"Let me tell one thing, sir," he said, savouring the irony to the last drop. "Let me tell one thing: never to neglect a loose-end."

THE PERFECT ALIBI

Paula Gosling

"Two beers, Charley."

It was a corner bar not too many steps from the precinct station, and the sergeant and the rookie, coming off an arduous tour, were in need of a little restorative refreshment. They carried their glasses to a booth and settled in with a sigh each, one tenor and brief, the other long, low and grateful.

"Gets worse every day," said the sergeant.

"You said that yesterday, Sarge."

"Yeah, and I'll probably say it tomorrow, smart-ass. So? I got my rituals, you got yours." The sergeant's voice was filled with the gravelly sediment of many years' service, and the rookie grinned.

There had been a rush of business just before they'd come off duty, to say nothing of a fist-fight breaking out between a man and wife, and a visit from Granny, who had been reporting the same B and E for fifteen years – lost, one diamond tiara (she was the *real* Princess Anastasia). The sergeant had a special report sheet he pulled out for her, like clockwork, and wrote everything down with a leadless pencil, going over the old words so many times that they were wearing thin in places. It was, he said, her only entertainment and it allowed them to keep an eye on her, for she was frail, and lived alone.

There were a lot of people in this slum precinct that the sergeant kept an eye on. Currently, one of them was the rookie, who showed promise, but was inclined to be swept away by the excitement of it all. As far as he was concerned the sergeant was the font of all wisdom, and he was always ready to listen to another story. The sergeant was flattered by this, naturally, being a childless widower and lonely, but he saw it as his duty to select incidents that would instruct rather than amuse. One day this freckle-faced bundle of energy would be in charge of a case, and he didn't want to see it go down the toilet just because the kid forgot the basics. In some ways, the young man's good looks would be useful – nothing disarms a female suspect quite as much as a handsome arresting officer. The sergeant didn't have that advantage, being thick in the middle and thin on top. However, the evening stretched ahead, and for some reason, the boy was in the mood for more learning.

Many steps, the sergeant always told him, many careful steps make a case.

He was telling it to him again today.

"Take, for instance, the line-up," he said. The rookie frowned with frustration. They'd had a line-up that morning, in an attempt to identify a mugger and, as happened so often, the witness hadn't been certain enough to make an identification.

"Waste of everybody's time," the rookie complained.

The sergeant shrugged. "People don't like to make mistakes, don't like to take responsibility. They see all them scowling faces, they get confused. But sometimes that works for us, too."

"I don't see how," the rookie said. "A lawyer can really milk a failure to ID."

"Sure. But I'm not talking about failure, here, I'm talking about a wrong ID altogether, see? Take, for instance, the Excelsior diamond robbery in '56," the sergeant continued. The rookie, smiling, leaned back to listen. This was History. He hadn't even been *born* in '56, for crying out loud.

"Torn down now, the old Excelsior Building. Was over on Third and Oakland, I think. Or was it Third and Elm?" the sergeant mused. "Anyway, it had a lot of... Fourth and Oakland, that was it. Fourth and Oakland."

"Where the McDonald's is," the rookie said, encouragingly. He knew the location, he was on the ball.

"Yeah, yeah, where the McDonald's is," the sergeant agreed. The rookie nodded.

"The Excelsior Building," he repeated, as if taking notes.

The sergeant looked gratified. "Yeah. Right. Well, it had a lot of jewellery wholesalers and diamond merchants in it, the Excelsior, and one morning we get a call that one of the biggest, called the Excelsior Diamond Exchange, had been ripped off. So, over we goes, and the place is like an anthill, people running around and yelling, everybody scared to death and like that. See, the minute they come in and hear the Excelsior has been ripped off, they figure *they* been ripped off, too, so we got to go from office to office, the whole damn building this is, looking, checking, and like that, OK?"

"Yeah, I get the picture." The rookie could see it, he really could, a wave of blue surging through the corridors, and the plainclothes dicks in those hats with the big brims they wore in the Fifties, taking notes, talking out of the side of their mouths, the whole bit. Two years in the Academy and two years on the beat had not dimmed the rookie's childhood images. Now was now, now was a bitch, but then, *then*, cops were cops. The sergeant was rolling on.

"So we do our thing, and we get to this little guy named Samuels, *his* name I remember to the day I die, and he says to us he was working late planning to cut a big diamond – did you know they take weeks to figure out how to do it? – and he maybe sees the thief. Gives us a description. Right away we're lucky, because this description, it had to be Buddy Canoli. He had him cold, down to a scar on the back of his left hand, which he saw as Canoli was on his way up the stairs."

"If this guy was in his office, how could he see somebody going up the stairs?" the rookie interrupted.

"He left the door open to get a breeze, it was hot, OK?"

"OK."

"It was August."

"OK! Summer, diamonds, Buddy Canoli. I got it."

"Right. So we pull in Canoli. He's got spit for an alibi, so we put him in a line-up with some guys we pull in from the street plus a few cops for flavour, and what do you think?"

"Samuels identifies a cop?"

"No. No." The sergeant looks disappointed in his protégé. "He identifies one of the guys we pull in from the street, name of Whitney. Don't forget *that* name, either. Walter Whitney. Anyways, this guy is *like* Buddy Canoli, I give you that, tall and thin and a lot of dark curly hair, plus on the back of his left hand, he has a birthmark. Not a scar, but close enough, maybe for a nitwit like Samuels, who swears this is the guy he sees going up the stairs the night before."

"Swell," sympathised the rookie.

"Yeah, right. Well, there we were, we had Canoli cold, we *knew* he did it, and he knew we knew, and he walks out laughing. I was burned. To add to which, you know the regulations, I got to check this poor guy Whitney's alibi out, right?"

"What regulations?" the rookie asked, nervously. Another one he must have missed.

"The one which states if a person is identified on a line-up, we got to check them out, is which one," the sergeant told him, impatiently.

"Oh yeah, that one," the rookie said, vaguely, trying to pin it down in his mind.

"Right. Well, obviously, this Whitney is pretty boiled about the thing himself, respectable guy and all that. It makes him nervous, it would make anybody nervous, but I get him calmed down. You know, have a coffee, stuff like that."

"Yeah, sure," the rookie agreed. Stuff like that he could do standing on his head.

"So, Whitney tells me he was home alone like ten million other people. He's separated from his wife, who's gone back to her mother in Chicago, he leads a quiet life, all that. Fine, I don't argue, I got no reason to doubt him, do I? He goes on his way, I pick up a phone, call the caretaker of his particular apartment building which I happen to know personally, ask is this Whitney on the up and up, very casual, and the caretaker, what do you think he says?"

"Whitney is a nutny?" the rookie suggested.

"Nah. But Whitney is not being a truthful person. Like he says, he lives alone, all that. Only Whitney *wasn't* home that night because the caretaker has to go up there about the air-conditioning which Whitney told him was broken, and when he goes up he gets no reply. Goes up twice, too."

"Maybe Whitney was asleep."

"Caretaker has a passkey. Went in, fixed the air-conditioner, no Whitney." The sergeant looked triumphant.

"Jeez. So why was he lying?"

"Exactly what I want to know."

"Yeah, right!"

"So, I go down to where this Whitney has an office, he's some kind of accountant, and I say, look, friend, you weren't home on the night in question, anything to say about that, and he gets very nervous again and he closes the door and asks me to sit down. Turns out he's shagging his secretary on the night in question, but he doesn't want to put it on the record because his wife is on the look-out for anything she can get on him for a divorce, which would ruin him financially. He points to a picture of the wife on his desk, and she is one mean-looking old broad, that's for sure. One of those thin hard mouths, you know, the kind that bites and hangs on for keeps?" The rookie nodded. They'd picked up a hooker the other day who'd had a mouth like that and had done exactly what the sergeant said. The marks were still on his arm. He looked at the sergeant warily, to see if he was kidding him about that, but the old man's eyes were misty with remembering, so he let it go.

The sergeant was continuing. "Well, Mr. Whitney, I says to him, we can be discreet. If you'd said that to me right away and explained, I could have saved some shoe leather. He apologises, asks me if I want to speak to his secretary and confirm it, and I say, well, OK, if you insist, and so he calls in this little redhead from the outer office and says tell this man about last night."

The sergeant smiled. "She was a cute little thing, name of Marylou Mason, and she blushes, which tells me nearly all I want to know right there, but she speaks her piece all right, and says, yes, they were together all night, so I say thank you, Miss Marylou Mason, and I come away and write up my report."

"Is that it?" asked the rookie, finally, when the sergeant took time out to drink some beer.

"No," the sergeant said. "We keep on at the thing, but we can't get a hold on Buddy Canoli on account of no solid forensic evidence and no ID from friend Samuels, the near sighted diamond king, and so the case stays open. We're stuck, we have to move on to other things, and gradually the subject fades away, so to speak."

"Gee," said the rookie. "That was interesting." His voice was bleak with disappointment.

"I ain't finished yet," the sergeant growled.

"Sorry." The rookie brightened again.

"Right. So a few months later, we got to do another line-up, and we pull in some guys from the street as usual – this was, I think, maybe November now. And guess who is third from the right?"

"Whitney?"

"No, *Samuels*, dumbo. But seeing him reminds me of the case, so to speak. Nobody IDs *him* for robbery, though. Damn shame, would have served him right. Point is, because the whole thing comes back to me, my mind is aware, you know? And the next thing is, I spot Whitney in a restaurant a few days later. Only he's thinner, so I don't recognise him at first. Especially wearing a five-hundred-dollar suit, when before it was thirty-seven-buck numbers off the rack. Well, he spots me and suddenly lunch is over. I say hello, Mr. Whitney, to him, as he goes by, being a friendly type. He gives me the fish eye and goes out of the place like his ass was on fire."

"Aha!" the rookie pounced on this as evidence of something sinister. He was nearly chewing hunks out of the beer glass, trying to second-guess the story. The sergeant sighed. Where do they get all this energy, he wondered, and pressed on.

"Well, he goes off so fast, he forgets his coat, see? I notice the waiter pick it up and take it to the manager, so, being a swell guy, as you know, I decide to take it around to Whitney's office for him, as it's only around the corner. But it's not his office any more, I discover. He's moved uptown, they tell me. So, uptown I go, 'cause I'm now stuck with this damned coat, and sure enough, there he is. Set up in some fancy office with a new secretary and all very nifty. He makes like he didn't see me in the restaurant, acts all surprised, very nervous, too, wants me to get out of sight. I don't like to be put out of sight, you know? I got my pride."

"You bet."

"So I look around, I get like, expansive, you know, just to needle the stuck-up bastard. I say, business must be good, this is nice. He says yes. You must have some pretty fancy clients, now, I say, not like the old days. Yes, he says, and no, he says. He obviously wants me gone, so I figure what the hell. I say here's your coat and he says thank you, and that's it and goodbye."

The rookie's eyes showed disappointment again. "Is this going to be another one of your stories about how no matter how hard you work on something it never comes right?" he asked, suspiciously. "Are you just building me up for the big let-down?"

"Would I do that?" the sergeant asked, his eyes twinkling.

"You did last week, said it was a salutary lesson," the rookie grumbled. "You got it in for me, I sometimes think. I'm not as dumb as I look." He caught the sergeant's eye, and grinned. "I know, I know – I couldn't be. OK, go on."

"Right." The sergeant leaned back. "I thought to myself about this new office business, and the new suit, and the new secretary, even classier than the one before, and how it all must have cost him an arm and a leg, so I ask around, and what do you think? Seems that Whitney suddenly has a lot of money to spend a few months back. And this new money of his makes an appearance right after the Excelsior robbery. Hey! I begin to think, maybe – just maybe – that little weasel Samuels made the right identification after all! Maybe it wasn't Canoli who ripped off the Excelsior, but *Whitney*, instead."

"Son of a bitch," the rookie breathed.

"I tell all this to the Captain and he says follow it up, things being what they were and him not liking a big case dangling unfinished like it was. So I go around to Whitney's bank and say what about all this money in August? And they say what about it? And I say was it cash? And they say, no, it comes by cheque from some insurance outfit in Chicago, which stops me, cold. What can I say? Oh, I say. They tell me he's got three accounts now, one personal with his wife, one for the business, and one for what's left of this big lump of money, which ain't much, but they don't let me look at no details because I ain't got no court order, only nosiness and my badge."

"Bastards," the rookie growled.

"You got to go by the rules," the sergeant said, pointedly, then relented. "But that doesn't mean you have to go by the main road, either." The rookie lit up. He knew the sergeant wasn't going to give up *now*.

The sergeant let his halo glitter for a moment, then went on. "I went around to Whitney's apartment, which was as new and fancy as his office. I ask to speak to his wife. The guy on the Security desk, who happens to be an old cop I know, tells me Whitney's wife has left him, and I say, *again*? And he says as far as he knows this is the first time she goes, and now Whitney, the bastard, leads the life of Riley with a new girl every week. He doesn't seem to think too much of Walter Whitney, and I decide maybe I should push this button a little. Well,

I say, I don't blame Whitney for kicking up his heels after having a wife that looks like a bad-tempered anteater, and this is the right tack because my old friend gets real mad, all of a sudden, and I wonder what's going on, here? Mrs. Whitney is a lovely girl, he tells me in a loud voice, and who should he proceed to describe to me but Marylou Mason, Whitney's old secretary."

"No!" said the rookie, with highly satisfactory surprise.

"Yeah. My old friend gets pretty excited about it – I guess sitting at a security desk in the lobby of some fancy building all day is kind of boring, at that – and bangs his fist, even. He didn't deserve her, he says. Turns out she was nice to my old buddy, and looked a little like his granddaughter, you know? This kind of thing is a big help when you're pushing a witness, believe me. Anyway, he gives me her new address, which is a little dump on Nineteenth. I think maybe I'm lucky at last, and I go over there. Sure enough, it's little Marylou, and boy, is she sour on Whitney. I ask her about the alibi she gave Whitney for the night of the Excelsior job and eventually she breaks down and says it was all a lie."

"Got him cold!" said the rookie, banging his own fist down on the table top and nearly knocking over his empty beer glass.

"Jesus," said the sergeant. "Don't *do* that, you'll give me a heart attack one of these days."

"Sorry," said the rookie, looking around to see if anyone had noticed. One had – the new girl from Records who was sitting in the corner with some other clerks. She was laughing at him. He turned his attention back to the sergeant and tried to look as if they were on to something big. "Go on."

The sergeant, who had seen the girl in the mirror at the back, and knew how the rookie felt about her, went on. "So tell me the truth, I says to Marylou, all braced to hear about the robbery. 'He wasn't with me,' she says. 'He went to St. Louis to meet someone he told me would mean big money. I got the feeling it was some kind of fast deal with this "insurance business" he was getting into.'

"'What kind of business is that?' I asked her.

"'I don't know, but there were some very funny people involved. He wouldn't let me stay in the office when he talked to them. I think they must have been criminals or something. He thought I was stupid, but I'm not. He was always talking big, like he was so tough and knew what was what. He said when he got back we could get married, and we would be on Easy Street. He always bragged about the important people he knew, but *I* never met any.' You could see he'd cut her up pretty bad, emotionally, you know? Poor kid. I hate guys like that."

"Me, too," said the rookie.

"But I had to go on. Was it like he promised, I asked her, and she says yes and no. The money showed up, all right, and he married her quick enough, and put her into that fancy apartment, but that was it. Like he had her where he wanted her and so he wasn't interested any more. He never talked to her, never took her anywhere or introduced her to anyone, expected her to stay home alone all day. She'd only lied for him because she thought he loved her, but now it seemed to her like the lie had been all he'd really wanted her for. Seemed to me, too. After a while, she says, there started to be other women and she couldn't stand that, so she ups and leaves. Didn't take anything with her, either, but what she stood up in. Marylou was a real nice girl. She's a grandmother, now, would you believe? I put her on to another retired cop I know ran a security firm and she married his son. Anyway, back then I ask her will she tell the truth about Whitney in court, and she says, sure, as far as she's concerned he's a rat and we can have him."

"But a wife can't testify against her husband…" interrupted the rookie.

"Sure, she can, if she wants to," the sergeant said. "The law says that a wife can't be *forced* to testify against her husband. That's a big difference."

"And had Whitney gone to St. Louis that night?" the rookie asked, feeling this foray into jurisprudence wasn't getting them anywhere.

"Yeah, just like she said. She'd booked the ticket herself, using the name Mason, and drove him to the airport."

The rookie's eyes lit up. "Ah," he said, with great emphasis. "But did she actually *see him get on to the plane*?"

The sergeant's expression was a patient one. "Yeah," he said. "She did."

"Oh," said the rookie. "Damn. But why didn't Whitney just *say* he'd gone to St. Louis the night of the robbery?"

"I'm coming to that, dammit. She waved him bye-bye at around six that night, and as far as she was concerned, that was where he had been, St. Louis. That was what she had been lying for him about – going to St. Louis. If she couldn't maintain the first lie for him, that they'd spent the night together say, because she was worried about her reputation or something, she could *still* give him an alibi because she'd seen him leave town, right? He had *two* alibis, one behind the other. He figured that was perfect."

"Right," said the rookie, but he sounded dubious, which pleased the sergeant.

"Yeah, right. How did he know he was going to *need* two alibis?"

"I was just going to say that."

"I thought you were." The sergeant smiled kindly. "Because you know and I know that planes not only fly *into* St. Louis – they also fly *out* of St. Louis. He had plenty of time to turn around and come back – the Excelsior job wasn't pulled until around midnight."

"And did he take another plane out?"

"As a matter of fact, he did. After I left Marylou, I called St. Louis and confirmed that 'Mr. Mason' took a flight out almost immediately after he got in. Bingo. A few days later, we arrest Whitney. I get a commendation, and that's how the line-up can sometimes work for you, although not always the way you expect it will."

"So you broke the Excelsior case all on your own?" the rookie said, much impressed. "That's real good."

The sergeant shook his head. "Hell, no. Deakins and Brady broke the Excelsior case, got Canoli cold through a fence that traded the information in exchange for a light sentence."

"But you said…"

The sergeant leaned forward and tapped the table. "The trouble with you is, you don't listen. Many careful steps make a case. I had to check Whitney out because of a false identification. He lied, so I had to go on checking. He told me he lied because he didn't want to drag the girl into divorce proceedings. That was another lie. Marylou said he married her as soon as he got back from his trip to St. Louis. A trip *in* that was just a blind to cover another little trip *out*. He came into a lot of money very soon after this second little trip, which happened to take place the night of the Excelsior job, which is how he happened to come to my attention in the first place by getting identified in the line-up the next day." He was beginning to wheeze, slightly. "I wouldn't have had to check him out, otherwise, would I?" The sergeant leaned back, waved to the bartender for another two beers, then watched the rookie expectantly.

The rookie was confused. "But you said he didn't do the Excelsior job."

The sergeant sighed. "He didn't. Walter Whitney had a third and even more perfect alibi for the Excelsior robbery. At the time the diamonds were being lifted, he was in Chicago – murdering his wife."

CUCKOO IN THE WOOD

Lesley Grant-Adamson

A cuckoo in the wood. When the sound of the machinery stopped Tom could hear it across the fields. Every year the same, as long as he could remember. A cuckoo sang in the wood in the month of May. It had sung when...

A shadow sloped across him as a fat man lumbered out of the bar and into the pub garden. Kear, it was, the one who'd been a policeman up at the town and retired to the village to be near his grandchildren.

Tom saw Kear settle himself on a stout wooden bench and put his tankard carefully on the table. Tom was a cider drinker himself. He watched as the pint was raised and flecks of foam stayed on the former sergeant's moustache. Then he slid his gaze away, up the hill beyond the elder hedge with its white parasols. Soon, when it suited him, he'd accept Kear's presence and they'd grunt a greeting. In the past, they'd had long conversations but not pleasant ones, what with Kear in uniform and paid for suspicion. Tom didn't like to think of that, it had been a bad time. Every year, though, the cuckoo brought it back to him.

Thirty-something years ago it had begun, when that girl, Mary, had come to live with her sister in the cottage by the wood. Unwelcome, the memories returned.

Tom had got ideas about Mary. Couldn't help it at all. And no wonder, for Mary was always about the place, popping into the garden to the washing line or the chickens; stretching up to gather armsful of lilac, white and mauve; crossing the fields on a short cut to the village. And he was always there too, riding the tractor or ditching or whatever task his father set him to.

Tom and Mary were always there, and her sister and brother-in-law were always out at work. Tom would sit in the shade of a May tree, open his cider jar, look down the hill to the cottage and make believe there was no other young man in the world but himself and no other girl but Mary. Occasionally she noticed him and waved, and how much he made of her distant wave! His dreams, his nonsense about her, carried him through her first season in the village. By the time the harvest was in, those dreams had grown into intention. He would have her for himself.

Tom did nothing about it, unless staring into the flames of the kitchen fire and conjuring a future can be called doing something. And then...

Another shadow fell across him, another man entered the pub garden, glass in hand. Bullman, who'd run the village shop until his retirement. Tom hadn't retired, not entirely. How did men retire on a family farm that was forever short-handed?

"Hot day, Tom," said Bullman, wiping a hand over tanned skin.

"'Tis hot enough for I." Tom no longer noticed his accent, the quirks of grammar and dialect. There'd been a time when they'd shamed him to his tender core.

Bullman turned his head to Kear. A sheen of sweat prettified the fat man's bald head. Bullman said to him, "Hot enough for you, Mr. Kear?"

"Couldn't be better," said Kear. "Who needs to go to Spain when England's got weather like this?"

Bullman went on. "The hottest May I can bring to mind. Not a time to be working out of doors, eh?" He waited for Tom's response and Tom remarked on hotter Mays, disastrous harvests, droughts, and the hills above the village alight with spontaneous fires no one could douse.

Kear attended to Tom, and Tom ignored him and spoke to Bullman. As Tom paused, the afternoon was filled with the heaviness of summer: damp grassy smells, bees fussing over yellow roses on the grey stone wall at his back, the excitement of small birds questing nest-building materials, and the call of the lonely cuckoo.

"*Cuckoo. Cuckoo.*"

Tom's other memories occupied the pause too. Mary, that first autumn, wide-eyed, not exactly mocking but caught off balance by him asking her – if in fact he *had* asked her. What he said was oblique, confused. Later he'd seen that and smarted at his own waste of an opportunity, not at her mild rejection. He continued to look down on her, when the field he'd reaped was stubble and when the stubble was ploughed in. Christmas, he decided, he'd ask her again at Christmas.

In November he spied her in the wood, in the arms of the salesman from the animal feed company. By spring she'd stopped walking over the farm to the village. When Tom met her in the lane one May afternoon the cuckoo punctuated their words.

"Why does it sing for just a few weeks?" she asked.

"'Tis calling for a mate," he said and felt the blood rise to his wind-browned face.

"Oh, yes." She chanted the old rhyme. "*The cuckoo comes in April, it sings its song in May, it lays its eggs in June and then it flies away.*"

"'Tis so, Mary."

She said, "I wonder where it flies to."

Tom didn't know, but he knew that Mary was pregnant. He...

Bullman was speaking to him. "Isn't that so now, Tom? A bad bend, a very bad one."

Tom latched on. The road-widening for the village bypass, that's what Bullman meant. Tom muttered agreement and sucked at his cider. An ant was coursing along the worn fabric of his working trousers. He brushed it aside, his hand broad and strong, a hand that heaved sheaves, steadied a ploughing team and lifted stone for walls.

Kear said, "Forgive my saying so, Tom, but it'll be a good day for this village when the new road opens."

Tom's family had resisted the scheme. It was robbing them of a swath of land and a greedy part of the wood. The cottage where Mary had lived, and which weekenders now owned, would survive but its outlook would be tarmac.

Tom let Kear's comment float by. He picked up Bullman's point about the dangerous bends in the lane and recited the names of the locals who'd misjudged it, not fatally but sufficiently to damage property and pride.

Bullman laughed, plucking at his throat where age had let down the skin in leathern folds. "I'll bet you wouldn't mind a jug of cider for every time you've put the stones back in that wall."

"'Tis so," said Tom. "Mind, I always had a taste for walling. There be some tasks about a farm I can't abide, but walling, now there's one I do enjoy."

"Just as well," contributed Kear, still trying to join in. "Remember when the cattle truck ripped a great section of it down, back in...oh, when was it now?"

They both knew. It was the year they had the difficult conversations, the year Mary's baby disappeared.

Tom shut his eyes against the burden of sunlight and called up a thirty-year-old picture of Kear. Slimmer, lean almost, and sweating in his regulation shirt sleeves. "Tom, are you quite sure you didn't see anyone near the cottage?"

"Quite sure, Sergeant."

And because no one else had seen anyone, Tom had never needed to veer from that denial. There was a search, there was repetitious questioning and there were appeals in the newspapers for information. But the baby remained missing and the village drew its own conclusions.

Sergeant Kear had put it to him: "Tom, the mother claims the pram was in the garden. Says she put it in the shade of the laburnum tree and walked into the village. Too hot to push the pram, she says. Are you sure you didn't see anyone go near that pram?"

"Quite sure," Tom repeated.

So Mary became known as a careless, ignorant mother who left her baby unattended in the shade of a poisonous tree, who delayed reporting him missing for two hours because she feared the wrath of authority and because she bred the wild hope that her sister had come home from work early and taken the baby somewhere with her. In days, rumour hardened against her: Mary had killed her own son and was concealing the body and the truth.

"Tom, you're the only one who doesn't accuse me," she blurted out when he met her crying in the lane while he was repairing the ravages of the cattle truck. Usually vehicles toppled a few stones at the apex of the bend but the truck had flattened yards of it. Tom, always slow, was taking his time, making a good strong job of it, making sure it didn't all come down again.

"What do folks say to 'ee, Mary?"

She scrubbed a balled handkerchief over her eyes. "Oh, it isn't what they say. They don't *say* much but they look. It's the way they look at me."

He touched her then, for the first time. His fingers marked her bare arm with stone dust. "Don't 'ee cry, Mary. That's the way folks do be. It don't mean nothing."

She pulled away, slightly, exactly enough for his hand to fall free. "Oh, Tom!" And she bowed over the broken wall and cried, not a delicate weeping that he might have attempted to console but passionately, with all the rawness of her anger and her loss.

Tom stepped away from her. Her grief put her beyond reach. He understood then that she had always been out of his reach. Firelit dreams and nonsensical plans evaporated before her intensity. Tom stared as she wailed, oblivious of him. Then he stretched out a roughened hand and took up a jagged hunk of grey stone which he added to his wall.

Bullman cocked an ear. "A short break they gave themselves."

The machinery had started up again, drowning out the cuckoo and the murmurous wood pigeons. Out of sight, round the flank of the hill, men were destroying the landscape in preparation for the new road.

Kear said, "The sooner they get it done the better."

"Won't be long, the speed they're going," said Bullman. "They're up to the copse field already. Could finish that stretch today, maybe."

Tom didn't think they would. He sensed Kear peering at him. The fat man used to watch people while pretending to be doing no such thing, but since leaving the force he'd abandoned pretence. Kear had used his special way of watching when Tom was made to point out the places on the farm where a baby might have been hidden. The pond in the bottom field, the brook, the clamps. But the weed on the pond was unbroken, the nettles by the brook untrampled, the clamps undisturbed. In a day or two Kear's superiors had other work for him and he went away, not necessarily satisfied.

Tom breathed the spiciness of the pub's honeysuckle that was just breaking into flower. A reddish flower, it was. The one at the cottage was a golden tumble from the porch to the stone seat by the old-fashioned pump. If the bird annually conjured Mary for him, then it was honeysuckle that revived the day the baby vanished.

The pram hadn't been visible from where Tom was working. The porch cut off his view. He ate his lunch in the field, the combination of sun and cider spurring him to call on Mary again. Several times he'd done so and several times she'd said no, the baby took all her time.

Kear was wrong about the pram being in the shade. No doubt it was when Mary left it but the protection had crept away. The handle burned Tom's palm as he swung it round to wheel it into the lee of the house, once he realised Mary was out.

The jerk woke the baby. It cried, screamed. Tom lifted it, to pacify. The baby stiffened itself over his arm, resisting him with all its puny strength. Its bawling frightened him. He shook it. Silenced it. Killed it.

Thirty years he'd lived with the secret. For thirty years...

The silence he was expecting came. Sun scorched his cheeks and a bee brushed his ear. He stirred, opened his eyes.

Bullman was looking into his glass as he drank. Kear had his eye on Tom. Tom squirmed to rub his shoulders against the stone behind him and made a show of relaxing.

"*Cuckoo. Cuckoo.*"

Presently a car droned along the lane to the village, right up to the pub. Through the door to the bar they heard one of the men from the roadworks asking for a telephone. He tagged on an explanation. "We've found something up there, under a wall." The landlord took him to a back room where there was a pay-phone.

Tom drank the last of his cider. Bullman was admiring swallows slicing the sky. Kear and Tom studied each other.

Kear said softly, "I wonder what they've found." He said it like a man who wasn't wondering at all.

Some fragments of bone, some shreds of rag, thought Tom. Nothing to show who hid the tiny body there. He met Kear's eyes with a look that said nothing. Then, as the church clock struck two, he said goodbye to Bullman, took his glass into the bar and began the slow trudge down the lane and up to the top field where his brothers were turning hay.

IN THOSE DAYS

Liza Cody

11 Dock Road,
London

Dear Mr. Harvest,

I am writing to you on the very sad occasion of your sister's death because it may be a comfort for you to understand what actually happened. I know that in my own case, when my poor Arthur went with his kidneys, I could not really lay him to rest until I had found out exactly what went amiss. Afterwards I felt better. I don't know why. But in those days there were people to talk to, especially the Kings next door. You can get things out of your system if there's someone to talk to. Don't you agree? I hope you have someone. A death in the family is hard to bear when you are on your own.

I know you are Selina's brother because of that postcard I took to the letter-box two weeks ago, the one with the old-fashioned picture of bathing beauties with paper bags over their heads which said 'Shame about the face' on the back. I shouldn't have read it, I know, but I was struck by the picture and wondered who your sister could be sending it to. Someone with a sense of humour, I decided. Anyway, people don't write secrets on postcards, do they? I wasn't entitled, but I wasn't really prying either.

Anyway, as you know, Selina came to live in my house four months ago. Well, you know she came to live at this address, but you probably don't know that it is my house. It was all my poor Arthur had to leave me and I have hung on to it through thick and thin ever since. Your sister must have told you a lot about it, and I can't imagine what you must think of me. But I would like you to know that it has only recently become the sort of house it is now.

You see, the neighbourhood has come down from what it was. A few years ago there were still business gentlemen staying here and one or two engineering students and a dental nurse. Respectable people, all of them. But times change and, what with container transport and everything, the area isn't what it was. I couldn't afford to sell the house even if I wanted to, not with the property market the way it is.

Beggars can't be choosers, I always say. The government doesn't look after old people the way it used to when this country was a welfare state. In those days, a pension was a pension. Not any more. I would be out on the streets if I didn't take rent from whoever is willing to pay it. I can't be as fussy as I'd like. I don't approve of what goes on here but I suppose it is a service of sorts. The only thing a person like me can do is maintain some small standards in the way of cleanliness, safety and hygiene.

It always puzzled me why Selina chose to come here. I know she said that photographers needed authenticity. But wouldn't it have been safer for her to stay closer to her home and take nice pictures of the people she knew? Then she wouldn't have had to come so far out of her way to find authenticity, and what happened wouldn't have happened. Really, a well-educated, nicely spoken young lady like herself has no place in Dock Road. I know, because I do not really belong here myself any more even though I have lived here for over seventy years. I should have moved out when Mr. and Mrs. King left for their son's place in Slough. They were the writing on the wall, if you get my drift. But I didn't move and now it is too late. Maybe if I hang on long enough the district will come up again. They have started developing about a mile down the river and built some lovely little flats and shops. But they seem to have missed out Dock Road, which is a pity.

Your sister used to say that this area was 'the real thing'. Although why it is any more real than Slough or Theydon Bois I honestly couldn't say. It seemed real enough to me when the only girl staying in one of my rooms was a dental nurse. I mean, things don't have to be dirty to be real, do they? Or girls, for that matter. I have always been respectable and I'm not less real for that.

I hope you don't think I'm criticising. I enjoyed having Selina here. She raised the tone, and heaven knows it needed raising. And she never talked down to the girls, although to be honest most of them won't understand you if you don't talk down. But of course, as her brother, you know Selina better than I did, so it won't surprise you to learn that some of her conversations were over people's heads. I myself was never quite sure what she meant at any given moment and, though I say it as shouldn't, I regard myself as being quite well read – by Dock Road standards, anyway. Certainly I was one of the few who knew where to find the public library in the days when there was one. The girls these days leave school scarcely able to read the names of their lipsticks let alone a newspaper or a magazine. No wonder the poor little things are reduced to what they are reduced to.

All they ever care about is money. I honestly don't think your sister ever realised how much. They do what they do for money and that's the be-all and end-all of it. They aren't interested in their customers. They aren't even interested in the job. They just want to do it as quickly as possible, get paid and on to the next. You can't blame them, can you? Not when you see the sort of customers they get in Dock Road. What on earth is the point, I often ask myself, of paying good money for whatever it is they pay for when they are so drunk they throw up all over my stair carpet? I wouldn't have allowed my poor Arthur inside the house in that condition, let alone my bed. And who has to clean up after them, I ask you? Well, it isn't the girls. They wouldn't even know how.

I mustn't judge. Girls these days aren't brought up the way they were in my youth. We were taught how to polish a stair rail and how to turn a mattress. These girls don't even think it's necessary.

But I do think the old ways are the best so please don't think I've let things go completely at 11 Dock Road. As I said to Selina when she first came, I said, "I can't vouch for what has gone on in this room but I can say, hand on heart, that the sheets were fresh on this morning. And you won't find dust balls under any of my beds." I always scrub the baths out with Flash every day because you never know, do you? A person with a superior education, like your sister, will have appreciated that. Even if her clothes and shoes left something to be desired, she kept her books beautifully. There was never a speck of dust on them. But you can't get nasty diseases from books, can you? Whereas sharing a bathroom with a dirty person might give you something catching.

I am returning the books under separate cover. No one touched those.

They are intact and just the way she left them. I can't answer for the clothes and toiletries though. There seems to be a shortfall somewhere in spite of the police locking the door.

What really worries me is your sister's camera. I know it was very valuable, and I can't seem to put my hands on it at all. If you ask me that camera went walking long before the police arrived. None of the girls will admit to even seeing it, but you can't trust what they say. I know for a fact they all had their pictures taken. And got paid for it too. To tell you the truth, those pictures weren't the sort you'd want to frame and put on your mantelshelf, I'm afraid.

I like a nice photograph. It was lovely when photos stopped being black-and-white and you could see the colour of the hats and frocks. I always wore a hat for any picture taken of me. Young ladies wore hats then. Now all my old hats are on top of the wardrobe in plastic bags, but no one wants to take my picture any more, not even Selina, so I suppose it makes no odds. When the time comes I'd like to be buried in a hat – the lavender one with the feather which I wore to Mrs. King's eldest's wedding. I used to love a good wedding but you don't get them in Dock Road any more, and I can't see any of the girls at No. 11 getting wed. I mean, who would want to marry them after what they've done?

But you can't tell them anything. They think of me as a silly old woman, as if I was always the age I am now and as if No. 11 was always the sort of house it has become. And sometimes I ache for someone my own age to talk to. Yet, when I think of the shame of it I'm glad there's no one left. You see, I remember Mrs. King – Susan Brown as she was then – I remember how we sat in the stalls of the old Majestic and watched Bing Crosby and Grace Kelly sing 'True Love' in the moonlight. We were young women then and nothing much had happened to us, but we sat in the dark with tears in our eyes for the romance of it all. I know she had tears in her eyes because of the way she took her handkerchief out of her sleeve. That's another thing you don't see any more – a lady's handkerchief. And gloves. I sometimes ask myself where all those little white gloves and hankies went to. Hats, gloves, hankies and romance all disappeared from Dock Road years ago, and I wish I knew where they went.

I did try to explain it to Selina once. She kept photos pinned to a cork board in her room where she could see them. I was in there with the vacuum one day, and I said, "How can you bear to look at these awful things all day?"

And she said, "They aren't awful. This is the most fundamental transaction in the world." Or something like that. We were always talking at cross-purposes.

But they *were* awful. They were of the girls and their boyfriends and the customers. There was one photograph I particularly hated. She must have taken it from her window because it showed the derelict house opposite. One of the girls was leaning against the wall smoking a cigarette. And the man had just got out of his car and was sort of looming over her, talking to her. You could see from the way he stood and from the expression on her face just what they were talking about. It's funny, isn't it, how a picture can be disgusting without being actually rude.

So I said, "Why don't you take pictures of nice, pretty things?" Because I suppose I was thinking of Bing Crosby and Grace Kelly, and how in the old days you used to see pictures that made you want to weep they were so lovely: things like brides and waterfalls and swans. Your sister's photos had the opposite effect, I'm sorry to say. It wasn't as if they were bad photos: you could see every detail, even the brand name on the cigarette packet and the number plate on the car. But you felt miserable and not quite clean just from looking at it.

She said, "This is reality, Mrs. B. Reality isn't nice or pretty."

"It used to be," I said and I finished vacuuming her room. I was wondering if your sister ever suffered a personal tragedy in her life to make her so bitter against reality. Because Selina was a well-spoken young lady with lovely manners, and she should have been married with a family, and not taking photos about the terrible things that happen in Dock Road. I mean, she had the chance, didn't she? She had all the advantages. She wasn't like the girls here who, I sometimes think, were born for trouble.

I'm afraid I won't be able to send the photographs with the rest of her things. It's just as well really because I'm sure they would have depressed you as much as they did me. That cork board disappeared before the police came, and when I asked about it the girls all said none of them had seen it. It was such a muddle that night. Everyone shouting and screaming and running every which way. And when the police and ambulance finally arrived, a good twenty-five minutes after I phoned, I was the only one left to talk to them. The girls and their customers had scattered to the four winds and left me to cope on my own.

They don't want the police in Dock Road any more. It isn't like the old days when people wanted to see the constable walking down late at night to try the warehouse doors at the end of the road. People used to say hello then, and many's the time we saw him chatting to customers outside the Prince of Wales of a warm evening. Nowadays nobody wants to know. It's the same with the ambulance men, although what on earth the ambulance men could have done to harm them I'll never know. Maybe they are allergic to uniforms.

I called the ambulance myself. As soon as I saw Selina at the bottom of the stairs I went back in my room and phoned. There used to be a phone in the hall, but I had it taken out for obvious reasons. You can't trust these girls even with a telephone, and I can't tell you the awful things I overheard in my very own hall.

I must confess that it was only the ambulance I called. The police came on their own. I may be a silly old woman, but I am not senile and I know the trouble I would be in if I had called the police to this house. My life wouldn't have been worth living. The girls and their boyfriends can be quite vindictive if they think anyone is getting at them. Especially the boyfriends. You might think I am a coward. But you don't have to live here. I do. Which is why I never mentioned the missing camera or the photos. I do hope you understand and that you don't think I am keeping them from you. I am an old woman, and I'm not very brave any more. In the old days I would have had my poor Arthur to turn to. But now I'm by myself in a house I can barely call my own. Things go on here which I can't alter. I should be able to, seeing as it's my house, but I can't.

I would have liked to send you everything Selina left, no matter how depressing. After all, her property should be yours by right. I would also like to be able to vouch for the honesty of all my lodgers, but I can't do that either.

I am very careful with my own things, and I always keep my door locked even during the day whether I am in my room or not. I advised Selina to do the same but I don't think she listened to me. I am not often listened to in my own house.

Nowadays I am especially careful on the stairs. I mean if a healthy young lady like your sister can have an accident then think what could happen to an old woman like myself. It is quite dark on the landing and anyone could miss their footing. There used to be a light there, but I got so tired of replacing the bulb.

I hate to think what you must be imagining about me and my house, but you must understand what I mean by not being able to vouch for the honesty of the lodgers. Fancy stealing light bulbs! If you can't trust a girl with a light bulb, what chance has a camera got, I ask you?

You see, in a way your sister died for the want of a light bulb. I do feel bad about it, very bad, but at the same time I can't really blame myself. No sooner did I put one in than it went missing again. How many times can an old lady climb a stepladder on a gloomy landing at the top of a long flight of stairs? I wouldn't want to fall and break my neck the way Selina did. In the old days I would have asked one of my lodgers to do it for me. Some of them were ever so obliging. But I couldn't ask those girls to do it. The stepladder might go missing too and I need that stepladder to dust around the top of the wardrobe where I keep my old hats. I know they are in plastic bags, but even so, nice things get ruined no matter how hard you try to protect them.

But I mustn't go on about my hats, must I, when this is supposed to be a letter of condolence. I am most awfully sorry about your sister. I miss her too. And as I said at the outset, I do hope you have someone to talk to about it. It will make your loss much easier to bear.

Yours faithfully,
Rose Bratby (Mrs.)

TURNING POINT

Anthea Fraser

If I hadn't been so vulnerable it wouldn't have happened; but Clive and I'd been having one of our periodic bad patches, and to add to my misery Jamie, our youngest, had just started boarding-school. It seemed I was at one of life's turning points, and needed to stop and consider what lay ahead.

On the face of it, it didn't seem promising. I'd given up my job when we married; Clive's income was more than adequate, and as I'd always been a mother-hen rather than a career girl I was only too happy to stay home. In any case we'd started a family almost at once. Now, though, with all three children away at school and Clive busy with trips abroad and business entertaining, time would hang heavy. I needed an interest of my own.

And then, coming out of the library, I saw the poster. In a blaze of red and gold, it announced an exhibition in a nearby town by the artist whose biography I'd just finished reading.

Fate! I told myself, little realising the danger in submitting to it. For here was a chance to get away for a few days and sort myself out. My mind raced eagerly ahead. I'd find myself a B&B, visit the exhibition, and, since Sandham was on the coast, perhaps spend an hour or two on the beach. And maybe by the time I came home I'd have some idea what I wanted to do.

"I'm going away for a few days," I said casually over dinner that night.

Clive looked up in surprise. "To your mother's, you mean?"

"No, to Sandham, actually. There's an exhibition on by a Mexican artist, Sancho Perez. I've just read his biography, and I'd like to see it."

He regarded me suspiciously. "Is this tit-for-tat? Because I'm off to Brussels?"

"Nothing so childish. I simply need a break and you're not free to come with me. And you're not interested in art, so it wouldn't appeal to you anyway."

"When are you going?"

"Tomorrow; it's only on this week."

"So you'll be back at the weekend?"

"I don't know; I might stay on a few days, since you'll be away."

Clive shrugged, losing interest. "Fine, if that's what you want." And he reached for the cheese.

So the next morning, quite excited at the prospect, I packed swimming things, jeans, an assortment of shirts and sweaters, and a solitary dress in case I visited a restaurant. I also tucked in some paperbacks as insurance against loneliness. Thus provisioned, I reckoned I could last up to a week in Sandham if it took my fancy. And if I didn't like it, I'd come home.

But I did: I liked it very much. It was a pretty, grey little town tucked into the shelter of some cliffs to protect it from the strong east winds, and at the end of the summer it had a clean, fresh feel about it.

Most of the holiday-makers had left with the start of the school term, and already beach cafes and amusement arcades were boarded up. But the inhabitants of the town, who had been skulking in their gardens during the summer invasion, were beginning to reappear, breathe a sigh of relief, and take up their normal lives again.

There was a long promenade, with old-fashioned shelters positioned along it where, doubtless, the local youth conducted their love affairs. Bordering it were colourful gardens, bright now with chrysanthemums and dahlias and late-blooming roses, and seats where you could sit and look at the view, or read, or doze in the still-warm sunshine. The art gallery, smug behind its stone façade, overlooked a square boasting a variety of shops, some selling buckets, spades and cheap souvenirs, others dealing in designer clothes. And on one of the headlands an imposing hotel stood sentinel, its grounds sweeping in a series of terraces down to the sea.

"Why in heaven's name don't you stay at the Grand in comfort?" Clive had asked, when I'd mentioned my intention of a B&B.

"Because I don't want to have to dress for dinner and sit in solitary splendour."

Again he'd shrugged, as though despairing of me, and said no more.

Though it was late September, there were still plenty of bed-and-breakfast signs in evidence. I selected a tall, whitewashed house on the front, with a long path lined by seashells. It proved a good choice. Its owner, a Mrs. Carlisle, was delighted to welcome a guest at the end of the season, and her home was spotless – brass shining, furniture gleaming with polish, linen crisp and smelling of the salt winds that had dried it. I felt immediately at home.

The next morning, refreshed after the best night's sleep I'd had in months, I set off to view the exhibition – and it was all I hoped it would be. The large, rather austere rooms leading out of each other were exploding with colour – hot pinks and purples, acid greens and yellows, deep shadows and blazing sunshine such as this grey English town could never have known. Peasants dozed in doorways under large-brimmed hats, naked children played on white sand, girls clapped their hands, buildings shimmered in the heat. All the vividness, the vibrant life of Mexico was pulsating in the canvases, reaching out to ensnare the passer-by and fill him with undefined yearning.

I spent the morning alternately wandering round or sitting in a bemused, colour-washed daze consulting my catalogue and trying to get my tongue round the titles of the paintings. And when I finally left, satiated for the moment, it was with the intention of returning when I was ready to take in more.

Outside on the pavement I stood for a moment, drawing a deep breath and reacclimatising myself to the muted tones of an English autumn. Then, unbelievably, I heard my name called.

"Melanie – as I live and breathe!"

I spun round as the voice echoed down the years, rekindling in that first instant all the forgotten hopes and dreams of my romantic teens. It couldn't be – but it was.

"Philip!" I said, glad of the support of the warm stone wall behind me. With the sun in my eyes it was hard to see the blurred figure striding towards me, which added to the unreality.

"What a fantastic coincidence!" he was exclaiming. "Whatever brings you here?"

He had reached me now, and, with his hands on my shoulders, was staring down at me with a wonderment matching my own. And now that he was between me and the sun, I could see the face I'd thought never to see again: older, of course, than I remembered, but as strong, as ruggedly good-looking as it had ever been, and the eyes as piercingly blue.

"God, it's been years! I can't believe it, running into you like this. Let's have a coffee, and you can tell me what you've been doing with yourself." He took my arm and led me down the road to one of the few cafes that remained open, where, seated opposite each other, we exchanged cautious smiles.

"It's really great to see you," he said. "Do you live round here?"

"No, I came to see the art exhibition."

He glanced at my wedding ring. "Your husband with you?"

I shook my head. "He's not interested in art." I added hesitantly, "And you – are you married?" As I asked the question, I remembered that I'd once hoped he would marry me. My face grew hot, but Philip didn't notice. His eyes were on the coffee as he swirled his spoon in his cup.

"No; I tried it briefly but it didn't work. I'm not the marrying kind, Mel, as you might remember!" He grinned at me ruefully, and I weakly forgave him all those nights of heartbreak.

"So my mother warned me!"

He laughed. "Mothers always know best. So – what have you been up to for the last fifteen years?"

"Bringing up children for most of them – twins of thirteen and a boy of ten. He's just started boarding-school."

"Poor little devil," Philip said carelessly.

Since he was obviously not interested, I didn't elaborate. "And what about you?" I asked instead. "What have you been doing?"

"Oh, this and that. Making a fast buck when the chance offered."

As footloose, apparently, as he'd been at twenty. "No staying power, that lad," my father had observed. "Don't get involved with him, Mellie, he'd only bring you heartache." Perhaps fathers also knew best.

"How long are you here for?" Philip was asking, possibly to forestall further questions.

"It depends on the weather, really. My husband's away so there's no rush to go home."

"You're at the Grand, I suppose?"

"No, just a boarding-house; I wanted somewhere informal. Are you on holiday?" It seemed an odd choice for someone as restless and mercurial as Philip.

"Sort of, a short break."

I wasn't sure I believed him. "I'd have thought you'd have gone for the bright lights," I remarked.

He looked up then, and there was an expression in his eyes that I couldn't fathom. "Sometimes I prefer the shadows," he said. Then he smiled quickly. "Specially when I'm with a pretty woman! What do you say, Mel? You've no immediate plans, have you? Shall we spend the day together, for old times' sake?"

I could hardly have declined, could I, when he knew I was alone in a strange town. And to be honest, I didn't want to. There was a touch of the old magic about Philip – perhaps, for me, there always would be. So coffee stretched into lunch, and afterwards we went for a long, exhilarating walk over the cliffs, where the gulls were screaming and where, out on the headland, the wind tore at our hair and clothes, catching our words and flinging them to the wide blue sky.

We talked constantly, not of personal matters but of the world in general: art, music, politics. Whatever his lifestyle, Philip proved knowledgeable on a variety of topics and was an entertaining companion.

We stopped for tea at a village along the coast and caught the local bus back to Sandham. Philip proposed dinner at an Italian restaurant he'd discovered.

"No need to dress up, it's quite informal," he assured me. "I'll meet you outside the art gallery at eight and we'll have a drink somewhere first."

*   *   *

It was dusk when I closed the front door of Bay View behind me and set off down the path. The first stars were pricking through and a golden sickle of moon hung over the sea. But there was a hint of chill in the air; the wind we'd encountered on the cliffs had, in diminished form, followed us back to town and I pulled my jacket closer as my thin dress swirled round my legs. I should have followed Philip's advice, and kept on my jeans and sweater.

As I turned the corner by the gallery I saw him under a street lamp, his hands deep in his pockets. He looked up at the sound of my footsteps and, straightening, came towards me with a smile.

"Let's see about that drink," he said, slipping my hand through his arm. We walked quickly, heads down against the wind, and turned into the lighted doorway of the Three Pigs. Loud laughter came from the public bar but Philip guided me to the saloon, where more subdued customers sat at tables and talked in quiet voices.

He brought the drinks over and sat down. "Here's to old times," he said, raising his glass. It was not the toast I'd have chosen, but I nodded and drank, the cold liquid making me shiver.

The two-hour break had, I realised, dissipated our ease with each other and we were constrained, strangers again. It would have been wiser not to have met this evening; an afternoon together was all that was called for in the circumstances. Perhaps, though, he'd thought I expected it. The idea made me uncomfortable.

Philip was frowning into his glass, his face withdrawn and older than it had seemed earlier. Then, suddenly conscious of my gaze, he looked up and smiled.

"Sorry, Mel!" he said, with a swift return to his easy manner. "I'd some business to attend to after leaving you, and my mind was still on it."

I smiled back, reassured. Another fast buck, no doubt. My eyes drifted past him to the bar. It was L-shaped, and in the mirror I could see the reflections of the men in the public bar on the far side; and of one man in particular, tall and red-haired, who was staring intently at my own reflection. As our eyes met in the mirror he moved quickly back out of sight.

Philip was saying, "You do like Italian food, I hope? If you'd rather go somewhere else—"

"I love it," I answered, turning back to him.

"Good. Drink up, then, and we'll be on our way."

The wind was waiting for us, undeniably cold now, sending leaves scuttering in the gutters and unlatched gates banging. Scraps of paper swirled through the air like birds, swooping and dipping above our heads as we hurried up the road.

"And it's only September!" Philip commented. "Imagine it in winter."

I was glad to reach the shelter of the restaurant, warm and welcoming with its candles and lamps. Philip ordered a bottle of Chianti and we settled down to study the menu, relaxed and at ease again.

The meal was delicious, a mouth-watering concoction of lamb, garlic and olives. The waiter kept refilling my glass and the empty bottle of wine was replaced. I could feel my inhibitions slowly dissolving, all the restrictions, disappointments and responsibilities of everyday life slipping away until I was a different person entirely from the rather dull woman Clive would have recognised. In short, I felt young again.

Over coffee, Philip unwrapped a handful of amaretti and put a match to each flimsy paper in turn, watching as it curled into a spiral and took off to float up to the ceiling. Like children, we made bets with each other as to which colour would rise the highest.

I was laughing at the game when I happened to glance towards the window. The lower half was covered by net curtains, but above them darkness pressed against the glass. And as I looked, I could have sworn that someone moved swiftly aside, someone who had been standing looking into the lighted room. Briefly I wondered if it was the man from the bar, but dismissed the idea as ludicrous. My senses, blurred by good food and wine, were playing tricks on me.

It was time to go, and reluctantly, not wanting the evening to end, we went once more into the cold darkness. I clung to Philip's arm as the wind leapt on us, buffeting and intrusive as we battled our way along the narrow pavements back towards the seafront. Once, I thought I heard footsteps behind us, but the wind distorted sounds, and when I turned there was no one there.

"What are you doing tomorrow?" Philip was asking.

"I want another look at the exhibition. I couldn't take it all in at once."

"If it's as good as that perhaps I should see it myself. How about meeting there about eleven?"

"Fine," I agreed, glad of the prospect of his company.

"We can have lunch afterwards and then, unfortunately, I must be on my way."

"You're leaving?"

"Afraid so. I did say it was only a short break."

So once again he was going to walk out of my life. Yet what did I expect, a married woman with three children? The Melanie who had loved Philip, I reminded myself, was long gone.

The wind gusted suddenly, throwing a handful of sand into our faces. Philip reached for a handkerchief, but when he withdrew his hand he was holding a buff-coloured envelope. "Damn! It's the final demand for my gas bill. I meant to buy a stamp for it."

"I have some in my room," I said, "and there's a pillarbox at the gate. I'll post it for you."

"Are you sure?" He felt in his pocket again. "I can give you—"

"Twenty-four pence? Don't be ridiculous. Think what you've spent on me today – coffee, lunch, tea *and* dinner."

He laughed. "Put like that, we seem to have spent most of our time eating. Well, if you're sure, thank you. I don't want them turning the gas off, with cold weather on the way." He handed me the envelope and I slipped it into my handbag. We had now reached the gate of Bay View, but although we came to a halt, he did not release my hand.

"I wish you were staying at that nice, anonymous hotel," he said wryly, "instead of a boarding-house where every movement is noted."

"What if I were?" I asked, my mouth dry.

"I'd suggest a nightcap in your room, and no doubt one thing would lead to another."

"You're very sure of yourself," I said.

"Oh, Mel!" He pulled me suddenly against him, and for long moments we clung together, while the wind tore at our clothes as though trying to separate us.

"Why the hell did I let you go?" he said against my hair.

With an effort I pulled myself free. "Good night, Philip. And – thank you."

He sighed and, lifting my hand to his lips, kissed the base of each finger in turn. "Till tomorrow morning, then."

"Eleven o'clock at the gallery," I confirmed.

"I'll be there."

As I walked alone up the path, I knew – and the knowledge filled me with shame – that had I been at that 'anonymous hotel', I should happily have spent the night with Philip.

I awoke with a headache, and at first thought the low, persistent humming was in my head. Then I identified it as a lawnmower. At this hour? I thought grumpily. I reached for my dressing gown and went to the window with some half-formed intention of complaining. But my view of the garden was obscured by the fire escape, and while I waited for the perpetrator to come into sight my annoyance evaporated and, abandoning the hope of further sleep, I went for my bath.

"You start work early round here," I commented to Mrs. Carlisle, when she brought the tea and toast which was all I could face for breakfast.

"The grass, you mean? My son cuts it before he goes to work. I hope he didn't wake you, but it's the only chance he gets."

After breakfast I went to the pillarbox with Philip's letter. It was still early but, feeling in need of fresh air, I continued walking along the promenade. In the cold light of morning, the memory of my behaviour the previous evening was deeply embarrassing and again I doubted the wisdom of another meeting with Philip. But there would be no chance of amorous dalliance today. We'd look at the exhibition, have lunch, and then he would go.

And I? I'd be guided by the weather, as I'd told him. If it became warm enough to sit on the beach, I'd stay on a few days. The wind had dropped this morning, and the air felt as sluggish as I did.

I walked as far as the boating pool, stood for a while watching small boys sailing their yachts, then made my way slowly back to town. The library clock was striking eleven as I turned the corner by the gallery, but this time Philip was not there. Nor, though I stood waiting with increasing impatience, did he appear.

Perhaps, I thought eventually, he'd meant us to meet inside? I bought a ticket and hurried in, but a quick search proved he wasn't there either. Disconsolately I began my solo round of the paintings.

But though I was looking at the same pictures as the day before, my reactions were very different. The sizzling colours no longer seemed joyous but discordant, violent even, and the stinging yellows and throbbing reds hurt my eyes. Every few minutes I went back to the door, from which I had a clear view of the steps and the lamp-post outside. But Philip did not appear.

By twelve o'clock I had to accept he wasn't coming. He could at least have phoned, I thought irritably; the staff would have passed on a message. But as I knew to my cost, Philip had never been considerate.

No, something else must have come up and he'd abandoned me without a second thought.

Because it was the only place I knew, I went to the cafe we'd visited the previous day. He'd mentioned lunch, and there was a faint hope he might be there. He was not. I was served a leathery omelette and a tepid cup of coffee. Had the fare been as poor yesterday? I'd been too engrossed in Philip to notice. Well, that was what I got by behaving as though I were eighteen again.

Annoyed, humiliated, and with a by this time blinding headache, I returned to the boarding-house. Mrs. Carlisle was out, but she'd provided me with a front door key. As I went up the stairs I was composing a withering speech to Philip, though I knew I'd never have the chance to deliver it. But the moment I entered my room, it went out of my head.

Someone had been there, I knew it instinctively – someone other than Mrs. Carlisle, who'd made the bed and cleaned the basin. I stood stock still, looking for proof to back up intuition. And found it. One of the dressing-table drawers, which I'd noticed shut crookedly, was not quite straight, though I'd left it so.

Swiftly I checked my belongings, though fortunately I'd nothing of value with me. The intruder, whoever he was, must have reached the same conclusion, for though some items were out of place, nothing seemed to be missing.

I straightened, looking round the outwardly undisturbed room, and with a shiver realised belatedly that no burglar would have left things so tidy. It had been a search rather than a robbery, which I found even more disquieting.

Uneasy and bewildered, I walked to the window and stood staring down at the newly mown lawn. Then something closer at hand caught my eye. On both the windowsill and the top step of the fire escape were several blades of freshly cut grass. Altogether too easy a means of entry.

I began to pack, and by the time Mrs. Carlisle returned, was waiting to pay the bill. I didn't mention the intruder; there seemed little point.

Well, my bid for independence had not been a success, I reflected in the taxi on the way to the station. Not only had I made a fool of myself over a man I'd not seen for years, but I'd attracted enough attention for someone to think it worth searching my room. In retrospect, the whole venture had been sordid and degrading. I should have stayed meekly at home, as I'd always done before. My only consolation was that I could now put Philip out of my head once and for all.

But in that I was mistaken, as I discovered the next morning when I opened the newspaper.

MURDER AT RESORT, I read. Then, with increasing horror:

The body of a man in his late thirties was discovered yesterday morning in the seaside town of Sandham. Death had been caused by a stab wound and probably occurred overnight.

Identification has not yet been established, but a bus ticket from Lee to Sandham dated the previous day was found in his pocket. An incident room has been set up at Sandham Police Station, and police are asking anyone who might have any information to contact them there. The telephone number is—

The print swam before my eyes. Philip was dead. All the time I'd been seething at his non-appearance, he'd been lying murdered. But by whom? The red-haired man who'd watched us in the bar, and probably also through the restaurant window?

Then something occurred to me with the impact of a douche of cold water. The police were appealing for information: suppose someone reported seeing him with *me*? On the bus back from Lee, for instance – mention of the ticket might jog someone's memory – in the cafe, the pub or the restaurant? Looking back, we'd hardly kept a low profile.

Should I forestall any informer and go to the police myself? But there was nothing I could tell them – and how would Clive react to my involvement in a murder case? I shivered. Though deeply shocked by Philip's death, I had no wish to be dragged into its aftermath.

Philip's death, my brain repeated numbly. Philip, who had been so alive, so vital, was dead. In God's name, why? I remembered the footsteps I'd heard and our embrace at the gate. The watcher in the shadows would have seen that, and known where to look the next day. But for what?

The envelope. It had to be. Anyone following us would have seen

Philip hand it to me. Whatever he'd imagined it contained, it seemed likely Philip had died because of an unpaid gas bill.

Somehow the days crawled past. The murder, which had made the regional news headlines that first evening, was unaccountably dropped from subsequent bulletins, nor could I find any follow-up to the newspaper story. The clamp-down struck me as ominous; such items usually ran for days. Perhaps they'd caught the killer? But if so, why not announce it?

My conscience remained uneasy and I still felt I should contact the police. Yet even if I did, I argued with myself, I had little to report – I'd not even known where Philip was staying. No, I decided finally, I'd made enough mistakes in the last few days. Better to sit tight and volunteer nothing.

Clive arrived home at last, and I was overwhelmingly glad to see him. He looked tired, I thought, the few days apart lending an added perception.

"And how was your trip?" he asked, accepting my fervent kiss with some surprise.

"Not an unqualified success," I admitted.

"But you saw the exhibition?"

"Oh yes. It was—" How was it? Joyous and exuberant or stridently threatening? Which of my visits was the more discerning? But he wasn't really listening.

"I gather there was a bit of excitement while you were there," he said, tossing his briefcase on a chair. "Murder, no less. If I'd known where you were staying, I'd have phoned to check you were all right."

"You surely didn't think I was involved?" I hoped he wouldn't hear the tremor in my voice.

"Hardly. Though oddly enough, *I* was, in a way."

I stared at him, a pulse beginning to throb in my temple. "How do you mean?"

"By a freak chance one of our chaps was in the thick of it. It seems the man had been stalking him all week and suddenly sprang out and attacked him. He was lucky – the outcome could have been very different."

I felt I was floundering in a foggy sea. "One of your chaps?" I repeated blankly. "But – you're in electronics!"

Clive gave a tired smile. "You've never been interested in my work, have you, Melanie? If you had, you'd have realised that electronics covers a multitude of things. Listening devices, for example, and other bugging equipment, the use of which can be quite controversial. Sometimes we do odd jobs for the government and at others we're caught up in industrial espionage. Every now and then it backfires, which was what happened this time. One of our devices picked up some sensitive material which could net several big fish. Let's say they weren't anxious for it to be passed on."

I gazed at him speechlessly. My conventional, dull-seeming husband had been leading a double life which I'd never even suspected. How could I have lived with him all these years and not known? It wasn't that he'd deliberately kept it from me, just, as he'd said, that I'd never been interested.

Hot with shame, I remembered all the times he'd come home, full of the day's events, and started to tell me of something that had happened, only to be interrupted by a request to go and say goodnight to the children, or the announcement that dinner was ready.

Clive had been watching me, reading without difficulty the emotions crossing my face. "Don't look so stricken, love," he said gently. "It wasn't meant as criticism."

I said shakily, "How could I have been so – so blinkered and self-centred?"

"Well, you were involved with the children, weren't you? There's no harm done. I only mentioned it because of the coincidence of your being there and because the chap concerned is calling round any minute to put me in the picture."

The nightmare, it seemed, was not over. I said with difficulty, "So it was he who killed – that man?"

"In self-defence, yes. I gather he made a grab at the knife, and in the struggle the other man fell on it."

"Who – who was he, do you know?"

"Not specifically, but his outfit had been under surveillance for some time. They sell information to the highest bidder."

Making a fast buck when the chance offered. Tearing my mind from Philip, I realised with horror that Clive's colleague must be the red-haired man I'd cast as villain. He'd seen me with Philip – how would he react if I were introduced as Clive's wife? The sound of the doorbell cut into my panic.

"That'll be him now," Clive said.

"I'll go upstairs, then, so you can talk." I started frantically for the door.

"No, stay here," Clive said over his shoulder. "I'd like you to meet him."

Heart hammering, I stood immobile in the centre of the room.

Because of that one reckless day with Philip, my marriage, my whole future hung in the balance and there was nothing I could do to salvage it.

There were voices in the hall, and they were coming closer. Like a rabbit caught in car headlights, I fixed my eyes on the door. And as the visitor came into sight, felt myself jerk and sway. For there, regarding me across the room with an expression of disbelief, was Philip.

Dizzily I tried yet again to adjust. Ironic that I'd gone to Sandham to consider the turning point in my life; ever since my return I'd been spinning like a top, unsure from one moment to the next which way I was facing, while Philip, the red-haired stranger, even Clive, shifted and changed places in my perceptions, as though performing the intricate steps of a *danse macabre*. And yet, I thought, as the faintness passed, the only constant was, and had always been, Clive.

Over Philip's shoulder, he was saying, "Darling, this is Philip Barr, whom I was telling you about. My wife, Melanie. By an odd coincidence she was in Sandham herself last week."

Philip's eyes still held mine, and it wasn't difficult to read their message. "Really?" he said, and came forward to take my hand. "I'm delighted to meet you, Mrs. Roper. I hope our little melodrama didn't spoil your holiday."

I smiled back, sure of myself at last. "Not in the slightest. I knew nothing about it until I got home," I said.

THE HAND THAT FEEDS ME

Michael Z. Lewin

It was one of those sultry summer evenings, warm and humid and hardly any wind. The sun was just going down and I was grazing the alleys downtown, not doing badly. It never ceases to amaze me the quantity of food that human beings throw away. Especially in warm weather. The only real problem about getting a decent meal is the competition.

When I saw the old man poking in a barrel I said to myself, 'Here's trouble.' I was wrong, but I was right.

The old guy was grazing too and at first he didn't notice me. But when he did, though I couldn't make out the words, he was obviously friendly. And then he threw me a piece of meat.

It's not always smart to take meat from strange men, but this guy seemed genuine enough. I checked the meat out carefully, and then I ate it. It was good. Topped me up nicely.

I stayed with the old guy for a while, and we got along. I'd root a bit, he'd root a bit. And we'd move elsewhere.

Then he settled down to go to sleep. He patted the sacking, inviting me to sleep too, but it was early so I moved on.

★   ★   ★

A couple of hours later it was semi-dark, like it gets in the town. I didn't go back down the old guy's alley on purpose. Things just worked out that way. There are forces in a town at night. They push you this way, they push you that.

I could tell immediately that something was wrong. I approached cautiously, but nothing happened. Nothing could happen. The old guy was dead.

There was blood on his face. There was blood on his clothes.

Someone had given him a terrible beating. Beatings are something I know about.

I licked one of the wounds. The blood was dry on top, but still runny under the crust. The old guy's body was pretty warm. Whatever had happened wasn't long over.

Nosing around, I picked up the scents of three different men. They were all fresh, hanging in the tepid air. Three men together, three against one. One old man. That could not be right.

I set out after them.

They had headed away from downtown. Curiously, they had stuck to the alleys, these three men, though they hadn't stopped at any of the places I would have. The places my dead acquaintance would have.

The only time I had trouble finding the spoor was where the alley crossed a street near a couple of stores. Seems they went into one of the stores, then headed back for the alley.

After another block I began to find beer cans they had handled.

At first I picked each can up, carefully, and I put it where I could find it again. But once I had one can from each of the men, I ignored the rest. I followed the trail with increasing confidence. I figured I knew where they were going.

The long, narrow park by the river is popular on a summer's night. I could tell immediately that it was teeming with life, and not just because so many scents crossed that of the trio I was following. All you have to do is listen. A dozen human beings, not to mention the other creatures.

But my trio made it easy again. They were down by the riverside, whooping and hollering and throwing things into the water.

I was extremely cautious as I drew close. I wasn't quite sure what I would do. I only knew that I would do something.

I saw them clearly enough. Young, boisterous men, rough with each other and loud. They picked up stones and swung thick sticks to hit the stones into the river. Already drunk and unsteady, most of the time they missed, but when one connected they would all make a terrible din to celebrate the crack of stick on stone.

Lying in the grass behind them were more cans of beer and a pile of jackets. There was also a fire. A fire! On a hot night like this.

It wasn't until I crept near that I realised that in the fire they had been burning something belonging to the old man. The old man who gave me meat. The old man they had beaten to death.

I was sorely tempted to sink my teeth into the nearest one, maybe push him over the bank and into the water. But I was self-disciplined. A ducking was too good for these three, these murderers.

I edged close to the fire, to the beer cans. To the jackets.

The idea was to grab all three garments, but just as I made my move, one of the louts happened to turn around and see me in the light from the embers.

He yelled ugly things to his friends, and they reeled back towards me... I am not a coward but they did have sticks. And I am considerably bigger than a stone.

I grabbed the top jacket and ran for it.

They chased for a while, but they were no match for me running full out, even lugging the flapping jacket. And this was no small, lightweight thing. It was a heavy leather, and *not* clean.

But I got 'clean' away, and the last I heard of the three young killers was what I took for loud, angry swearing as it floated across the humid night air.

I went straight back to the body of the old man. I laid the jacket down by one of his hands and pushed a sleeve as best I could into its forceless grasp. I spread the jacket out.

I left the old man three more times. After each trip I returned with a beer can. Each can reeked of a killer. Other men might not be able to track them from the smell, but each of the cans bore a murderer's finger marks.

Then I sat and rested. I didn't know what it would look like from higher up, but from where I sat the scene looked as if the old man had grabbed the jacket of one of the men who had attacked him. Beer-drunk men. The old man had grasped and wouldn't let go. They, cowards that they were, ran off.

Cowards that they were, if one of them was brought to justice from his jacket, he would squeal on the other two from his pack.

I was pleased with my justice.

I raised my eyes to the moon, and I cried for the dead man. I cried and cried until I heard living men near the alley open their doors. Until I heard them come out into the still summer night. Until I heard them make their way to the alley to see what the fuss was.

Once I was sure they were doing that, I set off into the darkness.

COLD AND DEEP

Frances Fyfield

The ice had formed over eighteen hours. Sarah could sense it on the outside of the train travelling north from King's Cross to the Midlands. Fortunately, it was too cold to snow. Snow would only trap her for longer, and she was trapped enough already. What a fool, what a silly idiot she was to agree to help her sister when it wasn't as if she even liked children.

In a split second, on stepping from the train, Sarah examined her reasons for being where she was and found them lacking. It was simply that she was so successful at being single, she had nowhere else to go. Mary had asked, and Christmas was a nightmare anywhere.

There would be quite a crowd. Sarah struggled to remember how many. Mary, of course, with her husband Jonathan, plus two daughters aged six and eight, plus a baby. Then there was Richard, Jonathan's brother, and his utterly devoted fiancée, the lovely Fiona, who had been on site three days in advance to organise provisions and prepare the house.

Richard would follow her slavishly like the Magi in thrall to the star in the East, the way he always did. While the rest, Mary said in admiration, bowed to her practical wisdom and followed her order...

In comparison to this elegant paragon, the prospect of the elderly father was almost appealing in Sarah's estimation. He and she could celebrate their single status, with herself in the role of a hard-bitten aunty, and he as a hard-drinking Grandad. They could survive the season with the aid of a litre of gin. Since grandfather was recovering from a stroke, Sarah doubted the accuracy of this dream, but it was the best she could do.

The station of the small industrial town – foreign territory to a refugee from the fleshpots of central London – was ugly, chilly and not a place to linger. Sarah remembered her instructions to call the invincible Fiona, but somehow baulked at the idea when she saw the queue for the phone. Get a taxi, she thought, with the lazy London habits her successful career allowed her to afford. Ask the driver to stop at the end of the road, walk to clear her head from the foggy warmth of the train, anything to postpone the claustrophobic wretchedness of it all.

At least there would be a dog for company. A bitch, with puppies, Sarah recalled, and in the remembering, she was violently sick while standing at the rank. On that account, it took a while longer to get a taxi.

In a slow-moving car, approaching the same town from Manchester, weary bickering had trailed into dreary pauses. "I don't know why we have to do this," Mary was saying for the last time. Jonathan was beyond yelling and banging the wheel by now; all that had come earlier. He could scarcely speak. His head was full of the incessant calculation of how long his redundancy money would last, sums which buzzed and hummed like a persistent insect. The New Year beckoned like an old nightmare. Mary was trying to be noble, attempting to hide a kindred form of depression which left her constantly tired, often petulant.

"You know for why: because it's good for us. The girls get to run around. Dad can't come to us since he had his stroke, which is just as well for the sort of Christmas we'd be able to give him. And," he added cunningly, "with Fiona there, you don't have to do anything, except sleep. Surely Sarah will help?"

Oh clever, very clever, Mary thought. The prospect of sleep was unbearably appealing. Jonathan looked at Mary's face in the rear view mirror, and saw a pinched, exhausted look beyond his expectations or his curing. He envied the insouciance of his younger brother and the careless decade which came between them. He envied not only Richard's life, but his car and delicious, competent, caring Fiona.

"We got Sasha! With puppies, this time!" Beth shrieked, sick of the silence. "And I can go swimming in the lake!"

Mary winced. "I don't think so, darling."

"Can I tell you something, Daddy? Can I, can I, can I?" Beth continued. Mary's eyes closed. She was remembering the only holiday they could afford that past summer: a week with Richard and Fiona at Grandad's, just before his stroke. Fiona had been wonderful: so wonderful she had made Mary feel perfectly useless. Sylvie was always getting scratches, but somehow all the children's noisiest toys, such as Sylvie's recorder and Beth's drum, had disappeared.

Mary still wondered why it was that the children stayed so clean and mysteriously quiet around Fiona. It had been such a relief, herself so grateful, she had failed to question, and she was too anxious for peace to question now.

"What do you want to tell me, love?" Jonathan asked Beth. The child drew breath.

"I don't like Fiona, she wears horrible rings. Not after the summer holidays, I don't like her. Not much."

Mary's eyes opened and her voice rose in desperation.

"Don't be silly. Fiona's lovely. Everyone loves her."

"Sasha doesn't. Grandad doesn't. I doesn't."

Mary lost control. "Rubbish! You must be mad! Without Fiona, we don't eat or sleep for two whole days. So shut up... Just shut up!"

Silence fell until another small voice rose from the back.

"How very long till we get there, Daddy? How long? How long?"

"Soon. If you're good, you can play with Grandad's dog."

A yellow bitch, mostly labrador, called Sasha and still Richard's pet.

"We'll have to be very patient," Fiona was saying to him on his car phone. "But at least we've got the best bedroom and the best bed," she breathed seductively. Richard smiled like an idiot. He liked the sound of bed.

"Was Dad pleased to see you?"

"Oh yes, but not as much as the home helpers and the night nurse when I took over. I thought they were going to kiss me. But he doesn't really like me. You know that..."

Her voice was velvety, like the soft pouches beneath the labrador's jaw where Richard tickled until she rolled on her back, presenting her pink and yellow belly in ecstasy. Clutching the beloved car phone, his business as well as his delight, in lane three of the motorway, Richard checked the mirror at the same time and saw himself grinning. There was another BMW on his tail. He made it wait.

"You know your father doesn't like me," Fiona was saying sensibly, "but I thought I'd better warn you, he's much worse. Swears like a trooper, when he can talk at all. Says awful things about people, me included; you, even. Much worse than last month. He may not say much this evening because he's very tired, but he might blow bubbles." She kept thinking of bubbles.

"What kind of bubbles?" Richard asked stupidly, but the car lurched and the line began to crackle. No snow, his phone dead without apology, the BMW behind suddenly in front as he drifted left and he hadn't had a chance to ask about his darling golden bitch Sasha, and her late, aberrant pregnancy.

★   ★   ★

As he witnessed his father's judgement diminish, Richard saw himself losing one rudder to replace it with another. He shook his head and spurred the car into life. Fiona was simply a miracle.

The pudding was almost cooked. There was a brace of geese stuffed and wrapped in the larder. What an ugly house this is, Fiona thought. No country mansion, but pre-war Gothic, stuck on the edge of an awful conurbation once made rich by the industries of coal. The villa was the last in the road; a privileged position, with a field sloping down the bank to a pond in a gully – a stagnant stretch of water which Jonathan and his romantic brother still described as 'the lake'.

This puddle might have looked larger to kids, Fiona admitted condescendingly, but it was still only a pond. Small, but deep and cold, or so she had discovered as she warmed her hands in the sink after a second brisk walk to the crumbly edge, just to get out and see how the ice was progressing. It had been forming slowly ever since she arrived, more solid by the hour.

There was a keening sound from the dog's basket; a vague noise of distant thumping from the living room reached by a horrible lino passage. Sasha regarded Fiona with eyes of helpless misery. The bitch lay on one side with her milk-swollen tits exposed, the blanket beneath her freshly clean as a replacement for the torn and bloody newspaper of yesterday.

Fiona strode across and forced a pill between the unresisting pink jaws. The effort left her own fingers damp with saliva. She looked at them with disgust. "There," she said. "Vet's orders, you revolting beast.

You mothers are such a trial." She kicked the dog lightly with a small, well-shod foot. "Come on, show a leg, you stupid brute. Come on."

The almost labrador obeyed with ponderous reluctance, her unclipped claws clicking on the lino, which gave way to a tartan carpet. There was nothing here she would want to keep, Fiona thought, everything frightful. But it could make a beautiful and valuable dwelling.

We'll commute, Fiona planned. Have stone flags for the garden; gravel for the driveway. Plenty of ground. The pond could become a swimming pool. I could call Richard from there on his best mobile phone and ask him to bring down the champagne.

Sarah approached on foot, passing closed-up dwellings with eyeless windows set back from the road, the odd glimmering of light emphasising her own exclusion, until she reached the last house. The rutted drive was large enough for three cars in a row, containing only one, which must be Fiona's.

That single smart and feminine motor told Sarah she was the first of the other guests and made her reluctant to knock; left her standing in a state of uncertainty by the front door next to an enormous terracotta plant pot, pretentiously out of place and housing a small shrub on a bed of fresh compost. The shrub branches were festooned with tiny baubles, tinkling softly as she breathed, the whole decoration slightly repellent in its tasteful newness.

Still reluctant, inhibited by this sign of festivity, Sarah moved to her right and looked into a window. There were leaded panes through which she could see multicoloured fairy bulbs on a Christmas tree, hear muffled sounds, blurred like the lights, by the distortions of the glass.

An old man was sitting in an armchair, so far upright he might easily have risen with the aid of the stick which someone else had placed out of reach, leaning against the door sixteen feet away. He seemed to be yelling for his prop, screaming with rage and beating his wrists on the arms of his seat. There was a tall, fair-haired young woman about the business of shushing him, followed by a faded yellow dog with a pink underbelly.

Sarah stared and rubbed her eyes. She thought she saw a plastic bib ripped from the crêped neck, revealing a clean, white shirt; a hearing aid rammed in, the stick retrieved and placed where it belonged; a brush dragged through the thick, grey hair, yanking back a full, round face into a scream. He looked like a baby. Sarah felt sick all over again. The bright blue eyes in his face turned to the window as if for redemption, saw headlights behind her and began to focus.

Sarah scuttled towards the door. Her back was illuminated as she rang the bell, a dinky, irritating chime which defied the last illusion of ancestral splendour and also cut across the modern good taste of the expensive pot. One car pulled up behind her, another, more slowly behind that. Fiona flung open the door, framed in the light like an angel, laughing her hallos, uttering warm and lovely platitudes. "Come in, come in, how clever of you all to arrive at once, come and see Daddy…"

Father smiled at Richard. He was desperate to talk, it seemed, but Fiona was busy organising which room was whose, wash your hands and come and eat. Besides, father looked healthy, clearly so well cared for he must be content.

Then there was home-made soup; sandwiches, biscuits and Coke for the kids. Lots of red wine for the adults. Perfect for a family on Christmas Eve.

It was Beth, as usual, who created the discord by pointing at Sasha with a trembling finger. "Where are her puppies?" she shouted impatiently, forgetting her manners and the lecture in the car.

Grandad arched in his chair, looked as if he was about to shout, but hissed instead. "She didn't want…" he began. "She didn't want…"

"Oh dear," said Fiona, laying a hand on his arm, looking at Beth with sympathy. "I think it was a false alarm." She turned to Richard. "Hysterical pregnancy; Sasha's had them before, the vet told me. So I'm sorry, darlings, no puppies this time. The poor thing thought she was: her poor old body thought she was, but she wasn't. She just got fat."

Beth began to weep. Slow, solid tears of frustration.

I wish I was like that, Sarah thought wryly. I wish that my condition was the result of hysteria instead of careless fornication. I like my single, trouble-free life, my prospects of promotion to partnership over the heads of other accountants. I need nothing. I do not like spending Christmas marking time until I can find the right kind of discreet clinic for an abortion, so I can go on as before, and the awful misery I feel can only be because I always detested Christmas, anyway.

The dog raised a paw, suddenly acquiescent with a child warm against her throbbing flank. Dad thumped his stick. He shouted for scissors to deal with his sandwiches; ate with voracity the pieces which Fiona had cut so kindly and without comment or condescension, staring at her calm and beautiful face.

Yes, you are wonderful, Sarah thought. Richard's a lucky man. Mary's eyes were closed again. "He has such trouble with his speech," Fiona explained, leaning away from her prospective father-in-law, "since his stroke."

The children and Sarah were in one heap by now, as if Sarah had somehow acquired them all. How peculiar it was that little girls and boys should take to her so, Mary thought. They lollop towards her like puppies.

So it was Sarah who took them to bed soon after Grandad had been shepherded away by Fiona without protest, as if to give a good example.

The ugly house was strangely silent apart from the plumbing: the children spoke in whispers. They should be more excited, Sarah reflected. Suddenly protective of their dreams and against her better judgement, which applauded the convenience of their subdued behaviour, she found herself trying to stimulate some of the old and naughty fever.

"What's Santa bringing you? Will he be able to get everything down the chimney?"

"He was bringing me a puppy," said Beth savagely.

"No he wasn't, stupid," said Sylvie. Beth eyed Sarah in challenge.

Sarah was silent and the glance slid away as honesty prevailed.

"I wanted to see a puppy. That's all. Grandad said on the phone, it was the dog's last chance. He could speak all right then. Only Fiona says Sasha didn't have nothing. No puppies. Nothing."

"Dogs have lots of chances. So do people."

"No, they don't. I don't think they do. Grandad said they don't. You've got to grab chances, he said."

"Shush, now. Everyone's tired. Shush…"

As she tiptoed away down the corridor, full of relief, she saw a light beneath a door, prepared to creep past that too, until she heard the sound of sobbing. Grandad's room. She scarcely knew the man; she should leave him alone, she wanted a drink. But still she pushed the door and went in, cursing herself.

The old man lay on his side, foetally curled, his hand stretched out to a bedside light and a book which seemed too far from his fingers for easy reach. He turned his face to the door as she entered, and all at once she recognised that look of pellucid sanity in his blue eyes which she had seen before, distorted by the glass in the windows.

"Do something," he hissed. "She'll eat him up. Do something."

Sarah was embarrassed, arranged his blankets, smiled in the conciliatory way she imagined Fiona would smile, and put the lamp and the ever-elusive stick within reach, listening all the time to the laughter from downstairs which beckoned her to where she really belonged.

"Shall I turn off the light?"

He stuck two fingers in the air, a gesture obscenely at odds with his laundered fragility. Awkward old cuss, Sarah thought, retreating in good order.

Downstairs, there was no relief either. They were family; together they could only speak of their young and the old, and this was the season for both.

"Your dad can't cope," Fiona was saying gently, lying like a lioness at rest across Richard's knees. "He's determined he can, but he can't."

Richard bristled. "I could get him a mobile phone," he said, pointlessly, to universal silence. "We could get someone in to look after poor Sasha...how could he let her get into that state and not notice it was wrong?"

"But he should never go into a home, should he, darling?" Fiona murmured reassuringly. "We could always keep lovely Sasha for a while. You'd like that, wouldn't you?" Richard nodded.

"So I just think we step up the support for now," Fiona continued. "I mean, actually, we could live here, once we're married..."

"Yes," said Jonathan, relieved at the mere suggestion of solutions half as tidy. "Yes." Since the birth of his children and the even more momentous loss of his means to support them, he too had felt old. Sarah nodded and smiled: her contribution was not required. She was the only one distant enough to watch. So she did.

*　　*　　*

No snow on Christmas morning. A milky mist melted against the windows. By some miracle, it was as late as seven o'clock when the first piece of chocolate was presented by Beth; eight when Sarah rose and padded towards the Christmas tree like a pilgrim unsure of her religion. The old man was sitting there in his chair, haphazardly dressed.

"Did it all by myself. Easy, when I can reach the stick. What the hell does Richard think I normally do? I'm not mad, you know," he announced with surprising clarity. "Only as mad as a man with sons who are deaf and blind after all I taught them. Listen to me; you didn't listen to me, did you? They don't either."

"When?"

He seemed to slump, then rallied into a murmur. "I love Richard best. Is that so awful?"

"No. We all love someone best. It's allowed."

"Which is why it's important for him to know that she is trying to…" the voice declined to a mumble. Grandad's face contorted. "That woman…she's trying to kill… No, she's trying to…trying to…kiss me! Oh yes, she likes to kiss!" he shouted while his other hand waved in a mockery of greeting.

Sarah turned. Fiona was in the doorway. "Silly old Daddy," she said fondly. "You do go on." Her face was perfect, without a trace of tiredness. "Sarah, could you be an angel and help peel a few spuds before all hell starts? Then we can relax."

Sarah followed her out, looked back once. Grandad was slightly purple in the face.

"He's better in the morning," Fiona confided in a whisper. "But he does talk nonsense."

"Some of the time?"

Fiona responded sadly. "No, I daren't tell Richard. All of the time."

No one listens to the old, Sarah was thinking as they all opened their presents.

While Mary and Jonathan meekly exchanged books and records with a peck on the cheek before turning full attention to the pleasure of their children, Sarah lingered over the unwrapping of her token gifts to make them last, said thank you politely, delivered hers, then helped a listless Grandad open up a sweater, a shirt, and a tie, while the children tore into parcels like wild beasts. Even they had finished with the smallest and greatest of these long before Richard and Fiona ceased presenting to each other gift after perfectly wrapped gift.

"Oh, darling you shouldn't! A silk shirt! Sweetheart!"

There was a hunky suede jacket, a nightdress, jewellery for both, shoes, then more and more until the whole room was ablaze with their luxury.

Mary had begun to look a little stiff to remind Richard he seemed to have forgotten his nieces. From a forest of pretty paper, it took some time for him to remember where he was.

"Oh, I got this for the kids…"

Beth perked up, then her face assumed a stony expression of no expectation as Fiona handed her the parcel. Inside was a mobile phone.

"Oh," said Jonathan, doubtfully.

"There's another one for Sylvie," said Richard happily.

"I get a discount. They can try them in the garden."

"Crap," said Grandad suddenly and distinctly. "Crap."

"Lunch in an hour," Fiona announced brightly, gathering up paper. "Is it worth going out?"

"We'll go," said Sarah, desperate for air, feeling frantic with heat from the fire. "Won't we? Come on Sylvie, we'll take a phone and phone Grandad. He'll like that."

"Crap," said Grandad.

"If you must," said Fiona. "Do be careful with it, they're expensive, the very best. I should stay in the garden if I were you. No, don't take the dog. She's been out already."

Outside the mist and the mood cleared. Beth shrieked her way down the long, unkempt garden, holding the mobile phone as a kind of balance, yelling "Yuck" as she skirted the tentacles of the dripping bush, bellowing out of sight.

Sarah's arms clutched her bosom as she ran through a gap in the hedge, yelling after them, "Wait for me, wait for me!" There was no real cause for concern. The children were in awe of the lake they approached. Gingerly testing the steep, friable edges with the insensitive toes of wellington boots, both quieter than before, sulking with their feet because they could go no farther and dare not try the ice.

Sarah desperately wanted to revive for them the simple excitement which seemed to die indoors: felt the same desire in herself as the last evening, to make them noisily, joyously responsive.

"Let's break the ice," she yelled. "Come on, get stones. We can crack it!"

Sylvie threw a branch she had lugged to the edge; Beth threw lumps of earth. Then Sarah found a large stone, which was an effort even to lift. Beth helped. Between them, they dropped it rather than threw, watched it roll heavily down the side, bounce the last yard and make a hole in the edge of the ice. The water heaved and burped. Bubbles rose.

"Yeah, yeah!" Beth howled.

"I hate Fiona!" Sylvie shrieked. "She slaps me with her rings on! She steals stuff! She takes everything!"

She picked up the abandoned phone and threw it towards the hole.

"Stop it," Sarah shouted, but too late. Sylvie's aim was bad. The phone slid two, three feet distant from the hole. She began to cry.

Oh no, please don't, Sarah thought, I wanted to see you both happy: we were doing so well.

"Silly," she said sternly. "Don't be silly. We'll get it back."

It was unstated, but by some common instinct, they all knew that the wrath of Fiona would be terrible. Sarah scrambled down the bank and stood at the edge of the water, making an act of it, pretending it was fun. On the very edge, she was safe, until she looked at her feet.

A piece of sacking was protruding above the surface and with it the pink snout of a corpse. A pink and yellow body, bloated, pathetic, followed by another. Dead puppies. A whole litter of drowned puppies, the almost labrador's last chance.

Squatting over her freezing feet, Sarah shielded the sacking and talked brightly to the children over her shoulder to disguise the waves of fury which made her tremble.

"Listen," she said. "Listen, I've got an idea. Aunty Fiona can't get mad at me, right? I'm a guest and a grown up and I don't care anyway. Right?" They nodded, like two wise owls. "So you go back to the house, now, tell her I was carrying the phone and I dropped it on the ice.

"Say we don't want to tell Uncle Jonathan, in case he gets upset. Get Aunty Fiona in the kitchen, make it sound secret, right? And ask her to come here with a broom or something, so I can get the phone back. Then stay inside. It's too cold out here."

Beth grabbed Sylvie by the arm and they both fled, rehearsing lines. Sarah waited. She fished one of the dead puppies out of the water, repelled by the touch, but compelled to wipe the water away from its blind eyes and feel the softness under the chin. Then she dragged out the sack containing the rest.

The other six were still curled together. There was a pain in her abdomen and a fluttering in her chest. The stone had been too heavy, she felt sick, but she knew she would not wait long. Soon, down the slope, she heard the breathless panting of Fiona, booted, spurred, carrying a yard brush.

"The phone," Fiona said. "How could you? Richard lives for phones. We'll have a lousy Christmas if you upset him, how could you?"

She'll eat him up, was all Sarah thought, seeing in her mind's eye the sanity of the old man which they all ignored, concentrating on his weakness. She'll eat them all up; she likes to kiss. Possessions, other people's inheritance, other people's chances, she likes to kiss.

★   ★   ★

Sarah was halfway up the bank, scrambling with one hand, the other holding the sodden sack behind her back. Fiona saw it and stopped.

"How many did the poor bitch have? What a nuisance for you." Sarah tried to sound patient and understanding. Fiona pretended she had not heard, then relented, seduced into a sense of conspiracy by the concern in the other's voice, ignoring the prospect of the blinding, ice-cold rage beneath.

"Well, yes it was, a bit. The day I arrived. Can you imagine! He can't cope, you know. Richard would have wanted to keep them, take them home. Can you imagine how awful…mess on our carpets, the smell, everything…I mean you've got a nice flat, you see what I mean?"

"Yes, I do understand. Anyway, the phone's the most important thing at the moment, isn't it? I mean, it's valuable."

"Of course it is."

"Why don't you try to get it?" Sarah said, oozing sympathy. "I'm afraid my feet have gone numb."

"Fine, fine."

Oh, she was such a coper. Sarah squatted, winded with a pain far worse than the sickness outside the station the night before, clutching her chest where the gripe was sharpest, the sackful of sodden babies by her side. She was half-weeping, praying madly for the invisible foetus inside her.

Oh no, oh no; whatever the punishment to me, please do not die. I want you to live. That is what I want; whatever the purgatory, don't die on me. Every dog deserves its day, every bitch deserves a baby. Heaven help me.

Dazed, she watched Fiona stand up to her knees in icy water and fish for the phone, which lay like some ghastly talisman on the frozen surface. The slim body of the fiancée leant forward to sweep the brush over the ice, grunting. Then Sarah watched as Fiona slipped on the smooth clay surface; then Fiona was sliding under the ice up to the waist, her feet flailing for a hold.

Half the bank caved in behind her with a plop. The incline down was now very steep. The ice broke against her back. She slid further, bawling for help and for more than a moment, Sarah was tempted.

But it was a passing temptation. She hurt too much; she had too much to protect to fling herself down a slippery incline towards deep, cold water; she could not run for help anyway.

So she simply wondered about how to harness her small store of energy to bury the puppies in case the children should see them. Stayed where she was, full of the overpowering desire to preserve her own child and aware of the dimmest possible notion that it was better for a woman like Fiona to go like this.

Better in the long run for everyone. Knowing while she thought it, how a woman like herself was the slightest bit mad, but also knowing she couldn't, wouldn't, ever quite regret it.

It was not as if she even wanted to move; she wanted her own child to lie peaceful, but never as still as the cold puppies. Would it be better, she asked herself, if Richard saw these little corpses? She wondered briefly, dizzily, decided emphatically not, neither he nor his nieces.

As the new set of bubbles stopped rising to the surface, Sarah got up. She went round to the front of the house to the enormous planter on which she had stumbled the night before, lifted the tinkling shrub carefully, placed the sack with respect then went back to the bottom of the lawn behind and walked to the kitchen door.

"Where's Fiona?" Richard demanded.

"What? Isn't she here? I left her trying to fish a phone out of the lake. Went for a walk down the avenue. Isn't it remarkable how every house looks the same but manages to be so different? Are they 1930s or sooner? I never know. What's wrong? She said she'd give it five minutes. Isn't she back? Does she like the cold or something?"

He flung himself out of the house. Sarah washed her hands, went into the living room, where Grandad sat with the dog's head on his knee. Jonathan was on the floor, next to his suddenly animated, affectionate wife, with her arm round his shoulder as they laid out a game for the children, all four heads together. The baby was grinning in a carry cot, also studiously ignoring Sarah's glance. The atmosphere was suddenly lighter and brighter as though a stone had been removed and daylight introduced into a cave.

Sarah knelt by the old man's knee and watched while the dog lay down and transferred a trusting head into her own lap. Grandad watched too, with his crêpey hand trembling, Sarah's fingers interlaced with his.

"Trust me," she murmured.

"You'll have a nice pup," he said, loudly and clearly. "One day."

Sarah did not know if he spoke to her or the dog. Or even if it mattered.

MOVING ON

Susan Moody

i. Martin:

I see we're moving on. All three of us. Gerry and Susanna, who live in the big house opposite mine. And, as inevitably as Ivory follows Merchant, or Lybrand follows Coopers, me.

They put the For Sale sign up yesterday. I wonder where we'll go this time. I wouldn't mind being nearer London, I must say. Or even *in* London. Kensington, maybe, or Notting Hill Gate. Holland Park. Somewhere in there. It's not as if the bastard can't afford it, not with the amount he must be making from those crappy books of his. Perhaps I should suggest it to him. Walk right up the path and knock on the door. Say: "Look here, Gerry, old man. How about the metropolis this time, hm? How about bloody London this time?"

And I know what he'd answer. He'd raise those trademark eyebrows of his. He'd curl that famous well-shaped lip. He'd say: "Have you taken a look at yourself recently, Marty? Do you know what a pathetic figure you've become?"

If he did, I could say yes, I do. I could say that I'm every bit as disgusted with the way I am these days as he is. With the crumpled look which seems to have settled over me. With the stink of fags and stale booze and unwashed armpits that I carry about with me.

I could add that I blame him for it, that it's all his fault. But what point would there be? I don't want to give him the satisfaction. Anyway, he knows.

You could argue that I should have got over it by now. That my behaviour is immature and I'm only using Anna's death as an excuse to waste my own life. Maybe you'd be right. So many years ago, and I still haven't come to terms with it. Still haven't moved on from where I was then. Loving not wisely but too well is always a mistake. It blinkers you. Holds you back.

You may be wondering what I meant by that opening sentence: We're moving on... It's quite simple, really. When they sell up, I sell up. When they move on, I move on. Like Rachel and Naomi, in the Bible. Whither thou goest, I will go; and where thou lodgest, I will lodge. If you didn't know the reason for it, you might find it quite touching. Boyhood chums and all that. Still friends after all these years.

Still enemies after all these years, would be nearer the mark.

We didn't start out like that. Not at all. When we first met at university, we fell into a friendship of the warmest kind. I'm not talking sex here, of course. I'm not talking gays or poofters or queers or whatever you want to call it, though I've got absolutely nothing against homosexuality, male or female. I'm talking friendship. Maybe even love. Agape, though, not eros. We were both freshers, both on the same staircase, both reading Eng. Lit. Both grammar school oiks. We fizzed with enthusiasm for poetry, for cultural thought and, yes, for the idea of literature at its highest level. We spent hours together talking, discussing, arguing about the merits of words over music or painting, about the difficulty of manipulating language into the expression of emotion. We both wanted to be writers in those days. Authors. Whatever the difference is.

In the course of that first year, he came to my home and met my family. I went to his. During term-time, we did everything together. Went out with girls (often the same ones, though consecutively rather than simultaneously), drank, worked, walked, talked. About the only activity we didn't share was screwing. No, we didn't do that but we certainly talked about it afterwards. Extensively. Compared notes. Awarded points.

That went on for nearly two years. Until the second Long Vacation, in fact. Then he got a summer job with one of those market research companies, and I was taken on for six weeks as a general dogsbody by one of the national dailies. Old boy network, not merit. My father knew somebody who knew somebody. It still worked like that, back then. We wanted to find a place to share, Gerry and I, but our funds didn't run to that. But at least we were both in London, so we were able to meet up most days.

It was in July that I met Anna. July 29th, to be exact.

ii. Gerard:

"I don't want to move again," Susanna said.

"We have to," I said.

"I just can't face it, Gerry. Not again."

"I can't write," I said. "I haven't written a decent word since he tracked us down."

"This is absolutely the best house yet," she said. She squared her shoulders and stuck out her jaw and as usual, I experienced a surge of desire. We were sitting in bed reading the Sunday papers and the shoulder-squaring bit made her small breasts more prominent. Her nipples pushed against the dove grey satin of the nightdress she wore and made me want to fling aside the coloured supplements and the book review pages and yet again, as so many times over the years, make love to her.

Usually she was as eager as I was, but I knew that this morning it would be wiser to forego the pleasures of the flesh, however mutual they might be. The men from the estate agent had arrived yesterday afternoon to erect the For Sale board outside our house and Susanna had been restive ever since.

"The best house," she repeated. "Gerry, I'm happy here. Truly happy. I really don't want to move."

"Even with that maniac living down the lane?"

"Even with him."

"You know why he does it, don't you?"

"I know what you've told me."

"He thinks I was having an affair with his bloody wife."

"But you weren't."

"You *know* I wasn't. I didn't even like her that much, let alone want to jump into bed with her. But will he believe that? Will he hell."

"Can't you just ignore him?"

"Of course I can't. It's absolutely impossible. And while he's around, I can't write. Which means, my precious sweetheart, that I can't earn a living."

"Can't you bribe him to go away?"

"I tried that once. He just laughed in my face. The trouble is, he earns a fair old whack himself. Or used to, before he started drinking so much. And when his parents died, they left him quite a bit, too."

"Seven moves in ten years. I had enough of that with Daddy." Susanna's father had been a military man.

"I know, darling, but what else can we do?"

"The garden," wailed Susanna. "And the friends I've made. The people here are so warm and friendly." Tears started to fall down her cheeks. "Maria," she snuffled. "I haven't had a friend as close as Maria is since I left school."

"Darling…" I took her little hand in mind. "I promise you we'll find another house, just as nice as this. And other friends."

"How?" she demanded. She knuckled her eyes, looking as if she were about eight years old, instead of thirty more than that. "Wherever we go, he'll find us. He always has before. Every time I start to settle in, we're off again."

"I've been thinking about that," I said. "We could change our names, for a start."

"But you can't begin from scratch, Gerry. People wait for the new Gerard O'Connell the way they wait for the new Robert Ludlum or – or Danielle Steel." Even in her distress, my wife wasn't going to place me up there with the literary greats, with the Amises or the Rushdies. I didn't care. Her assessment of my talent just about matched my own and that wasn't particularly high. I made a hell of a lot of money and frankly, I wasn't too bothered about what the critics thought. You could say that I'd sold out, or you could say that I had moved on from my early unattainable goals, had come to terms with what I was, that I was an honest, even a happy, man, in that I made the very best use of what gifts I had.

Of course, in our university days, I had higher aspirations. Literature, no less. I was going to write the Great British Novel, the Great Global Novel. I was going to take the world by storm. And not just once, but many times as the years went by and I matured into Grand Old Manhood, as I drew round my more-than-worthy shoulders the mantle of literary genius.

Of course it didn't work out like that. I spent a year on the Great Novel, only to discover that in me, the seam of literary gold ran thin indeed. I mined it assiduously, buffed and polished it, spun it into fantastical filigree. Metaphor and allegory were my tools, myth and dream the scaffolding on which I erected my plot. Flimsy, you'll agree.

Insubstantial. Far too slight to carry the burden of my pretensions. Nobody, in short, would touch it.

I found myself a series of part-time, dead-end jobs, the sort of thing which kept body and soul together but little more. In my spare time, I wrote another novel, and another. The publishers remained distinctly unenthusiastic and I grew more and more depressed. We'd have starved if Susanna hadn't found a job as a PA to some high-powered executive in the oil business.

Then one cold winter, just before Christmas, my darling wife came home from work and said she'd been given a bonus. Why didn't we, she asked, splash out, spoil ourselves? Forget the bills, and blue it all on a package holiday to somewhere warm? So that's what we decided to do. Of course, after the first euphoria, common-sense prevailed. Package holidays cost an arm and a leg and we only had a small bonus to spend. We listed everyone we knew who lived abroad and might be prepared to let us foist ourselves upon them for a fortnight, and finally came up with South Africa, where Susanna had cousins she hadn't seen for years. That's where we went.

The cousins – a couple from Surrey with two young children – farmed acres of dusty red soil under wide blue skies. They lived among people whose skins were the colour of aubergines and whose expectations dared not rise above the next meal for their children. They lived inside a heavily walled and guarded compound, with a couple of fierce dogs prowling the perimeters of the grounds. There were cars, horses, tennis courts. There was a blue swimming pool and gardens kept green by constant watering. Conspicuous consumption. Conspicuous indifference.

While we were there, unrest bloomed in the cities. News came of bombs thrown, of troubles in Soweto, of houses burned and young men shot. It disturbed Susanna and me. The cousins said they had learned to live with it and we didn't like to ask at what price.

One afternoon, Susanna and I travelled by jeep to visit friends of friends of Susanna's parents. The house we visited was very similar to the one where the cousins lived and I thought then how strange it was that people could exist without worry in a situation of such contrast, such polarisation. We stayed the night, enjoying a barbecue out on the wide patio beneath stars far more significant than those we knew at home, served by silent young men with blank faces and expressive eyes.

The next day we drove back to the cousins' house. We would be leaving in two days' time. We agreed that we had enjoyed this glimpse of an alien way of life but we would not be sorry to return to our own much humbler existence.

Susanna said: "Do you suppose it was like this in India, during the Raj?"

"No," I said. "In India, the two separate cultures existed side by side. There was a lot of unfairness about the British rule, I'm sure, but they did at least attempt to be benevolent. There was none of this deliberate repression, this denial of the rights of others."

"I hate it," Susanna said, with a shiver. "There's something sinister about it. I'll never come back. At least, not while things are the way they are."

But while I never came to terms with South Africa – as it used to be under apartheid, I mean – I can't feel truly negative about the place. If I sound utterly callous about this, I certainly don't mean to, but it was entirely thanks to our visit that our fortunes changed.

Thanks to the visit, and, of course, to old Marty. I might still be working at some boring job during the day and trying, in my spare time, to fashion the crystalline prose of which I knew I was capable into something that a publisher would want to print, if he hadn't invited me to his birthday party.

But he did. And it was there that I met a young woman who was a commissioning editor with some publishing house. It was there that, in fact, I met his Anna.

iii. Martin:
July 29th.

The day I fell in love for the first – and it appears, the last – time. Totally, irrevocably, head over heels. All that crap. Anna was the light of my life, the icing on my cake, the song in my heart, the fairy on my Christmas tree. All that crap. I'd have crossed Saharas to see her, swum Hellesponts to reach her. I sighed for her. I'd have died for her. I loved her. The miracle of it was, that she loved me back.

She was a year older than I was. Just finished a degree at Bristol. Filling in time before taking up the job she'd got in one of the major publishing houses. Nothing grand. Secretarial work. But it would lead on to better things, she said. It always does, she said. Publishing is dominated by women. I'm going to be one of them, she said.

And, in due course, she was.

When we went back for our final year, Gerry and I, things had altered between us. He'd met Susanna somewhere during the summer and was much occupied with her. I'd got Anna. He told me all about Susanna. I told him little or nothing about Anna. At that stage, she was too precious to be shared, even with Gerry. Susanna visited him often, but I always went back to London to see Anna. She was preoccupied with her job, with learning the ropes, with working out how to get ahead. I was content just to be in her orbit. She had little time to spare and I was grateful when she spared it with me.

By the end of the summer term, Gerry and Susanna were engaged. As a wedding present, his parents bought them a flat in St. John's Wood. An aunt or something gave him a large sum of money, and he told me he was going to take a year off to write his novel. I was happy for him. I thought that some day soon I'd introduce Anna to the two of them.

Somehow, I never did. There wasn't time. I got a job on my local newspaper. I'd stopped worrying about being a novelist. Pragmatic, that's me. I just didn't have what it takes. Dedication. Doggedness. Self-confidence. I realised I wasn't a marathon man. More of a fifty yard sprint man. The short rather than the long haul. Journalism suited me. I had plenty of the rat-like cunning that is a prerequisite of the job. I moved on. Up to Manchester, then down again to London. A stint on the foreign desk in Japan, another in Germany. Back to London.

I got lucky. Wrote a piece or two which caught the attention of those who matter. Wrote theatre reviews for a prestigious magazine, then edited the book-pages of a Sunday. Got asked to do the restaurant critiques. Became a columnist on one of the dailies. Appeared regularly on a bookish game show on Radio 4. Became, eventually, famous. Not for very much, I admit. Except drinking. Got kicked out of the Groucho once. Picked a fight with Peter Ackroyd. Made acerbic comments on TV about the finalists for the Booker Prize. Threw up at some literary award luncheon. The *enfant terrible* of the chattering classes.

Anna and I set up together. Bought a house in Hampstead. The place smelled of dry rot and mice, but I didn't care, as long as she was there with me. And she was. She loved me. In bed, or out of it. Adored me. As I adored her. Looking back, I can see that it's not good. A love like that spoils you for anyone else. She was my hostage to fortune.

We gave a party. A celebration. Anna's birthday. A book she'd commissioned had reached the Top Ten in the *Sunday Times* Bestseller List. My own collection of pieces was doing well on the non-fiction lists. I invited Gerry and Susanna, who were recently back from a trip to South Africa. He still hadn't managed to get published. Anna had looked at his books but said that though they had good bits in them, the whole was distinctly less than the sum of the parts. That he was a gnat straining at a fly. Something like that. I can't remember exactly how she put it but it summed poor Gerry up.

I noticed them at the party, talking together in a corner, Gerry and Anna. They were still there, looking serious, half an hour later. When they'd gone, when we were in bed, Anna said: "I think we could have a bestseller on our hands."

"Who?" I said.

"Believe it or not, your mate. Your chum. Gerard O'Connell."

"Gerry? A bestseller? He's been trying for years to get published. Can't even get on to the slush pile."

"He just might," Anna said, "turn out to be the new Wilbur Smith."

"What's wrong with the old one?"

She fitted herself against me, her long limbs cool. "He'll need editing, of course. He's got literary pretensions, but we'll soon sort him out."

And she was right. The first Gerard O'Connell, assisted by judicious and plentiful publicity, got into the Bestseller list. So did the second, and the third. And all the ones after that.

At first I didn't mind the time he spent with Anna. Just part of the job. They went down each year to the cottage in Wales which Gerry bought with the proceeds from the fourth or fifth book. Editing. Ten days, two weeks. It didn't occur to me that anything was going on. I mean, he had Susanna. She was devoted. He was uxorious. The happy couple. Call me naïve, but it never bloody well crossed my mind.

iv. Gerard:

I told her, this Anna, whom Martin had not introduced to us before, what had happened. How we'd come back to find the gate of the compound hanging open. How we'd realised there was something wrong when the dogs didn't come running from the house at the sound of our car. How we pushed open the front door and seen – well, I'd seen. I'd managed to push Susanna away before she could step inside the house, ordered her to stay in the car. The shock…just telling Anna about it brought everything back, all the horror of it. Limbs. Severed limbs. A child's head. Three fingers lying on a table. A tongue. Blood everywhere. Absolutely everywhere. I found bits of them scattered all through the house. Just bits. The girls, Susanna's cousin and her little girl, had been raped in the grossest kind of way and then hacked to pieces. The other two, the boy and his father, had been treated even worse. All I could think of was that if we'd been there, Susanna and I would have suffered the same fate.

I wouldn't let her into the house. We got away as fast as we could, to the police station, to the consulate. Susanna drove. I was incapable of holding the wheel. Shivering and weeping, and occasionally getting her to stop while I spewed up my guts at the side of the road. Oh, God. It was impossible to describe the horror of that house.

Until, that is, Anna persuaded me to write it down, to turn it into a story. She said that at worst, it would be therapy for me, at best, it might even be a publishable book.

She was right. By the time I'd finished writing it, I was already thinking of a plot for the second book. There was an incident in my childhood, on a visit to an uncle in New Zealand… The books went on from there. The new Gerard O'Connell became as much a fixture in the publishing calendar as the annual Dick Francis. Anna helped me. I freely admit that I wouldn't have got off the ground if it hadn't been for her. It was a strictly professional relationship, whatever Martin chose to believe. I'm not attracted by those big women with long legs and manes of sweeping black hair. They frighten me, actually. I'm always afraid that one day they'll open their wide gashes of mouths and swallow me whole. Susanna is a little thing who needs my protection and therefore makes me feel like a man. She doesn't ask for independence, or even equality. She is as happy to let me take the decisions for us both as I am to make them.

Anyway…it became a regular routine. I'd write the new book in first draft. Go through and produce a second draft, send it off to

Anna for consideration then hole up with the computer in our Welsh cottage to come up with a third draft. After which, Anna would join me down in Wales and we'd go through the book again, line by line, until it was as good as I – as we – could make it.

We were rich, Susanna and I. I loved all the trappings that went with the money, all the fame and adulation, the invitations, the appearances on TV, the requests for my opinion on almost any subject under the sun. I never heaved a sigh for the great literary novels I might have written. I had found my proper level and I rejoiced in it. I felt no need to justify myself, not in any way.

One year, the book was to be about a man living quietly in the house where he was born, which had been handed down through the generations. A few hundred acres, country pursuits, sense of duty, wife and kids, no surprises. And then, *pow!* into his life comes a dangerous stranger, demanding, insisting, threatening everything that our hero holds dear. If he is to regain his peace of mind, he has no choice but to deal with the matter. Gun running came into it. Brazilian gold. Beautiful temptresses. Even drugs, though I try to keep off the subject since market research has shown that my readers don't want to know about them except in the most general and sanitised form. Gun running...

I went down to Wales to write the final chapters, taking with me, as part of my research, the Purdey my father had given me for my twenty-first birthday, and the Heckler & Koch P7K3 I borrowed from Martin which he had acquired in (according to him) rather strange circumstances while he was in Germany

The book went like a dream. I wrote ferociously, getting up early every day, working well into every night, existing on strong coffee and frozen meals. Every lunchtime, I went out for an hour with the guns, taking pot shots at crows and rabbits, experiencing for myself the pull and kick, noting the eye-hand co-ordination needed, the smell of the thing, the weight, the determination needed to aim at a target, to blow away a piece of vermin, be it animal or human. It was what gave my books that personal yet professional touch, according to Anna.

When I was ready, she came down to Wales to work on the typescript. As with Marty, all those years ago, we worked, we walked, we worked again. In the evening, we sat over a bottle or two of wine and talked, as always. I of my Susanna, she of her ambitions and of Martin. This time there was a new theme to her conversation: biological clocks, the running out of.

"I'm nearly thirty five," she said.

"Aren't we all?" I joked.

"Children," she said. "Until now, my career has been everything to me. I never thought I'd feel the urge to be a mother, but suddenly, I do."

"What will Martin think?" I asked.

"I'm afraid he won't like the idea. I'm afraid he won't want to share me. We love each other," she said simply, "we're everything to each other. We've always lived in each other's pockets, perhaps almost too much and I don't know how our relationship will stand the strain of enlarging the magic circle."

"It'll survive," I said.

"I'm sure it will. It would have to. I couldn't live without Martin." She picked up the H&K which was lying on the windowsill. "He's got a gun just like this."

"It's his, actually."

"Oh." Her mouth – that engulfing slash of a mouth – drooped. "Gerry, I'm so torn."

"Poor love," I said sympathetically.

"I mean, I really want a baby. Really really." Maybe she was a little pissed, maybe just being sincere. "But if anything happened to destroy the relationship between Marty and me, I might just have to kill myself." Before I could stop her, before I could do a damn thing about it, she had pointed the gun – laughing – at the side of her head and pulled the trigger.

Everyone knows you should never do that.

My fault. It was all my fault. I'm not usually so careless. Like anyone who's ever had anything to do with guns, I know how vital it is to remove the cartridges. Normally, I always do. This time...I could only plead pressure of work. I hadn't touched the damn thing for several days, since before Anna came down. And now – well, it was like South Africa all over again. She was dead long before she hit the floor.

v. Martin:

I might have bought it. Probably would have, if the next Gerard O'Connell hadn't featured a love affair between a man and his best friend's wife. Ostensibly, it was the usual bollocks about a bloke getting into and out of trouble in any political trouble-spot you cared to name. But this time, it was really a sex manual for retards. Lust in Leningrad. Sex and saunas in Sarajevo. Passion under the palm trees. An exposé, if you please, of his liaison with my wife. At the end of the book, she turns on him, spurns him, tells him she's moving on, that she loves her husband and it's all over. He picks up a gun – his best friend's gun, at that – and shoots her. "If I can't have you, no one else will," he grates. Gerry's heroes are good at grating.

I couldn't believe the brass neck of the man. Perhaps the results of the inquest, which, while noting his carelessness, exonerated him of any blame, made him feel that he was God. That he could get away with anything. It was clear that he'd seduced Anna, and when she tried to get away from him, his overweening vanity wouldn't allow it, and he'd shot her. I told the coroner this but he dismissed it. I wrote letters but nobody would take any notice. I spread the story among my pals in the newspaper world but they didn't want to know. Accused me of paranoia. I went to see Susanna, told her of my suspicions. She just laughed. Said I was jealous. Jealous? Of Gerry?

It was the perfect crime. He'd got away with it. Or so he thought. That's when I decided to do something about it. Follow him. Haunt him. He'd know that I knew. He'd never get rid of me, until death did us part. Just as it had parted Anna and me. So I went where he went. Where he lodged, I lodged as well. Always there, down the road, round the corner, across the lane. A reminder that there's no such thing as a free fuck. Especially not with someone else's wife. I'm not even discussing the emptiness I feel. The despair. The hole she has left in my life. The hole I fill with alcohol. The bottomless pit.

Yes. I have become disgusting. Red faced. Coarse featured. My hands shake most of the time. My clothes are not clean. I don't know when I last had a bath. I'm not proud of it. I smoke too much – first thing I do when I wake is to light up. Drink too much – most of the time I sit among the whisky bottles and think about Anna. About the fairy on my Chernobylled Christmas tree. About the icing on my poisoned cake, the dirge in my heart. When I don't think about her, I think about him.

And when I'm not thinking, I'm packing up my increasingly meagre possessions, ready to follow where they lead, ready to go where they go. Moving on.

vi. Gerard:

All right. It was insensitive of me. Damned insensitive. Even Susanna said so and she doesn't often criticise me. But Anna herself had taught me all about what she called the Fuck Mother factor. That is, the answer to the timid author's question: *But if I write that, what will Mother say?* A bestselling author, she told me, has no room for sensitivity. He is shameless, he uses the material to hand and never mind who objects. So I fucked Mother. Used Anna's accident. I know she'd have wanted me to. I dressed it up with an affair, added some steamy sex scenes in various places, had the man kill her when she spurns him, and then get away with it. He suffers, of course. He tries to expiate the crime and in the end dies nobly, sacrificing himself to save someone else. The critics thought it was the best book I'd done.

It honestly didn't occur to me for a single minute that old Martin would take it as some kind of confession. Anna and I had a professional relationship, nothing more. She wasn't my type. We could have shared a bed naked, and I doubt if I'd have raised a stand. She simply didn't turn me on. Martin can't believe that. Cock-ridden himself, he believes everyone else must have been too. He thinks I killed her for spurning my advances. I've tried to explain but he won't believe me.

The persecution started about ten years ago. Susanna and I decided to move, just because I couldn't bear the guilt of what had happened and wanted to get out of our house. When Marty turned up living practically next door, I thought at first that it was a bizarre coincidence. I found it impossible to write with him so close. Naturally I felt guilty enough about what had happened without him there all the time as well, a living breathing reproach. We sold up again before the place had even been redecorated and moved elsewhere. So did he. The third time, I realised it was deliberate. I've tried to choose places he'll hate; I've tried swearing the agents, the solicitors, my publishers to secrecy; I've even bought a new house without selling the old. It's no good; he always manages to track us down.

I've tried to persuade Susanna to move to Hollywood: it wouldn't be difficult, with the first three books under option to one of the major studios and principal photography already started on the first. Keanu Reeves, Sandra Bullock and Gene Hackman or Anthony Hopkins – it should be good. But Susanna doesn't want to leave England, or her family. The trappings of fame and fortune don't mean a lot to her, frankly. Our houses are always fairly modest, and so are our cars, though we splash out on holidays and own a place in Italy. I've told her that if we moved on, went upmarket, we'd be able to shake Martin off just because he couldn't afford the kind of place that we can, but she says that after what we saw in South Africa, she'd feel uncomfortable in anything too grand. As a matter of fact, so would I.

Now, with the For Sale sign up once more, with the wellsprings of creation dried up yet again, as I think of that poor sad bastard just down the lane, the quiet reproach on his face, the hatred I sense in his heart, I realise that something must be done. I've thought about it for a while. I've plotted it as though it were a book.

Given the condition he's sunk to, given the vices he increasingly gives in to, the fags, the booze, I don't think it will be terribly difficult. I know him too well. Starts the day on a fag, ends it at the wrong end of a whisky bottle. I can see exactly how to do it. I can't think why I didn't do it before.

THE SOUTHBURY & DISTRICT CHRONICLE

At the inquest today on Martin Blowers, 44, a journalist, of Linstead Lane, the Coroner paid particular attention to the deceased's lifestyle as having a significant bearing on his death. Peter Atkinson, landlord of the Three Feathers in the High Street, stated that Mr. Blowers was a regular customer and on the night in question, had consumed at least six pints of bitter followed by several double brandies. Asked if, in his opinion, the deceased was drunk, Atkinson said that he would not necessarily have said drunk but certainly well lit up. Since he knew that Mr. Blowers, who lived about half a mile from the pub, would not be driving home, he had not considered it necessary to limit the amount served to him. In answer to a question from the Coroner, he agreed that with hindsight, it might have been wiser to refuse to serve him.

Mrs. Maggie Clifford stated that she had worked as a domestic for Mr. Blowers for the past eight months, ever since he had bought the house in Linstead Lane. She said that in her opinion, he was an accident waiting to happen. *Asked by the Coroner to explain this remark, she said that for instance, she had come in one morning to find water coming through the ceiling, and on going upstairs, had found the bath taps full on and Mr. Blowers slumped asleep on the landing outside the bathroom. Just a week earlier, he had put a pan of water to boil on the gas stove and then forgotten about it. If a neighbour hadn't noticed the smoke and called the fire brigade, anything might have happened. She said that the deceased often forgot to lock the doors of his house at night, despite the fact that in recent weeks, he had been burgled twice. She added that the way he left lighted cigarettes lying around, it was a miracle that he hadn't either burned down the house or blown himself to bits long before this.*

Mr. Gerard O'Connell, the well-known thriller writer and a neighbour of Mr. Blowers, stated that he had known the deceased since their undergraduate days, and that in the past three or four years, Mr. Blowers' physical condition had deteriorated markedly. Asked to what he attributed this deterioriation, Mr. O'Connell said that in his opinion, following the death of his wife, Mr. Blowers had developed a serious drink problem.

Coroner: In other words, he was an alcoholic?

O'Connell: I don't think that would be overstating the case.

Asked if he had noticed any other indications of impaired faculties, Mr. O'Connell mentioned his friend's recent inability to meet deadlines at work, and an increasing degree of memory impairment. He agreed with Mrs. Clifford that Mr. Blowers often failed to secure his house at night, and said that it was he who had, on a recent occasion, seen smoke pouring from the kitchen windows and had called the fire services before entering the house to find Mr. Blowers passed out on the sofa in the living room. He added that it had been extremely difficult to rouse him.

Coroner: In your opinion, was he suffering, on that occasion, from the effects of alchohol?

O'Connell: In my opinion, for what it is worth, yes, I would.

Evidence was given by the chief fire officer, who stated that on the night in question, the gas fire in the living room had been turned full on but not lit.

Given Mr. Blowers' habit of smoking as soon as he woke up, before getting out of bed, he gave it as his opinion that by the time Mr. Blowers had struck the match for his first cigarette of the day, the whole house would have been full of gas fumes.

Verdict: accidental death, aggravated by the problems of a reliance on alcohol.

From the *Sunday Times*:

PERFECT CRIME *BY GERARD O'CONNELL*
Steven Laidlaw

Another thumping good read, the new Gerard O'Connell is very much the mix as before, with plenty of action in various exotic locales, the statutory gorgeous bimbo, evil villains, and right, in the end, overcoming might.

In this one, our hero — all jutting jaw and steely eyes — seeks to revenge the death of his best friend in what seems to be a domestic gas explosion. Best friend is a burned-out wreck who is slowly drinking and smoking himself into an early grave. Although the police consider it an accident, our hero is convinced that the forces of evil — possibly the Yakuza, whom his dead friend investigated during his days as a journalist in Tokyo — are responsible, having sneaked into the house while the best friend was sleeping off his most recent binge, turned on the gas fire and deliberately left it unlit.

There are plenty of the sort of thrills and spills which only O'Connell can provide, with much convincing technical detail, elegant sex, graphic fisticuffs and the hero conquering all. But there is more to it than this. In his most recent books, O'Connell has definitely moved on from producing mere hokum; there is a dark and satisfying edge to his recent work which transcends the genre in which he has chosen to make his mark and this latest example offers glimpses of a real — I might even suggest a great — novelist trying very hard to fight his way out from under.

*Steven Laidlaw's new thriller, **Root of Evil,** will be published by Hodder & Stoughton in September (£15.99)*

THE WOMAN WHO LOVED ELIZABETH DAVID

Andrew Taylor

On the evening that Charles died I actually heard the ambulance, the one that Edith Thornhill called. I was putting out the milk bottles in the porch. I didn't take much notice. Our house was on Chepstow Road and so was the hospital; we often heard ambulances.

He died on the day the rat-catcher came – the last Thursday in October. Our house was modern, built just before the war, but in the garden was a crumbling stone stable. Charles planned to convert it into a garage if we ever bought a car, which was about as likely as his agreeing to install a telephone. Meanwhile, we used it as a garden shed and apple store. Almost all the apples had been ruined by rats in the space of a week. Hence the rat-catcher.

Charles was late but I had not begun to get worried. After he closed the shop, he often dropped into the Bull Hotel for a drink. Then the doorbell rang and I found Dr. Bayswater and Mrs. Thornhill on the doorstep. I know Edith from church, and Dr. Bayswater is our doctor.

"I'm sorry, Anne," Edith said. "It's bad news. May we come in?"

I took them into the lounge. Edith suggested I sit down.

"Charles? It's Charles, isn't it?"

"I'm afraid he's dead," Edith said.

I stared at her. I did not know what to say.

The doctor cleared his throat. "Coronary thrombosis by the look of it."

"Do you mean a heart attack? But he was only forty-eight."

"It does happen."

"And he doesn't have a weak heart. Surely there'd have been some—"

"I'd seen him three times in the last month." Dr. Bayswater examined his fingernails. "Didn't he tell you?"

"Of course he did. But that was indigestion."

"Angina. Some of the symptoms can be similar to indigestion."

The doctor and Edith went on talking. I didn't listen very much. All I could think of was the fact that Charles hadn't told me the truth. Instead of grieving, I felt angry.

My memory of the next few weeks is patchy, as if a heavy fog lies over that part of my mind. Certain events rear out of it like icebergs from the ocean. The funeral was at St. John's and the church was full of people wearing black clothes, like crows. Marina Harper was there, which surprised me because she wasn't a churchgoer. The obituary in the *Lydmouth Gazette* was not a very long one. It said that Charles came from a well-respected local family and referred in passing to Nigel.

Unfortunately Nigel, Charles's younger brother, was in Tanganyika, looking at some sawmills he was thinking of buying. I never really understood what Nigel did for a living. Whatever it was, it seemed to bring him a good deal of money. Once I asked him and he said, "I just buy things when they're cheap, and sell things when they're expensive. Nothing to it, really."

I sent a telegram to Dar es Salaam. Nigel cabled back, saying he would be home as soon as possible. He and Charles had always been very close, though Nigel was my age, a good ten years younger than his brother. He was also Charles's executor.

Until Nigel came home, I could have very little idea of what the future held for me. I didn't even know whether I would be able to stay in the house. The family shop – Butter's, the men's outfitters in the High Street – was left in the charge of the manager.

What struck me most was the silence. In the evenings, when I sat by the fire in the lounge, there was a quietness that I could not drive away by turning on the wireless. After a while, I stopped trying. I would sit in my chair, with a book unopened on my lap, and stare at the familiar room which had grown suddenly unfamiliar: at my mother-in-law's dark oak sideboard, which I had always loathed; at the collected edition of Kipling, which Charles and Nigel had laboriously assembled when they were boys; at the patch on the hearthrug where Charles had left a cigarette burning one Christmas-time.

I don't know when I realised something was wrong. I think the first thing that struck me was the key, when the hospital sent back Charles's belongings. He had kept his keys in a leather pouch with a buttoned flap – keys for the house, for the shop. This one, however, was loose – a brass Yale, quite new. I tried it unsuccessfully in our only Yale lock, the one on the old stable. I took it down to the shop, but it didn't fit any of the locks there, either.

On the same morning, I went to the bank to draw some cash – something I had to do for myself now Charles wasn't here. The cashier said the manager would like a word. Our account was overdrawn. The manager suggested that I transfer some money from the deposit account.

As I was walking down the High Street on my way from the bank to the bus stop, Mr. Quale was sweeping the doorstep of the Bull Hotel.

"Morning, ma'am. Sorry to hear about Mr. Butter."

"Thank you."

"Very nice gentleman. I saw him just before it happened."

"How did he seem?"

"Right as rain. He popped in for a quick drink – left a bit earlier than usual. Thought he must be in a hurry for his supper."

"Earlier?" Charles had collapsed on the pavement outside the Thornhills' house in Victoria Road a little after seven-thirty. "You mean later?"

Quale shook his head. "It was about a quarter-past six."

"I expect he looked in at the shop on the way home."

I said goodbye and joined the queue at the bus stop. Charles had never worked in the evening. I was standing there, turning over in my mind what Quale had said, when there was a loud tooting from the other side of the road. It was Marina Harper in her little two-seater.

"Hop in, Anne. I'll give you a lift."

I was tired, and it was beginning to rain. Otherwise I might have tried to find an excuse. I never knew quite what to make of Marina. She had fair, coarse hair and a high-coloured face with small, pale eyes. She was comfortably off – her father used to own the local bus company. We had known each other since we were children but we weren't particular friends. And I was old-fashioned enough to feel that a wife should live with her husband.

Marina talked unceasingly as she drove me home. "I've just had a couple of days in town." Her husband worked in London. He and Marina had a semi-detached marriage: his job kept him in London while she preferred to live in Lydmouth. "...and you'll never guess who I met at a party last night. Elizabeth David – yes, really. Absolutely wonderful. Such style. She looks how she writes, if you know what I mean."

"Elizabeth who?"

Marina raised plucked eyebrows. "Elizabeth David. The cookery writer. You know, she's always in *Vogue*. And she's written this super book about Mediterranean food. Why don't you come to lunch tomorrow? We can try one of the recipes."

Marina dropped me in Chepstow Road. After lunch, I went into the dining room. Charles kept cheque books and other documents relating to money in the top drawer of the bureau. I settled down and tried to work out how the money ebbed and flowed and ebbed again in our lives. I found the most recent bank statement among the pile of business letters which I had left on the hall table for Nigel. How I wished Nigel were here now.

At the date of the statement, our personal account had not been overdrawn, but it now was. In the week before his death Charles had made out a cheque for one hundred and eighty-nine pounds, nineteen shillings and eleven pence.

I leafed through the cancelled cheques enclosed with the statement. The one in question had been made out to H.R. Caterford Ltd and paid into a branch of Barclays Bank in Cardiff.

Feeling like a detective, I put on my hat and coat, walked to the telephone box on the corner of Victoria Road and consulted the directory. H.R. Caterford Ltd was a jewellers in the Royal Arcade. Suddenly the solution came to me: Charles must have bought me a present. The dear man knew I had been a little low since coming out of hospital in September. (Knowing one will never have children is a little depressing.) But in that case, where was the present?

On impulse I dialled the number in the directory. The phone was answered on the second ring, just as I was beginning to get cold feet about the business.

"Good afternoon," I said. "May I speak to Mr. Caterford?"

"Speaking."

"This is Mrs. Butter, from Lydmouth. Mrs. Charles Butter. I believe my husband—"

"Mrs. Butter. How pleasant to hear from you. You're well, I hope?"

"Yes, thank you. I was wondering—"

"Oddly enough, I was just thinking of you. Only yesterday afternoon the lady who sold us the brooch came in with the matching ring. Platinum and opal. Said she didn't want that either, because her daughter had told her that opals are unlucky unless you're born in October. Not that you need worry about that, of course."

"Oh?"

"As you're one of the favoured few."

"Oh," I said. "Oh yes."

"It's rather a lovely ring. The opals are a perfect match for your eyes, if I may say so. Would you like to have a word with Mr. Butter about it? Then perhaps he could telephone me. I'll hold it for a day or two. It's always a particular pleasure to oblige an old customer."

"Yes, thank you. Goodbye."

I put down the phone and walked home. A platinum and opal brooch. Charles knew I didn't like platinum. Then the opals: unlucky unless the wearer had been born in the month of October. My birthday was in March. And how could opals match my eyes? They are brown. Finally, Mr. Caterford had spoken to me as if he knew me. But until this afternoon I had never even heard of him.

The following morning, I found a rat. The rat-catcher had warned me this might happen. "That's the trouble with them, look," he had said. "You can never tell where they're going to pop up."

The rat was lying on the path by the old stable. It was dark, with a long tail. There had been a frost in the night and its fur was dusted with droplets of ice, like sugar. Actually, it looked rather sweet. Because of the frost, the ground would not be easy to dig, so I decided to bury it after my lunch with Marina Harper.

Marina lived in Raglan Court, a modern block of flats overlooking Jubilee Park. The place was very nice, I'm sure – if you like hard, modern furniture and American gadgets. There was a lounge-cum-dining room with a huge picture window overlooking the park and a serving hatch to the kitchen. The air stank of garlic.

"I've just made dry martinis," Marina said. "You don't mind if I put the finishing touches to lunch, do you? We can talk through the hatch."

As she poured the drinks, light glinted on a silver brooch she was wearing. Rather a pretty brooch with opals set in it.

Not silver: platinum?

"That's a lovely brooch," I said.

"Yes, it is pretty, isn't it?"

"Aren't opals unlucky?"

Marina laughed, a gurgle of sound like water running out of a bath. "Not if you're born in October. Then they're lucky. Now why don't you sit here while I finish off in the kitchen?"

I watched her through the hatch – the flash of a knife, the glint of platinum – and all the time she talked.

"I thought we'd have filet de porc en sanglier. It's one of my Elizabeth David recipes. Pork that tastes like wild boar. The secret is the marinade. It has to be for eight days. And you can't skimp on the ingredients either – things like coriander seeds, juniper berries, basil. There's a little shop in Brewer Street where you can get them. I think it must be the only place in England."

While Marina talked, the rich, unhealthy odours of the meal wafted through the hatch into the living room. In my nervousness, I finished the drink more quickly than I should have done.

"Can I get you a refill?" she called.

I stood up. "I wonder if I might – is it along here?"

"Second on the left."

In the hall, I opened my handbag and took out Charles's Yale key. Holding my breath, I opened the front door. I slipped the key into the lock and twisted. The key turned.

I drew it out of the lock, closed the door quietly and darted into the sanctuary of the bathroom. Marina was wearing the brooch. The jeweller in Cardiff had thought that Marina was me, had thought that she was Charles's wife. So they must have been in Cardiff together, and acting as if they were a married couple. The key in Charles's pocket fitted Marina's door. There could be only one explanation for all that.

It is strange how in a crisis one finds reserves of strength one did not suspect existed. Somehow I went back into the living room and accepted another dry martini. Somehow I made myself eat the ghastly, overflavoured pork which Marina served up with such a triumphant flourish that I wanted to throw the plate at her. I even complimented her on her cooking. She said that she would give me the recipe.

The meal dragged on. It was far too heavy and elaborate for lunch. Marina served it in the French manner, with salad after the main course, and then cheese before the pudding. So pretentious. What was wrong with our British way of doing things?

When at last it was time to go, Marina came into the hall and helped me on with my coat. She bent forward and kissed my cheek.

"I have enjoyed this," she said. "Let's do it again soon. I'm running up to town for a night or two but I'll be in touch as soon as I get back."

I walked home. The rat was still lying on the path between the house and the stable. I manoeuvred its stiff body into a bucket with the help of a spade. The ice had melted now, so the fur gleamed with moisture. I carried the bucket into the stable. I looked at the various places where the rat-catcher had left the poison. All of it had gone. I wondered whether there were more rats. It was then that the idea came into my mind. I remembered the Kipling story.

Nigel and Charles thought Kipling was the greatest writer of the century. They were particularly fond of his *Stalky* stories, which are about unpleasant schoolboys at a boarding school. I had read them in our early days, when I'd been friends with both Charles and Nigel, just before Charles and I became engaged. A wife should try to like the things the husband likes. But I hadn't much liked these stories.

Their favourite story was one in which the boys kill a cat with an air gun. They push its dead body under the floorboards of a rival dormitory. The cat decomposes, and gradually the smell fills the dormitory, growing stronger and stronger, and more and more loathsome. If a cat could do that, I thought, so could a rat.

It was just a silly idea – childish, undignified and in any case impossible to carry out. I left the rat in the stable and went inside for a cup of tea. During the rest of the day, however, I could not help thinking about the dead rat. And about Marina.

Marina was going to London. I had a key to her flat, which she did not know I possessed. If I went there tomorrow evening, after darkness, there would be very little risk of my being seen. As the evening slipped past, the idea seemed more and more attractive. It wouldn't harm Marina to have another smell in that evil-smelling flat. And it was a way of making a point about her beastly behaviour. There was no excuse for adultery. There was no excuse for stealing my husband.

The following evening, I wrapped the rat in newspaper and put it in my shopping bag. Fortunately I'm not squeamish about such things. I slipped a torch into my pocket, walked up to Raglan Court and let myself into the flat.

I was not afraid. Indeed, I had the oddest sensation that it could not be me, Anne Butter, doing this. I went into the kitchen. This was where Marina's nasty foreign smells came from – so this was the place for the rat. I didn't turn on the light. I unwrapped the rat and let it fall to the linoleum.

The gas cooker was raised on legs a few inches above the floor. I used a floor mop to push the body underneath. The torch proved to be a blessing. With its help I was able to see that there was a gap between the wall and the back of the cupboard beside the cooker. With a little manoeuvring of the broom, I pushed the rat into the gap. Even if Marina looked under the cooker she would not be able to see anything. I didn't think it would be long before the rat began to smell: the flat was centrally heated, and the kitchen was the warmest room.

I went home. Then it was simply a matter of waiting. Waiting for Nigel and waiting for the rat.

A few days later, Marina arrived on my doorstep with a small parcel in her hand.

"For you," she said, smiling. "Just a little something."

I had to ask her in for coffee. The parcel contained a copy of Elizabeth David's *A Book of Mediterranean Food*.

"The lovely thing about cooking is that when the pleasure's shared it's somehow doubled," Marina said. "You won't be able to get a lot of the ingredients in Lydmouth. Perhaps I can find what you need in London."

During the next two weeks, I saw Marina regularly. I even asked her to lunch. Many of Elizabeth David's recipes were really very simple. I found one – tarte à l'oignon et aux oeufs – which turned out to be very like the flans I used to cook Charles. Marina said my tarte was quite marvellous.

Why did she do all this? Why was she such a hypocrite? There were two possible explanations: either she felt guilty about stealing my husband, or she was doing it because she derived a malicious pleasure from pretending to be my friend.

On the second occasion I had lunch with her, I was sure I could smell a faint blueness in the air, an uneasy hint that lingered in the nostrils. After the meal, I helped Marina carry the plates into the kitchen.

I sniffed.

"Can you smell something?" Marina asked.

"Well..."

"I keep thinking I can. I must turn out the cupboards. And the larder."

No more was said about it until a day or two later, when Marina drove me up to Cheltenham for a matinée at the Everyman. In the interval she brought up the subject again.

"Do you remember that smell in the kitchen? I think it might be drains."

"Have there been complaints from other flats?"

"Not as far as I know. I've got someone coming to have a look."

Two days later, she came to tea and gave me the next instalment. Unfortunately the plumber had turned out to be rather good at his job. He had soon realised that the smell was not from the drains. He pulled out the cooker and found the decaying body of the rat squeezed between the cupboard and the wall.

"It was quite disgusting," Marina said. "It looked as it smelled, if you know what I mean. Anyway, the plumber was quite marvellous. He got the wretched thing out of the flat and now things are beginning to return to normal."

"Isn't it odd having a rat in a modern flat?"

"Apparently they are very agile creatures, and you never know where they are going to turn up. The plumber suggested that I get someone in." Marina shivered, rather theatrically. "Just in case there are any more."

"We had rats in the stable," I said. "The rat-catcher soon sorted them out. I've got his address if you'd like it."

Marina took out a little leather-bound diary and made a note of the details. As she jotted them down, the brooch gleamed on her cardigan. Platinum and unlucky opals.

The rat man came and left poison under the cooker and in the larder. Marina told me all about his reluctance to leave the poison in the kitchen, about the strictness of his instructions to her. This was just before she went up to London for the weekend. She was going to a party, she said, where she hoped Elizabeth David might be present.

"I know I've only met her once, but I feel I know her really well – as well as I know you – just through her writing." Marina patted my arm – she was always touching me, which was one of the things I disliked most. "I'll tell Mrs. David I've been making converts in Lydmouth."

I was in a quandary for the whole weekend. Should I or shouldn't I? It was such a good opportunity, presented to me, as it were, on a plate. It would make up for the rather tame performance of the rat. I didn't want to hurt Marina, of course, or not seriously. But there would be very little risk of that. The amount of poison that would kill a rat would surely give a human being nothing more than a mild bilious attack.

All weekend I toyed with the idea. *What if? What if?* On Sunday evening, when it was dark, I put on the headscarf and the raincoat and left the house. I had the torch and the key of Marina's flat in my pocket.

Everything went as smoothly as last time. In the refrigerator was a saucepan containing what I now knew was ratatouille. It smelt quite disgusting. The rat poison was on saucers, one under the cooker and the other in the larder. I took a little of the poison from each and rearranged what was left on the saucers so that they both looked untouched. I stirred the poison into the ratatouille. To my relief, it seemed to dissolve very quickly. I wondered if it would taste. With luck the ratatouille was so strongly flavoured that it would mask any additions.

I went home. That night I dreamed of Nigel. Funnily enough I had always dreamed more about Nigel than about Charles. On Monday morning, I woke with a light heart. Now I could put the past behind me and look to the future. In a sense, there had been nothing personal about what I'd done at Raglan Court. It had not been a question of being vindictive – merely of doing my duty.

I was washing up after breakfast when a man walked past the kitchen window and knocked on the back door. It was the rat-catcher again. He was a grubby little man with a baggy tweed jacket and a collarless shirt.

"Morning, ma'am. Just come to see how the little fellows are getting on."

"I really don't know."

"No dead 'uns?"

"Who knows?"

"Shall I take a look? See if they need a second helping?"

A few minutes later, the rat-catcher came back. "They took it all. I put down a bit more."

"Good." I opened my handbag and took out my purse. "Were there – were there any bodies?"

He chuckled. "Gone back to their nests. Give 'em a choice, they like to die in their own beds – just like us, eh?"

I paid the man. He wanted to stay and gossip – in my experience, men are far worse gossips than women – but luckily we were interrupted by the ring of the front doorbell.

It was a telegram. My heart lurched because telegrams usually mean bad news, apart from those connected with births and weddings; and I had nothing to do with either...I tore it open.

BOAT DOCKED LATE LAST NIGHT. COMING DOWN TODAY. ROOM BOOKED AT BULL. SEE YOU FIVEISH. NIGEL.

That was typical of my brother-in-law. Nigel was so thoughtful. When Charles was alive, of course, Nigel used to stay at the house. But now Charles was dead, the situation was different. Lydmouth wasn't London. If Nigel and I were alone at night under the same roof, tongues might wag. People might even remember that before I had become engaged to Charles, I had seen a good deal of Nigel.

By half-past four I was as ready as I could be – the lounge fire burning brightly, the brasses in the hall gleaming, the water near boiling point in the kettle, the tea tray laid. As I sat waiting, all sorts of foolish thoughts about Nigel chased through my mind. *What if? What if?*

He rang the doorbell at twenty-three minutes past five.

"Anne – wonderful to see you." He swept me into his arms. "I'm so sorry about Charles." He hugged me tightly, then stood back. "Sorry I'm late. Train was delayed. Nothing works properly in this country."

Nigel was taller than Charles had been, and age had been kinder to him. As a young man, he had been gawky and had difficulty in talking to a girl without blushing. The war had changed all that. I brought the tea in and we chatted for a while – mainly about Charles.

"You must be wondering about the money side," Nigel said. "No need. As far as I am concerned, you can stay in the house for as long as you like. You own fifty per cent of it now, anyway. And Charles's share in the shop comes to you, so that should give you a decent income, even if we have to pay out a bit more in wages."

I asked him how long he was staying in Lydmouth.

"Only a couple of nights, I'm afraid. I'm popping over to Paris on Thursday." He grinned at me. "I'll see if I can find you some perfume."

"It's a shame you can't stay longer."

His eyes met mine. "I'll be back."

"I wonder – could I ask you to help me with Charles's things? His clothes, for example. And I've not really been through the business papers in the bureau."

"Of course. When would suit you?"

"Come to lunch tomorrow – we can sort everything out afterwards." He hesitated.

"I'll see if I can do something interesting," I said brightly. "I've been experimenting lately. I love Elizabeth David. Her recipes are mouth-watering."

"Yes." He glanced at his watch. "Elizabeth David, eh? You've been acquiring cosmopolitan tastes in my absence."

"I try." I smiled at him. "Even with the shortages, there's no excuse not to be a little adventurous in the kitchen."

Nigel stood up and tossed his cigarette end in the fire. He ran a fingertip along the spines of the Kipling edition in the bookcase. I shivered. He turned to face me.

"Oh – by the way: I owe you some money."

"Really?"

"I asked Charles to pay a debt for me. He mentioned he'd done it in his last letter. A hundred and ninety-odd pounds."

A hundred and eighty-nine pounds, nineteen shillings and eleven pence?

I felt as if a horde of insects were crawling across my skin. "I'd noticed the cheque. To a jewellers, wasn't it?" With immense effort I forced a smile. "Who was the lucky lady?"

Nigel's cheeks darkened. The young man I had known before the war was suddenly not so very far away. "I – I suppose I'd better tell you. I hope you won't be shocked. The thing is, in the last few years, when I've been in Lydmouth, I've had a sort of on-and-off friendship with a woman. A special friendship."

"And Charles knew?"

He nodded, took out his cigarette case and fiddled with the catch. "But I went to Paris on a business trip in the spring, and I met Ghislaine. One thing led to another – well, in fact she and I are getting married in the new year."

He paused, looking at me, waiting for congratulations. I couldn't speak.

"But there was still this – this other lady. That had to end, obviously. But I wanted to get her something as a keepsake. Unfortunately, I had to go to Tanganyika…"

He managed to open the case at last. He took out a cigarette and rolled it around in his fingers. Crumbs of tobacco dribbled down to the hearthrug.

"So I asked dear old Charles to buy her a present. It was while you were in hospital. A piece of jewellery – something quite decent. I gave him a rough idea of how much I wanted to spend and left him to get on with it. We were going to settle up when I got home. I – I do hope you don't think too badly of me."

Nigel looked at me. I shook my head, which seemed to satisfy him. Men are so easily satisfied.

"It wasn't serious," he said, as if that excused it. "Just a bit of fun. Men tend to sow a few wild oats before they settle down. Women are different."

Were they? If all women were different, how on earth could the men sow their wild oats?

He looked at his watch again. "Oh lord, I must go. I'll see you tomorrow."

We went into the hall. He bent towards me and his lips brushed my cheek.

"You've always been a good pal. You're not shocked? Charles thought you would be."

"Don't be silly." I smiled up at him. "Boys will be boys."

I closed the door behind him. There was nothing left of Nigel in the lounge except crumbs on a plate, a puddle of tea at the bottom of a cup and golden flecks of tobacco on the hearthrug. I ran my finger along the spines of the Kiplings. I tried to think about Ghislaine but she was too abstract, too foreign for me to grasp. She wasn't flesh and blood like

Marina. Marina, I thought idly, would be home by now.

One of the books was a little out of line. It was *Stalky and Co*, those silly schoolboy stories which had been Nigel and Charles's favourite. Boys will be boys. A buff-coloured slip of paper protruded from the pages, presumably a bookmark. I took out the book, suddenly curious to re-read the story about the dead cat and the smell. I glanced at the bookmark. It was a telegram.

For a moment, I thought that Nigel's telegram to me must have found its way into *Stalky and Co*. But that telegram was still propped up on the mantelpiece behind the clock. This one was addressed to Charles. It was dated in September, while I was in hospital.

YOU'RE WELCOME OLD BOY. WHILE THE CAT'S AWAY. HAVE FUN. NIGEL.

I sat down in the chair that was still warm from Nigel's body. I read and re-read those eleven words. Nigel had sent the telegram from Suez, when he was on his way to East Africa. Suddenly many things were clear. Nigel, Charles and Marina – they had all betrayed me in their different ways, even Nigel.

Nigel worst of all.

It was growing very cold. I stood up and put more coal on the fire. *A Book of Mediterranean Food* was on the sideboard. I riffled through the pages, looking for a suitable recipe for tomorrow. Something with a strong flavour. I knew that, whatever I cooked, whatever it tasted like, Nigel would eat it with apparent relish because he felt guilty.

A little later, I went outside. It was a cold night, with stars like diamonds. Frost gleamed on the path to the stable. I opened the door. Moonlight streamed across the floor and showed me the untouched saucer in the corner. I picked it up and left the stable.

As I was walking back to the house with the saucer in my hand, I heard the sound of an ambulance. The bell drew closer and closer. It was coming down Victoria Road from the direction of Raglan Court and Marina's flat.

In the freezing night air, I stood still and listened to the ambulance as it slowed for the junction with the Chepstow Road. It turned left and sped towards the hospital.

What if? What if?

NOWHERE TO BE FOUND

Mat Coward

The last word he said to me was 'topography'.

When the phone rings late at night I always look at the clock first and *then* answer the phone. A sign of chronic pessimism, according to my last girlfriend – always anticipating bad news. Well, there's an obvious retort to that.

"Jerry? You've got to come and get me. How soon can you get here?"

Seven minutes past two in the morning. It was November, and big winds were herding hailstones against my bedroom window. "Alan? What do you mean, come and get you? Where are you?"

"I'm at home, of course. Wake *up*, Jerry. I really need your help here, man. I'm leaving Jackie, right now, and I…are you *awake*, Jerry?"

"I'm awake, calm down. You and Jackie are splitting up? What's happened?"

"I'm leaving her, you've got to come and get me. You should be here in under two hours if you put your foot down. OK?"

He rang off. I sat there thinking for a while, feeling slightly sick from a combination of the sudden awakening and the beer I'd drunk the night before. Then I had a shower, got dressed, and set off for Wiltshire.

The drive down from London took me just over three hours door to door, in terrible weather and over unfamiliar terrain. Alan was hopping by the time I arrived.

"Where have you *been*, Jerry? I've been leaving messages on your bloody machine for the last hour and a half." He didn't shake hands, or smile, or even say hello. He'd been waiting for me outside the cottage, at the far end of what was little more than a mud lane. I was impressed with myself for having found the place; I'd only been there once before, when I'd helped Alan and Jackie move in.

"Got here as quick as I could, mate," I said, opening the car door but not getting out – I wasn't sure if I was *supposed* to get out or not. "So, what's the plan? Got any luggage?"

"Yeah. Wait here." He turned and walked back up the path towards the cottage. His back was as soaked through as his front. He looked freezing cold, but he also looked as if he was unaware that he was freezing cold.

Just as he reached the cottage door, I called after him. "Alan?"

He paused without turning, his irritation visible even through that weather. "Yeah?"

"Good to see you, mate."

"Just wait there, OK?"

I waited there, the car radio playing, the motor thrumming, for five minutes before I eventually thought *Sod it, the least I'm due is a slash and a cigarette.* I got out of the car, walked up the path and knocked on the door. *Cup of tea and a piece of toast wouldn't hurt, either.*

Jackie opened the door. She yanked it towards her as if it was sticking from flood damage, then let her hand slide off the doorknob as she turned and walked away. She didn't look at me.

I followed her into the kitchen, at the back of the house. She was wearing a dressing gown over a pink nylon nightie. Blue nylon slippers. The general air of someone who has realised that giving up smoking all those years earlier did not, after all, placate the gods sufficiently that they would evermore keep sadness from her hearth. Her face was grey, except where it was red. If a half-decent paramedic had turned up at that moment, he'd have prescribed a dozen full strength fags and a pint of vodka. *Then* breakfast.

"Sorry to intrude, Jackie," I said, from the kitchen doorway. She sat at the table, her back to me. "I just wanted to…obviously, I don't know what's going on here, that's your business. I just wanted to use the loo, if that's all right?"

She didn't answer, but then it was a pretty daft question. No matter how much someone's life is falling apart, they're hardly likely to respond to such a request with: "No, you bastard! Go and do it on the compost heap!"

I had a pee, a bit of a wash and brush up, drank some cold water from the tap in cupped hands; I didn't reckon a pot of tea and a plate of scones were going to be appearing in that kitchen any time in the near future.

I could hear Alan still moving about upstairs, so I sat down at the kitchen table. Eventually Jackie did look at me, but she needn't have bothered: there was nothing in the look that said anything.

"Well," I said. "This is a bad day."

She began crying, silently, her eyes fixed on mine. Now that she'd started looking at me, it seemed, she couldn't stop.

"Do you know where I'm taking him to, at all?" I asked. "Because I don't."

She shook her head, very short, surprisingly careful shakes, and wrinkled up her face and cried some more. I'd thought she *wouldn't* speak, but I realised now that she couldn't speak. Another gulping of sobs caught her by surprise, like sudden vomit. She clamped two fingers over her lips, as if fearful that if she allowed her mouth to fall open even a crack, all her vitals would slip-slide out and pool around her feet.

I reached over and patted her arm, which didn't seem to help enormously. I didn't know what else to do – I hardly knew the girl, for God's sake, I'd only met her once before. Twice, maybe.

Footsteps clattered on the carpetless stairs, and Alan appeared. He was carrying nothing but a duffel bag. "What are you doing here? I said wait in the car."

"I needed to use the loo," I said, and immediately wished I hadn't offered him an explanation at all. The rude, ungrateful bastard! It wasn't even as if we were close friends. We were *old* friends, certainly, known each other forever, and I loved him like a brother. But your brother isn't usually your closest friend, is he?

We went out and got into the car. Neither of us said goodbye to Jackie, and she didn't speak to, or look at, either of us. It was still raining. People often say, "I must be mad to do this," but at that moment I really did wonder if I was actually mad. Or if one of us was, anyway.

"Is that all you've got? One duffel bag?"

Alan looked down at the duffel bag between his knees. "That's it," he said. He didn't seem inclined to say more, so after a brief pause to search for loose cigarettes in the glove compartment (there weren't any), I fired up the motor and headed off in what I hoped was the direction of the motorway.

"You got any smokes, Alan? I ran out on the way down."

He shook his head. "I packed it in."

"All right," I said. "I'll stop somewhere. Anyway, be breakfast time soon, right?"

He wasn't talkative – he wasn't in fact saying anything, which is untalkative by anybody's standards – but that didn't surprise me. He'd been with Jackie a good few years, on and off, and any breakup that occurs in the early hours of the morning is, by definition, a sudden break-up.

I couldn't keep silent, though. Not on a journey of that length. Not with no sleep, no breakfast and no cigarettes. Time dragged. So did distance – I didn't know my way around there, the weather was no better, I was driving slowly.

Every minute or so I'd say something like "Well, this is a bad night," or "Maybe things'll look better in a day or two". But I had to be careful what I said; careful not to sound too disapproving. Because the truth was, I *did* disapprove. I didn't know the ins and outs of this particular situation, obviously, but I couldn't help feeling that a man like Alan, who'd had three wives before he was thirty, was more often than not likely to be the author of his own misfortunes.

And he knew I disapproved. Which is why I tried to keep things light.

"So where is it I'm taking you?" I said, after a few more silent miles, and with the bloody motorway still playing hide and seek in the country darkness. "Back to my place, is it? Because that's fine if it is, goes without saying, my floor is your floor. Might even find you a spare pillow if you're good."

"Stop here," said Alan, and I was so shocked that I obeyed him immediately. He started struggling with the seat belt. Its release catch had always been dodgy.

"What's the matter? You feel sick?"

"You can drop me here," he said.

I peered out of the windscreen. I couldn't see much because of the weather, but I got the impression that there wouldn't be much to see even on a clear day. Just hedges and fields. No houses for miles around. "Alan, we're in the middle of nowhere. We're on a road with no pavements, for God's sake. We're on a road with no pavements, it's raining and we're Londoners."

He freed himself from the death-trap seat belt, and started struggling with the door handle. A deeply non-mechanical man, Alan; never learned how to ride a bike, let alone drive a car.

"Look, Alan, I don't feel happy about leaving you here. I mean, at this time of night, in this weather – what are you going to do, hitchhike? I can take you where you want to go."

He got out of the car, slung his duffel bag over his shoulder, and ducked his head down to speak to me. He started with a half-smile, the nearest thing to a friendly face I'd seen all night. "No, don't worry, Jerry, I'm not hitching. I've got a friend lives just near, I'll crash there for a day or two while I sort myself out."

I'd never seen anyone lie so obviously in all my life, but what could I do? "What's this place called, then?" I asked, trying for a tone somewhere between sceptical and jokey.

Alan shook his head. "I don't know it by name, exactly, I just recognise the topography." He began walking in the opposite direction to the one in which the car was pointing. Within a very short time he was invisible.

I called after him, "I can drive you to your friend's house, that's no problem," but I don't know if he heard me.

What could I do? You can't force a grown man to stay in a car, no matter how hard it's raining. As I leant over to close the door that he'd left ajar, I spotted a cigarette, bent but unbroken, under the passenger seat. So I sat and smoked that, and after a while the sky became lighter and I was able to find my way back to the motorway and home.

*   *   *

It wasn't until three years later that I went looking for Alan. Perhaps I should explain that.

Alan never became a Missing Person, except in the crudely literal sense that he was a person, who was missing. No official body ever listed him as missing, because nobody ever reported him gone. He hadn't had a regular job in years. He had no mortgage, no driving licence, no credit cards, no bank account. Alan Hallsworth was one of those people whose only proof of existence is their heartbeat, who never trouble the computers of the world, either with their presence or their absence.

His parents had divorced when he was twenty, long after he'd left home, and Alan had achieved the impressive feat of becoming permanently estranged from both of them. I remember him boasting to me about that, one sober night. "I have literally," he told me, "*literally* got an address book with no addresses in it." Another night, equilibrium restored by Guinness, he'd changed his mind about that. "I didn't mean that I'd *literally* got an empty address book," he explained. "I just meant that I don't know where my parents live, either of them, and don't wish to know. I haven't actually got a *literal* address book, empty or otherwise. Don't need one – don't know anyone."

His wife, of course, might have reported him missing, but when I once suggested it to Jackie, on the phone, she sounded puzzled. "But I kicked him out, Jerry. I mean, you know, him not being here sort of goes without saying, doesn't it?"

Missing Person, of course, is a definition rather than an occupation, and it's one that not every person fits, even when they do happen to be missing.

And me? I never reported Alan missing because I never believed for a moment that he was a missing *person*. Almost from the start, I thought of him as a missing corpse.

*   *   *

Two weeks after my pointless journey to and from Wiltshire, I still hadn't heard from Alan and I was beginning to get worried. He didn't know many people, and I'd been certain that he and his duffel bag would end up on my sofa before long. After all, where else do you go when you're running away from home but to London? No offence to Wiltshire, but it's definitely a *from* place, not a *to* place.

That was when I phoned Jackie. She was no longer unable to speak without crying, and made it unambiguously clear to me that her marriage, her husband, her husband's duffel bag, and her husband's friends were all part of her past, not her present. Goodbye.

So, I thought: he must be dead. If he was alive and well, he'd have been in touch with me. If he was alive and in trouble, the authorities would have been in touch with his wife. Therefore, he must be dead – and undiscovered. A missing ex-person.

As weeks and months passed, Alan's supposed death and disappearance faded from the forefront of my mind, the way even the biggest things in life will under the daily onslaught of little matters. I thought of him most at Christmastimes, when he didn't send me a card. He never *had* sent me a card, you see, not once in all his life, and I'd always sent him one, and it had always rankled. But now, I couldn't really blame him for not sending me a card, because there wasn't really much he could do about it.

And then, as the fourth Christmas approached, I suddenly thought: *I've got to know.* Just like that, really: *I've got to know.* After all, it was my car he got out of.

The drive down still took me three hours. The weather was OK this time, but I still didn't know the way.

The cottage in which Alan and Jackie had served the greater part of their marital sentence was uninhabited now, empty and boarded up. I sat outside it for a while, smoking, listening to the shipping forecast, wondering where to start.

Three years earlier, I'd asked Jackie on the phone "Was there another woman?"

"*A*nother woman?" she'd replied. "There were *several* other women. But not one that would have taken him in."

If Alan was alive he'd have been in touch. I'd known him since we were both kids, and I don't think there'd ever been a period of three consecutive months during which we didn't speak to each other at least once.

He had been killed deliberately, because if it had been an accident his body would have been found, and word would have trickled through to me eventually, through one twisting conduit or another.

I finished my cigarette, turned the car in the craterous road, and set off slowly to try and retrace the route we'd driven on the night he left. After about an hour of dawdling, reversing, peering and swearing, I gave up. One bit of rural road looks much like another, unless it's where you live.

Once winter's early darkness had turned my mission from futile to farcical, I stopped at the next pub, which happened to be one I'd seen a few hours before, on my drive down. I reckoned it was about ten minutes' walk from Alan and Jackie's old place. Their local, by any chance?

I needed a drink. Until that day, I hadn't said the word "murder" to myself – not out loud, so to speak. The logic was solid enough, and had been there all along, but I suppose acknowledging it was just one of those jobs I'd preferred to put off indefinitely, like fixing a leaky tap.

Murder, I thought, as I sipped a pint slowly. In which case, given the truncated nature of Alan's social circle, there could only be two categories of suspect: his wife, or one of his girlfriends. (Not a wronged husband? No – Alan put it about a bit, before, during and after his various marriages, but he never to my knowledge slept with anyone else's wife. "I have my standards," he used to say. "They're twisted ones, I know, but they're the only ones I've got, so I keep 'em.")

In my mind, as I drank, I auditioned Jackie for the part of vengeful assassin. Supposing, when Alan got out of my car, he had walked or hitched back to the cottage. He'd changed his mind, he wasn't leaving home after all. It had just been one of those rows that ignite in marriages, and then burn themselves out. Now I thought about it, his lack of luggage perhaps suggested a certain lack of resolution. You don't walk out of a marriage with just a duffel bag, do you?

All right, I thought, towards the bottom of the beer. He arrives back on his own doorstep, tells his briefly abandoned wife the good news: "I've decided to give you another chance, you lucky cow." So why does she kill him?

Well, for all I knew he performed the same show once a month. Leaving, coming back, expecting (demanding?) gratitude. And this time was once too often. Being left by your husband would be bad enough, I imagined, but being left on a regular basis would be even more humiliating. Worse – it'd be *irritating*.

So much for the wife. What about the mistress?

When he insisted on getting out of my car, Alan had claimed that he was going to seek shelter with a friend. At the time, I hadn't believed him. It had crossed my mind then that perhaps he was going home, and was embarrassed to have me drive him there, but now it struck me that there really could have been a friend. She'd have had long, dark hair and big buttocks, no doubt, as did Jackie, and Susan before Jackie, and the Spanish one, whose name I could never recall, before Susan.

But then, what was the story there? Alan gets out of the car, walks to his girlfriend's house, says "I've finally left my wife, let me in, it's raining" – and she kills him? No, that doesn't work. All she'd have to say, if she wasn't keen on the idea, was "Grow up, Alan. Go home and sleep it off, kiddo."

By the time my pint was dead beyond doubt, I'd talked myself out of the murdering mistress scenario. Which, unavoidably, meant that I'd talked myself into the murdering missus...

I needed another drink, and maybe a sandwich to soak it up. While I was waiting for the sole barmaid to serve a man at the other end of the counter with a bag of peanuts (a transaction which seemed to involve a longer conversation than most people have with their mothers on Christmas Day), I eavesdropped a large, red-faced man with a local accent giving directions to an elderly couple who had wandered into the pub holding a road map upside down.

"Excuse me," I said, when the old folk had departed smiling, with their map the right way up. "You seem to know your way around these parts."

"I should do, yeah. Been running deliveries round here for years. Plus I live just up the road. Why – you lost?"

"Well, not exactly. Look, could I buy you a drink, if you've got a moment? I'd really like to pick your brains a bit."

He shrugged. "I wouldn't say no to a lager top."

We took our drinks over to a table, and I pondered my approach. *I need some village gossip* probably wasn't tactful. I decided to rely on ritual and feel my way.

"Cheers."

"Cheers."

"Jerry, by the way." I stuck out my hand.

"Oh, right. Norman. Cheers."

"Cheers." We drank, smacked our respective lips, put down our respective glasses. I leant my elbows on the table. "Look, Norman, hope you don't mind me waylaying you like this. Thing is, I've driven all the way down here from London to look up some old friends."

"Round here?"

"Right, yep, just up the road here. Haven't seen them for ages, and obviously I should have phoned first, because when I got to their cottage I found it was abandoned. I mean, you know, actually boarded up!"

Norman shook his head sadly. "Lot of that round this way. No jobs, see?"

"Ah? Right, right. Terrible, really, what's happening to the countryside. But the thing was, I was wondering if you might have known them – might know what happened to them. Alan and Jackie Hallsworth."

He looked at me suspiciously then, I thought, and I wondered if I'd underdone the subtlety, or whether I was merely receiving the standard amount of suspicion awarded by a villager to an outsider who asks questions. I couldn't tell, having never lived in a village.

Norman took his time swallowing a few mouthfuls of beer before he replied. "Well...Alan and Jackie. Yes, I did know them. Not to talk to, like, but to nod to. They used to come in here now and then, weekends and that."

"How long have they been gone?"

"You're an old friend, you say?"

"Yeah, you know, we sort of lost touch. The way you do, you know."

He drank some more, and watched me over the rim of his glass as he did so. "Well," he said eventually. "If you've not been in touch for some while, then you probably won't know. They split up."

"Alan and Jackie?"

"Yeah. Afraid so. Few years ago now, must be."

"Oh God, that's awful! What happened, do you know?"

Norman shook his head. "Didn't know them that well. From what I heard at the time, Alan just walked out one night, and a month or so later Jackie was gone, too. Back to her mother's, apparently. She waited around for a while, I daresay, just to see if he was coming back."

"Which he never did?" I asked.

Norman studied me again, but this time without using the beer as camouflage. His suspicion now was overt, though not, I thought, hostile. "Never saw him again. Took off with one of his women, I suppose. No offence, what with you being a mate of his, but – well, he was a bit of a lad, if you know what I mean."

I couldn't believe my luck. This was exactly the conversation I wanted: a discussion of Alan's infidelities, preferably with names and places. But as I started to assure Norman that I knew exactly what he meant about my old friend's ways, he abruptly stood up.

"Got to be going now. She'll be expecting me back soon." He stuck out his hand. "Nice to meet you. My advice, look for Jackie at her mum's. Cardiff, somewhere, I seem to recall. Can't help beyond that, I'm afraid."

Damn, I thought. I must have asked one question too many. Enough to turn a natural gossip into a loyal neighbour. Even so, I felt that what Norman had said – and what he had presumably left the pub in order to avoid saying – told me quite a lot. Alan was a known philanderer, active locally. He had disappeared, and shortly afterwards, so had his wife.

I left my second pint half-finished on the table, and walked out to my car. I couldn't put this off any longer: it was time to visit the scene of the crime.

Whoever had boarded up Jackie and Alan's cottage – the landlord, presumably – had done a thorough job. I quickly saw that I wouldn't be able to get into the house without some difficulty, not to mention some tools. For now, I'd have to make do with a quick look round the garden. The body was more likely to be in the garden than the house, anyway, I figured. I couldn't really imagine Jackie burying her husband beneath the floorboards.

There was a fair bit of garden, very overgrown now. Most of the land was at the side of the house, with only a small stretch at the front. The back yard was mainly laid to patio – and that, I remembered, had already been there when Alan and Jackie moved in.

I kept a torch in the car, but not a spade, so a proper search was out of the immediate question. As I prodded around more or less aimlessly amid the brambles and frost-blackened weeds, I felt fear, as well as frustration – fear that I wouldn't have the guts or the constancy to come back again, better prepared. And fear that I would.

To do either would be to confront a question about myself that I would sooner have left unanswered: was I a man who believed that one is obliged to make sense of death? I'd never made, or especially tried to make, any sense out of life. But death, especially someone else's death, was somehow a different kettle of ball games.

"I've got a spade here."

The words, quietly spoken somewhere behind my left shoulder, made me leap, gasp and drop the torch, which landed a few yards away in a patch of mud. Norman picked it up and shone it in my face.

"I saw you here earlier today, sitting outside in your car. I come by once or twice a week, to check everything's still as it was. I followed you around the lanes, and into the pub. I'd have spoken to you if you hadn't spoken to me. And now here you are, back again. Didn't need to follow you this time. Guessed where you were headed."

I cleared my voice before speaking, but still it croaked. "From what I said in the pub?"

Norman dropped the torch's beam from my face, to the ground between us. "Didn't know how much you knew. Still don't know how you found out. But you know something, that's clear." He passed me a heavy, agricultural spade, blade end first, and said: "Over here."

The spot he led me to was deep in a small thicket of horticultural neglect, hidden from any view, not too near the house or the road. I could see his logic. As I took a moment to gather my thoughts before beginning the sweaty task of digging my own grave, I went through the motions of considering my options. What it came down to was this: Norman was a big bloke, a physical-looking man, and I wasn't. I hoped he had a gun, or a blunt object, or at worst a knife. He hadn't struck me as the naturally violent type. If I did what he wanted me to do, I hoped he'd end it quickly. End *me* quickly. If I tried to escape, he'd catch me, and probably finish me with the spade.

That was what it came down to, my last attempt to make sense of death: that I'd rather die by a gun than by a spade.

"It was your wife, then, was it? Alan was seeing your wife?" I was playing for time, of course, but only for more time to rest before beginning the digging. I was too far gone in fear and listless despair to try for a higher prize.

"My wife?" said Norman. "I'm not married. I can't be, see, I have to look after my mum, she's been poorly."

As I turned the first sod, I was thinking: "I don't know that many more people than Alan did. How long will it take them to realise I'm dead?" And I was thinking, if this bloke's a psycho killer, he's a bloody bone idle one. Two victims in three years? You wouldn't think they'd allow it in these deregulated days. You'd think they'd have got some guy in Korea to do it for half the wages, twice the productivity.

But then I realised that I was making too many assumptions. Norman had only two victims that I knew of – he could have had four hundred that I didn't know of. I might be doing him an injustice, he might be the archetypal New Model Worker. I was pleased to think that. There's comfort in numbers, even when there isn't safety. Stupid, but true. Stupid, but human.

Anyway, I dug down a few more feet, and after a while I unearthed Alan.

"I'm to be sharing then, am I?" I said, putting down my spade. I was quite pleased with that. It showed a certain character, I thought, to go out with a quip on your lips.

Norman reached into his coat pocket. Gun or knife, I wondered. Gun, I hoped. Blades are too personal.

It was a mobile phone.

"You call them," said Norman, handing me the phone. "I'm no good at all that."

"Call them…?" My croak became a whisper.

"The police," said Norman. "Would you mind? I get all, you know, tongue-tied. With officials."

I looked at the phone. I didn't know what it meant. I looked at Norman. I didn't know what he meant, either. "You *didn't* kill Alan?"

"I didn't mean to!" he said, his face flushing in the torchlight as if I'd offended or embarrassed him. "You know what these roads are like, round here, in winter. I never even saw him. First I saw of him, was when I stopped and went back to see what the noise was." He choked, snorted his nose clear. "I thought it was a badger."

"When was this?" I said. To my relief, I found that my hands had stopped shaking sufficiently for me to light a cigarette. I drew the smoke in deep, and felt it save my life. I offered the packet to Norman.

"Ta. I'm supposed to have given up last Christmas, but you know… When was it? Three years ago. Found out later Jackie'd kicked him out that same night. He must have been hitching, I suppose, though he was going in the wrong direction, silly bugger. Probably pissed or stoned, he usually was."

He took the cigarette down like an outfielder gulping water. I lit him another. "Ta, you sure you got enough? Ta, then."

"Why didn't you call the police? After the accident, I mean."

Norman shook his head, as if to dislodge the shame from his face. "I'd been made redundant three times in five years. Company I was with then, they've got this policy – you have an accident and you're out. Doesn't matter if it's your fault or not. I couldn't allow it, do you see that?" He nodded towards the open grave. "If I'd lost that job just then, the debt would have buried us. I'm not kidding, me and my mother, we'd have been buried alive." He laughed. "Got the push a year later, anyway. Rationalisation. It's just me and my old van now."

"So you put him here."

"Not straight off. I kept him in my shed for a while, but then when Jackie handed in the keys to this place – well, it belongs to my mum, you see. And I knew we'd not be able to let it again in a hurry, not with the way things are."

I was still holding the phone, and I still couldn't make sense of it. "I thought you were going to kill me, Norman. I thought that was what the spade was all about."

"Jesus!" Norman threw his cigarette away. "Bloody hell, man, where could you get an idea like that? I'm not a nutter!"

"Of course not," I said, quickly. "It's only that—"

"It was you asking questions, see? I mean this –" again he nodded towards the grave – "this was never intended to be permanent. Just until, you know…my mum. But then you came down, looking for Alan."

"I don't get it." What I meant was: I don't get why you're not going to kill me. Always assuming you're not.

"I knew Alan and Jackie a bit. More than what I said earlier in the pub. We weren't real mates or anything, but when I came round to get the rent sometimes we used to have a drink, like, bit of a smoke, bit of a chat. So I knew Jackie wouldn't miss him, see what I mean? Even if she hadn't kicked him out, she'd just have thought he'd walked out. He would have sooner or later, too."

True, I thought. Alan wasn't one for sticking at things.

"And I knew there was no one else gave a shit about him, dead or alive. No family, nothing like that. So I thought – well, bit hard on him, bit hard on me, but no point in making matters worse. It wasn't as if I was causing anyone else pain, do you see? By keeping quiet."

"But then I showed up."

Norman nodded, and tears appeared on his cheeks. "At first I thought maybe you were a debt collector. Child Support, whatever. But debt collectors don't go looking for bodies in gardens. See, if he had someone who cared about him enough to come looking…well, that changes everything, doesn't it?" He gave a huge, rasping sigh, and sat down on the wet earth. "You call the police, then, will you?"

The mobile phone still didn't make sense. It did to Norman, perhaps, but not to me. I gave it back to him. I gave him the spade, too.

"You can fill in," I said. "I've done enough digging for one lifetime."

*   *   *

When I got home, there was a Christmas card waiting for me. Just one. It had a return name and address on the back: Jackie Peters (Hallsworth), Cardiff. I read it without taking my coat off.

"Sorry not to have been in touch for so long," she wrote, "but it's taken me a while to sort myself out. Hope you're still at the same address! I hope also that things are OK with you, and that you might drop me a line some time." Then she came to the point. "Are you in touch with Alan at all? I don't have an address for him. If you hear from him, could you give him my address? Tell him not to panic, nothing heavy, it's just that I feel we have some unfinished business."

I got myself a drink, opened a new packet of cigarettes. Finally I took my coat off, and switched the central heating on.

It had occurred to me during the drive home that the only reason Alan got out of my car on the night he died was that he was being driven mad by my silent nagging. So he'd got out, walked along a country road in the dark, and got himself killed.

"Dear Jackie," I wrote. "It's good to hear from you. I have often wondered what became of you. I'm afraid I can't help you regarding Alan. I haven't spoken to him since the night you and he parted. I have come to believe, Jackie, that it's not always possible to make sense of death—"

I swore, screwed up the letter, and started again.

"...not always possible to make sense of loss, and that sometimes it's best not to try. It sounds like you've got yourself a life there in Wales, and I truly believe that you should concentrate on the present, not the past. I hope you don't find my advice impertinent. And I do hope you'll keep in touch. There's not many of the old crowd left, we should stick together! With love from Jerry."

I hadn't bought any Christmas cards, so I put the letter in an ordinary envelope, addressed it and stamped it and went out to post it before I had a chance to do a lot of useless thinking.

INTERIOR, WITH CORPSE

Peter Lovesey

Her chestnut brown hair curved in an S shape across the carpet, around a gleaming pool of blood. She was wearing an old-fashioned petticoat, white with thin shoulder straps. The lace hem had been drawn up her thigh, exposing stocking-tops and suspenders. The stockings had seams. Her shoes, too, dated the incident; black suede, with Louis heels. One of them had fallen off and lay on its side, close to the edge of a stone fireplace. The hearthstones were streaked with crimson and a blood-stained poker had been dropped there.

But what really shocked was the location. Beyond any doubt, this was Wing Commander Ashton's living room. Anyone who had been to the house would recognise the picture above the fireplace of a Spitfire shooting down a Messerschmitt over the fields of Kent in the sunshine of an August afternoon in 1940. They would spot the squadron insignia and medals mounted on black velvet in the glass display cabinet attached to the wall; the miniature aircraft carved in ebony and ranged along the mantelpiece. His favourite armchair stood in its usual place to the right of the hearth. Beside it, the old-fashioned standard lamp and the small rosewood table with his collection of family photographs. True, some things had altered; these days the carpet was not an Axminster, but some man-made fibre thing in dark blue, fitted wall-to-wall. And one or two bits of furniture had gone, notably a writing desk that would have been called a bureau, with a manual typewriter on it – an Imperial – and the paper and carbons under the platen. It was now replaced with a TV set and stand.

DI John Brandon stared at the scene in its gilt frame, vibrated his lips, stepped closer and peered at the detail. He had to act. Calls had been coming in all morning about the picture in the window of Mason's Fine Art Gallery. Some, outraged, wanted it removed. Others, more cautious, inquire d if the police were aware of it.

They were now. Brandon understood why people were upset. He'd drunk sherry in the Wing Commander's house many times. This oil painting was a near-perfect rendering of the old fellow's living room. Interior, with corpse.

Brandon wasn't sure how to deal with it. Defamation, possibly. But defamation is usually libel or slander. This was only a picture. Nothing defamatory had been said or written down.

He went into the gallery and showed his ID to Justin Mason, the owner, a mild, decent man with no more on his conscience than a liking for spotted bow-ties.

"That painting in the window, the one with the woman lying in a pool of blood."

"The Davey Park? Strong subject, but one of his finest pieces."

"Park? He's the artist?"

"Yes. Did you know him? Local man. Died at the end of last year. He had his studio in that barn behind the Esso station. When I say 'studio', it was his home as well."

"Did he give the picture a title?"

"I've no idea, inspector. He wasn't very organised. It was left with a few others among his things. The executors decided to put them up for sale, and this was the only piece I cared for. The only finished piece, in fact."

"How long ago was it painted?"

"Couldn't tell you. He kept no records. He had some postcards made of it. They're poor quality black and white jobs, nineteen-fiftyish, I'd say."

"You realise what it shows?"

"A murder, obviously. You think it's too gory for the High Street? I was in two minds myself, and then I remembered that series of paintings by Walter Sickert on the subject of the Camden Town murder."

"I wouldn't know about that," Brandon admitted.

"I only mention them to show that it's not without precedent, murder as the subject of a painting, I mean."

"This is a real location."

"Is it? So was Sickert's, I believe."

"It's Wing Commander Ashton's living room."

Mason twitched and turned pale.

"Take my word for it," said Brandon. "I've been there several times."

"Oh, good Lord!"

"People have been phoning us."

"I'll remove it right away. I had no idea. I'd hate to cause offence to Wing Commander Ashton. Why, if it weren't for men like him, none of us would be living in freedom."

"I'll have to take possession of it. You can have a receipt. Tell me some more about the artist."

"Park? A competent professional. Landscapes usually. Never a big seller, but rubbed along, as they do. Not an easy man to deal with. We expect some eccentricity in artists, don't we?"

"In what way?"

"He drank himself to death, so far as I can make out. Was well known in the Crown. Amusing up to a point, and then after a few more beers he would get loud-mouthed and abusive. He was more than once banned from the pub."

"Doesn't sound like a chum of the Wing Commander's," Brandon commented. The Battle of Britain veteran, not far short of his ninetieth birthday now, was eminently respectable, a school governor, ex-chairman of the parish council and founder of the Town Heritage Society. He'd written *Scramble, Chaps*, reputed to be the best personal account of the Battle of Britain.

"They knew each other in years past, I believe, but they hadn't spoken for years. There must have been an incident, one of Davey's outbursts, I suppose. I couldn't tell you the details."

"I wonder who can – apart from the Wing Commander?"

Brandon left soon after with the painting well wrapped up. Back at the police station, he showed it to a couple of colleagues.

"Nasty," said DS Makepeace.

"Who's the woman supposed to be?" said DC Hurst.

"A figment of the artist's imagination, I hope," said Brandon. "If not, the Wing Commander has some awkward questions to face."

"Have you spoken to him?"

"Not yet. It's difficult. He's frail. I'd hate to trigger a heart attack."

"You're going to have to ask him, guv."

"He's a war hero. A gentleman through and through. I've always respected him. I need more background before I take this on."

"Try Henry at the Crown. He knew Davey Park better than anyone."

Henry Chivers had been landlord for most of his life, and he was seventy now. He pulled a half of lager for the inspector and gave his take on Davey. "I heard about the painting this morning. A bit of a change from poppy fields and views of the church. Weird. Davey never mentioned it in here. He'd witter on about most things, including his work. He had an exhibition in the old Corn Exchange a year or so before he died. Bloody good artist. None of that modern trash. It was outdoor scenes, mostly. I'm sure this one with the woman wasn't in the show. The whole town would have talked."

"They're talking now. He must have been inside the Wing Commander's house, to paint it so accurately. It's remarkable, the detail."

"In years past they knew each other well. I'm talking about the Fifties, now, half a century ago. They had interests in common – cricket, I think, and sports cars. Then they fell out over something pretty serious. Davey wouldn't speak of it, and whenever the Wing Commander's name was mentioned in the bar, he'd look up at the beam overhead as if he was trying to read the names on the tankards. Davey had opinions on most subjects, but he wouldn't be drawn on the Wing Co."

"Could it have been a woman?"

"The cause of the argument? Don't know. Davey had any number of affairs – relationships, you'd call them now. The artistic temperament, isn't it? A bit saucy for those days. But the Wing Co. wasn't like that. He was married."

"When?"

"In the war, to one of those WAAFs who worked in the control rooms pushing little wooden markers across a map."

"A plotter."

"Right."

"She must have died some years ago, then. I don't remember her."

"You wouldn't. They separated. It wasn't a happy marriage. He's a grand old guy, but between you and me, he wouldn't move on mentally. He was still locked into service life. Officially he was demobbed in 1945, and took a local job selling insurance, but he wouldn't let go. RAF Association, British Legion, showing little boys his medals at the

Air Training Corps. And of course he was writing that book about the Battle of Britain. I think Helen was suffocated."

"Suffocated?"

"Not literally."

"What became of her, then?"

"Nobody knows. She quit some time in the Fifties, and no one has heard of her since."

"That's surprising, isn't it?"

"Maybe she emigrated. Sweet young woman. Hope she had a good life."

"Dark-haired, was she?" Brandon asked. "Dark, long hair?"

"Now don't go up that route, inspector. The old boy may have been a selfish husband, but he's no murderer."

Brandon let that pass. "You haven't answered my question."

"All right, she was a brunette. Usually had it fastened at the back in a ponytail, but I've seen it loose."

"You said Davey Park was a ladies' man. Did he ever make a pass at Helen Ashton?"

Chivers pulled a face. "If he did, she wasn't the sort to respond. Very loyal, she was. Out of the top drawer."

"That's nothing to go by," said Brandon. "So-called well-brought-up girls were the goers in those days."

"Take my word for it. Helen wouldn't have given Davey the come-on, or anyone else."

"She couldn't have been all that loyal, or she'd never have left the Wing Commander."

"I bet it wasn't for another man," said Chivers. "You'll have to ask the old boy yourself, won't you?"

Brandon could see it looming. How do you tell a ninety-year-old pillar of the community that half the town suspects he may have murdered his wife? Back at the police station, he studied that painting again, trying to decide if it represented a real incident, or was some morbid fantasy of the artist. The detail was so painstaking that you were tempted to think it *must* have been done from memory. The index and middle fingernails of the left hand, in the foreground, were torn, suggesting that the woman had put up a fight. The rest of the nails were finely manicured, making the contrast. Even the fingertips were smudged black from trying to protect herself from the sooty poker.

Yet clearly Davey Park couldn't have set up his easel at a murder scene. The background stuff, the Spitfire picture, aircraft models and so on, could have been done from memory if he was used to visiting the house. The dead woman – whoever she was – must have been out of his imagination, unless Park had *been there*. Was the picture a confession – the artist's way of owning up to a crime, deliberately left to be discovered after he died?

If so, how had the killing gone undetected? What had he done with the body?

The interview with the Wing Commander had to be faced. Brandon called at the house late in the afternoon.

"John, my dear fellow! What a happy surprise!" the old man innocently greeted him. "Do come in."

The moustache was white, the hair thin and the stance unsteady without a stick, but for an old man he was in good shape, still broad-shouldered and over six feet. Without any inkling of what was to follow, he shuffled into his living room, with the inspector following.

The room was disturbingly familiar. Little had changed in fifty years.

"Please find somewhere to sit. I'll get the sherry." He tottered out again.

Brandon didn't do as he was asked. This would be a precious interval of at least three minutes at the old man's shuffling rate of progress. With a penknife he started scraping at the dark strips of cement between the hearthstones. If any traces of dried blood had survived for half a century, this was the likely place. He spent some minutes scooping the samples of dust into a transparent bag and pocketed it when he heard the drag of the slippers across the carpet.

He was upright and admiring the dogfight picture over the fireplace when the Wing Commander came in with the tray.

"My, this is a work of art."

"Don't know about that, but I value it," said the old man. "Takes me back, of course."

"Did you ever meet the artist?"

"No, it's only a print. There are plenty of aviation artists selling to dotty old critters like me, nostalgic for the old days. We had a copy hanging in the officers' mess at Biggin Hill."

"I suppose it comes down to what will sell, like anything else. There was an artist in the town called Park, who specialised in landscapes. Died recently."

"So I heard," said the Wing Commander with a distinct change in tone.

"You knew him, didn't you?"

"Years ago." There was definitely an edge to the voice now.

"He painted a pretty accurate interior of this room. It was found among his canvases after he died."

"Did he, by jove? That's a liberty, don't you think? Abuse of friendship, I call that."

"He didn't remain your friend, I heard."

"We fell out."

"Do you mind telling me why?"

"Actually, I do, John. It's a closed book."

In other circumstances, Brandon would have put the screws on. "But you must have been close friends for him to know this room so well."

"I suppose he'd remember it. Used to drop in for a chat about cricket. We both played for the town team." The Wing Commander poured the sherry and handed one to Brandon. "Are you here in an official capacity?"

It had to be said. "I'm afraid so. The picture I mentioned wasn't just an interior scene." He hesitated. "I wish I didn't have to tell you this. It had the figure of a woman in it, lying across the carpet, apparently dead of a head wound."

"Good God!"

"There was a poker beside her. You don't seem to keep a set of fire irons any longer."

"It's gas now." The Wing Commander had turned quite crimson. "Look here, since you've come to question me, I think I have a right to see this unpleasant picture. Where is it?"

"At the police station, undergoing tests. I can let you see it, certainly, later in the week. What bothers me is whether it has any foundation in real events."

"Meaning what? That a woman was attacked here – in my living room?"

Brandon had to admire the old man's composure. "It seems absurd to me, too, but he was an accurate painter—"

"An alcoholic."

"... and wasn't known to paint anything he hadn't seen for himself."

"Don't know about that. Painters of that time used to use their dreams as inspiration. What do they call it – surrealism?"

"I have to ask this, Wing Commander. You separated from your wife in the nineteen-fifties."

"Helen? She left me. We found out we were incompatible, as many others have done."

"Did you ever divorce?"

"No need. I didn't want another marriage."

"Didn't she?"

"Evidently not."

"You're not in touch?"

"When it's over, it's over."

He's lost none of his cricketing skills, thought Brandon. He could stonewall with the best.

The dust samples went to the Home Office forensic department for analysis. In three days they sent the result: significant traces of human blood had been found. Normally, he would have been excited by the discovery. This was a real downer.

So a gentle inquiry was transformed into a murder investigation. Wing Commander Ashton was brought in for questioning and a scene of crime team went through his house. More traces of dried blood were found, leaving no question that someone had sustained a serious injury in that living room.

The Wing Commander faced the interrogation with the dignity of a veteran officer. He had lost contact with his wife in 1956 and made no effort to trace her. There had been no reason to stay in contact. They had no children. She had been comfortably off and so was he. No, her life had not been insured.

Brandon sensed that the old man held the truth in high regard. It was a point of honour not to lie. He wasn't likely to volunteer anything detrimental to himself, but he would answer with honesty.

When shown the painting that was the cause of all the fuss, he gave it a glance, no more, and said the woman on the floor didn't look much like his wife, what you could see of her. He was allowed to go home, only to find a team of policemen digging in his garden. He watched them with contempt.

A public appeal was made for the present address of Mrs. Helen Ashton, aged 79. It was suggested that she might be using another name. This triggered massive coverage in the press. Davey Park's painting was reproduced in all the dailies with captions like: *IS THIS A MURDER SCENE? and PROOF OF MURDER OR CRUEL HOAX?*

The response was overwhelming and fruitless. Scores of old ladies, some very confused, were interviewed and found to have no connection with the case. It only fuelled the suspicion that Helen Ashton had been dead for years.

The investigation was running out of steam. Nothing had been found in the garden. There were no incriminating diaries, letters or documents in the house.

"What about the book?" someone asked. "Did he have anything mean to say about his wife?"

Brandon had already skimmed through the book. Helen wasn't mentioned.

The answer to the mystery had to be in the picture. If the artist Davey Park knew a murder had been committed, and felt strongly enough to have made this visual record, he'd wanted the truth to come out. Then why hadn't he informed the police? Either he had killed Helen Ashton himself, or he felt under some obligation to keep the secret until he died. The picture was his one major work never to have been exhibited.

Either way, it suggested some personal involvement. He'd been known to have numerous affairs. Had Helen Ashton refused his advances and paid for it with her life?

Brandon stared at the picture once more, systematically studying each detail: the bloodstained fireplace, the pictures, the medals, the photos on the table, the armchair, the typewriter on the bureau, the dead woman, the blood on the carpet, her clothes, her damaged fingernails, her blackened fingertips. By sheer application he spotted something he'd missed before.

She wasn't wearing a wedding ring. The hand in the foreground was her left and the ring finger was bare.

"I deserve to be sacked," he said aloud.

Park had been so careful over detail that he wouldn't have forgotten to paint in the ring. And in the Fifties, most married women wore their rings at all times.

"You're joking, guv," said DS Makepeace when Brandon asked him to make a list of the women Davey Park had been out with in the nineteen-fifties.

"I'm not. There are people in the town who remember. It was hot gossip once."

"Did he keep a diary, or something?"

"If he had, we'd have looked through it weeks ago. All he left behind were pictures and unpaid bills. Start with Henry Chivers, in the Crown."

After another week of patiently assembling information, Brandon had the Wing Commander brought in for further questioning.

Sergeant Makepeace thought he should have waited longer, and didn't mind speaking out. "I think he'll stall, guv. You won't get anything out of him."

"No," said Brandon firmly. "He's one of those rare witnesses you can rely on. A truth-teller. With his background it's a point of honour to give truthful answers. He won't mention anything that isn't asked, but he won't lie, either."

"You admire him, don't you?"

"That's what makes it so painful."

So the old man sat across the desk from Brandon in an interview room and the tape rolled and the formalities were gone through.

"Wing Commander Ashton, we now believe the woman who was attacked in your house was not your wife."

A soft sigh escaped. "Isn't that what I told you from the beginning?"

"The woman in the picture doesn't have a wedding ring. I should have looked for it earlier. I didn't."

The only response was a slight shrug.

Brandon admitted, "When I realised this, I was thrown. The victim could be anybody – any dark-haired young woman without a ring.

There had to be some extra clue in the painting, and there is. She was the woman who typed your book. Her name was Angela Hamilton. Is that correct?"

He said stiffly, giving only as much as his moral code decreed, "I had a typist of that name, yes."

"She was murdered in your house in the manner shown in the painting. Davey Park saw the scene just after it happened and painted it from memory."

The Wing Commander spread his hands. "The existence of this painting was unknown to me until I saw it here a few days ago."

"But you confirm that Miss Hamilton was the victim?"

"Yes."

"I'm interpreting the picture now. It gives certain pointers to the crime."

"Like the typewriter."

"Just so. And the reason she was partially dressed is that you and she had been making love, probably in that room where she typed for you. Precisely where is not important. Your wife came home – she was supposed to be out for some considerable time – and caught you cheating on her."

The Wing Commander didn't deny it. He looked down at his arthritic hands. The passions of fifty years ago seemed very remote.

Brandon continued: "We think what happened is this. To use an old-fashioned phrase, Angela Hamilton was a fast woman, an ex-lover of the artist Davey Park. Park heard she'd been taken on by you as a part-time typist and found out that she didn't spend all her time in front of the machine. Perhaps she boasted to him that she'd seduced the famous Battle of Britain hero, or perhaps he played Peeping Tom at your window one afternoon. Anyway, he decided to tell your wife. He'd been trying to flirt with her, with no success. He thought if she found out you were two-timing, she might be encouraged to do the same. She didn't believe him, so he offered to prove it. They both turned up at your house when you and Angela were having sex. Is that a fair account?"

"They caught us in some embarrassment, yes," said the Wing Commander.

"You were shocked, guilt-stricken and extremely angry. The worst part was seeing Park and realising he'd told your wife. Did you go after him?"

"I did, and caught him in the garden and let fly with my fists." At last, the Wing Commander was willing to give more than the minimum of information. "I was so incensed I might have injured him permanently."

"What stopped you?"

There was an interval of silence, while the old man decided if at last he was free to speak of it. "There was a scream from the house. I hear it now. Like no other scream I have ever heard. The fear in it. Horrible. We abandoned the fight and rushed inside."

"Both of you?"

"Yes. He saw it too. Angela, dead on the floor, with blood seeping from her head and the poker beside her, just as it is in the picture. Helen had already run out through the back. Such ferocity. I never knew she had it in her."

"What did you do?"

"With the body? Drove it to a place I know, a limestone quarry, and covered it with rubble. It has never been found. I blamed myself, you see. Helen had acted impulsively. She didn't deserve to be hanged, or locked up for life. You'll have to charge me with conspiracy."

"I'll decide on the charge," said Brandon. "So you felt you owed it to your wife to cover up the crime. What did she do?"

"Packed up her things and left. She wanted no more to do with me, and I understood why. I behaved like a louse and got what I deserved."

"You truly didn't hear from her again?"

"I have a high regard for the truth."

"Then you won't know the rest of the story. Your wife took another name and moved, first to Scotland, and then Suffolk. Davey Park, always scratching around for a living, saw a chance of extorting money."

"Blackmail?"

"He set out to find her, and succeeded. We've looked at a building society account he had. Regular six-monthly deposits of a thousand pounds were made at a branch in Stowmarket, Suffolk, for over twenty years."

"The fiend."

"He painted the picture as a threat. Had some postcards made of it.

Each year, as a kind of invoice, he would send her one – until she died in 1977."

"I had no idea," said the Wing Commander. "He was living in my village extorting sums of money from my own wife. It's vile."

"I agree. Perhaps if you'd made contact with her, she would have told you."

He shook his head. "Too proud. She was too proud ever to speak to me again." His eyes had reddened. He took out a handkerchief. "You'd better charge me before I make an exhibition of myself."

Brandon shook his head. "I won't be charging you, sir."

"I want no favours, just because I'm old."

"It would serve no purpose. You'd be given a suspended sentence at the very worst. There's no point. But I have a request. Would you show us where Angela Hamilton was buried?"

The remains were recovered and given a Christian burial a month later. Brandon, Sergeant Makepeace and Wing Commander Ashton were the only mourners.

On the drive back, Makepeace said, "One thing I've been meaning to ask you, sir."

"Ask away."

"That picture contained all the clues, you said. Davey Park made sure."

"So he did."

"Well, how did you know Angela Hamilton was the victim?"

"She was on your list of Park's girlfriends."

"It was a long list."

"She was the only one who temped as a typist. The typewriter was in the picture. A big clue."

"Yes, I know, but—"

"You're not old enough to have used an ancient manual typewriter," Brandon added. "If you remember, her fingertips were smudged black. At first I assumed it was soot, from the poker, but the marks were very precise. In those days when you wanted more than one copy of what you typed, you used carbon paper. However careful you were, the damned stuff got on the tips of your fingers."

THE EGYPTIAN GARDEN

Marjorie Eccles

"But what has happened to the garden?" asked Mrs. Palmer.

"There doesn't appear to be one, I'm afraid, dear," replied Moira Ledgerwood, who felt obliged to take the old lady under her wing, as she'd frequently let it be known over the last two weeks. "Just a big courtyard."

"Well, I can see that!"

"No garden in Cairo houses," the guide, Hassan, asserted sibilantly, with the fine disregard for truth which had characterised all his explanations so far.

"But there used to be one here. With a fountain in the middle."

Hassan shrugged. The other twenty members of the cultural tour smiled tolerantly. They were accustomed to Mrs. Palmer by now, after ten days together in Upper Egypt. You had to admire her spirit, and the way she kept up with the best of them, despite her age. A widow, refusing to let the fact that she was alone limit her choice of holiday to Eastbourne, or perhaps a Mediterranean cruise. Intrepid old girl, eighty if she was a day. They were always the toughest, that sort. But her younger travelling companions sensed that this trip had turned out to be something of a disappointment. Egypt was not apparently living up to expectations, it wasn't as it had been when she'd lived here, though that would have been asking a lot, since it had been in the Dark Ages, before the war.

"Taking a trip down Memory Lane then, are you, Ursula, is that why you've come?" Moira had asked kindly, when Mrs. Palmer had let slip this fact on the first day, utterly dismayed at the tarmac road that now ran towards the once remote, silent and awesome Valley of the Kings, at the noisome phalanxes of waiting coaches with their engines kept running for the air-conditioning, the throngs of people from the cruise ships queuing up for tickets to visit the tombs of the Pharaohs, which were lit by electric light. Before the war, when her husband had taken her to view the antiquities, they had sailed across the Nile in a *felucca* from Luxor, and traversed the rocky descent and on to the Valley of the Queens and the Temple of Hatshepsut by donkey, accompanied only by a dragoman. The silence had been complete. Now, they might just as well be visiting a theme park, she said tartly.

"They're a poor people. The tourist industry's important to them, Ursula," Moira reminded her gently.

Mrs. Palmer had so far managed to bear Moira's goodness with admirable fortitude, but she was beginning to be afraid it might not last.

Strangers ten days ago, the tour group members were on Christian-name terms within a few hours, something it had taken Mrs. Palmer a little time to get used to. But nothing fazed her for long, not even the touts who pestered with their tatty souvenirs, and craftily pressed worthless little scarabs into your palm, or even slipped them into your pocket, and then held out their own palms for payment. Moira had asked her advice on what to say to get rid of them, but when she repeated what Mrs. Palmer had told her: "*Imshi! Mefish filouse!*", the touts had doubled up with laughter and Moira was afraid that Ursula had been rather unkind and led her to say something indelicate. Ursula, however, said no, it was only the prospect of a middle-aged English lady using Arabic, telling them to go away because she had no money, that amused them, when they knew that all such ladies were rich, and only addressed the natives loudly, in English. But then, they were easily amused – childlike, kindly people, who were nevertheless rogues to a man.

The group advanced through the courtyard and made an orderly queue at the door of the tall old Mameluke house near the bazaar, now a small privately owned museum with a cafe for light refreshments on the ground floor, buying their tickets from the doorkeeper, an enormously fat, grizzled old man who wore a sparkling white *galabeya* and smiled charmingly at them with perfect teeth. He kept his eye on Mrs. Palmer, gradually losing his smile as she lagged behind. He noticed her casting quick glances over her shoulder at the benches set in the raised alcove of perforated stonework, at the many doors opening off the large dusty inner courtyard, which itself held nothing but a couple of dilapidated pots haphazardly filled with a few dispirited, un-English-looking flowers. But after a while she turned and resolutely followed the rest of the party.

Inside the house, little had changed, except that it had been recently restored, and consequently looked a little too good to be true. Wide-panelled wooden doors; wrought iron and coloured-glass hanging lamps depending from ceilings elaborately carved with geometric designs; inlaid furniture and wide couches in balconies that jutted out over the once poverty-stricken squalor of the narrow street below. Mrs. Palmer was so overcome she was obliged to rest on one of these couches to try and catch a breath of air through the carved trellis screening, leaving the rest of the group to be shown around the house. She had no need to go with them, she knew every corner and every item in it, intimately. She had lived here once, she had been the mistress of this house.

And there had been a garden here. She had made it.

*   *   *

Impossible to count the number of times she'd sat here behind the *mushrabiyeh* lattice-work, a device originally intended to screen women of the seraglio from passers-by. Listening to the traffic that never stopped, the blaring horns, police whistles, the muezzins' calls to prayer, the shouts and sounds from the bazaar, to Cairo's never-ceasing noise, noise, noise! Longing for the soft, earthy smell of an English spring, to hear a blackbird or the call of the cuckoo, and the whisper of rain on the roof.

"Rain? What rain?" her husband had repeated when he had brought her here from England as a bride, dewy-fresh, hopeful and twenty years old. "It never rains." She had assumed he was exaggerating, but she quickly realised it was almost the literal truth. He rarely spoke anything else.

In the short time since her wedding, she had already begun to wonder, too late, if her marriage had perhaps not been overhasty. Such a good catch, James Palmer had seemed; courteous, well-connected – and well-off, something that Ursula had been taught was of paramount importance in a husband. She knew now that he was essentially cold and reserved, and humourless, too. He was tall and thin, handsome enough, and his only disadvantage, it had seemed to Ursula, was an

Adam's apple that seemed to have a life of its own. She had decided she could learn to ignore that disconcerting lump of cartilage, and also the fact that he was twenty years older than she. His lack of warmth and humour, his pomposity, however, were things she didn't think she would ever get used to.

As time went on, longing for the smiles and laughter that had hitherto been a natural part of her life until then, she began to throw herself into the pursuit of amusement, easy enough to find in the cosmopolitan Cairo of those days. It was 1938. Somewhere, beyond Egypt, the world was preparing for war, but here expatriate European society carried on as though it would go away if they ignored the possibility. Her time was filled with countless dinner parties, afternoon tea at Shepheard's, gossip, charity functions, tennis parties if the weather was supportable. When James was away, there was always someone to escort her, to take her dancing and dining every night.

But fun of this sort turned out to be an ephemeral gratification. For a while, she had believed such frenetic activity could obliterate the loneliness and dissatisfaction with her married state, but it very soon palled. Increasingly, when James was away and she was left entirely to herself, a pensive melancholy fell upon her. As an oriental export merchant, eldest son of his family business, he travelled all over the Middle East in search of carpets, carved wooden furniture, alabaster and metalwork to ship to England, and it had pleased him to furnish this old house he had bought with the best of what he had found, so that one had to accustom oneself to reclining on couches and eating off low tables, as if one were a woman in a harem. Indeed, her disappointment with the life she had let herself in for made Ursula reflect ironically that James might have been better pleased if she had been such a woman.

Spending most of her time listlessly in this very room, which was open entirely to the air on one side, drinking thick Egyptian coffee or mint tea, longing for Earl Grey, which could be bought if one knew where to look, but never, for some mysterious reason, in sufficient quantities, she had gazed over the balustrade to the barren expanse of sandy earth around the edges of the courtyard, the drifts of dust obscuring the lovely colours of the tiles, wondering if this was all life had to offer. Not even a sign of a child as yet, though her mother, in her weekly letters, constantly assured her there was plenty of time.

Time, it seemed, stood still, an hour as long as a day. A huge expanse of space, and inside its infinity, she sat alone, while the friendly chatter and laughter – and noisy, if short-lived, quarrelling – sounded above the continuous wailing Arab radio music that issued from the kitchen quarters and made her feel more alone than ever. What was she to do? Nothing, it seemed, but assume a stiff upper lip and get on with accustoming herself to the inescapable facts of her new life. The food, for one thing: the tough, unidentified meat she was tempted to think might once have been a camel, the sugary cakes that set her teeth on edge, and the unleavened bread. She must get used to the heavily chlorinated water that James insisted upon, too. The flies. The beautifully ironed napkins, so fresh from the *dhobi* that they were still damp. And especially to the *khamsin* that blew from the south west, hot and dusty, giving her a nasty, tickling cough that wouldn't go away. Oh, that eternal dust and grit that insinuated itself everywhere!

When she had first arrived, she'd been determined to emulate her mother and maintain an orderly English household, with the dust outside, where it belonged, but she was defeated. In their attempts to clean, the servants insisted on using whisks, whose only effect was to distribute the dirt from one place to another. The grit ground itself into the beautiful mosaic floor tiles and the silky carpets under your feet. The cushions gave off puffs of dust whenever you sat on them. Even simple tidiness was beyond her capacity to convey to them, and theirs to accept. Elbow grease was a substance as entirely unknown as the Mansion Polish and Brasso she ordered from Home. Gradually, despite all her natural inclinations and her mother's training, inertia overcame her and she began to think: what does it matter, why fight the inevitable? Perhaps the servants were right, perhaps it was as Allah willed, *inshallah*.

Even more did she feel that now, sixty years later, when ghosts, and her own perceptions of violent death, were everywhere.

Sometimes, for air, she used to sit in the cool of the evening on the flat roof of the house, overlooking the expanse of the lighted city, watching the achingly beautiful sunsets over the Nile, with the ineffably foreign domes and minarets of the mosques piercing the skyline, as the darkness mercifully masked the seething squalor of the ancient, dun-coloured city. There was an especially low point on one particular night, when she almost considered throwing herself off, or alternatively taking to the bottle, but she was made of sterner stuff and didn't really take either proposition seriously. Instead, when it eventually became too cold for comfort, she took herself down the stairs to her usual position overlooking the courtyard, where she faced the fact that, unless she did something about it, her life would dry up as surely as the brittle leaves on the single palm that gave shade to the dusty square below, that she might as well take to the *chador* and veil. Despite the lateness of the hour, she went outside and, picking her way over the rubbish that seemed to arrive by osmosis, stared at the gritty, trampled earth and thought of her father's hollyhocks and lupins and night-scented stock.

"Of course the courtyard's dark," James said when she later began by mentioning, tentatively, how the walls seemed to close in on her. "That's its purpose. Oriental houses are traditionally built around the concept of high walls providing shade. The natives like nothing more than to live outdoors whenever they can, and the shade makes it bearable."

"No one lives outdoors in this establishment," Ursula pointed out.

"We are not natives, Ursula. And while we're on the subject, it's not a good thing to get too friendly with the servants. They'll lose all respect for you."

It wasn't the first time she'd been tempted to laugh at his pomposity, but she knew that it would have been a mistake. She didn't laugh now, she was only half listening, anyway, absorbed by her new idea. She didn't bother to point out that the only friend she had in the house was Nawal, the one female among all the other servants who, as one of Yusuf the cook's extended family, had been brought in to work for her. At first sulky and unco-operative, she had gradually accepted Ursula's friendly overtures. Now she was all wide Egyptian smiles and good humour; she delighted in looking after Ursula, making her bed, taking care of her silk underclothes, and being allowed to brush her mane of thick, red-gold hair. She brought magical, if foul-tasting, syrup for Ursula's cough when it became troublesome, and had become fiercely protective of her, pitying her, so far from home and with no family around her, no one except that cold and distant husband.

The next day, Ursula obtained – with difficulty – a spade, a garden fork and a hoe, took them into the courtyard and began to dig the hard, flattened earth around the edges of the tiles, where surely there had once been plants and trees growing – and would be again, after she'd arranged for a delivery of rich alluvial soil from the banks of the Nile, in which anything grew.

James predictably disapproved strongly when he'd got over his first disbelief at this crazy notion of actually tackling the making of a garden, alone. It was unnecessary. She could occupy herself more profitably elsewhere. Why not take up sketching, or Byzantine art, his own particular passion? But Ursula's inclinations didn't lie either way; she couldn't draw for toffee, and she found Byzantine art far too stylised to be either comprehensible or interesting. For once her stubbornness overcame his disapproval. Very well, he said reluctantly, but had she considered how such eccentricity would reflect on him in the eyes of their European acquaintances? They needn't know, said Ursula. And neither was it, he could not resist reminding her yet again, ignoring her interjection, something calculated to enhance her authority with the servants.

And, of course, he was right about this last, as he always contrived to be. They came out in full force to see what she was doing, and laughed behind their hands at the prospect of an English lady wielding a spade, even sometimes going down on her knees, getting her hands filthy, grubbing in the earth for all the world like one of the *fellaheen*. She didn't care, but was nevertheless a little discouraged. Digging in the heat was harder work than she'd anticipated, and meant she could only do it for short periods. It did not seem as though her garden would progress very fast.

On the third day, she saw the boy watching her. He watched her for a week. She didn't know who he was, why he was here, how he'd arrived. If she spoke to him, or even smiled, he melted away. He appeared to be about sixteen or seventeen, slim and tall, liquid-eyed, with curly black hair and skin as smooth as brown alabaster. A beautiful youth in a *galabeya* white as driven snow, with a profile straight off a temple wall.

"Who is he?" she asked Yusuf, at last.

"He Khaled," Yusuf said dismissively, and Ursula, intimidated, asked no more questions. She wondered if Khaled were dumb, or perhaps not entirely in his right mind, but dismissed this last, recalling the bright intelligence in his face.

The first time he spoke to her was early one morning, when he said shyly, "I deegéd the kennel for you." His face was anxious.

Kennel?

Following his pointing finger, she saw that the first of the series of blocked irrigation channels, which led from the source of the fountain, had been cleared. He had anticipated her intention, to clear the conduits so that she could draw water for her thirsty new plants. She smiled. He smiled back, radiantly. He took up the spade and began on the next one.

Miraculously, he persuaded the fountain to work. Water began to jet into the basin again, and at once the courtyard was transformed with possibilities: colour and scent, visions of lilies and lavender, marguerites, blue delphiniums and phlox in white and pink swam about in her head. Roses, roses, roses. She saw her dream of a lush and opulent garden coming true at last, the tiles clean and swept and glowing with colour, with the reflection of light and shade dappling through the leaves on to the dark walls, under the burning blue sky, the cool, musical playing of the water into the basin.

He came most days after that to help her, unselfconsciously tucking his *galabeya* up between his legs. She discovered he had a sly wit, and they laughed together, sharing their youth as well as the work – she was not, after all, so many years older than he. He sensed quickly what she wanted done, but shook his head when she showed him the plant catalogues her mother, overenthusiastically, had sent from England. Roses, yes, Khaled made her understand – his English was picturesque but adequate as a means of communication, and he learned quickly – roses would flourish. Were not the first roses bred in Persia? But lupins, hollyhocks, phlox – no. She thought it might be worth a try, however, if she reversed the seasons, pretended the Egyptian winter was an English summer, then for the fierce summer heat planted canna lilies and bougainvillea, strelitzia, perfumed mimosa, jacaranda and jasmine, oleander... The names were like an aphrodisiac.

She arranged, mistakenly as it turned out, to pay Khaled for his work, and though it seemed to her pitifully little, after some hesitation he accepted gravely, while making her understand he would have done it for nothing. "It help pay my bookses," he said ingenuously.

Nawal, with a blush and a giggle and a lowering of her eyes whenever she spoke of Khaled, had told Ursula that he was hoping to attend the University of Al Azhar, to study architecture, in order some day to build good, clean houses for poor people, both of which ambitions his uncle, Yusuf, regarded as being impossible and above his station. Nor was Yusuf, it seemed, pleased with Ursula's arrangement to pay the boy. Shouting issued from the domestic quarters shortly after she had made him the offer. When she asked Nawal what was the matter, Ursula was told that Yusuf, while able to shut his eyes to the help Khaled gave freely, could not entertain the idea of his accepting payment for it. The noise of the altercation in the kitchen was so great it brought James from the house's upper fastness, where he immured himself whenever he was at home. After a few incisive words from him, an abnormal quietness was restored. He then turned to deal with Ursula.

"When will you learn?" he shouted, marching out into the courtyard, his face red with anger, his Adam's apple wobbling uncontrollably, his patience at an end. "Don't you see that paying him money, when he freely offered his services, is tantamount to an insult? You will abandon this ridiculous project at once, *do you understand*? No wonder the servants look down on you, working out here like a peasant! If you want a garden so much, I can have one made for you, dammit! There's no need to make such an exhibition of yourself."

"No! You've missed the point, that isn't what I want at all." Now that she had found her *raison d'être,* something that gave meaning to the enforced idleness and aridity of her life in Egypt, Ursula was in a panic at the thought of losing it.

Khaled had followed them outside. He had endured Yusuf's shouting with equanimity, but when James turned on Ursula, those liquid eyes of his flashed, simply flashed. He plucked out the garden fork that was driven into the earth nearby and for a terrified moment she thought... But he merely dashed it to the ground with a dramatic gesture worthy of the wrath of God. Before anyone could say anything, after another murderous look, he was gone.

And that's the last I'll see of him, Ursula thought sadly.

She had no prescience then of the dark future, otherwise she would have left, too, taken the next available ship. Left Egypt then and there and gone back to England, as James had been urging her to do for some time, in view of the ever-increasing talk of war in Europe. But that would have been admitting failure, and a certain innate stubbornness was keeping her here, a refusal to admit defeat. A tacit awareness by now had arisen between herself and her husband that their marriage was not a success, but divorce in those days was not to be contemplated lightly. Paramount was the scandal, as far as James was concerned. As for Ursula, it would have felt as though she were being sent home in disgrace, like a child, for not being good, which she knew was unfair. She had been too young for what she'd had to face, and her marriage had been a foolish leap in the dark, but no one had attempted to warn her. And for another, although James simply would not, or could not, understand, Ursula was not going to abandon her project at this stage. He could not *make* her give it up.

The garden had become an obsession. Ignoring his disapproval, she worked every day, until the perspiration poured off her and her thick hair became lank as wet string, until the sun or the *khamsin* drove her indoors. Sometimes she was so hot she took off her hat in defiance of the sun and her fair skin got burnt. Her English rose looks faded and she was in danger of becoming permanently desiccated and dried, as English women tend to be, under the sun. It was obvious that James was beginning to find her less than attractive. But her garden was starting to take shape.

She had been wrong about Khaled. Eventually, without explanation, he returned. Nothing was said, he simply took up where he had left off. Ursula bought him books and gave them to him as presents, so that honour was satisfied. James, surprisingly, said nothing. Perhaps he hoped the garden would be completed all the more quickly and Ursula would regain her sanity. Then, one day, he announced, "I've found a live-in companion for you."

"What?" She was so furious she could scarcely speak, in a panic, imagining a stringy old lady who would torment her with demands to play two-handed patience, and prevent her from gardening. How could he do this to her?

But the stringy old lady turned out to be a bouncy and athletic young woman not much older than Ursula, called Bunty Cashmore. Three months out of England, with short, dark, curly hair, hockey player's legs and a healthily tanned complexion enhanced by the fierce Egyptian sun rather than ruined by it, unlike Ursula's. And then Ursula understood the reason for James's sudden concern for her friendless state.

Rather than regarding the brisk bossiness of her new companion as a threat to his own authority, he seemed amused by it, and showed not a trace of disapproval of her, or impatience with her meaningless chatter. In fact, he paid more attention to her than to Ursula, no matter that she showed enthusiasm for the garden project. But then, Bunty was enthusiastic about everything, most especially when it came to learning something of Byzantine art, about which she cheerfully admitted she was ignorant.

She knew nothing about gardening, either, but it didn't prevent her from interfering – or pitching in, as she cheerfully put it. She pulled up tiny, cherished seedlings, believing them to be weeds. Oops, sorry! Surveying the garden through its haze of dust, which was hosed off each night when the garden was watered, she informed Ursula that she needed bedding plants to provide more colour in the courtyard, that the yucca in the corner, chosen for its architectural form, was ugly, and should go. She suggested that 'the boy' was no longer needed, either, now that she was here to help Ursula, now that the garden was at last almost finished, apart from the very last strip of bare earth which Ursula was reluctant to deal with, since that would leave little else to do but tend the garden while waiting for it to mature.

Khaled bent over his work at hearing what was proposed for him, hiding his thoughts and the resentment in his eyes.

And Nawal, meanwhile, noted every look that passed between Bunty and James, enraged on behalf of her mistress, fiercely jealous of the time Ursula was now forced to spend with the usurper, Bunty.

As for Ursula herself, she gritted her teeth at Bunty's insensitivity and refused to let her get on her nerves, hoping that all she had to do was wait, and the untenable situation going on in her own house would resolve itself. For England had declared war on Germany in September 1939, and Bunty was forever talking of going back Home and becoming a WAAF. Ursula, entirely sick of her, couldn't wait. Yet talk, it seemed, was all it was. Something held Bunty here, presumably in the person of James Palmer: she was by no means as naïve as she seemed, she knew very well which side her bread was buttered.

Though he was too old to fight, James was presently offered a job with an army intelligence unit, and was threatening to close the house and pack his wife off Home whether she wanted it or not. An ugly atmosphere developed at her point blank refusal to do his bidding. Egypt was neutral, maintained Ursula, she would be safer here than in England. Depend on it, James countered, sooner or later the war would be on their doorstep, and who knew what would happen then? But it wasn't her safety that was in question, they both knew that; it was a face-saving ploy for getting rid of her.

Yet how could she have willingly left the only thing she had ever created, her garden?

★   ★   ★

What had it all been for, the struggle and the unhappiness? More than sixty years later, despite all the love and dedication lavished upon its creation, that garden, that bone of contention, but still the one shining star in an otherwise dark night, had disappeared as though it had never existed. The old feeling of melancholy overwhelmed Ursula as she contemplated where it had once flourished. It wasn't only, however, that the garden had gone and the courtyard had reverted to its original air of sad, dark desolation, with the fountain in the middle as dried up as when she had first seen it, one could cope with that. It was something about the atmosphere itself that provoked such thoughts, a sort of pervasive accidie. A stain on the air, left by the events that had happened here. She felt oppressed by the thought, and the weight of her years. Or perhaps it was just that the last ten days had taken it out of her.

"Mrs. Palmer?"

She turned with weary resignation, but it wasn't Moira Ledgerwood, being responsible. There was still half an hour of interesting things to see on the upper floors before the group descended for glasses of tea in the cafe. It was the doorkeeper who stood there. He said softly, "I'm sorry the garden is no longer there. It grew wild. They cut it down, during the war, when the house was occupied by English officers."

The filtered light from the windows fell on the ample figure of the doorkeeper in the white *galabeya,* and as he turned slightly, she saw his profile. He knew her name. And suddenly, she knew his. It was a shock. The dark curls were silvered now, but the smile was the same. She saw the young, slim, beautiful youth inside the grossly fat old man. And he, what did he see? A scrawny old woman in her eighties. "Khaled? How did you know me?" she asked faintly.

"By your hair, first of all."

Involuntarily, her hand went up to her white, serviceably short locks. "How could you? I had it cut off years ago, and it turned white before I was forty."

"I recognised the way it grows."

There was a silence between them. A feeling of what might have been, had they been born in other times, other places. Perhaps. Or perhaps not.

"Mrs. Palmer." He came forward with both hands outstretched and she saw he wore a heavy gold ring with an impressive diamond on his little finger. He clasped both her hands, something he would never have done in the old days, and she allowed him to. "It is so good to see you." Something had radically changed, apart from the fact that his command of English was now excellent. He didn't look like a *boab*, a doorkeeper, a man who sat at a table and took money. He looked like the sort of man who made it.

"But next year would have been a better time to come," he went on. "Then, there will be another garden. The men come next week to begin. I needed to have the house restored first."

She stared at him. "Khaled, are you telling me—?"

"Yes, the house belongs to me now, Mrs. Palmer. After the war, after the officers left, that is…" He paused. "It stayed empty, as you must know, until seven years ago, when I bought it, through your lawyers. The condition, the neglect!" He threw up both hands. "But I was too busy to do anything about it until now. A retirement project, you might say, hmm?" He smiled.

She digested the information that he was rich enough to do all this. "You did go to university, then? You became an architect?" The guilt that she had carried around for more than half a lifetime began to shift a little.

"Alas, no, that was not possible, in the circumstances."

There was a long pause. "And did you marry Nawal?"

His soft, dark eyes grew inscrutable. "No, I never married anyone at all." He shrugged. "*Malish*." That unquestioning submission to fate.

Malish – never mind – it doesn't matter. Then he laughed. "I became successful instead. I sell souvenirs to tourists. I have co-operatives to make them, and also shops now in New York, Paris, London. Many times I have thought of you when I am in England."

The hopeful young man with his lofty ambitions, now an entrepreneur, a curio seller, in effect – albeit a rich one. To such do our hopes and aspirations come.

"Why did you run away, Khaled?"

He looked at his feet. "It was necessary. Who would have believed me?"

"There were no questions asked, you should have stayed."

"I heard that, but I was far away by then." He smiled again.

Death due to extreme sickness and diarrhoea in this land wasn't so unusual as to cause many inquiries to be made, especially when it was known that the victim was not Egyptian and had been suffering from stomach upsets for ten days or more before dying. It had been put down to one of the many ills European flesh was heir to, and for that matter Egyptian flesh, too, in this land where clean water was unknown and a mosquito bite could kill.

*　　*　　*

She and Khaled had been pruning the shrubs. The jasmine had already grown into a tangle, and the pink, white and red oleanders, though pretty, needed to be kept in check. Bunty, decidedly under the weather, was sitting in the shade of the stone alcove, too unwell to do anything but watch. Ursula threw her a long, speculative glance and pensively snipped off an oleander twig, careful not to let the milky sap get on to her hands. "That's a nasty cough you have there, Bunty," she said eventually. "Why don't you ask Nawal for some of her cough syrup?"

"It's this wretched dusty wind," said Bunty, coughing again, her eyes red and sore. "This *khamsin*. I'm going indoors."

"Go and lie down, and I'll bring you the medicine. It's very good."

"We-ell, all right. Do you think she might have something for my gippy tummy at the same time?"

"I go bring," said Khaled, and departed with unusual alacrity.

The dry, rasping cough came again and another griping pain almost doubled Bunty up. It wasn't only cholera and malaria, or worse, that one had to fear, here in Egypt. Stomach upsets, and quite often being slightly off-colour for unspecified reasons, were unavoidable hazards, facts of life. Bunty looked wretched, but Ursula had little sympathy for her predicament. She had a passion for sticky native sweetmeats, and one didn't care to think about the flies. Ursula had actually seen her carelessly drinking water from the earthenware chatty by the kitchen door because it was always cool, and because the water which Ursula and James forced themselves to drink tasted so nastily of chemicals and didn't, as Bunty pointed out, necessarily make them immune; James himself hadn't quite recovered yet from the same sort of malaise that Bunty was suffering from now, and was still extremely queasy, even with the care he took. As for Bunty, it was hardly surprising that her usual rude health sometimes deserted her.

Death, though! No one could have foreseen that. These things took unexpected turns, however, madame, they said at the hospital, shrugging, affected different people in very different ways. A constitution already weakened by bouts of sickness and diarrhoea...*inshallah*. There were few formalities.

Afterwards, the desire to shake the dust of Egypt from their feet had been mutual. Home was all there was now, wartime England. It had been Ursula, after all, who joined the WAAF, taking a rehabilitation course in horticulture when she was demobbed.

"I made another garden, Khaled, in England, in Surrey. It became a commercial success. Hollyhocks and lupins, as well as roses." They smiled, remembering. "But no oleander. The climate is too cold there for oleander."

"Ah." The smiles faded as their glances met.

That day, after she'd administered Nawal's medicine, which Khaled had brought, Ursula had come downstairs again and sat on the carved wooden bench where Bunty had sat, to wait. The garden was tidy, and so still, apart from the splash of the fountain. The oleander twigs which had lain scattered on the brightly patterned tiles had already been swept away and cleared, she noticed.

Nerium oleander. All parts of which, including the nectar, are deadly, even the smoke from the burning plant, and especially its milky sap. Causing vomiting if ingested, sweating, bloody diarrhoea, unconsciousness, respiratory paralysis and, finally, death.

The memory of that day was etched into her brain forever: the sultry heat, the metallic smell of dust, the perfume of the roses. The silence in her head, as though the habitual din of life beyond the high walls had been stopped to let the world listen to what she was thinking. Even the Arab music from the kitchen was stilled. The waiting.

Within half an hour, the sickness had begun, and twenty-four hours later, it was all over.

*   *   *

Khaled was looking at her earnestly. "And you, Mrs. Palmer? Have you had a happy life, Mrs. Palmer?" he questioned acutely.

A happy life! How could that have been possible? Living with the tedium of Bunty's bright inanities, year in, year out. But there were many ways of expiating guilt. In the end, she'd become quite fond of her. A delicious irony indeed.

"I have – had no regrets."

"Meesees Palmer!" Hassan's voice, rounding up his flock, echoed down the staircase.

"Ursula!" Moira Ledgerwood was coming in, looking for her protégée, finding her. "Oh, the things you've missed! What a pity you didn't come with us." She looked curiously from the old lady to the old doorkeeper.

Ursula held out her hand. "Goodbye, Khaled. Good luck with your project."

She turned to go and then turned back, as he said softly, for her ears only, "Your husband should not have died. Nawal's medicine was good."

She smiled. "It must have been intended, Khaled. *Inshallah*, hmm? He must have been too ill for it to make any difference. Who knows?"

Khaled watched her go. And perhaps Bunty Cashmore would have died, too, if she hadn't been so violently sick again, immediately after swallowing her own dose.

"Who knows, Mrs. Palmer?" he said into the empty room.

MELUSINE

Martin Edwards

On the hillside, bodies were burning. As Jason drove down into the valley, he glanced across and saw the outlines of the bloated carcasses. Their stiffened legs protruded through the flames and pointed to the sky. On a fresh June morning, smoke and fire had turned the sky a strange purple hue that, until the coming of the plague, he had never seen before. A steamy white vapour hung close to the ground. He kept the windows of the van wound up, but the stench from the corpses on the funeral pyre was inescapable. It choked his sinuses and made his gorge rise.

The fields were deserted. Cows and sheep should be everywhere, but only their ghosts remained. All the footpaths were barred with tape and official notices; ramblers had been asked to stay at home. The winding route to Sidebottom's Farm was closed, a red sign blocking the middle of the lane. KEEP OUT – FOOT AND MOUTH DISEASE.

The grey stone cottages where a couple of the farm workers and their families had lived were shuttered and silent. When blisters were found on the tongue of one of Mick Sidebottom's bullocks, the men had been given forty-eight hours to pack their bags and leave. Folk said it was worse than going on evacuation, during the last war. This time the enemy drifted through the air, silent, ruthless and invisible.

His head was pounding and he kept taking the bends in the road too fast. At least there was no other traffic around; the Ministry kept warning against 'non-essential movement'. As he had driven through the smoke and vapour up top, a couple of tiny patches of unburned flesh had landed on the bonnet of his van. He clipped a hedge as he skimmed round a tight bend, but only when he struck a pothole did the bits fall off. At last he slowed as he reached the disinfected matting stretched over a cattle grid. In the distance he could see Gordon Clegg power-washing his tractor for the umpteenth time. Anything to keep the plague at bay.

Five minutes later, the squat church tower came into view. He glanced at his watch. Twelve o'clock. Time for a quick drink at the Wheatsheaf before he called home for half an hour. He had done enough killing and maybe he'd done enough drinking, too, but alcohol helped in a way nothing else did.

Dave Sharpe's rusty Vauxhall was the only other vehicle in the pub car park. He hesitated and thought about going straight to the house. Part of him wanted not to see Dave, not to speak to him, not to have to think about him ever again. But at least if he was swilling beer, he wasn't doing anything more dangerous. Jason took a breath and headed for the saloon.

Sally Binks was behind the bar, wearing a low-cut pink top and flirting with Dave. Apart from a couple of old men in the corner, no one else was in.

"Usual, love?"

He nodded. "And one for him."

"Cheers, mate," Dave said.

Funny, that. They had disliked each other for years, and still they called themselves mates. They had met on the first day of school at the age of five and on that very morning, Dave had pulled his hair and made him cry, then pretended it was all some kind of joke. As they grew up together, anyone listening to their lazy banter would never have a clue about what went on inside their heads. Jason wondered if he actually hated Dave. He never cared to analyse his feelings, but he thought probably he did hate him. For many reasons, not least because Melanie had said last week that he looked like Kurt Cobain.

"All right?" he asked.

As Sally moved to pick up the tankards, Dave reluctantly shifted his gaze from her cleavage and gave a shrug. "Feller from Padgett's was in here a few minutes ago. He said that when the rain came after they buried the sheep out Settle way, the bodies exploded. They exploded, literally exploded. He said, if you watched the ground, it looked as though the earth was sweating blood."

"Wicked," Sally said as she pulled the levers. Her breasts wobbled, hypnotising Dave again. "Wicked."

In the corner of the bar, the television was murmuring. The midday news. A government spokesman, carefully compassionate in a Paul Smith suit, was promising that everything was getting better. The detail of his explanation was lost as the old men in the corner hooted with scorn.

"'Back under control?'" one of them said. "Tell that to Jack Wilson's widow. No wonder the poor bastard hung himself. Took him and his dad forty years to build that herd."

"Aye," his toothless companion said.

"Nothing even wrong with the animals. Slaughter on suspicion, that's what it was."

The other man supped his pint. "Aye."

"See that bugger?" the old man said, jerking a thumb at the screen. "Pity he's never had blood and brains splashed all over him."

"Aye."

Dave winced. He was a postman and his work was already finished for the day. He'd never worked on the land and was one of the few people Jason knew whose life had not been touched by the coming of the plague.

When Jason said nothing, Dave nudged him in the ribs. "So how are you, mate? And how's the missus?"

His wolfish features gave nothing away, but was there a touch of mockery in his tone? Jason thought so. It wasn't just his imagination.

"I'm all right. So's Melanie."

"Great. Glad to hear you're looking after Mel. Did I ever tell you how I used to fancy her when she was a kid?"

Dave would have fancied Godzilla if it had worn a skirt. His late mother had fondly described him as *incorrigible*, a favourite word. He'd finished up getting Cheryl Stringer pregnant and marrying her before the baby was born. It wasn't in his nature to do the decent thing, so everyone assumed that it was because he'd never found anyone with a sexual appetite to match Cheryl's. Jason had never cared for Cheryl – she was so in-your-face – but these days she was proving impossible to avoid. In January she had started working as a classroom assistant at Melanie's school and the two couples had fallen into a habit of seeing each other regularly. Melanie said that Cheryl was fun, but Jason couldn't help wondering if it was an excuse, an opportunity for his wife to spend more time with Dave. She said that he made her laugh.

"Yeah, you told me."

"Course, she was too posh for me. For all of us. No offence, mate, but I never figured out how you managed to catch her eye."

He'd often asked himself that very question, never quite worked out the answer.

Dave drained his glass. "Same again?"

Jason hadn't finished his drink, but his headache was no better and he decided he'd had enough. Especially of Dave. He pushed the tankard across the counter to Sally and shook his head. "Another time."

"Off to kill a few more?" Dave mimicked the Sundance Kid firing his six-shooter.

"Later."

Dave treated him to a knowing leer. Jason could smell the ale on his breath. "Popping back to the nest for a quickie, then? Don't blame you, mate. Give my love to Mel, now, don't forget."

Jason loathed the easy familiarity of that *Mel*. He turned away, not trusting himself to answer. When he reached home, Melanie was in the front room. She used it as a study and was tapping on the keyboard of her computer. It was half-term, supposed to be a holiday, but she always found plenty to do. As he walked into the room, she glanced over her shoulder.

"You left early this morning."

"I tried not to disturb you."

"I heard the van when you set off."

"Sorry."

"Doesn't matter. How did it go?"

"Well, you know. The usual."

He'd never been good with words, not like Melanie. Anyway, how could you describe what he saw, what he felt? Nothing could have prepared him for this. The terror on the faces of the beasts, the staring eyes, the hoarse panting, the blood seeping from the wounds where they had in panic crashed through strands of barbed wire.

"Ready for a sandwich? There's cheese in the fridge."

She turned back to her computer. He wondered if he should go up behind her and kiss her on the neck. At one time, that would have melted her in a moment, but they had been married four years. Four years! Time to start a family, though she had always been reluctant. Weren't teachers supposed to like kids? But she never behaved like all the other girls he'd grown up with. Always, Melanie was different.

"Good morning?"

"Not bad," she said, still focusing on the text on the screen. "There's such a lot of work to do with the national curriculum. By the way, I wouldn't mind a sandwich myself."

In the kitchen, Jason found the bread knife. He hadn't expected marriage to be like this. What had he expected? He wasn't sure, perhaps he'd never thought clearly enough about it before asking Melanie to share his life. Marriage was what people did, but he had assumed that, because Melanie was different, their life together would somehow be different from everyone else's. After all, she was his fairy bride.

He ran his forefinger along the serrated edge of the knife, remembering how young Kevin Nolan had slit the throat of a terrified lamb the previous afternoon. The lamb was healthy, like all the other creatures down Beggarman's Lane, but that was not enough to guarantee survival. Tests on blood and tissue taken from animals at an adjoining farm had proved positive and the rules of contiguous culling meant that their neighbours had to die.

"I wouldn't mind a cup of tea while you're at it," Melanie called.

She talked like a woman of fifty, he thought, switching on the kettle. Not that she looked a day over twenty. Her face didn't have a single line. Three years older, he'd only been vaguely aware of her existence during her teens. He'd never spoken to her until the night of a dance in the village hall, a couple of weeks after she finished at college. He'd watched her, with her friends, and found himself hypnotised. She seemed delicate and aloof from their chatter, a slim, almost boyish figure in a simple dress lacking all the slits and embellishments favoured by her companions. Something prompted him to talk to her, even though he had watched her reject overtures from a number of the other young men. Including Dave Sharpe.

A couple of months later, when their unlikely romance was turning into something more than a fling, he tried to explain how he admired her, how he loved to watch her when she was watching something or someone else. There was a stillness about her that entranced him, and something more: an air of not belonging that was neither loneliness nor isolation, but a sort of serene uniqueness with which he had fallen hopelessly in love.

Of course, he found it impossible to describe his feelings. At first she had teased him, but when she realised that he meant to be deadly serious, her tone had softened and she had said that she thought she knew what he meant.

"I never wanted to be one of the crowd," she said, squeezing his hand.

"You're not," he said. "You're almost – well, not quite human."

"Thanks a lot," she laughed, withdrawing her hand in mock indignation. "Sort of alien from outer space, am I?"

"No, no," he said, his voice becoming hoarse with embarrassment. "But you're not like Dawn and Becky and all the rest. You're not like anyone I ever met before."

"I'll take that as a compliment, shall I?"

"You better had," he said. "I want to marry you."

To his amazement, she said yes. No play-acting, no messing. He could not believe his good fortune. Why him? In the past, he'd done all right with the girls, even if he would never be in Dave Sharpe's league. At least he was muscular and fit and poor tubby little Hannah Stott had once told him that his hazel eyes were the most beautiful she had ever seen. He was never mean with money and no woman would ever feel the slap of his hand, which was more than you could say for many men, even in this day and age. But Melanie had a brain and wanted to use it. She could make something of herself.

As for Jason, he didn't think he'd ever find a job that truly suited him. Perhaps his old Maths master had been right in branding him as lazy. It went deeper than a visceral loathing of algebra. Above all, Jason admired beauty. He admired it in a landscape, in a summer sunset, in the face and body of a gorgeous woman. How easy to become lost in rapture, to pass the hours in quiet adoration. But there was no beauty in work. Routine bored him and so he moved from job to job. He had been a garage mechanic, a gardener, a farmhand, a butcher's assistant, a slaughterman at an abattoir.

A week before the wedding, he asked Melanie if she'd ever loved anyone else. Idle curiosity, no hidden agenda – but for some reason, his inquisitiveness upset her out of all proportion. She was usually calm, unworldly even, and he was surprised to see her eyes filling with tears.

"Listen," she said gently as he stammered an apology. "It doesn't matter. But you must promise me one thing."

"Anything," he said. His worst nightmare was that she would pull out of their engagement. Twice already he had dreamed of her failing to show at the church on the day itself and of his mortification as everyone in the congregation stared at him in horrified sympathy.

"You must keep this promise and never break it." She thought for a moment. "I don't suppose you ever heard of Melusine?"

He shook his head. She often treated him as a pupil; it amused her to teach him things. He didn't mind; he was content simply to let her words wash over him, not absorbing the lessons, just luxuriating in her company.

"Melusine was a beautiful fairy but she had a terrible secret." A faraway look came into her eyes. "One day each week, she became half-woman, half-serpent. A man fell in love with her and she agreed to marry him, on one condition, that he never saw her on a Saturday."

"What happened?"

"Someone poisoned his mind, and said that was the day Melusine met her lover. When her husband broke his word and found out the truth, he lost everything. Including Melusine."

"I don't get it."

"Listen, I'm like Melusine. I ask just one thing of you. You must promise never to be jealous."

"So you've got a terrible secret?" His tone was jokey, but her flights of fancy baffled him. "It's not the new vicar, is it? I saw him across the street the other day. Quite a hunk. The church shouldn't allow it."

She put a finger to her lips. "Shhh, darling. No, I don't fancy the vicar, but I do want you to trust me. Now, are you going to promise or not?"

"You really want me to?"

She nodded seriously and he realised that he must not get this wrong. Not now, when he was committed to her. Even though he did not know why, he had to make his promise.

"I swear."

Her face broke into the loveliest smile and within moments he forgot about Melusine. In the years that followed, there was no hint that Melanie might have a terrible secret. She did not smoke, did not drink, and she had to be persuaded into any bedroom games that were not pretty conventional. Even now, he told himself he was crazy to believe that she was deceiving him.

He took the sandwich and cup of tea into her. "Here you are."

"Thanks. So when are you going back?"

"Five minutes."

"I'll have your tea ready by half six."

"Great."

"No problem."

She was still glued to the computer screen. He drank in the sight of her. Her hair was the same rich chestnut shade he had always loved, her skin was as white and unsullied as when they first kissed. Yet something had changed. He was no longer special to her; she had stopped trying to educate him to understand what appealed to her. Nowadays he featured in her life in much the same way as their shabby old furniture or the framed views of Brimham Rocks that hung on the wall of their living room.

"See you later, then."

"Mmmmm."

He closed the door quietly. As he rooted in his jacket pocket for the keys to the van, he wondered who had stolen her affections. Dave Sharpe? Checking the map in his glove compartment, he told himself for the hundredth time that life was not so cruel, that the only reason he was obsessed with the fear that Dave was cuckolding him was because such a betrayal would be too hard to bear.

Heading for the next Infected Premises, he couldn't rid his mind of Dave's gloating smile. As lads, they had played rugby together in winter and cricket in summer. They had so much in common and people regarded them as bosom buddies. Dave was fun and he was generous, but there were moments when the mask of good nature slipped. Taking a short cut along a single-track lane, Jason remembered a game one July when he and Dave had batted in partnership. It was one of those days of which cricketers dream. The ball kept speeding off his bat to the boundary. Even the best bowlers on the other side were helpless in the face of such a sustained attack. When he was one run short of his century, Dave called him for a quick single. The ball was in the hands of the cover point fielder, a farmer with a famously strong arm. Jason hesitated for a second, then put his head down and ran. His stumps were shattered when he was two yards short of the safety of the crease at the far end. In the bar afterwards, Dave had bought the drinks and said he took the blame. Jason argued with him, saying that if he had set off straightaway, he would have made his ground. But secretly, he knew that Dave was right. It was a reckless call, his fault. Perhaps he had been too anxious to see Jason achieve his moment of glory. Or perhaps he had wanted to deny it to him forever. Jason had never scored a ton since.

When he arrived at the site, the man from the Ministry came up as he was slipping on his white biohazard overall and rubber boots. "You took your time."

Jason's wave took in Kevin Nolan standing by a picket fence, supping Coke from a can, and Bob Garrett sitting in the cab of his van, reading *The Sun*. "Better things to do with my day than spend hours hanging around here, waiting for the word."

"Look here, you know the score. We have to get the go-ahead from the vet. But if you keep buggering off, we don't know where we are."

Jason shrugged. He was freelance, and right now the Ministry needed as much help as it could get. Three million animals didn't kill themselves. None of the slaughtermen liked the Ministry blokes. They were pen-pushers, more comfortable in a warm office than on the land. Most of the slaughtermen had learned their trade on farms, they were countrymen. They didn't have to like what they were doing or the people who paid them to do it.

Bob Garrett jumped down from his cab. "Eh up, pal. Wipe that smirk off your face. We all know you've been off giving your old lady a good seeing-to."

Garrett's ex-wife lived across the road from Jason. The previous summer, Jason had spotted him eyeing up Melanie when he brought back the kids and she was sunbathing on the lawn. No matter how many times he told himself that other men were jealous of him, it never helped, never made him feel good. What was wrong with him? Why did he feel damaged by the way they lusted after his lovely fairy wife? And things were getting worse. He couldn't shake off the fear that people were laughing at him behind his back. They knew something that he did not.

Kevin Nolan was sniggering, but Jason didn't rise to the bait. "How many are we doing this afternoon?"

The man from the Ministry consulted his clipboard. "Eighty-five cattle. Not a big job. I just spoke to the vet. We should be set to go in a couple of minutes."

Jason opened the door of his van and picked up the gun from the passenger seat. "Better get ready, then."

Their task did not take long. They were using captive bolt guns rather than rifles. A blank cartridge fired a four inch steel bolt into the animal's skull and a spring retracted the bolt. Once the animal had been stunned in this way, it was pithed, by means of a steel rod being thrust through the hole and into the brain.

As usual, not everything went according to plan. One bull had to be shot and pithed four times. The more he fought for life, the more Jason's temper frayed. What was the point of struggling? The bull wasn't sick, but it had to die anyway. Those were the orders. He wanted it over as quickly as possible and resented the doomed bull for delaying the inevitable. The more time you had to think about what you were doing, the worse it was for everyone.

"Where next?" he asked the man from the Ministry.

"There's a couple of dozen lambs penned up the other side of the barn at the end of the lane. You and Garrett head off there now, I'll catch up once I've had a word with the farmer."

The farmer had turned up during the killings. He'd stayed over by the fence, watching the destruction of his herd. Jason could tell the man was close to tears. In the early days, he had talked to the farmers whose herds he shot, tried to console them. But what could you say? Most people round here reckoned that it would be enough to vaccinate the animals and claimed the culling was unnecessary. But the powers-that-be in London thought differently, and that was what mattered.

Jason held the lambs while Bob Garrett shot them. He took care not to look at the faces of the creatures, settling his gaze instead on fields in the middle distance. The countryside was full of death, but Nature didn't seem to notice. Ragged robin, elderflower and foxgloves still bloomed.

"These fellers in the Thatched Tavern were talking last night," Garrett said. "They'd killed fifteen hundred sheep and cattle on one farm and then they were told to disinfect round a jackdaw's nest for conservation reasons. Christ, would you bloody believe it?"

Jason grunted. Perhaps all wars were like this; everyone had an anecdote to tell. Live lambs suffocating to death under the corpses of sheep with cut throats. Wagons driven by young squaddies, carrying the carcasses to the burial pits and leaking blood all along the country lanes. Each storyteller liked to spin a yarn more absurd or more horrific than the last.

"You all right?" Garrett asked. "You look – sort of glazed. On a promise for tonight, then?"

Jason felt his chest tightening. He wanted to grab the man, shake him by the neck until he choked, demanding to know why he kept talking about Melanie. What was going on – something that he, the poor old husband, was the last to know?

He strode away, unable to trust himself to speak. Surely he was wrong in suspecting Dave. What about Garrett himself? He was an older man and Jason supposed he was good-looking if you like that sort of thing. Or even Kevin Nolan? Kevin's last year at the school had been Melanie's first as a teacher. Jason remembered her saying that he was a rascal, but somehow she couldn't find it in her heart not to like him. That was the trouble with Melanie. She never saw through people, she was too naïve to realise that the men she liked were only interested in one thing.

"Where are you going?" Garrett demanded.

Jason pointed to the heap of bodies on the ground. "I've had enough of this."

"If you don't wait for whatsisname to show up and sign you off, there'll be hell to pay."

Jason shrugged. "So what?"

He'd walked away from jobs before. Even as he clambered out of his overall and boots, his headache was easing. Garrett gave a disgusted shake of the head. Kevin Nolan was grinning. Surely, *surely*, Melanie couldn't have slept with that lad?

Even as he sped back to the village, he told himself that he couldn't confront her. It wasn't so much that he lacked the balls to do it, but he remembered what she had said about Melusine. He dared not demand to know if she had taken a lover. What he needed was reassurance.

It could still be OK, he thought, as he jolted over the disinfectant mat. We can start again. Soon, maybe, she'll be ready to try for a family. That will make all the difference.

"I didn't expect you back so soon," Melanie said when he opened the door of the study.

"I've jacked it in," he said. "The money's good, but I'm sick of the smell and the faces of the animals as I kill them."

She swallowed. "What are you going to do?"

"Dunno. I'll find something."

"But there's no work! Haven't you heard? The countryside is closed. No tourists, no trade, nothing. People are going bankrupt right, left and centre."

"All right, it might take a while." He thought for a moment. "What's up? Don't you want me under your feet all day?"

"It's not that!" Two pink spots appeared in her cheeks. It wasn't like her to be flustered. "We can't go on like this."

"Me spending cash we haven't got at the Wheatsheaf, you mean?"

"Don't shout! I know you need to unwind…"

"Too right," he said, and marched out of the house.

Ten minutes later, nursing a pint in the saloon, he was wondering if he'd been too rough with her. They hardly ever argued; neither of them were natural combatants. When Sally asked him if he was OK, he bit her head off.

"Why? Don't I look OK?"

"I only asked," she said in an injured tone. "And if you want to know the truth, you look as miserable as sin."

It dawned on him that he hadn't been happy for a long time. Not since before the coming of the plague, that was for sure. Maybe he should offer Melanie an olive branch. It wasn't a Yorkshireman's habit to say sorry, but he wasn't proud. He would do anything, if it would help to recapture the love they had shared at one time. Maybe even work out his contract with the Ministry. He pulled his mobile out of his pocket and dialled home. He would apologise right now, and then go back and see what else he could do to make amends.

The number was engaged. He tried again a couple of minutes later, with the same result. Her parents were dead and she seldom socialised. The head teacher was on holiday and her two closest colleagues had taken a party of pupils to France. Who could she be talking to?

"Dave not in tonight?" he asked.

Sally shook her head to show that she bore no grudge for his sharp tone earlier. "He said that he would be busy in the garden until it got dark. He's building a rockery, you know."

Oh really? Jason's head was swimming and it wasn't just down to the beer. "Same again, then."

As darkness fell, Dave showed up. He spotted Jason and gave him a wicked grin. "What's up, mate? Abandoned your old lady? I dunno, you'd better take care. You know, women are like cars. You've got to keep their engines tuned."

"You've been looking after Cheryl?" a fat man at the bar demanded.

Dave found this amusing. "Matter of fact, I've been out in the garden."

"Oh yeah? Planting a few seeds?"

The fat man and Dave roared with laughter and fell into ribald conversation. Jason sat glowering and monosyllabic for a couple of rounds before summoning up the energy to head for home. If Dave had been with Mel, she would need time to have a bath, make herself decent. He didn't want a confrontation this evening. He had to think things through.

Although he could hold his beer better than most, he was swaying slightly as he walked through his front door. All the lights were out. It wasn't late, but Melanie must be in bed. She would probably say she needed the sleep, after he had woken her so inconsiderately that morning. Perhaps she was already fast asleep; she was bound to be tired.

On tiptoe, he made his way into the study. At night she left her mobile on her desk. He lifted it up and checked the list of recent calls. It was the first time in the marriage that he had ever snooped on her, but he couldn't help it. A familiar set of digits came up at once. His guts lurched. The number belonged to Dave Sharpe.

He started to climb the stairs, wanting to have it out with Melanie, but halfway up he changed his mind and went back down again. Better leave it until morning. He couldn't sleep beside her, though. Not after what she'd done. *Dave Sharpe.* His thoughts were as gridlocked as an urban motorway, but he could still guess what had happened. Dave and Melanie must have had a fling, but he'd two-timed her and got Cheryl pregnant. Perhaps Melanie had been too stingy in bed for him.

Melanie must have lost her heart to Dave. Yes, that explained everything. How she had fallen for Dave's mate on the rebound, her lapses into frigidity, even the story about Melusine. She did have a terrible secret after all.

He spent the night dozing fitfully on the lumpy sofa in their living room. At about four he woke from a nightmare. A dead bullock had risen like a zombie from the pile of carcasses and come towards him, intent upon taking revenge. The room was chilly in the middle of the night, but sweat was sticking his shirt to his chest. His head was pounding and the stale taste of beer lingered in his mouth.

Why had she done this to him? Dave was no fool; he must have picked up a hint that Melanie still held a torch for him. For all Cheryl's famously voracious appetites, he wouldn't have been able to resist the opportunity to be able to turn Jason into a cuckold. Humiliating his old 'friend' at the same time as enjoying the sweet pleasures of Melanie's tender flesh would double the fun.

At ten to seven, he heard the alarm shrilling in the bedroom. Moments later, Melanie came hurrying down the stairs, calling his name. When she saw him, her face turned crimson. In that instant, he knew that she knew he knew.

"What are you doing?" Her voice was croaky, uncertain.

"You should have told me the truth," he said. "We never should have got married."

"What are you talking about?" She was no good at feigning innocence. He thought she was naturally honest. Living a lie must have been a torment, but things had gone too far for him to feel a spurt of sympathy.

"Admit it. You're in love with Dave Sharpe, aren't you? That's always been your secret, hasn't it, *Melusine*? But you never had the bottle to tell me."

No actress could have faked the horror in her eyes. "You've got it all wrong."

"You lied to me," he said quietly. "But I found you out in the end."

"You don't understand!"

"Believe me, I do. You slut."

Tears were dribbling down her cheeks. For a moment she seemed transfixed and then she gave a little cry and ran out of the room and up the stairs. He heard her locking the door to their bedroom. No problem. He wasn't going after her just now. There was something else – this came to him in a slap of understanding – that he must do first.

He didn't bother to wash or shave; he was past all that. From upstairs came the sound of loud racking sobs, but as he unlocked his van, he felt a strange sense of calm, as if for the whole of his life he'd been wandering aimlessly, but now he'd found a mission.

Where could he find Dave Sharpe? At one time Dave's round had covered the village and its outskirts, but now he was a floater and covered for colleagues who were sick or on holiday, so he moved around the area. He said he preferred this; he liked the variety, but more than that, there was often a chance to meet new women. Countless times he regaled the Wheatsheaf saloon bar with anecdotes of nymphomaniac housewives who asked him in while their husbands were out at work. If only his restless womanising hadn't encompassed Melanie.

As Jason turned on the ignition, he saw the bedroom curtain twitch. His wife, furtively watching him drive out of their marriage. He slammed his foot down on the accelerator and the van shot out into the road, narrowly missing a milk float. His plan was to follow a circular route, heading out west first and then up and around the hillside before returning to the village. Sooner or later, he was sure to come across Dave Sharpe.

It took longer than he expected, but five miles from home he finally spotted his target. Dave was delivering a parcel to an isolated cottage at the end of a short lane. The woman on the doorstep was white-haired and frail, so Dave would not be lingering. The lane was narrow and Jason parked his van across to block it. He watched the woman go back inside her home and Dave climb on to his bicycle. Jason picked up the bolt gun from the passenger's seat. Keeping it behind his back, he shuffled out of the van to face his enemy.

"What...oh, it's you! Christ, Jason, what are you playing at?"

Jason said nothing. Dave dismounted and leaned his bike against the hedge. He marched up and stared into Jason's eyes.

"Lost your tongue?"

"I've lost everything," Jason said.

An odd light came into Dave's eyes. "Is this about Mel?"

Jason showed him the gun. They were within touching distance of each other. Jason caught a whiff of the other man's aftershave. Aftershave! What sort of a postman doused himself in that muck when he went out on his round of a morning? Only one who wanted to shag any woman stupid enough to give him the glad eye.

Dave's cheeks lost all colour. Hoarsely, he said, "What are you doing? Put that down."

Jason lifted the gun and put it to Dave's forehead. "You think I'm stupid, don't you?"

"I think you're mad. You've lost it, mate, totally lost it."

Dave tensed. Jason knew that he was going to try to grab the gun. He would only have one chance to do this. As he fired, he tried to close his eyes, but they wouldn't shut. He saw agony in Dave's eyes as well as hearing his scream. Just like my first day at the abattoir, he thought.

The pithing was over so quickly. Even as the old lady opened her door, coming to see who or what had screamed, Jason was back in the van, reversing over the body just to make sure before turning for the village. Some of Dave's blood had splashed over him, but he didn't care. His mind was as empty as the fields as he raced along the narrow winding lanes to his home. What was he going to say to Melanie? Was she truly lost to him forever? Ought she to die as well?

Within minutes he was back. The front door was ajar. Bolt gun in hand, he kicked it wide open and strode inside. He could hear Melanie weeping. Well, now she had something to weep about. He took the stairs two at a time. The bedroom door was shut. If she'd locked it, he meant to kick it down. But when he smashed the gun against the door, it swung on its hinges.

A woman cried out. Then he heard another voice, softly murmuring. As he stepped inside the bedroom, something occurred to him. *This is all wrong*. Melanie was with someone. Yet he had killed Dave Sharpe.

Melanie was in bed. Her eyes were puffy, her cheeks wet. Her companion had wrapped a plump arm around her shoulders. They were naked, both Melanie and Cheryl Sharpe. *Yes, I got it so wrong*. Helpless as doomed lambs, neither of them able to move or speak, the lovers stared at him.

His hand shaking, he pointed the gun first at his wife and then at Cheryl, before changing his mind and raising it instead to his left temple. The cold steel nuzzled his skin. This, at least, was a necessary death.

TOP DECK

Kate Ellis

November 1965

At ten past six on a rainy Tuesday evening, Keith O'Dowd witnessed a murder.

Up until then it had been an ordinary Liverpool Tuesday, a day like every other. At half past five Keith had left the portals of the Liver Building and hurried across the Pier Head in the rain to catch his bus home. His boss, Mr. Kelly, was leaving at the same time, in the company of his secretary, Linda. Kelly had given Keith a distant nod of acknowledgement on the stairs before heading off in the direction of the car park and his brand new Ford Cortina. Keith experienced a pang of envy. He could never afford a motor like that on the meagre wages he earned as a shipping clerk. But maybe one day things would be different. Maybe one day he would join the police force like his granddad and become a detective. Everyone has to dream. And, according to his mother, Keith dreamed more than most.

That evening it was pouring with rain and the number eighty bus was ten minutes late arriving at the terminus. When it finally turned up Keith clattered up the metal stairs to the top deck, his wet trouser legs flapping cold around his ankles, and made his way straight to the front seat, the seat with the best view on the bus. He sat down by the window and lit a cigarette, then he sat quite still for a few moments, inhaling deeply before wiping the misted up window with the sleeve of his coat. Looking out of the window was better than reading the paper. And you never knew what you might see.

The bus set off through the city centre, past stores closing up for the night. The glow from the bright shop windows reflected golden on the glistening pavements and umbrellas danced up and down the streets, their owners hidden beneath. Soon they were hurtling past the

Philharmonic Hall and the Women's Hospital with its rows of brightly lit windows. Then past the faded Georgian elegance of Catherine Street where the houses of wealthy merchants and ship owners had long ago been claimed by the poor and the Bohemian, bedsit dwellers and students. Keith stared out of his lofty mobile watchtower, wiping the window from time to time to get a better view.

Keith took this bus every night, rain or shine, winter or summer, and there was nothing that Tuesday night to tell him that this journey was going to be different from any other. There had been no omens of death as in the horror films he loved so much. No howling wolves or circling ravens; no mysterious gypsies issuing cryptic warnings. It had been a normal day; a good day. He had been to NEMS in his lunch hour to buy the Beatles' latest LP, *Help*, for his girlfriend Susan's birthday. He had bought some cigarettes too…and a packet of Durex from Boots just in case his luck changed when Susan saw the record. Keith patted the plastic record bag: Susan loved the Beatles so he felt rather pleased with his choice.

Once they were away from the bright, artificial lights of the city centre the scene outside grew darker…but then it was the beginning of November and the clocks had gone back. As they crawled down Princes Road Keith closed his eyes but he opened them again when the bus swung too fast round the bend at Princes Park gates, throwing him against the man who shared his seat. He restored his dignity by lighting a calming cigarette and the next time he looked out of the window he saw that they were passing the shadowy acres of Sefton Park heading down Ullet Road. His boss, Mr. Kelly, lived on Ullet Road, so he'd heard from the office gossips. He owned flats there. Flats and a new Cortina. Mr. Kelly was a lucky man.

When the bus stopped briefly in Ullet Road to let somebody off Keith found himself staring straight across into a lighted upstairs window. The curtains were wide open and two people were silhouetted behind the glass; a man and a woman who, for a split second, seemed faintly familiar. The man seemed to have both his hands raised up to the woman's throat and they were moving slowly to and fro as if the woman was trying to ward him off, trying to save her life. Just as one of the figures appeared to collapse to the floor, the bus suddenly pulled off and tore away from the bus stop at speed.

It had all been over in a matter of seconds and Keith sat there, dazed, wondering if he'd imagined the whole thing. He turned to the man sitting next to him, a thin, middle-aged man in a shabby raincoat who smoked nervously. He was reading a newspaper, the *Liverpool Echo*, and appeared to be engrossed in the small ads. Keith contemplated asking him whether he'd seen the couple in the flat but he decided against it. The man would probably think he was mad.

He turned round and saw two girls sitting in the seat behind, one peroxide blonde and the other henna red, both with mini skirts that left little to the imagination. It would do no harm to ask…if he could phrase the question so that he didn't sound like a complete lunatic. "Excuse me, love, did you see that murder back in Ullet Road?" might result in the men in white coats carting him away.

But from the way the two girls were chatting away, it was obvious that their minds were firmly fixed on gossip and there was no way they'd have seen anything out of the ordinary. And he guessed that, judging by the bored looks on the faces of his fellow passengers, nobody else had either. The blonde girl caught Keith's eye but she ignored him, pulling her mini skirt down to the middle of her thighs as she carried on pointedly chatting to her friend. But attractive girls were the last thing on Keith's mind at that moment. Some woman might be lying dead in the house they'd passed; a woman whose profile had triggered a bat squeak of recognition. But had he really seen her die?

As they stopped at the traffic lights in Smithdown Road, Keith felt a sudden urge to get off the bus, to hurry back to the spot where he'd seen the couple: he could remember the exact house and the exact window and for all he knew the woman might still be alive and in need of help. Perhaps he should tell the police. That would be what his mother would tell him to do. And Susan…she would always play things by the book. He stood up and the *Echo* reader beside him looked flustered as he juggled with lighted cigarette and open newspaper before swinging his legs out into the aisle to let Keith pass, thinking he was getting off at the next stop.

But Keith hesitated and sat down again, murmuring an apology. As the *Echo* reader mumbled, "Make up your mind, pal," and rearranged his newspaper, Keith sat on the edge of the seat, feeling foolish. Looking round the damp, smoky top deck he was quite sure that nobody else had seen what he had seen. He was the only witness. Or had he been watching too many Hitchcock films? Had his mind been playing tricks?

In all Keith's seventeen years, he had always possessed a streak of caution. He had never gone in for games of dare at school, never played on railway lines or played chicken with cars like some of his classmates. And in his heart of hearts he knew that there was no way he was going to investigate that flat in Ullet Road alone while there was a chance that a murderer might still be hanging about. But he still felt he should do something. Perhaps he should find a phone box when he got off the bus and call the police. Or venture into Allerton police station and report it.

He sat staring out of the window and by the time he passed Penny Lane he had managed to convince himself that he had probably imagined the whole thing. After all, if nobody else on the bus had seen it, it was likely that he was mistaken. Perhaps the couple had just been having a fight...or even dancing. If he went to the police, he might make a complete fool of himself. And besides, he wouldn't have time that night. He was taking Susan to the Odeon to see *Dr. Zhivago*: she'd been on at him to take her to see it for ages but it didn't sound like Keith's cup of tea. He preferred something like *Psycho*; just the sort of film that would make Susan terrified enough to want to cling to him in the dark. As he thought of the evening ahead he told himself to forget about the upstairs window. He had imagined it. Or it had been a trick of the light.

As he predicted, Susan adored the film's exotic romance. And when he had kissed her in the back row she had responded eagerly and allowed his hands to explore parts of her body not previously available to him. As he walked her home he wondered whether to mention what he'd thought he'd seen from the top deck of the bus but he decided against it: she would only have told him that he was imagining things and that he'd seen something quite innocent; a man taking a speck of dirt out of a woman's eye; or a couple kissing. And she would probably have been right. Instead Keith concentrated on a long and passionate goodnight, one that might have held a promise of something more if Susan's father hadn't been watching from the front bedroom window.

But that night it wasn't Susan who featured in his dreams. Instead he dreamed about murder. Dreamed that he was on the top deck of the eighty bus, outside the house in Ullet Road watching a shadowy figure stabbing a woman in a shower. Blood was spurting from the open flat window and landing in rivulets on the windows of the bus and Keith was wiping it away with his sleeve. He shouted but no sound came from his mouth. Then the man in the raincoat next to him on the bus suddenly turned, with mad staring eyes, and began to drive a knife into his defenceless body.

*　　*　　*

Keith felt exhausted when his mother woke him up the next morning but he hauled himself out of bed and dressed by the paraffin heater in his bedroom. His mother nagged him to have a proper breakfast, just as she did every morning, but Keith had no time. He grabbed a slice of toast and took a sip of tea before hurrying out into the chilly, bright morning, making it to the bus stop just in time.

He hopped on to the pea-green bus with the Corporation coat of arms painted on its side and made his way up the stairs, clinging to the handrail. The fog of morning cigarette smoke hit him as he reached the top deck and he was glad to see that his favourite seat was still free – the seat at the front with the panoramic view. He settled himself down and lit his first cigarette of the day, then he sat back, enjoying the fresh rush of nicotine and trying not to think of the dull routine of the day ahead.

As the bus chugged down Ullet Road he felt a thrill of anticipation. He had made sure he was sitting on the right-hand side of the bus so that he would have the best view of the upstairs window as the bus drove past. But he wasn't sure what he expected to see. A body lying on a brightly illuminated bed, perhaps? Or a screaming woman clawing at the window? Or, more likely, nothing at all.

The bus shuddered to a halt opposite what he'd started to think of as the murder house and the diesel engine throbbed while the queue of passengers climbed on. He focused on the window – the bay window on the first floor – but the thin cotton curtains were drawn, hiding the scene within. Keith studied the house: it was a large Victorian building: a corner house, probably divided into flats like most of its neighbours, standing at the end of a row of similar houses next to a side road. Red brick and vaguely Gothic in style, it was a house to grace any horror film. Just the sort of place to harbour a killer – or his victim. As the bus set off, Keith noticed a car parked close to the corner – a shiny blue Cortina, probably brand new. It looked exactly like his boss, Mr. Kelly's car, but Keith told himself that it couldn't be: Mr. Kelly always arrived at work early so he would be on his way by now. There must be a lot of brand new Cortinas around: a lot of lucky bastards who didn't have to queue at the bus stop every morning.

For the remainder of the journey Keith stared out of the window, watching the city awake from its slumber under the blue autumn sky. The bus pulled in to its allotted spot at the Pier Head bus station and cut its noisy engine. Then Keith walked the short distance to the Liver Building, accompanied by a fanfare of screaming sea gulls. Another day, another dollar, as he had once heard someone say.

When he reached the office he sensed a strange undercurrent of excitement. The clerks kept their heads down but the secretaries talked in whispers, as if they were sharing forbidden secrets…secrets too juicy for general consumption. Keith sorted through the papers on his desk, watching and listening. Something was going on in that smoky shipping office. And he wanted to know what it was.

He realised that he hadn't seen Mr. Kelly that morning, which was unusual: he was normally there in his glass-fronted office keeping an eye on things. Not that Kelly had much to say to the young clerks. He was old, at least thirty-five, tall with glossy black hair and a snub nose. But the girls in the office seemed to like him.

It was lunchtime before the clerks had a chance to get together. As Keith took a ham sandwich out of the lunch box his mother had packed for him first thing that morning, Mike Fry hurried over. Mike had joined the firm around the same time as Keith and he had a shock of red hair and a face that couldn't keep a secret. He perched on the corner of Keith's desk and looked around before leaning forward.

"So what do you think?" Mike began in a whisper.

"Think of what?"

"Mr. Kelly and Linda."

Mr. Kelly's secretary, Linda, was a tall, dark-haired young woman, beautiful in an unconventional kind of way. Striking, Keith's mother would have called her. None of the young clerks knew Linda well. She was way above them…as distant as a goddess.

"What about them?" Keith asked innocently.

"They've not come into work. Someone rang Kelly's house and there was no answer."

"What about Linda?"

"She's not on the phone."

"Perhaps she's ill then…and she couldn't get to a phone box."

Mike grinned knowingly. "Perhaps. Funny though, them both being off at the same time. Maybe they've gone on a dirty weekend together."

"It's Wednesday."

But this inconvenient fact didn't deter Mike. Soon others had gathered around the desk and in due course the verdict was that Kelly and Linda were holed up in a hotel in Blackpool living off the fruits of passion. A small, fair-haired typist, wise beyond her tender years, announced solemnly that they'd fancied each other for at least a year; certainly since the death of Mr. Kelly's wife…or maybe even before. There's nothing like office gossip for exercising the imagination.

"Perhaps the big bosses know where Mr. Kelly is," suggested Keith. "Perhaps they just haven't told us minions."

Mike leaned forward. "I saw Mr. Davies before and I asked him if Mr. Kelly would be in…trying to sound all innocent, like…but he didn't say anything. I reckon Kelly's gone AWOL. And so has Linda," he added with a wink.

"Kelly lives somewhere in Ullet Road, doesn't he? Near Sefton Park?" Keith said innocently.

"That's right," Mike piped up. "I heard he owns some flats down there."

"I heard that too," said Keith. This was old news.

"Someone said they belonged to his late wife. She inherited them from an aunt or something."

"What did his wife die of?" Keith asked. But nobody knew the answer.

The conversation ground to a halt. They'd covered the sum total of their knowledge about their boss's private life. Mike had done well to glean the information about the late wife's inheritance. He'd make a good detective, Keith thought, with a slight pang of envy.

"I'm sure I saw his car parked off Ullet Road this morning," said Keith.

But the clerks had lost interest and turned their attention to their sandwiches and the subject of Saturday's football match.

That afternoon Keith found it difficult to concentrate on his work and he kept looking at his watch, longing for five thirty. Longing for his homeward journey on the eighty bus. He kept thinking of Kelly and Linda. Why hadn't they turned up at work? He had to check out the house. And he was impatient to get it over with.

He would be late home, of course, and his mother would be annoyed because his tea would be spoiled. But she had refused to contemplate having a telephone put in so it couldn't be helped. He wanted to discover the truth. And the more he thought about it, the more he was convinced that the woman he saw being murdered might have been Linda. But had the man been Kelly? It had all happened too quickly to see.

The bus went out on time that night. Keith was first on and he hurried up the stairs to the top deck and headed for the seat at the front. He lit a cigarette. He needed one. He was afraid...afraid of what he might find. He sat there in the fog of smoke and crushed homeward-bound bodies, chain smoking and fidgeting with the clasp on the cheap leather briefcase his mother had bought him last Christmas. Somehow the journey seemed longer that evening. Like the journey to a place of execution.

When they reached the top of Ullet Road, Keith stood up and stubbed out his cigarette on the dirty grey floor. Grabbing the handrails, he made his way down the bus which rocked and lurched so much that he almost took a tumble down the stairs. The conductor stood on the platform, watching him with a smirk on his face. Keith jumped down on to the pavement outside the big red brick house as the smirking conductor rang the bell and the pea-green bus pulled away in a cloud of diesel fumes. From now on he was on his own. There was no going back.

He stood at the bus stop for a few minutes looking up at the house. The curtains were still drawn across the upstairs bay window but the light was on, a single bulb shining through the thin cotton. And he could see a shadow moving behind the flimsy material. Somebody was at home.

Keith knew he had to check if the Cortina was still there. He had been so certain that it was Mr. Kelly's car, but now he was there on the spot he began to have his doubts. What if he was leaping to conclusions? Adding two and two and making five? The road was a long one – Kelly might live anywhere. And he and Linda might both have come down with some illness or other and been unable to let the office know. He walked to the corner and looked down the side road. But there was no sign of the Cortina he had seen that morning.

Keith was beginning to feel rather stupid. His mother would tell him that he had been watching far too many Hitchcock films and maybe she was right. What did he have to go on? He knew Mr. Kelly lived in that particular road and owned flats in the area. And he had seen what he believed to be his car parked next to the house where he had seen a man murdering a woman, who may or may not have borne some vague, passing resemblance to Linda. And Kelly and Linda had not turned up for work that day, apparently without explanation. He had put all these facts together and come up with a scenario straight from the movies. Kelly had been having an affair with Linda and he had murdered her – for reasons unknown – in full view of the top deck of the number eighty bus before going to ground, a fugitive from justice.

It had all seemed so plausible sitting in the smoky warmth of the top deck but now, here in the cold November air, it began to seem rather far-fetched and ridiculous. He made his way slowly back to the bus stop. Perhaps he should just wait for the next eighty and go home.

And yet he had seen the couple struggling...the man possibly strangling the woman. It had just been a glimpse, over too quickly and too far away for any sort of identification. But he had seen it – he was certain of that. And now the light was on in that very room. There was somebody up there.

He took a deep breath. He had come this far so he might as well check, just to satisfy his own curiosity. He would concoct a story. He would be looking for a friend called John who lived next door and he would apologise profusely when he was told he had the wrong house. He loved detective stories and he felt rather pleased with himself for thinking up this ingenious ploy.

He pushed open the wooden gate and walked slowly up the path to the front door. The house was divided into flats like so many of its neighbours and there was a row of doorbells at the side of the flaking front door. Beside the row of bells a fat spider was sitting in the centre of a large web. Keith peered at the labels, trying to make out names in the dim glow of the streetlight. There was one in the middle that stood out, however. A neatly typed label gave the name of the occupier of flat number three as 'Kelly'. Keith's heart began to beat faster. Had his instincts been right all along? But then he told himself that there must be hundreds of Kellys in Liverpool, a city where at least half the population had Irish ancestry. The spider shifted slightly as he stared at the bell, pondering his next move.

He turned to go. It had been a stupid idea. But as he turned he came face to face with a young man, roughly the same age as himself, maybe a year or two older. The young man's hair was long, Beatles style, and he wore a donkey jacket and a Liverpool University scarf.

"How do?" he said with a grin. His accent was Yorkshire and he had an open, freckled face. "Who are you looking for?"

The young man was obviously a student, and he hardly looked like a murderer. "Er, I heard there was a flat going. Is it this one? Kelly?" He pointed at the bell.

"No, that's the landlord. Look, I don't think any of the flats are empty...unless the landlord's decided to move up in the world. He works in town and he inherited this place from his first wife so he can't be badly off. And he's just bought a brand new car so he must be in the money," he added bluntly, extending his hand. He seemed the chatty type, which suited Keith fine. "Jim Watts...doing medicine," he said, looking Keith up and down, noting his jacket and tie. "Are you a student then?"

"Er, no. I work in town. Thought it was time I got a place of my own...you know how it is." He took Jim's hand and shook it. "John McCartney," he said without quite knowing why he felt so reluctant to use his real name.

His heart was beating fast: he'd been right all along. Kelly did live there. And now he had disappeared...so had Linda. And Keith had seen him kill her.

"Just ring that bell there." Jim pointed to a bell marked 'Kelly'. "The light's on so one of them should be in."

"One of them?" Keith was aware that his voice was quivering with nerves. He had come too far to back out now.

"Either Mr. or Mrs. Kelly. Landlord or his wife. They've got the big flat on the first floor."

"I thought you said his wife was dead."

"That was his first wife." Jim winked. "He's remarried. Much younger than him. Linda, her name is. Lovely legs."

Before Keith could stop him, Jim had pressed Kelly's bell, trying to be helpful. "I'll leave you to it, then, " said the student. "One of 'em should be down in a minute. Good luck."

With that he closed the front door and Keith was left standing on the doorstep, stunned. Kelly was married to Linda – or at least that's what he told his tenants. He was living with her in a flat on the first floor, a flat he owned. And she was calling herself Mrs. Kelly. The situation would have provided hours of office gossip...if he hadn't murdered her. And he was upstairs now, probably getting rid of the evidence. Or disposing of the body. It was really time to go to the police. He had played detective but he felt he couldn't go it alone any more.

He turned to go. The next eighty bus should be due shortly. He'd report his discoveries at Allerton police station...on home ground. Perhaps this display of initiative would count in his favour if he ever applied to join the police force.

Keith had just reached the gate when the front door opened. He swung round and stared at the figure framed in the doorway.

"Hello, Keith. What are you doing here?"

Keith opened and closed his mouth, lost for words. This was the last thing he had expected.

"Seeing you're here, why not come in for a cup of tea? I'd no idea that you knew where I lived."

As he walked back up the path, Linda smiled and smoothed her mini skirt down over her shapely legs. And a fly landed in the web of the fat spider by the doorbells.

*　　*　　*

April 2003
"I hate these bloody cold cases." Detective Sergeant Bob Jones took a packet of cigarettes from his jacket pocket but, seeing the disapproving

looks of all those around him, put it back again. It was time he gave up anyway.

"So how long does the pathologist reckon it's been under the floorboards then?" DC Burns asked, looking at the photographs of the crime scene and wrinkling his nose in disgust.

"Donkey's years. I'm surprised nobody noticed the smell. We found a receipt from a record shop by the body dated 1965. It could have fallen out of the murderer's pocket – then again it might not. Everything's been sent to Forensics anyway: there might be fingerprints, even after all these years. The clothes are quite well preserved...considering." Jones smiled. "Didn't half give those builders a turn when they found it."

Jones flicked through the papers on his desk. "In 1965 the place was owned by a Kevin Kelly, a widower who inherited various properties from his late wife who, in turn, had been left them by an aunt. There was a bit of a question mark over the wife's death apparently, but nothing was ever proved. Kelly was found dead in 1965. His brand new Ford Cortina had been driven into the Mersey with him inside it... when I say driven I mean the handbrake was left off and it was given a shove. But he was already dead when it hit the water – stabbed in the heart. And there were a number of defensive wounds: he'd put up a fight. Don't expect his killer thought he'd be found until time and tide had destroyed the evidence. Matter of luck, really."

"So was anyone charged with Kelly's murder?" Burns asked, leaning back in his chair.

"Kelly had a mistress who lived with him in the flat where our new body was found – Linda Parker: she was his secretary but their relationship wasn't common knowledge at work. He'd recently altered his will so that she got everything and she disappeared around the time Kelly's body was discovered. It was thought at the time that she'd killed him during a domestic and did a runner – disappeared into thin air – so they never really bothered looking for anyone else." Burns looked at the sergeant and raised his eyebrows. "But this new development changes things a bit, doesn't it. The case'll have to be re-opened."

"Who else was living in those flats back in 1965?"

Jones looked pleased with himself. "I managed to track down a Doctor Jim Watts; he trained at Liverpool University and he had a flat on the ground floor. He's now a GP up in North Yorkshire. Nice bloke. Very helpful. He was interviewed by the police at the time Kelly was found dead – and Linda Parker went missing. I've dug out his original statement and in it he says that a young man, aged around eighteen, called at the house the evening before Kelly's body was found and asked about vacant flats…which Doctor Watts thought was strange because they were all occupied at the time. Watts told him to ring the landlord's bell and he heard the door being answered and the boy going up to Kelly's flat. The statement mentions the name the boy gave – John McCartney. Watts had remembered it because of the Beatles – John Lennon and Paul McCartney. They were never able to trace this John McCartney at the time; not that they made much effort because Kelly's murder seemed to be an open and shut case."

DC Burns picked up the photographs of the body found under the floorboards of the first floor flat in Ullet Road. The builders had been gutting the place in preparation for its metamorphosis into luxury apartments when they had made their grim discovery. The body had been found next to the hot water pipe and the dry heat had caused partial mummification of the remains. It was still recognisable as a human being. "John McCartney, eh. Think he could have killed her?"

"Who knows after all this time? But it was strange that she was found with a knife clutched in her hand and the postmortem found no sign of stab wounds on the body or the clothes. The pathologist reckoned she died of an injury to the back of her skull that fitted exactly with her falling against the marble hearth in that room – it's got an unusual moulded edge."

"So she could have gone for someone with the knife and they pushed her away so she fell backwards? And then they panicked and pulled up a few loose floorboards and hid her underneath. Case solved, sarge?"

Jones smiled. He doubted if it would be that easy. "I'd better let the Chief Inspector see the papers…see how he wants to proceed. If he can be bothered – it's his retirement do next week."

*   *   *

As his car was in for service, Keith O'Dowd perched on the front seat on the bottom deck of the eighty bus and looked out of the window at the passing urban scenery, so much smarter now than all those years ago: cafe bars and gentrification had taken their toll on the city. The bus still ran down Ullet Road…just as it had all those years ago. But now it had lost its pea-green livery; times had changed. And these days Keith avoided this route when he drove into town. The sight of that house made him feel uncomfortable.

As the bus turned into Ullet Road Keith gave an involuntary shudder and felt a sudden longing for a cigarette. But he'd given them up years ago. Susan, his wife, wouldn't allow them in the house and the office was a no smoking zone so it was no use swimming against the tide.

Kelly's old house was a mess with skips and builders' rubble everywhere. And police crime scene tape had been festooned around the place like a Christmas garland. The time he had been dreading since 1965 had finally arrived: she had been found. And with modern forensic technology – he was sure he must have left some trace somewhere – it would only be a matter of time before the truth came out.

But it had been self-defence. When Linda had come at him with the knife and he had pushed her away, he hadn't intended to kill her. They already thought that she had got rid of Kelly after he had altered his will in her favour and his statement would just confirm it…surely. He was bound to be believed.

He stared out of the window at the blur of shops and streetlights. When his involvement was discovered it would be an ignominious end to a successful career but he couldn't avoid the truth. He only hoped that Susan would understand and that all the questions could wait until after his retirement party.

When Detective Chief Inspector Keith O'Dowd reached the bus stop near his home, he climbed down stiffly from the platform, holding firmly on to the rail. Then he stood and watched as the bus disappeared down the road in a cloud of diesel fumes.

SINS OF SCARLET

Robert Barnard

Cardinal Pascona stood a little aside from his fellow electors, observing the scene, conjecturing on the conversations that were animating every little knot of cardinals. The elderly men predominated, of course. The young men were not only in a minority, but they were unlikely to want any of their number to be elected. A long papacy was the last thing anybody wanted at this juncture. So instead of forming up into a clique of their own, they separated and mingled with the older men. They were all, in any case, related in some way or other to earlier popes, and their opinions for that reason tended to be discounted. That was unfair but understandable.

Cardinal Borromei.

That was the name that kept coming towards him, through the sticky and fetid air of the Chapel. It was clear to Pascona that opinion was drifting – had already drifted – in that direction. Borromei was related to a previous pope, like the young men, but his promotion to the rank of cardinal at the age of twenty-three was now so long ago that everybody had discounted it. He had proved his worth to the College by a long life of steady opinions, safe hands on the tiller, and general mediocrity. He was a man to ruffle no feathers, stir up no hornets' nests, raise no high winds.

Ideal.

Or ideal in the view of most of his fellow electors. And promising in other ways too: aged sixty-seven and obese from a fondness for rich and outré foods. That, and a partiality for the finest cognac, marked him out as likely to be present before long in the Chapel in mummified form only.

Cardinal Pascona stepped down from the chapel stalls and began mingling with the knots of his fellows. The conversations were going as he had expected.

"The situation in France is becoming worrying," that old fool da Ponti was saying to a little group of like-minded ciphers. "Borromei has been used to a mediation role in Venice. Couldn't be bettered at the present time." He turned with mischievous intent to Pascona. "Wouldn't you agree?" He continued looking at him, and Pascona knew that any dissent would be discounted as the bile of an unsuccessful candidate. Everyone in the Conclave assessed Pascona as *papabile* but there was a distinct reluctance to vote for him.

"Absolutely," Pascona said with a smile. "A perfectly safe pair of hands, and accustomed to bringing peace to warring factions." He could not restrain himself from adding: "Though whether the Bourbons – fair weather friends to us, at their best – deserve the services of the Church's best mediator is another matter. The unkind might suggest that they deserve to stew in a juice of their own making."

And he moved on, with a peaceful, delightful glide as if, having just dispensed a Christ-like wisdom, he was currently walking on air.

The bowls from their light supper were just being cleared away.

Pascona nodded in the direction of the robed and cowled figures who silently served them and waited for them to bring the silver goblets with their nightcaps in them. A vile red wine from Sicily in all probability. It was generally agreed among the cardinals that everything was done to make their stay incommunicado from the real world (if Rome and the Vatican was that) as unpleasant as possible. The aim of the Vatican officials was to persuade them to make a decision as quickly as they reasonably could so that a return to normality could be achieved. After all, for those officials, it was only a matter of one old man being succeeded by another old man.

Nothing much happened during the last reign, and (unless a surprising choice was made) nothing much would happen in the next one.

Cardinal Pascona took up his goblet. It was indeed a vile wine, quite incredibly sour and thick. Prolonged indigestion or worse could well be the consequences for many of the elderly and infirm electors if they did more than sip at such muck. Confident in his own stomach the Cardinal drank, then went over to another group.

"It is a sobering thought," he injected into their small-talk that was by now a mere prelude to slumber, "that the world is waiting on our decision, but when the choice is announced everyone will say 'Who?'"

The cardinals smiled politely, though one or two of the smiles were sour. Not all of them liked to be thought totally insignificant in the wider scheme of things. Now the cowled figures were going round extinguishing the nests of candles on the walls. They rolled out the down mattresses and put on top of them a pillow and a pile of blankets hardly needed in the close atmosphere of the Sistine. Beside these bundles they put a nightlight. No great comforts for a long night. Cardinals removed their red robes and lay down in their substantial undergarments. Bones creaked as they levered themselves down. Cardinal Pascona took great care not to creak himself. He was still fit and active in every way. That ought to be noticed. He was not going to live forever, but he had a few years yet in him, and good ones too.

He lay on his back looking up. Nothing could be seen of the ceiling, but in the murky light cast by the few remaining nightlights he could distinguish the contours of the Chapel. He had loved the Chapel since he had first seen it, fifty years before. It spoke to him. Twenty years before, when he was barely forty, he had become part of a commission to report on the state of the Chapel, in particular on the state of Mazzuoli's restorations at the beginning of the century. Pascona had sat on the scaffolding day after day, eventually dressing as a workman, sharing their bread and wine, getting to *know* every inch of the ceiling and the altar wall and the Last Judgement fresco. The Commission had reported, but nothing had been done. Business as usual at the Vatican!

He altered the position of his bed so that his head was towards the altar. He did not want to think of the Last Judgement. Fine, terrifying, but the Christ was not his Christ – too commanding, too much an obvious man of action. A general, an organiser, that was Michaelangelo's Christ. Whereas his was gentler, more of a healer, more forgiving. He would be forgiving, surely?

He lay in the darkness, his eyes fixed on the panels he could not see, recreating the scenes he knew so well, that had been imprinted on his soul some twenty years before. The drunken Noah, a rare scene of comedy, and to the right of that panel his favourite of all the *ignudi* – the naked men holding medallions. A boy-man, infinitely inviting, conscious of his own appeal – delightful, inexhaustible.

But then he let his eye sweep across the darkness of the ceiling and fix on the central panel. The masterpiece among masterpieces in his opinion.

The moment of creation. And in particular Adam: beautiful, languid before full awakening, holding hope and promise for all those of Cardinal Pascona's tastes. And so like his own beloved Sandro! The yearning face, the beautiful body – it was as if Sandro had been created for him in the likeness of our first father.

He slept.

He awoke next morning to the sounds of disturbance – shouting, choking, vomiting and groans. He leapt from his bed. The Chapel was now fully illuminated and he ran to a little group of cardinals in a circle, gazing down in consternation. In the middle of the circle, writhing on the stone floor, lay the obese figure of Cardinal Borromei. Pascona could only make out one word of his cries.

"*Aiudo!*"

He immediately took control.

"Help he must have. Summon a doctor!"

Cardinal da Ponti stepped in with his usual statement of the obvious. "You know we cannot allow one in. The best we can do is get him out of the Chapel to be treated there."

"And that of course is what we must do."

"But he should be here. Today might be the day when… And it might be just indigestion."

Cardinal Pascona paused, momentarily uncertain.

"Cardinal Borremi is someone who enjoys the pleasures of the table. But there have been few pleasures of the table on offer here in the Chapel. Spartan fare every day so far. The wine last night was disgraceful."

He was about to put aside his indecision and insist that the tormented man be removed and treated outside the Chapel when the whole body of cardinals was transfixed by a terrible cry. The flabby body on the floor arched, shuddered, then sank motionless back to the floor.

"*E morto?*" someone whispered.

Dead was certainly what he seemed to be. Cardinal Pascona knelt by the body, felt its chest, then put his face and ear close to its mouth. He shook his head.

"Dead," he said. "We must – with the permission of the Cardinal Chamberlain – remove the body. Then we must put out a statement to the waiting crowds. I think it should specify a *colpo di sangue* as the cause of death. A stroke."

"But it didn't look—"

Cardinal Pascona put up his hand and turned to Cardinal da Ponti.

"I specify that because it is easily understood by the least sophisticated member of the crowd. Everyone there will have had some family member – a grandfather, an uncle – who has died of a stroke. It is a question of getting the message across with the least fuss. If some amendment is needed after the doctors have examined him – so be it. But I do not anticipate any need for it."

"But a death in Conclave – and *such* a death: a man who, if I might put it so, was the *favourite*."

Cardinal Pascona was brusque in the face of such tastelessness.

"But what could be more likely? A large number of elderly men, shut up together in an unhealthy atmosphere, on a diet which – to put it mildly – is not what they are accustomed to. And the candidate in a state of extreme excitement. It has happened before, and it is a wonder that it hasn't happened more often."

The thought that there had been a precedent excited them all.

"Oh, *has* it happened?" asked Cardinal Morosi, a new boy of fifty-five.

"Indeed. The procession from the Chapel out to the great Square at the time of Pope Benedict XIV's inauguration was delayed for two hours by one of the cardinals falling dead. Excitement, of course."

"But then the choice had been made," muttered Cardinal Morosi.

Pascona ignored him. He addressed the whole College, summoned from their beds or from the *prima Colazione* by that terrible last cry.

"The need now is to remove, with all appropriate ceremonies and mourning, the deceased brother, and then to continue our deliberations. The whole world awaits our decision. We must not be found wanting at this crisis in our history, and that of the world."

It struck nobody that for Cardinal Pascona "the whole world" meant effectively the Western half of Europe. They busied themselves, summoned the waiting monks who were clearing away the breakfast things, and had Cardinal Borromei removed from the Chapel. Having someone willing and able to take charge enlivened their torpid and aging intellects, and they settled down to discussions in groups with zest and vigour. What was a death, after all, to men for whom it was only a beginning?

Yet, oddly, the initiative and address of Cardinal Pascona had an effect on the discussion which was the reverse of what might have been expected. Put bluntly (which it never was in this Conclave), it might have been summed up in the phrase "Who does he think he is?" The fact that they were all grateful to him for taking charge, were conscious that he had avoided several hours of indecision and in-fighting, did not stop them asking by what right he had taken control at that moment of crisis in the affairs of the Church.

"He takes a great deal too much on himself," one of them said. And it did his chances no good at all.

For though Pascona was *papabile,* he was not the only one to be so.

There had been a minor stir of interest in the early days of the Conclave in favour of Cardinal Fosca, Archbishop of Palermo. He was a man who had no enemies, usually spoke sense, and was two or three years on the right side of senility. True, there was one thing against him. This was not the fact that he had something of an obsession about a rag-tag-and-bobtail collection of criminals in his native island. It was the Mafia this, the Mafia that the whole time, as if they were set to take over the world. That the cardinals shrugged off and suffered. But what was really against him in many cardinals' eyes was his height. He was barely five feet tall (or 1.5 metres, as the newfangled notions from France had it). Just to be seen by the crowd he would have to have several cushions on his throne when he went out on the balcony to bless the masses. It was likely to cause ridicule, and the Church was aware, since Voltaire, of how susceptible it was to wit, irony and proletarian laughter.

But suddenly, it seemed, Fosca was a decidedly desirable candidate.

Pascona watched and listened in the course of the day. Ballot succeeded ballot, with nothing so democratic as a declaration of the result. But the word went around: the vote for Fosca was inching up, that for Pascona slowly ebbing away. The Cardinal went around, talking to all and sundry with imperturbable urbanity – amiable to all, forswearing all controversy. He was among the first to collect his frugal evening meal. By then his mood was contemplative. He gazed benignly at the monks serving the *stufato,* then looked down in the direction of the Cardinal from Palermo.

As he helped himself to the rough bread there was the tiniest of nods from one of the cowled heads.

"Dear Michaelangelo, help one of your greatest admirers and followers," he prayed that night on his narrow bed. "Let the vote go to a follower of yourself, as well as a devout servant of Christ."

Before he slept his mind went not to the *ignudi,* nor to the awakening Adam in the great central panel, but away from the altar to the expelled Adam as, with Eve, and newly conscious of sin, he began the journey out of Paradise.

He smiled, as thoughts of Sandro and their forthcoming pleasures when they were united again warmed his aging body.

The morning was not a repeat of the day before.

Over breakfast there was talk, and before long it was time to take the first test of opinion, to find out whether straw should be added to the burning voting slips to make black smoke, or whether it should be omitted, to the great joy of the crowds in St. Peter's Square as the white smoke emerged. One cardinal had not risen from his bed, and he was the most important of all. Cardinal da Ponti went to shake him awake, then let out a half-suppressed gasp of dismay. The cardinals, oppressed by fear and horror, went over to the bed.

Cardinal Fosca lay, a scrap of humanity, dead as dead. He looked as if he could be bundled up, wrapped in a newsheet, and put out with the rubbish from the Conclave's meals.

"*Dio mio!*"

The reactions were various, but more than one started to say what was on everybody's minds.

"But he too was the—"

This time they hesitated to use the term from horse-racing. But one by one, being accustomed to bow to authority, they looked towards the man who, only yesterday, had set the tone and solved the problem of what should be done. Somehow Pascona, with his long experience of curias and conclaves, knew they would do that, and was ready. He cleared his throat.

"Fellow cardinals. Friends," he began. "Let us pray for our friend whom God has called to himself. And let us at the same time pray for guidance." There was a murmur of agreement, along with one or two murmurs of something else. After a minute's silence Cardinal Pascona resumed, adopting his pulpit voice.

"I believe we all know what must be done. I think God has spoken to us, each and every one, at this crisis moment – spoken as God always does speak, through the silent voice of our innermost thoughts." The cardinals muttered agreement, though most of them had had nothing in the interval for silent prayer that could honestly be called a thought. "He has told us that what must be thought of first at this most difficult moment is the Church: its good name, its primacy and power, and its mission to bring to God all waverers, all wrong-doers, all schismatics. It is the Church and its God-given mission that must be in the forefront of all our minds."

There was a more confident buzz of agreement.

"We are in a crisis, as I say, in the history of ours, the one true Church. In the world at large doubt, distrust and rebellion seethe, distracting the minds of the unlettered, provoking the discontent of the educated. Ridicule, distrust of long-held beliefs, rebellion against the position of the natural leaders of society – all these evils flourish today, as never before. At such a point any event – even an innocent and natural occurrence such as we witness here" – he gestured towards the human scrap on the bed – "will be taken up, seized upon as a cause of scandal and concern, distorted and blackened with the ingenuity of the Devil himself, who foments and then leads all such discontents and rebellions. Let us make our minds up, let us make our choice quickly, let us conceal what has happened until such a time as it can be announced and accepted as the natural event which in truth it was."

This time there was a positively enthusiastic reception for his words. "Come, my friends," resumed Pascona, delighted at the effect of his words, "let us get down to business. Let us vote, and let us vote to make a decision, and to present to the world a front of unity and amity. And let us treat our friend here with the respect that a lifetime of faithful service demands. Put a blanket over him."

It worked like a charm. A blanket was thrown over the body of the dead Cardinal Fosca, leaving his head showing. Not dead, only resting, seemed to be the message. The living cardinals proceeded to a vote, and even before the last vote was in and counted it was clear that the straw would no longer be required: the smoke would be pure white.

The excitement was palpable. While they remained cloistered in the Chapel the other cardinals thumped Pascona on the shoulder and indulged in such bouts of kiddishness as were possible for a collection of men dominated by the dotards. After five minutes of this, and as the Chapel was penetrated by sounds of cheering from crowds in the Square, the new Pope proceeded to the passageway from the Chapel to St. Peter's, pausing at the door to look towards the altar and the massive depiction of the Last Judgement behind it. Magnificent, but quite wrong, he thought. And perhaps a silly superstition at that.

Then he proceeded into the upper level of the great Church, then along towards the door leading on to the balcony. He stopped before the throne, raised on poles like a sedan chair. He let the leading cardinals, led by the Cardinal Chamberlain and helped by the monks who had serviced the Conclave, robe him and bestow on him all the insignia of his new office. He behaved with impeccable graciousness.

"What name has Your Holiness decided to be known by?" asked the Chamberlain. Pascona paused before replying.

"I am conscious of the links of my mother's family to this great, this the *greatest* office. The fame of Alexander VI will live forever, but the name is too precious for me, and for the Church, for me to assume it. In truth it would be a burden. I shall leave that sacred name to my ancestor, and I shall take the name of the other Pope from her family. I shall be known as Calixtus IV."

The Chamberlain nodded.

From the Square there came sounds. Someone, perched somewhere, with good eyesight, must have been able to see through the open door of the balcony. A whisper, then a shout, had gone round.

"It's the Borgia. The Borgia!"

The fame of his mother's family easily eclipsed that of his father's. The tone of the shouts had fear in it, but also admiration, anticipation. What a time Alexander VI's had been! Bread and circuses, and lots of sex. Calixtus IV smiled to himself, then ascended the throne. As he was about to nod to the four carriers to proceed through the door and on to the balcony, one of the monks came forward with a bag of small coins, to scatter to the crowd below. As he handed the bag to the Pope, he raised his head and the cowl slipped back an inch or two. There was the loved face: the languid eyes of Michaelangelo's Adam, the expression of newly awakened sensuality, and underneath the coarse robe the body, every inch of which Calixtus knew so well. He took the bag, and returned his gaze.

"Grazie, *Ales-Sandro*," he said.

ALL SHE WROTE

Mick Herron

The Head of Section had Daisy's report right there on the desk. Marked *Eyes Only*, it began without preamble:

♠

The General is uglier than he appears in photographs. His face is pockmarked and cratered; ruined by an adolescent inflammation, I suppose, and up close presents a palette of angry purple outbursts. He has thick black curly hair – too black to be natural. Vanity is not the prerogative of the attractive. His teeth are yellowing, and his eyes, too, have that same unhealthy light, as if he were a carrier of something we don't yet have a name for. When he speaks, it is in a voice used to command but of a slightly higher pitch than might be expected. When he walks, it is with neither grace nor lightness. His reputation as a man of subtle moves could hardly be less deserved.

The Imperiale, on the other hand, is everything its brochure promises. Its rooms are large and cool, with overhead fans that beat like a metronome, so that you fall asleep in the comfortable knowledge that the building's heartbeat never falters. The lifts are splendid, and in constant working order, and the lobby is a marketplace for information; I never crossed its tiled floor without registering at least three furtive conversations in corners. As for the bar – which occupies a patio overlooking the bay, and is lined by friendly palm trees – this is where the foreign correspondents gather, pretending they're relaxing. All wear sunglasses, even in the shade, and an air of expectation hangs heavily over the tables, as assorted possible headlines compose themselves in journalists' heads. Last year, both Greene and Hemingway stayed here. I expect it will turn up in a novel before long.

On my first afternoon, the General walked through the lobby while I was reading an English paper. His gaze rested on me for a long while. I kept my expression blank, I trust, though his inspection was unpleasant.

It might seem odd that Rubello keeps a suite at the Imperiale, but it is somewhere he feels secure: far enough from the President's palace for him not to feel overshadowed; close enough that his driver can deliver him there in ten minutes. When on the premises, he keeps only a brace of guards with him. The Imperiale is regarded as neutral territory by all, as any horror taking place within its walls would harm the island's tourist trade. Besides, the General has little to fear from the correspondents. Most of them only leave the bar to waddle as far as the casino. They tend to be on their next-to-last legs, their stomachs as padded as their expense accounts.

The General was my first assignment since recruitment. He will also be my last.

♠

I have been told that a report should *cover the background* – that was the phrase. Cover the background. So. The General is General Marc Rubello, fifty-two years old: much loved by the army he commands; much feared by the people. Feared, too, I think by our own dear Majesty's Government – or at least, feared by our American cousins, and therefore held to be fearsome by us. It's no secret that Rubello's rival for the Presidency, Chief of Police Andrea Nabar, is the horse Whitehall and Washington back. As far as the islanders are concerned, the race lacks a favourite. Nabar is much loved by the police force he commands; much feared by the people. But less likely to steer east were he to take up the reins of power.

There is a saying I've heard: better the bastard on your side than the bastard on the other. I won't ask you to forgive the vocabulary. There is worse to come.

As for the President himself – the former President, I should call him now – he was the weakling son of a stern leader, with rarely a thought to call his own. Presidents' sons should never be Presidents themselves. They either splash about helplessly – so shallow, they're constantly out of their depth – or indulge in wars to exorcise their fathers' ghosts.

There was never any doubt that the Presidential Palace had a temporary resident. It was simply a question of which bastard would replace him.

♠

The assignment was straightforward: I was to pose as a guest at the Imperiale, and "gather information". When would Rubello make his move? Would he aim for a bloodless coup, or take the opportunity to exterminate opposition? Given that this included the police force, civil war would result if he took that route, and Her Majesty's intelligence services like to know in advance about such events. I assumed similar information was being gathered regarding Nabar's intentions. As it turned out, I underestimated the degree of interest being shown in the General's rival.

It's a peculiar affectation – to pose as something you truly are. For whatever my motive for being there, there's no doubt I was a guest at the Imperiale. I had a room on the third floor, and a balcony overlooking the square. There was nothing unusual in being a tourist there at any time of year, and political unrest was never spoken of in front of visitors. There were always groups of soldiers and policemen on street corners, but they were largely keeping an eye on each other, and taking turns beating up beggars and thieves. Tourists were off limits; rarely, if ever, arrested.

And as far as my actual task went, I was not without resources. The service has long had an asset in place at the Imperiale. Maria is a maid. She has heavy eyebrows, and for some reason this lends a certain foreboding to many of her utterances. The first time we talked she launched, without invitation, into a discussion of Rubello's vices.

"The General is a man of fearsome appetites." She was looking at me directly when she said this. "When he takes a lover, this requires his full attention. The same when he takes a prisoner."

"Is there a difference between the two?"

"You might say not. Sometimes I see them leaving in the morning. They look as if daylight will strike them dead."

"You have no sympathy for them."

"They come asking favours. They leave having suffered more for those favours than they expected." She shrugged. "Life is hard."

"I imagine he does not have to look far for his conquests."

"He is a powerful man," Maria said. "And many people require favours."

"And you?" I asked. "You have not…attracted his attentions?"

She laughed. "I am not his type." She was still looking at me. "You are the type he enjoys."

I remembered the gaze he'd bestowed on me the previous afternoon, and suppressed a shiver.

"And you have fair skin," she said. "He likes fair skin."

I did not want to pursue this topic.

"Daisy," she said.

"Yes."

"It is pretty name."

I smiled uneasily. "Thank you, Maria."

She became businesslike. "Anyway. You have device, I understand, yes?"

The sudden change of subject threw me, and for a moment I had no idea what she meant.

"Listening device? To hear the General's conversations?"

"Oh. Yes. Yes, I do."

"I tell you when is safe to put in room."

"I thought—"

She waited me out.

"I thought perhaps you would put the device in place."

But she was shaking her head before I finished speaking. "No. That I cannot do."

"But you would have a reason for being in his suite. If I were caught—"

"If you are caught, you are lost tourist. If I am caught, I am dead maid."

It seemed unarguable. My only rejoinder – that I would have to be a very lost tourist indeed to end up in the General's suite – failed to reach my lips. There was a limit to what Maria was prepared to do for her stipend, and this exceeded it.

I said, "I have never done this before."

I'm not sure why I told her this.

She said, "No. But do not worry. I tell you when is safe."

♠

She tell me when is safe. That should have been a comfort, but over the next days, I felt anything but secure. The game of being a tourist – of taking the dangerously overloaded bus into the hills to the famous caves; of wandering the market, buying coins from "centuries-old pirate hauls" – felt like its rules had changed. Those soldiers: were they eyeing their police counterparts, or watching my every move? That pair of policemen, pacing behind me – was that coincidence? The second evening I dared not venture out of my room, which was very un-tourist-like behaviour. Not appearing at the bar without a doctor's certificate was unheard of.

That night I slept badly. It seemed I heard noises in the hillsides; beasts engaged in combat over the same dry bones.

But in the morning, Maria was waiting when I went for breakfast. "Tonight," she said.

I looked around. There was no one in sight. Nobody cared I was talking to a maid. "Is it safe?"

"He go to casino. Every week, this day. He leave at nine. He not return before two, three. You have all evening."

"It won't take ten minutes."

I was fairly certain of this. I had been shown many times how to plant a bug.

She said, "You are not scared."

It didn't appear to be a question. I answered, anyway: "A little scared, yes. I've never done this before."

The eyes beneath those heavy brows glanced briefly towards heaven. "You go in at ten, yes? I wait on stairs. I keep you guard."

"What about his soldiers? Don't they watch his room?"

"They watch his back. They go to casino also."

She bustled off, on maidly tasks. I had no appetite for breakfast, and returned to my room.

♠

I don't remember much about that day. I examined the eavesdropping device I had been equipped with, I'm sure of that – it was smaller than a watchface – and practised attaching it to the mouthpiece of my telephone. After a few dry runs, this took no more than a minute. I would also have to search the General's suite. There might be documents or photographs that I, in turn, should photograph. The camera I had used as a tourist was of the normal size, but the one I had been supplied with for this purpose fitted in a pocket. This, too, I practised with. The rest of the day is a blur.

The balcony. I expect I sat on the balcony, looking down on the square below. All those people milling about. One way or the other, my mission would affect their lives – did that responsibility weigh on me? I don't think so. I think it just added to my nervousness.

At 9.55, Maria knocked softly on my door.

"It's time?" I asked her stupidly.

"He not here for hours. Now is safe."

I nodded, meaning it as thanks. Then I took the stairs to the fifth floor, and the General's suite.

The hallway was empty, Rubello's guards nowhere in sight. As Maria had said, they watched his back and not his rooms. I knocked on the door. No answer. If there had been, I'd have fainted on the spot. I looked over my shoulder to see the top of Maria's head, a few stairs down the well, then used skeleton keys to open the door, my heart pounding louder than any overhead fan. The room was cool. It faced the bay, and the balcony doors were open, the curtains fluffing in the breeze. Noises drifted upwards: gossip from the bar, and distant music.

I stepped to the phone, but could not unscrew the mouthpiece.

It was something from a dream – the gate that comes no closer, no matter how fast you run; the corridor that stretches endlessly ahead. No matter how hard I twisted, the mouthpiece remained immovable. Downstairs, disassembling the phone had been the work of seconds; here, it felt like one of Hercules' tasks. From the patio, conversation drifted: I heard laughter and singing. The laughter might have been aimed at me.

But I had hours. There was surely somewhere else I could place the transmitter. The trouble was, I had been given no alternative instructions; no standby location. The bug was small, but not invisible. I could fix it beneath a table, but it might be found by a maid other than Maria. And would not overhear both sides of a telephone conversation.

After what can't have been more than ten minutes, but felt as many weeks, I cursed my luck and gave up. But there were still the General's papers to look for. I was halfway to the desk when I heard voices from the hallway. I think my heart stopped at that moment. Before it could start again, I did the only sensible thing of my life. I dropped the transmitter on the floor, and with my foot nudged it under the bed.

The door opened.

♠

This is my report. I have covered the background. There are things that happened you do not need to know.

♠

Up close, the General is uglier than he appears in photographs. His face is pockmarked and cratered; ruined by adolescent inflammation. When he speaks, it is at a higher pitch than might be expected.

"How did you get in here?"

"The door was unlocked," I stammered.

"No. My door is always locked. Did Maria let you in?"

He knew about Maria.

I shook my head. Nodded. Shook my head.

"So. You come for a favour, yes?"

I had no other answer. "Yes."

"You are tourist. For my people, I do many favours. What favour can I do a tourist?"

"I am a writer," I said. "A journalist."

"You have no press card. You are not registered as journalist. Your visa, it says tourist."

I nodded again, dumbly.

"I notice you in lobby, you see. I ask about your papers."

"I plan to become a journalist," I amended. "I hope to sell a story soon."

"But you do not belong to newspaper."

"No," I said.

"I see." He considered the matter. "They call this word freelance?"

It was a glimmer of light in the darkest of rooms. I groped towards

it. "That's what they call it, yes. Freelance. I hope to write a story and
sell it to a newspaper. And then I will be a journalist."

"I see. And so you come to my room."

"I…I was hoping for an interview."

"We have many journalists here. Many stay at this hotel. You want
interview? I give interview every week."

I said, "You give the same interview every week."

He smiled at that.

"I was hoping for something a little more…"

My mouth was dry. Vocabulary failed me. This man had tortured
prisoners to death.

He said, "Something little more private."

"…Yes."

"Something little more intimate."

"…Yes."

"So you become famous journalist. First to interview man who will
be next President of little island paradise."

I said, "Yes."

He nodded. He unbuttoned his jacket. Through the window behind
me, laughter and song drifted.

"So," he said. "I do you this favour. What you do in return?"

Without waiting for a reply, he picked up the phone I had been
unable to master. "No calls," he said.

♠

Some men use sex as power. I don't need to tell you that.

Perhaps the worst of it was, I could not pretend to be there against
my will. If the General knew I was a spy, he wouldn't waste time on a
trial. He would have put a bullet in my head, and had me carted through
the lobby in a basket. When your men loot villages on your word, the
disposal of a body is a domestic trifle. His type or not.

And besides, besides, besides – even if my wants had aligned with
his, he was not the man I would have chosen to enjoy them with. He
takes his pleasures as roughly as he treats the island he would rule. He
expects his commands to be fulfilled instantly. And there is no apparent
limit to the degradation he inflicts.

Sometimes I see them leaving in the morning. They look as if daylight will strike them dead.

♠

That night, as we both know, Chief of Police Andrea Nabar seized power in a bloodless coup. No shooting, no explosions – a polite signing over of power by a dimwit long stupefied by Presidential responsibility. I stumbled from Rubello's suite at five; by six, the General was under arrest. His "No calls" was more than a suggestion to the switchboard – long practice had established it as code for total privacy. The armed guards on the stairwell brooked no interruption. The first inkling they had of regime change was the new Presidential guard arriving, with heavy artillery.

And we both know too that what happened to me was deliberate. It was no accident I was chosen for this mission doomed to fail; no accident I was the General's *type*. And no accident he returned early from the casino that night. Maria was not simply our asset; she would hardly have been suffered to continue working (indeed, living) if she were. She was also the General's pander. Intelligence assets, like whores, indulge more than one master. Some while after she glued his telephone's mouthpiece to its receiver, she had told Rubello I was there. That she had done both on your orders did not interfere with his lusts.

Rubello was well and truly occupied while the island's future slipped into his rival's hands.

And me? Once able to do so without obvious pain, I took a flight home. To write this, my first and last report.

What should I have expected, working for a service whose practice is deception?

May you, and all who work for you, rot in hell.

♠

The Head of Section laid the report on the desk and paused for a moment. Then she sighed, picked up a pen, and initialled James Daisy's report.

And that was all she wrote.

BIOGRAPHIES

Robert Barnard (1936–2013) had a distinguished career as an academic before he became a full-time writer. His first crime novel, *Death of an Old Goat*, was written while he was Professor of English at the University of Tromsø in Norway, the world's most northerly university. Under the name of Bernard Bastable he also wrote novels featuring Mozart as a detective. He regarded Agatha Christie as his ideal crime writer and published an appreciation of her work, *A Talent to Deceive*, as well as a book on Dickens and a history of English literature. He received the CWA Diamond Dagger Award in 2003.

Simon Brett OBE is the author of over one hundred books and many plays for radio and the theatre. He has published four series of detective novels (the Charles Paris, Mrs. Pargeter, Fethering, and Blotto & Twinks mysteries) as well as stand-alone novels such as *A Shock to the System*, which was adapted into a film with Michael Caine in the lead.

John Dickson Carr (1906–77) is widely regarded as the most gifted of all exponents of the locked room mystery. A native of Pennsylvania, he relocated to Britain after marrying an Englishwoman, and pursued a career as a detective novelist with a taste for the baroque. His first great detective, the French examining magistrate Henri Bencolin, was succeeded by Dr. Gideon Fell, a rumbustious character modelled on G.K. Chesterton, whom Carr much admired. As Carter Dickson, he wrote primarily about Sir Henry Merrivale, a baronet and barrister who shared Fell's penchant for solving baffling impossible crimes. Carr also created Colonel March, and a television series, *Colonel March of Scotland Yard*, ran from 1955-56, with Boris Karloff cast as March.

Liza Cody is an artist trained at the Royal Academy Schools of Art as well as a crime novelist. *Dupe*, her first novel, won the John Creasey

Memorial Dagger, and launched a series about the female private investigator Anna Lee, which was televised with Imogen Stubbs in the lead role. She has also published the Bucket Nut Trilogy featuring professional wrestler Eva Wylie, as well as stand-alone novels such as *Rift*, *Gimme More*, *Ballad of a Dead Nobody*, and *Miss Terry*. She has won a CWA Silver Dagger, an Anthony award, and a Marlowe in Germany.

Mat Coward writes crime fiction, SF, humour and children's fiction. He is also the gardening columnist on the *Morning Star* newspaper. His short stories have been nominated for the Edgar and shortlisted for the Dagger, published on four continents, translated into several languages, and broadcast on BBC Radio. Over the years he has also published novels, books about radio comedy, and collections of funny press cuttings, and written columns for dozens of magazines and newspapers.

Marjorie Eccles is the author of a series of thirteen contemporary novels about Inspector Gil Mayo; the stories were adapted for television by the BBC in 2006 with the actor and impressionist Alistair McGowan cast as Mayo. A prolific short story writer, she has won the Agatha award, and currently writes crime novels set in the first half of the twentieth century.

Martin Edwards is the latest recipient of the CWA Diamond Dagger. His new novel, *Mortmain Hall*, is a sequel to *Gallows Court*, which was both shortlisted for the 2019 eDunnit award for best crime novel, and longlisted for the CWA Sapere Books Historical Dagger. He was honoured with the CWA Dagger in the Library for his body of work and has received the Edgar, Agatha, H.R.F. Keating and Poirot awards, two Macavity awards, the CWA Margery Allingham Short Story Prize, and the CWA Short Story Dagger. He is consultant to the British Library's Crime Classics, a former chair of the CWA, and current President of the Detection Club.

Kate Ellis's first novel, *The Merchant House*, launched the long-running DI Wesley Peterson series set in Devon. She has also written five crime novels featuring another cop, Joe Plantagenet, set in a fictionalised version of York, and a trilogy set in the immediate aftermath of the First World War, as well as many short stories. She won the CWA Dagger in the Library in 2019. *The Devil's Priest* is a stand-alone historical mystery set in Liverpool.

Anthea Fraser's first professional publications were short stories. Her first novel was published in 1970, and she wrote books with paranormal themes and romantic suspense stories before turning to crime fiction. She has created two mystery novel series, the first featuring DCI David Webb, and the second featuring Rona Parish, a biographer and journalist. She has also published novels under the pseudonym Vanessa Graham.

Celia Fremlin (1914–2009) was born in Kent and educated at Berkhamsted School for Girls and Somerville College, Oxford, where she read classics and philosophy. During the Second World War she worked for the Mass Observation project, an experience that resulted in her first published book, *War Factory*, which recorded the experiences and attitudes of women war workers in a radar equipment factory outside Malmesbury, Wiltshire. Her first published novel of suspense was *The Hours Before Dawn*, which won the Mystery Writers of America's Edgar Allan Poe award for best crime novel in 1960. Over the next 35 years she published a further eighteen titles, including three collections of stories.

Frances Fyfield worked as a solicitor for the Crown Prosecution Service, thus 'learning a bit about murder at second hand'. Later, writing became her vocation, although the law and its ramifications have influenced many of her novels. Her Helen West books have been adapted for television, and she is a regular contributor to BBC Radio 4. Her non-series novel *Blood from Stone* won the CWA Gold Dagger.

Michael Gilbert (1912–2006) received the CWA Diamond Dagger in 1994 and was made a Grand Master of the Mystery Writers of America. His experience as a prisoner of war in Italy provided background material for *Death in Captivity*, one of the finest British "impossible crime" stories of the post-war era, and filmed as *Danger Within*. By the time of its appearance, Gilbert was well-established as a partner in a prestigious law firm, and had also made a name for himself as an author of considerable talent. His urbanity is reflected in the smooth, readable prose of his whodunits, thrillers, spy stories, legal mysteries, and police stories. He was equally adept at writing novels, stage plays, radio plays, and television scripts.

Paula Gosling is American, but moved to England in the 1960s. A former copywriter, she received the John Creasey Memorial Dagger for her debut, *A Running Duck* (which has been filmed twice, once as *Cobra*, starring Sylvester Stallone), and the Gold Dagger for her first Jack Stryker novel, *Monkey Puzzle*. She is also the author of the Luke Abbott and Blackwater Bay series, and of several stand-alones.

Lesley Grant-Adamson gave up her job as a feature writer on the *Guardian* to write fiction. Her first novel, *Patterns in the Dust*, was shortlisted for the CWA's John Creasey Memorial Dagger for first crime novels. Like several of her early novels, it featured newspaper folk and their ailing industry. She has written further crime novels of various types, and her wide experience of writing crime fiction led to a commission for a book in the Teach Yourself series, *Writing Crime and Suspense Fiction*, subsequently updated as *Writing Crime Fiction*.

Mick Herron is a novelist and short story writer whose books include the Sarah Tucker/Zoë Boehm series and the stand-alone novel *Reconstruction*. He is the author of the acclaimed Jackson Lamb series, the second of which, *Dead Lions*, won the Gold Dagger. His novels have regularly appeared on award shortlists and *Spook Street* won the CWA Ian Fleming Steel Dagger and the Last Laugh Award.

H.R.F. Keating (1926–2011) published five stand-alone novels before introducing the Indian policeman Inspector Ghote in *The Perfect Murder*, which won the Gold Dagger. The Ghote series continued for over forty years. Another novel set in India, *The Murder of the Maharajah*, also won the Gold Dagger, and Keating received the Diamond Dagger in 1996 in recognition of his lifetime achievements in the genre. He was also a leading critic and commentator, whose books include *Writing Crime Fiction* and studies of Agatha Christie and Sherlock Holmes.

Bill Knox (1928–99) was a Scottish author, journalist and broadcaster, best known for his crime novels and for presenting the long-running STV series *Crimedesk*. He began writing crime novels in the 1950s and often wrote under pen-names such as Michael Kirk, Robert MacLeod and Noah Webster, especially for the American market. He published over fifty crime novels, notably the Thane and Moss series. His final novel, *The Lazarus Widow*, was unfinished at the time of his death, and was completed by Martin Edwards.

Michael Zinn Lewin is an American-born author perhaps best known for his series about the private detective Albert Samson, based in Indianapolis. Lewin himself grew up in Indianapolis, but has lived in England for more than forty years. Much of his fiction continues to be set in Indianapolis, including a secondary series about the cop Leroy Powder. A series set in Bath, England, features the Lunghis, who run their detective agency as a family business.

Peter Lovesey had already published a successful book about athletics when he won a competition with his first crime fiction novel, *Wobble to Death*, which launched a series about the Victorian detective Sergeant Cribb. Since then, his many books and short stories have won or been shortlisted for nearly all the major prizes in the international crime writing world. He was awarded the CWA Diamond Dagger in 2000 and is also a Grand Master of the Mystery Writers of America.

Susan Moody's first crime novel, *Penny Black*, was published in 1984, the first in a series of seven books featuring amateur sleuth Penny Wanawake. She has written a number of suspense thrillers, and in 1993 introduced a series of crime novels with a new central character, Cassandra Swann. *Misselthwaite* was shortlisted for the Romantic Novelists' Association Award in 1995, while *The Colour of Hope*, the story of a family struggling to cope with the loss of their daughter in a boating accident, was written under the name Susan Madison, as is her most recent title, *Touching the Sky*.

Julian Symons (1912–94) was an eminent crime writer and critic of the genre as well as a biographer, poet, editor, and social and military historian. His early detective novels were relatively orthodox, but he soon became dissatisfied with the conventions of the classic form and began in the early 1950s to develop the British psychological crime novel. He received the Gold Dagger for *The Colour of Murder* and an Edgar from the Mystery Writers of America for *The Progress of a Crime*. In 1990 he received the CWA Diamond Dagger in recognition of his outstanding career in the genre, and he was also a Grand Master of the MWA. He wrote an influential history of the genre, *Bloody Murder*.

Andrew Taylor's crime novels include a series about William Dougal, starting with *Caroline Miniscule*, which won the John Creasey Memorial Dagger, the Roth Trilogy, which was televised as *Fallen Angel*, the Lydmouth series, stand-alone novels such as *The American Boy*, and much else besides. He has won the Historical Dagger three times and in 2009 won the Diamond Dagger, as well as earning awards in Sweden and the US.

SOURCES